ADRIAN CHAMBERLIN
FAIRLIGHT

Published by Crystal Lake Publishing—Tales from The Darkest Depths

Website: www.crystallakepub.com/

WELCOME
TO ANOTHER

CRYSTAL LAKE PUBLISHING
CREATION

Join today at www.crystallakepub.com & www.patreon.com/CLP

All warfare is based on deception.
Sun Tzu – The Art of War

DAY ONE: SEPARATION

CHAPTER ONE

"What do you see when you cut yourself?"

It was a strange question, Tony Collins thought. Surely the psychiatrist had meant to ask Rachel *what do you* feel *when you cut yourself?*

Rachel didn't answer, but there was no change in her expression to indicate she shared her father's bewilderment with Nicholas Quinn's question. Her clear blue eyes stared distantly through the window behind him, a faint smile on her lips. She cocked her head, as if she could hear something beyond the soft humming of the groundskeeper's lawnmower. Her left eyebrow lowered slightly, a patch of flaxen straw resting on a cornflower. Apart from the scars, she looked so much like her mother that Tony wanted to cry.

"Did you hear me, Rachel?" Quinn's high-pitched voice was even higher now and Tony knew that the clinical psychiatrist was fighting to remain calm. Quinn's narrow shoulders were hunched together, the top half of his body bent over the desk. His slender fingers clutched the Parker ballpoint too tightly, his fingertips showing white beneath the barrel of the pen.

Seeing Quinn's anxiety made Tony aware of his own, that he too was leaning forward, hunched over the desk. He forced himself back into the seat; the leather upholstery squeaked in protest.

The heat of the June morning didn't help but was a good excuse for the pools of sweat trickling from his armpits to the waistband of his work trousers. He was thankful that his dark polo shirt hid most of the stains. Quinn didn't have that luxury. His crisp white shirt was thoroughly soaked under the armpits. Under his neatly trimmed black beard the collar was crumpled where he kept nervously running a finger between the material and his neck.

"Yes, Mr Quinn. I heard you." Rachel's tone betrayed irritation, as though she'd been asked a ridiculous question by a schoolteacher. The teenage rebelliousness remained with her; Tony could imagine her mother giving the same backchat and stonewalling to her own teachers when she was that age.

But this wasn't school. Rachel wasn't here because she'd bunked off class or given her teacher some lip.

Rachel's attention remained fixed on the window, but it wasn't petulance that kept her eyes away from the psychiatrist's. Tony followed her gaze. Quinn's eyes nervously flicked to his and then back to his notepad, determined not to meet Rachel's unwavering, blue-eyed stare. Tony understood all too well how unnerving that stare was. What Quinn saw on the lawns of Fairlight would not be the same thing Rachel saw.

The windows of the ground floor office were slid back fully, the retracted blinds rattling slightly in the light breeze that sprang up from the sea beyond the sloping lawns. Tony could smell the refreshing hint of salt water amongst the freshly mown grass and the blossoming roses in the neat borders. He saw the ride-on mower make a gentle turn, coming back their way and ready to tame another section of lawn.

The groundskeeper looked cheerful, grinning, his hips rocking back and forth on the seat to the music in his headphones. The sunlight beating down from the cloudless sky caught the pale pink dome of his bald head, shining as brightly as the whitecaps of the rolling sea beyond.

He was in his early forties, Tony guessed. A well-fed beergut spilled through the groundskeeper's green-spattered T-shirt, joining in the dance.

Tony seethed. How the fuck could that man be so happy? Knowing what was happening in the world, to its children?

He wanted to leap from the sweaty leather swivel chair, launch himself through the window and grab the groundskeeper. Drag his stupid, fat, grinning face from the mower, throw him to the ground. Hold his head up to the main entrance of Fairlight and scream *is this funny? Do you know the suffering those poor kids are going through in here? Do you?*

Quinn raised his eyebrows questioningly, but not in a judgemental manner. That told Tony that Quinn understood the anger the parents felt, the impotent fury that came with the terrible condition. Of course, you wanted to take it out on something – or someone, anyone. Quinn understood because he had seen these cases time and time again, had dealt with despairing parents like Tony.

Which was what made this morning's appointment so odd. If Quinn was as experienced as he said he was, why did Rachel make him so nervous? Why was he so reluctant to meet her eyes?

What do you see when you cut yourself?

Rachel blinked slowly, pausing before she opened her eyes. Then she lowered her head and stared at the recent scars that criss-crossed her wrists. She ran a fingernail down the largest one, just beneath the leather strap of her wristwatch. The smile this time was a wistful one, with a sigh of memory.

The smile of someone reminiscing about a happy event. But

opening up your wrist, coming so close to death, should not have been a happy memory. Tony was chilled by that smile.

"I came *so* close to seeing all of it then," she said. "The more blood came out…the clearer it was."

The smile vanished, replaced with a petulant pout. She glanced angrily at her father; Tony almost wilted under her cold blue glare.

"And you spoiled it, Dad. You stopped me seeing it."

"Rachel, I – I saved your life," Tony stammered. "That cut was so deep…"

Quinn's eyes narrowed as he raised his head from the notepad, his nervousness slowly replaced with interest in this new case. He lowered the Parker and leant back in the chair. He clasped his hands in his lap but couldn't keep them still. They twitched as though he was trying to keep a butterfly prisoner without harming it.

"What your father's trying to say, Rachel, is that you didn't see anything, that you were hallucinating because of the blood loss."

"He would." A sullen answer, a normal teenage strop. "Because he doesn't understand. None of you do."

Quinn's mouth opened, then closed. He looked at his clasped hands again.

You're right, Rachel. None of us understand. That's why you're here.

The thought was shared by Quinn and Tony, and their uneasy silence made Rachel pick it up.

"I'm not like the others. You know this, don't you?" She traced the deep line in her wrist once more. "They cut themselves for different reasons. Reasons you don't understand…so how can you hope to understand why *I* do it?"

Neither man had an answer to that. Quinn tried to smile reassuringly, but it came out as a sickly, patronising grimace.

"That's what you're – that's what *we're* - here to find out."

Rachel gave the clinical psychiatrist a contemptuous sneer and turned back to the window. It wasn't long before her eyes glazed, and her smile returned. The same faraway smile as before, which had made Tony and Quinn so nervous. Because Tony had only ever seen that look when she was about to cut herself.

She was seeing something else, Tony realised. The sea breeze stiffened, shaking the retracted blinds and pushing them into the office. The sunlight vanished momentarily behind a solitary cloud, casting a veil over the office. A veil that didn't dim the brightness of Rachel's eyes. The cornflower-blue of her irises glowed, a brilliant sapphire.

Tony blinked, then the cloud passed, the breeze subsided, and the glow in Rachel's eyes faded. Quinn was on his feet, hastily sliding the windows closed. He paused at the window, his stiffened back towards the soon-to-be patient and her father, reluctant to turn.

I didn't imagine it. Quinn saw that light in her eyes as well.

The eyes were now their normal cornflower blue, no trace of the strange illumination. She blinked slowly, then turned to her father.

"Don't worry, Dad. Now's not the time."

Tony swallowed noisily and nodded. Even the knocking on the door didn't shake her. Tony twisted around in the swivel chair, surprised to see the stocky figure of a woman in her late thirties enter without waiting for an answer. The late-morning sun coloured her unkempt curls of hair into a shining tangle of copper. It did little to brighten her pale features, though. The sunlight emphasised the dark rings around her eyes and clearly showed the bloodshot eyes that spoke of little sleep. She wore beige combat trousers, white Nike trainers and a grey vest top that was soaked down the front, highlighting her pendulous breasts and spreading hips. A small, pinned badge read the name BETHAN. No uniform, Tony noted, so common with mental hospitals. An attempt to break down the barrier between staff and patient.

"Dr Quinn, I'm sorry I'm late. There was an incident in the Springbank ward." Her harsh Cardiff-accented voice contained no trace of an apology. She narrowed her eyes at the sight of the smiling Rachel.

"Nothing serious I hope, Bethan?" Quinn looked relieved by the ward nurse's interruption.

"No, just a blocked sink. Site Services weren't answering the phone, so I had to…well, it's resolved now." She pulled her wet top forward a few inches and shook it, anxious to stop the clinging and revealing.

Quinn sighed. "Not the first time they've let us down. Very well, I shall have a word with Rogers shortly. Mr Collins, this is Bethan Appleton, our head nurse."

"Pleasure," Bethan said curtly. "And this must be Rachel."

Now Rachel turned. She eyed the woman warily, and Tony saw Bethan flinch under her gaze.

"Yes, this is Rachel."

"Will she be staying?" Bethan's voice cracked slightly, and Tony knew then that the answer the nurse wanted to hear was a negative.

Quinn rubbed his left earlobe. "That depends on Mr Collins."

Decision time. Tony looked at Rachel helplessly. The rising sun lit up the loose strands of her hair and turned them into threads of gold.

Quinn smiled reassuringly. "Rachel, Bethan's going to take you for a little walk around the grounds. Just to show you that there's nothing to fear here. And we can help you. You won't be locked away for the rest of your life, no matter what you've heard. Fairlight isn't a prison. It's not even an asylum."

Rachel looked at Bethan. The nurse gave a brief, tight smile; it was more of a grimace.

"Just for half an hour."

Rachel turned back to her father. He forced a smile that was more reassuring than Bethan's attempt.

"Go on, Rache. Get some fresh air - the smell of us old farts must be rank."

Rachel sniffed and half-smiled. "Don't give up the day job, Dad."

His smile was easier with her answer. Almost normal again, the same reply she used every time he told a bad joke.

Rachel rose gracefully from her chair, no trace of the sweat stains or dampness on her shorts or the chair that had plagued the two men. The door closed, leaving Tony and the clinical psychiatrist alone with no trace of Rachel but a faint scent of perfume.

Trésor. The same perfume Becky had used. Tony told himself not to be angry; Rachel didn't use it to taunt him with her mother's memory. She used it because she liked the smell, she said. More likely it was another way of keeping her memory alive. He didn't need Quinn to tell him that one.

The psychiatrist appeared more relaxed now that Rachel was out of the room. But a long time passed before he spoke, his ear cocked to the doorway and listening to the fading footsteps on the polished tiled corridor outside.

"Okay, Doc. Now what?"

Quinn stared again at his notepad. The blue ink was smudged in places. Not that there would have been much worth reading anyway.

"Be honest. You don't know." Tony felt the tremble of emotion in his words but wasn't certain if it was anger or fear. Both, maybe. *For God's sake, this man's a mental healthcare professional! Fairlight is supposedly a state-of-the-art facility for researching and treating these cases – so why the hell does he look so lost?*

"No, Mr Collins. I don't." There was relief in his features with the admission. "Rachel is a…rather unique case."

"She's not a *case!*" Tony's eyes blazed.

Quinn raised a hand. "Forgive me, Mr Collins. A poor choice of words, I know. But please try and understand this from my perspective."

Tony released pent-up breath. "Go on."

Quinn cradled his hands and sat back in the leather chair. He stared out of the window. The grey cloud bank had disappeared, and sunlight brightened the summer scene. The sea in the distance was calm.

"Rachel is the only self-harmer who reports positive hallucinations when she cuts herself. I don't need to remind you of what the other poor youngsters say they've seen, do I?

"You've heard the news reports, read the interviews. Believe me, Mr Collins, those are *nothing* compared to the descriptions I've come across in my career."

Tony noted the momentary tremble of the shoulders. He gazed into Quinn's eyes and saw not just an anguished man but a haunted one also.

"It's been going on for years, hasn't it?" Tony said. "Even longer than we've been told."

Quinn was silent. Only the muted scything of the returning mower broke the silence.

"And you're nowhere nearer to working out what causes it – shit, you don't even know how to stop it!"

"That's not quite true, Mr Collins. The psychotropic medications will slow the condition, give us time to...to -"

"Drug them up, secure them and then they're unable to hurt themselves. That's not treatment."

"It's a start," Quinn said quickly, his tone betraying irritation. "At the very least, it prevents them doing further physical damage to themselves."

"And how long can you keep them like that? Until they hit eighteen? Until they get their bus passes? For Christ's sake, how long does the condition last?"

Quinn slowly got to his feet. He passed the desk and placed both palms on the windowsill. He leant forward, his forehead pressed against the glass, his eyes closed.

"We don't know, Mr Collins." He spoke to the glass, obviously afraid to meet the parent's eyes while he admitted his helplessness. "We've had some of the children in here for over three years – yes, that's how long this thing has been going on."

"Three years - oh, my God. And no signs of a cure..."

Quinn opened his eyes and watched the mower complete another strip. The groundskeeper still bounced along in his seat to whatever internal music was jollying him along. Tony saw Quinn's eyes narrow, a sudden flash of anger directed at the worker – or was it envy? That a Fairlight employee could be so blissfully happy while working in an institution that incarcerated young people who suffered such inner torment?

Tony sympathised with the psychiatrist then. He remembered his own feelings of anger at the groundskeeper's happiness. But that wasn't his immediate concern.

Three years. What about the new intake? How long would they be here?

"I don't want Rachel here."

"Of course you don't, Mr Collins. *I* don't want anyone here – but let me ask you this." He raised his head from the glass and looked over his shoulder to face Tony. A sweat smear remained on the glass.

"Can you look after her twenty-four hours a day, seven days a week? Can you be with her at all times, ensure that she has no access to any sharpened edges, or even blunted ones?" Quinn's face was grim. "How can you go to sleep at night, convinced that she won't leave her room and try to harm herself again? How could you do that without sedating her – or even restraining her?"

Tony closed his eyes. He felt tears well up again.

"The simple answer, Mr Collins, is that you *can't*. None of the parents and guardians of the children could – that's why they come here."

Tony fought back a sob. He knew where this was going.

"And that's those with large families – with siblings,

and…partners." Quinn left that hanging, allowed Tony to fill in the gaps.

Your parents are dead. Your wife is dead. You are alone, with no one to look after Rachel when you're at work, the supermarket, sleeping – even taking a shower. You can't help her.

"When did you last get a proper night's sleep, Mr Collins? And how long have you been off work now? This will be for your own good as well as Rachel's, believe me."

Tony bit his lip. "I don't need any help. I can take care of her. I can…"

"But for how long? You're not the first, Mr Collins. Parents have refused to admit their children before. Like you, they thought they could provide all the assistance required, guard them from themselves. You know all too well those cases."

By keeping his eyes closed, Tony could see the newspaper reports, the news websites, the grim-faced anchors reciting more dreadful statistics. One lapse of concentration, allowing the guard to drop for a single moment, and that was when the children defeated their parents' care and reached for the blades.

He opened his eyes again and saw Quinn as a tear-stained blur.

"That's why the Mental Health Act had the new amendment. Legally, I can force her to stay here – but I don't want to do that. Treatment is even harder if it's given without consent. But these are desperate times. The government's first priority is to stop the self-mutilation, the suicides. If that means curtailing certain civil liberties, so be it, they say."

The mower had stopped. Tony saw the groundskeeper

wave to the two approaching figures and dismount the machine. Quinn turned back and opened the window.

Rachel was in front of the nurse Bethan, her head tossed back, playfully kicking up clumps of freshly mown grass. Tony heard her tinkling laughter, saw the obvious joy on her face.

Bethan wore a weary but relieved smile. She turned back to the window and gave a brief wave to Quinn. A sign of confidence. *She'll be fine.*

That was when Tony knew.

"Bethan!" Quinn cried. "Bethan, NO!"

Tony could see the next few moments before they happened, see in painful slow-motion Rachel throw clumps of the grass in Bethan's face, toss another handful at the lawnmower's driver. Saw him splutter and stagger away from the still-running machine.

Saw Rachel extend both hands and with a joyful laugh thrust them under the guard of the mower.

Tony's scream muted Quinn's cry of horror.

CHAPTER TWO

Callum Hayes felt a sharp prod in his ribs. At one time he would have found it painful, but compared to the recent injuries it was nothing. It was just irritating.

He turned and glared at the woman who had dealt the blow. His mother was barely recognisable behind the black veil, but the disapproving scowl and lack of tears from narrowed eyes was just like her. Her lips moved soundlessly, and the black gloved finger pointed to his ears before it jabbed his ribs again.

He sighed and removed one earphone without hitting the pause button. He pulled out the other earpiece and let the cord dangle over his shoulder. 'Archives of Pain' from the Manic Street Preachers' album *The Holy Bible* spilled onto the wooden pew. James Dean Bradfield's voice was metallic and distorted in the silent church, but the line about preaching extinction was perfectly audible.

There. That should piss 'em all off. He turned away from his mother and grinned at the man on his right.

His father glowered at him but didn't raise a finger. He wouldn't dare. Instead, Michael Hayes clenched his fists and pressed the heels of his palms harder onto his knees. He always did that when he tried to bottle up his anger. Never a harsh word, never a slap, never even a *Callum! Do what your mother tells you to!*

Other heads had turned in the nave to stare at him, just as disapprovingly as his parents. He faced them down, his cold, grey-eyed stare forcing some of them to hastily turn their attention back to the vicar standing over the coffin.

He allowed himself a small smile of triumph, which broke out into a full smirk when his mother gave up prodding his ribs and turned away.

The vicar met his eyes once, having heard the tinny sound from Callum's iPhone. His bushy eyebrows furrowed and met in the middle, looking to Callum like a disapproving, sanctimonious caterpillar on a rosy-cheeked globe of pious piss and wind.

A victory of sorts, he considered, an entire village scared stiff of a sixteen-year-old boy. Nothing new there; these bastards shat themselves every time they came near the council estate or deliberately crossed the road to avoid a bunch of WKD drinking teens congregating outside the Londis. Callum didn't fit the media-defined image of a working-class teenager. No shaven scalp or piercings, no tattoos or bling, no street wear or expensive trainers. In his normal uniform of Primark jeans and three-for-a fiver T-shirts from the local market, the cheapest spectacles his parents could find and imitation-Vans trainers that squeaked whenever he walked, he was fair game for the teenage thugs himself, in or out of school. Consistently high grades, a love of literature and cack-handedness at any form of team sports made him an irresistible target. In another time he would have been the victim of them, rather than a source of fear and apprehension.

Another time, he mused. *Might as well be on another planet.* The coffin was proof of that.

He pressed the pause button on the iPhone's music app. Not out of respect for the mourners, but because it amused him to hear what the priest had to say.

One more kid went too far when they harmed themselves.

Go on, explain that *as part of God's plan!*

He stretched leisurely and leaned back on the hard wood of the pew. His black T-shirt lifted over his smooth abdomen, revealing well-toned abs. He saw his mother open her eyes in surprise. A previous look of disapproval at his refusal to wear a suit and tie, now changed to a look of bewilderment. Her baffled gaze swept over the bulge of his biceps and the taut skin that barely contained the new muscles, but she didn't see the bandages and plasters that covered his own self-inflicted wounds.

Of course she hadn't noticed the change in him. Too busy fussing over the girl when she started to self-harm, too wrapped up with researching the condition online, seeking answers from dedicated Facebook pages and message boards when the media and the mental health professionals admitted they didn't have a clue. And then the grief as her daughter became one more statistic, one more hole in the ground. All this time, neither she nor the old man bothered asking *him* how he felt when his sister died. Why he'd abandoned the chess club and had attended the local gym instead.

His father had vaguely noticed. He'd probably even approved, maybe considered that pumping iron and ten-mile runs every morning were a good way of burning off the excess energy and the rage that built inside the boy. A positive way of coping with grief.

But that wasn't the reason Callum had forced the physical change on himself. He didn't give a shit that his sister was dead.

"Megan's passing has been a terrible blow to us all." The vicar's words hung in the oppressive atmosphere of the church, held firmly in place over their heads as though stuck in the wall of heat that blazed from the June sun. Sweat poured from the vicar's forehead, ran down his cheeks to join the tears.

"It is at times like these that we look deep into our hearts and ask the question: *why? Why* has God allowed this to happen? *Why* did He not prevent this terrible, terrible affliction? *Why* has such a wonderful young woman, with such intelligence, compassion and love for life been taken from us in such an obscene way?"

He saw his father lift his fist to his mouth and bite his knuckles to stifle a sob. Callum grinned.

"There *are* no answers," the vicar continued. Callum shook his head and looked at his father. Michael Hayes's eyes were squeezed shut, but the tears still found their way. They mingled with the blood that trickled from the knuckles. His stifled sob escaped, too. High pitched and wheezing.

No answers, Dad? What, not even you, Mister-fucking-know-everything? Callum's grin faded as contempt for his father returned. He knew what his father had been thinking over the last few days. Knew he was blaming himself, questioning his role as a father – as a protector. *If I can't save my own daughter from herself,* his face said every morning, *what good am I?*

The vicar's eyes turned to the bereaved parents, and his eyes softened at the sight of Michael Hayes.

"There are no answers, and *no one to blame.*" A sympathetic, watery smile.

There. That was it. *Console yourself. It's not your fault. You're a good man, and still a good father.* Callum sniggered. In the silence of the vicar's pause the sound was loud, amplified by the cold stone walls of the packed nave. The priest's smile froze, and Callum delighted in the shocked glares from the rest of the congregation. Disapproval mingled with fear.

Still a good father. Shame that it was Megan who went rather than that bastard son of yours.

Callum glared back, turned in the pew to face the rest of the congregation whose hate-filled eyes quickly sunk to their laps.

"Megan Hayes's tragic passing is devastating to us, but we must remember that ours is not the only community to be shattered in this way. The shock and grief we all feel may seem unique to us, but we must remember that what has happened here – and the service we are performing today – is being repeated throughout the country." The vicar sighed and glanced at the coffin. The floral tributes looked tired and wilted, the wreath in the shape of Bongo the cat, sagging as though overcome with the heat from outside or the despair facing the community.

All but one. Callum wasn't surprised by how packed the church was. With a small community of fewer than six hundred people, everyone in Haverton knew each other and Megan had had the knack of being loved by all. Even brighter than her brother, her acceptance by Trinity College Cambridge to study European Literature was no surprise and indeed a cause for celebration. But then, Callum grudgingly admitted, she never flaunted her academic brilliance and managed to be friends with the geeks and the cool kids. Shit, even the thugs that milled around the Londis store showed her some respect. But that may have been more down to the fact that they'd fancied the pants off her.

Funny how no one had ever tried it on with her, though.

Not that she had this I'm-out-of-your-league-so-don't-even-try-it vibe about her which would've turned the other blokes on even more. Neither did she prick-tease. There'd been something otherworldly about her, something that distanced her from the rest of her peers no matter how friendly and charming she was to them.

That otherworldliness was something he understood now. Something he had feared when it had first whispered to him, gave him the impression that it was not the same thing that had spoken to his departed sister. But he knew now it was not to be feared. If anything -

Bloody hell, there was one of the Londis twats over there, just at the rear pew. Sobbing like a fucking girl.

What's up, Wayne? The fantasy-fuck image all gone now that the last memory of her you'll have is of her being lowered to the ground in a wooden box?

Another prod, this time accompanied with a whispered warning.

"For God's sake, Callum!"

Callum sighed. That prod had *hurt.* The fingernail pressed into a gap between his ribs, and he felt the recent wound open up beneath the Elastoplast. Shit. Just as well he'd worn black today to cover the ever-reddening plasters and bandages. Hard work to hide his self-harming, knowing that if his parents noticed, he'd be whisked away to one of the recently built government institutions. But it didn't matter anymore.

The Presence wanted him inside. Why, he didn't know - he'd always thought that his purpose was on the outside. Surely he could follow his as yet unknown destiny to greater effect in the real world? But no. The Presence had been very clear. Only when the coffin was taken out of the hearse and carried into the church by the sombre-faced pallbearers, his tear-faced father in the lead, had it made its decision known to him.

Now was the time to show them. Now was the time to let them all know that the vicar was wrong when he said there were no answers.

"For *God's* sake, Mum? What has God got to do with this exactly?" He grinned at her flinch. Her mouth opened with a shocked gasp; a gasp taken up by the other grievers.

"Callum," his father hissed. Michael Hayes's eyes blazed with fury and fear. "I don't know what you're playing at, but it ends now. D'you hear me?"

Callum stood. He stared directly ahead, looking at the stained-glass window behind the vicar. The crucifixion of Christ was a beautiful, shimmering collection of jewels with the sun blazing behind it. The rivulets of blood were glistening, liquid rubies.

The beauty of death and self-sacrifice, he thought. *Pain and suffering have a light of their own. And it's beautiful.*

"No, Dad. It doesn't end here. It's only beginning." He pushed past his stunned father, forced the clutching, sweat-and-tear-soaked fingers from his T-shirt. He strode down the aisle, an arrogant swagger. The palpable hatred and fear of the congregation fired him up even more.

He pulled off his T-shirt and tossed it onto the coffin. It landed with a wet slapping sound, a mixture of sweat and blood from his wounds. Even he was surprised by the amount of scarlet that oozed from the collection of bandages and plasters on his otherwise immaculate torso. Sharp, horrified gasps and mutterings echoed in the nave. His audience.

Tough crowd. The vicar was the support act, the warm-up. Now was the main gig.

"Cheers, Vic. You can go home now. There's nothing more you can do."

The priest took an involuntary step backwards. "I beg your pardon? What on Earth -"

"On Earth as it is in Heaven. As above, so below, and all that shit. No longer." He grinned as he took the vicar's place behind the lectern. He glanced briefly at the open pages of the Bible and shook his head. He lifted his left arm and pulled off the plaster he'd freshly applied this morning to his shoulder. It came away with a wet sucking sound, pulling away pieces of skin and reopened a wound which gaped like a hungry red mouth.

"Things are changing, boys and girls." He slapped the soaked plaster onto the spread pages of the Bible and moved it in a slow, circular motion, just like his father cleaning the family Passat. Within moments the typed script on the thin pages became illegible.

"Forget the Word of God. He can't help you now. In fact, words will be pretty much meaningless in the days to come. What's coming for us doesn't use language the way we do." He pressed the damp sponge of the plaster firmly into the centre of the Bible, lifted the left cover and then slammed it shut. Blood oozed from the spine and dripped onto the lectern. Callum smiled darkly as he lifted the heavy crucifix.

"Solid gold, eh? Waste of precious metal. Let's put it to some real use." He hefted it in his right hand and turned on his heel. The vicar ducked, just in time to avoid the heavy object striking his sweating forehead. But he wasn't Callum's intended target.

The shattering of the stained glass filled the nave like a bomb exploding. The central panel of Christ's Passion fragmented, and daggers of glass fell from the lead panes, their further destruction muffled by the thick red carpet. Callum knelt down and picked up the closest piece.

Two feet long and curved like an Arabian scimitar. Every edge gleamed in the fierce sunlight that poured through the hole in the window, glistening with a warning of sharp pain to any who dared pick it up.

Callum dared. He was no stranger to pain. And this was for a truly noble cause.

He turned back to his audience. Some were still shaken by the assault on this sanctuary, but none had dared to leave their pews. He had expected a sudden rush from the male mourners, an attack before he could begin his journey. It wouldn't be long, though. He had to act quickly before they recovered their wits.

"My sister is dead. She killed herself but not because she'd had enough of life. Not because she was in despair. She self-harmed like so many others of us do…she just went too far. Didn't know when to stop.

"That's the story, anyway. The truth? Truth is, she didn't believe. She chose the wrong side. The side that's going to lose. And she didn't want to be around to see the final battle."

His fingers caressed the curved side of the fragment. Fresh blood welled from his fingers as he tightened his grip. He brandished the fragment like the scimitar it resembled, swung it round his head three times. Blood flicked from his damaged fingers and flecked the Sunday-Best clothes of the front row of mourners.

When he felt the glass grate against the exposed bones of his metacarpals, heard the grinding, he knew it was time.

"One thing this guy got right. Self-sacrifice. Shame he did it for the wrong reasons."

He raised his left hand, palm outwards. Then he turned it at an angle, just enough for the audience to see the point of the fragment pierce his palm. With no trace of pain or exertion on his features, he pushed the piece of glass right through. His impaled fingers twitched in time to the rasping sound from the bones of his ravaged right hand powering the sword of glass.

He pulled it back quickly and the glass retreated with a wet, meaty sound. He showed the palm to the audience.

"*I am the way,*" he said. "*It is through me that life eternal shall be granted.*"

There were new sounds in the church now. The cries of horror mingled with the shouts of rage and hatred at the blasphemy and the desecration of Megan Hayes's service.

Silence returned in an instant. Because now the mourners saw what was in Callum Hayes's pierced palm.

"*I am the gateway. It is through me that* they *shall come. It is through me that their lives will be eternal...at the cost of your own.*"

The warning – or the promise – was underlined by the thing that emerged from the gaping hole in Callum Hayes's palm.

CHAPTER THREE

The sound of breaking glass followed Tony Collins's scream. Instinct took over from rational thought. He didn't even consider his next actions when confronted by the sight of Rachel thrusting her hands under the flimsy guard of the ride-on mower.

The sliding windows were half closed. His work boot caught the left pane and fractured it, the steel toecap pushing pieces of the safety glass through the spider web window, but the pane didn't hold him for long. He fell through onto the mown grass outside, his splayed hands gouging chunks of earth from the well-tended borders while the rose thorns scratched his face.

"Rachel! NO!"

He knew he wouldn't get there in time. Knew it would be mere seconds before the blades tore into his daughter's hands, ripping the flesh from the bone before yanking the bones from their sockets, churning them into fragments and splinters to be expelled like shrapnel.

The vehicle's driver had finally removed the mown grass from his eyes. He spat out the cuttings that had fallen into his mouth, rubbed his eyes which had turned scarlet from the pollen irritation, then realised he was no longer in control of the vehicle.

He cried out at the young girl kneeling on the grass just to the left of his machine, saw her hands stretching outwards, saw the same chillingly beatific smile that her father saw.

He grabbed the wheel and twisted it violently to the right.

It wasn't quick enough, Tony knew; he saw Rachel's fingers hidden by the red plastic guard plate, knew what was coming next.

He saw the twitching figure of Bethan Appleton, spitting out the cuttings of mown grass from her mouth. Saw her eyes widen in the direction of Rachel.

She can't get there in time, surely, Tony thought, his feet pounding on the soft grass.

Bethan turned in Rachel's direction, thrust herself forward, leaping into the air and crashing to the ground with her arms around Rachel's legs in an impressive rugby tackle that would put an international fly-half to shame.

The landing took the air from Rachel's lungs in a shuddering gasp. Her feet kicked the air, her trainers beating feebly on the nurse's face, but the sit-on mower had turned, and her arms were clear from the machine.

Almost. Her left arm struck the ground and her fingers dug into the soft grass and the blades of the mower swallowed the tips of her right-hand fingers.

Beneath Tony's halting feet the ground seemed to shudder in time with the grinding, spitting noise of the mower. Tony's despairing eyes saw the mower stall and shudder violently, just the way Tony's old Flymo shuddered and groaned whenever he'd run over a stone on their lawn at home.

Blood sprayed Bethan's hair, darkening the coils of copper. She turned away, gagging at the fluid filling her mouth, her eyes squeezed shut. Tony sank to his knees.

The mower finally regained its momentum, overcame the mere hiccup of something that was no greater barrier to its progress than loose stones or pieces of rubble. It left a thin red smear behind which glistened in the bright June sun. The driver jumped off and staggered towards the fallen pair.

Tony wasn't certain if there was screaming from the two women. His head rang with the echoes of his own screams, trapped within a breathless chest. His breath tore from under-exercised lungs in painful gasps and his head swam with the heat that savagely beat down on him, his eyes blinded by sunlight and horror.

He wasn't sure how long he remained on the grass. Oblivious to the shouts and screams in his private world of despair and pain, only the summer scents intruded. He smelt the sweet perfume of the roses in the borders, Becky's favourite flower. He smelt the freshly mown grass, a reminder of picnics and school sports days. He smelt the muted tang of sea air, further reminders of family holidays and joyful, priceless times spent with Rachel and Becky before the dark days. Smells that were so painfully tied in with his cherished memories of happier times that they were a mockery now. He kept his eyes shut, rocking back and forth on the lawn, oblivious to the tears that streamed down his face.

Now the sounds came. Sounds that forced him to open his eyes. The buzzing of flies and wasps and the hyperventilating breathing of his daughter.

Two bluebottles squatted on the red path, lazily soaking up Rachel's precious blood. A wasp buzzed past Tony's head and hovered arrogantly over the bleeding stumps of Rachel's hand, held up to the golden sunshine.

While the groundskeeper stood silent and awkward, Bethan knelt behind Rachel, her meaty arms clasped around the girl's shoulders, rocking her back and forth slowly, smoothly.

Soothing. Ignoring the greedy attentions of the yellow-black invader.

Bethan crooned to Rachel; comforting words delivered in a sweet voice that belied the sharpness of her Cardiff accent. But when he saw Rachel's face, Tony was uncertain as to whether the comfort was for Rachel or Bethan herself.

His daughter's face was paler than before, with the all-too-familiar sight of blood loss and shock. But her features weren't creased up in agony as anyone else's would be at the severing of three fingers above the second joint. Instead, there was a look of wonder in her blue eyes, sparkling with the joy that turned her open mouth into a smile.

The source of her joy drew a gasp of shock and disbelief from Bethan, who tried to fasten a handkerchief around the stumps as a rough tourniquet to prevent further bleeding.

Because there was no need. The blood that dribbled down her knuckles and spotted the waistband of Rachel's shorts slowed and came to a full halt. Nubs of white bone glinted above ravaged chunks of flesh, but no fresh blood appeared.

Bethan frowned and loosened the pressure. Then she squeezed Rachel's palm, her mouth dropping in disbelief as not a single droplet emerged.

"It's wonderful, Dad! She looks so beautiful…" Rachel's eyes turned towards her disbelieving father's, and Tony was overcome. But no relief surged through him at the sight of the impossible arrest of blood flow. Despair churned in his guts, because that joyful expression on Rachel's face did not belong to a fifteen-year-old girl. It was ancient. Ecstatic, beatific and unearthly.

And the words that followed added to Tony's horror.

"Mum is here, Dad. She's here, and waiting for me..."

Tony knew that he shouldn't have been surprised that Fairlight had its own intensive care unit. With all the self-harming cases here it was the law of averages that some would slip through the net of restraints and drugged sedation; some would find a sharpened edge somewhere.

Even so, this was a mental health facility. Surely it would be better to send Rachel – hell, anyone else, come to that – to an outside A&E department?

He pressed his fingers over the small glass window that showed him his unconscious daughter. He traced an imaginary line from the IV line attached to her wrist to the flowing tresses that fanned over the pillow like the hair of a drowning victim. Colour had returned to her cheeks, a healthy pink. Her eyes were closed, in a deep sleep and oblivious to the bleeping of the monitors that crowded around her in mechanical vigil. Oblivious to the white bandages and surgical dressing that covered her mutilated hand.

Pristine, white, and immaculate. There were no spots of red, no sign of fresh bleeding.

He felt a hand on his shoulder. Until then he hadn't realised he was pressing his finger harder on the glass. Too hard.

"Mr Collins."

Tony didn't turn. She looked so beautiful there, so at peace. So...normal. Now the tears came.

How could this be normal? *And why am I so terrified by this...this miracle that stopped her healing?*

"Mr *Collins*." Quinn's voice was even more high-pitched. "We need to talk. Please."

Tony sighed, and with one last, despairing look through the window, turned away from his daughter.

"Okay, Doc. Let's talk." He followed Quinn through the tiled corridor, noting the number of unoccupied beds that surrounded them. The blinds that formed cubicles around each one were drawn backwards, each metal-framed bedstead covered in crisp white sheets that reeked not of disinfectant but lavender fabric softener and the faint odour of freshly opened plastic packaging. Even the plump pillows looked new and unsullied.

No new patients in the recovery ward. That meant the therapy Fairlight offered was working. He hoped so, anyway. The alternative wasn't one he wanted to consider.

The double doors slid open with the activation of the motion sensor. Quinn stood in the lobby, blinking in the fierce glare of the midsummer sun. The stiffening breeze ruffled his swept-back black hair, and combined with his white features, widened eyes and trembling hands, he looked like some mad prophet who had just realised his god had abandoned him. He had put his suit jacket back on despite the summer heat, and Tony knew that was to hide the sweat patches on his shirt.

Tony joined him and reached into his pocket for his tobacco tin. The fresh breeze felt good against his skin, cooling him more naturally than the clinical air conditioning of the recovery ward. The salt air whistled in his ears and coated his lips with a pleasing tang. He took his time rolling the cigarette, cursing the flakes of dry tobacco when they spilled from his shaking hands.

He put the cigarette to his lips and touched the end with his Zippo. The flame fluttered in the stiff breeze, pushing it back to the filter and burning a line all the way through the paper. He sighed and crushed the cigarette into the wall-mounted ashbin.

"What now, Doc?"

Quinn stroked both sides of his neatly trimmed beard with trembling fingers. He kept his eyes fixed on the jagged headline of the coast over the bay. Tony glanced in that direction. The sun turned the lively, incoming waves into a dazzling confusion of diamonds and white-edged sapphire. The bank of low clouds had long disappeared, carried inland and to the town by the sea breeze. The sky was clear and unsullied, as brilliant a blue as the sea water and the closed eyes of Rachel.

"The simple answer, Mr Collins, is that we don't know. I've never seen anything like this before. Rachel's power of healing after such a traumatic incident…well, it's unprecedented."

"That's good, right?" Tony turned his back to the sea and began rolling another cigarette. This one was easier, and the lighter behaved itself. He took the smoke deep into his lungs, held it for a moment while the nicotine flooded his system to give a small measure of calm. He exhaled; the sea breeze whisked the smoke into the lobby.

"If I was a religious man, Mr Collins, I'd say it was miraculous. Not just the immediate halting of blood loss. You didn't see, but the stumps of her fingers healed themselves."

"What?" The second inhalation of smoke escaped Tony's mouth before he could draw it in.

"Exposed bone and flesh — we didn't see them anymore when her wounds were dressed. There was a fresh coating of tissue and even skin. Red raw, obviously – but that's a sign of new tissue growth. A sign you wouldn't expect to see until weeks after such a trauma. We saw it within minutes."

"Jesus Christ."

Quinn stared at him, unblinking. "Mr Collins, why are you pretending you've not noticed this before?"

Tony froze.

"Rachel's psychiatrists and her GP gave me a detailed medical history of her self-harming. There have been no less than twelve recorded incidences. Mostly minor injuries up until now, certainly – but with some of her lacerations she should have much more scarring than she does."

Tony didn't answer. He took another drag of his cigarette. When reduced to numbers, cold statistics like that, the history of his daughter's mental health was even more disturbing. Twelve *recorded* incidences. Mostly minor.

Mostly.

"The deepest laceration was across her abdomen. Last Christmas, I believe? The report stated that the cut was so deep – and so wide - that her lower intestine was perforated. And yet the scar is barely visible."

Christmas. Carving the turkey, another vain attempt to maintain the illusion of normality within the Collins household. Rachel beaming happily, wearing the expensive sweater he'd bought her, the new earrings.

And then the change in her smile. From normal, happy teenage beaming to beatific, unearthly joy as she reached across the table and pulled the carving knife from him. Lifting the jumper before she cut herself – out of respect for her father, not wishing to ruin the Christmas gift he had bought her – the blood jetting over the sprouts and parsnips, splattering the TV set where the Queen's mouth opened, pausing in her speech to the Commonwealth to take Rachel's life fluid.

The stench of opened intestines and their contents, the shriek of ecstasy from Rachel and the cry of despair from her father mingled with the sound of Kate Bush's *December Will Be Magic Again* from the kitchen and the Queen's spoken wishes for a peaceful Christmas and a Happy New Year.

"I…I hadn't noticed, Doc. You've got to remember, I spent so much time patching up – shit, even preventing her new wounds that I lost track of all the cuts she'd made in the past." *How the hell did I forget that one? She almost died with that, the ambulance taking over an hour to get through the snow.* But of course, as soon as she'd been released, he'd had her new injuries to deal with. The abdominal scar had faded like his memory.

"But…there are so many scars on her. Some have been there for years, they haven't faded. And even the most recent injuries…the scars are still there, even more noticeable than the belly scar. So that one…down to the skill of the surgeons, surely?"

"If it wasn't for this morning's incident, I would agree with you. But I telephoned the surgeon who dealt with her case. He had a very interesting story to tell, told me that the intestines and liver had healed *before she arrived in surgery.* The cuts to her belly were large and ragged, no surprise with the serrated blade she'd used. There were chunks of her flesh *missing,* Mr Collins. He did the best he could but wasn't expecting the recovery she had."

There was silence between the two men. Above, a lone

seagull cried as it made its way to roost in the Victorian turrets of the older building that lay in the centre of the Fairlight complex. Tony followed its rapid flight, watched with detachment as the implications of what Quinn had told him sank in. The seagull, aided by the stiff breeze, vanished behind a shadowed chimney stack. Now he felt cold. Perhaps that breeze was too strong after all. And the sun was dipping behind the buildings, about to paint the west wings with red and gold.

"So today's recovery…"

"It changes everything, Mr Collins. It gives us hope. If we can find out just what is accelerating the physical recovery – regrowth, even – we could be on our way to a solution to the self-harming."

Tony drew on the cigarette, but no smoke filled his lungs. The breeze had extinguished the light. He tossed it onto the gravelled ground and looked back to the Victorian battlements of the older hospital building.

"Just because she can heal herself doesn't give much hope for this 'condition' as you guys put it. She's still harming herself, isn't she? No matter how good her body is at mending, *she's still cutting herself.*"

Quinn looked at the ground. There was defeat in his eyes. The mad prophet had found a last glimmer of hope for his faith and saw it fading from view. Like the light of Tony's cigarette, extinguished by the sea breeze.

Tony looked back to the Victorian battlements that towered over the newer buildings. The shadows lengthened and the sun sank behind the cliff tops.

CHAPTER FOUR

"Another one, chap?"

Tony stared at the dregs of his pint glass. When he realised the question was aimed at him, he looked up into the speaker's face. The barman wasn't rushed off his feet – apart from two old boys in their fifties who sat staring with dull eyes at the television and a willowy blonde in the corner nursing a glass of red, he and Tony were alone. Oddly, the barman's features were as tired and drawn as his own.

"You got any rooms vacant?" Tony asked.

The barman nodded. "Eighty quid a night. That includes breakfast."

"I'll take it. And another pint. Fuck it, give me a whisky as well."

The barman nodded solemnly and refilled Tony's glass. While waiting for the Guinness to settle Tony glanced around him. Above the doorway was a glass display case that contained what he took to be a preserved Moray eel, its teeth exposed in a ferocious snarl. Other display cases arranged at strategic spots in the saloon were coffins for other species of preserved fish, various record and prize-winning catches back in the day when Fairlight had been a fisherman's paradise. A *long* time ago, he realised. The cases were dust-free but old, bearing light scratches and signs of over-zealous polishing.

Through the saloon window the sun set on the waters of the harbour, turning the ebbing tide into rippled sheets of gold and crimson. The fishing boats tugged at their moorings, as though desperate to escape from the harbour. Tony closed his eyes at that dark thought and tried to concentrate.

"Usually this quiet?"

The barman shrugged as he handed Tony his whisky. "Been slack for a while now. We could always rely on the summer trade to make up for the winter months, especially with food. But now…"

There were three sets of dining tables and chairs, the white tablecloths pristine and starched, and the black leather-bound menus resting on a chair in the far corner, next to the doors leading to a silent, odourless kitchen, looked like they'd been unopened for a very long time.

The glass had two fingers of whisky. Tony nodded his thanks and drained it. Without asking, the barman refilled it to the same generous level.

"Don't worry, chap. These are on the house. The minute you came in I reckoned you'd need a good drink." There was a haunted, distant look in his bloodshot eyes. His hair was completely grey and yet he couldn't have been older than Tony.

"You know where I've been, then." Tony's voice cracked. His fingers tightened on the tumbler.

Another solemn nod. "That's why we don't get much summer trade. Very few families come and have a meal before their consultation with the doctors at Fairlight. Even fewer come back afterwards with all members in tow. The parents are usually too upset to eat or stay – they just want to get back home."

"Not all, though."

"No. Not all. Some don't want to go home and face the empty house…shit, I'm sorry."

"Don't worry." Tony drained the whisky and turned his attention to the Guinness. *If Becky was still here, would she have insisted we go straight back? Or would she've wanted a drink first?* He knew the answer to that one; the Guinness now tasted sour, and he lowered his glass.

"I'm Adam." The barman extended a hand. Rough and calloused; Tony suspected that he had other, more physical work on the side to keep the failing pub going.

"Tony." They shook hands briefly, and Tony realised just how sweaty his own palm was. Jesus, ever since leaving the institution he hadn't stopped sweating – even though the air temperature had cooled significantly.

The blonde placed her shoulder bag on the counter and unzipped it. Tony glanced at her and considered offering her a drink but could see she was in a hurry to get off. The grey trouser suit and high heels put him in mind of an office worker until he saw the contents of her bag. He saw paperbound exercise books and a copy of Thomas Hardy's *Jude the Obscure.* A schoolteacher.

Adam took a bottle of red wine from behind the counter. He passed it to her with disappointed but non-judgemental eyes.

"Thanks, Adam. I'll settle up with you next week." She placed it in the bag and hefted it. One of the exercise books fell to the floor. Tony reached down to pick it up and frowned at the words, underlined in red marker pen.

We shall meet in the place where there is no darkness.

It was like a punch in the gut. The last words Becky had spoken to him, when she lay dying in her blood and his arms.

"Can I have that back, please?" Her voice betrayed her

wariness. He realised how he must appear.

"Sorry," he said. "That's Orwell, *Nineteen Eighty-Four*, isn't it? That line gets me every time." He sighed and passed the book back to her.

She placed it in her bag, gave him a quick, tight smile and headed for the door. She walked with the self-conscious gait of someone who knows they've had too much to drink and feels sober eyes are watching; judging.

He followed her with his eyes, but not lasciviously. He saw her slumped shoulders silhouetted in the doorway, rogue greys in her too-blonde hair turned silver by the setting sun.

He looked at the two old men. Apart from a disinterested glance in his direction when he entered the pub – as though seeing a grown man on the verge of tears was an everyday occurrence in the Day Gone Down - they hadn't moved. Their pint glasses were half full; the cider within must be at room temperature by now.

"Good game, boys?" He tipped his half-empty glass in their direction.

A slow turn of heads, watery grey eyes as lost and as hopeless as Adam's – or his own, come to think of it – stared straight through him. He considered offering a drink, but then thought better of it. *Just a few drinks, then crash out. Worry about everything else tomorrow when it's time to go back.* The change of scenery wouldn't do him good, exactly, but it would be better than staring at the four walls of his even-emptier house.

"Dark days indeed," an unfamiliar voice said from the television corner. The interruption caused him to forget himself; he turned around and faced the nearest of the old men.

He saw that the TV channel had been changed. Now, a grim-faced reporter outside a church graveyard had replaced the football.

"Happening all over again." He shook his head in disgust, and gestured towards the TV screen, his thin, liver-spotted hand flapping like a dying fish. "Looks like another one. Turn it up, Ad."

The volume display bar on the screen jerked to the right as though trying to obscure the digital banner proclaiming BREAKING NEWS. Tony felt the alcoholic haze slip from him like autumnal mist dissipating in the sun. Except there was no warmth from the TV report. Instead, the cold seeped deeper into his bones.

"...police are at present interviewing many of the witnesses..." behind the reporter, flashing lights painted the gravestones and the yews a sickly blue colour, and the urgent cry of the sirens moved from the left to the right speaker.

Tony's hand shook. His pint glass rattled on the well-polished oak.

"...so soon after the tragedy of a young woman taking her life, this is the second traumatic event to rock the quiet community of Haverton. The funeral of Megan Hayes, who died two days before her sixteenth birthday, was violently disrupted by the actions of her brother, Callum."

The reporter's eyes were cold pieces of flint, her lips tightening as she forced the words out. Tony froze. This wasn't just another self-harming episode. Something else had happened, something that even this hardened newswoman had difficulty accepting.

The other occupants of the Day Gone Down leant closer to

the television in wary silence. The reporter's hand shook on her microphone, and she tossed her hair back to divert attention from the lump in her throat and the tears that had formed in the corners of her eyes. The chips of slate were shiny.

"Yet another victim of the self-harming epidemic that is sweeping the country. And yet..." a pause as she swallowed and steeled herself. "This is the first recorded incidence of a – a *public* self-harming episode."

Tony pressed the rattling glass hard on the counter and gripped the rail with his other hand. He glanced at Adam. Adam's eyes were rooted to the screen, his lips parted slightly. Even he looked shocked.

"Callum Hayes cut himself in...in imitation of stigmata victims."

In a church, at his sister's funeral service? Tony felt colder than he ever thought possible. Not because of the religious connotations, although even in this secular age he found that disturbing in itself.

It was the memory of the last funeral he attended, the weeping and despair of Becky's family, the tears from his own sister who'd seen Tony's wife as the sister she'd never had...that service would haunt him forever. It was his final goodbye to the woman who had saved him from his own self-destruction. As painful as it had been, it was dignified, respectful, and heartfelt.

And the thought of a family member interrupting it with even a cough filled him with cold fury. He remembered glaring at the senile aunt who'd unintentionally farted during the eulogy. That had seemed the worst possible thing to do at such an occasion. But this...

"Another one, Tony?" Whisky followed, drained as quickly and shakily as it had been poured.

"…the motive for this…bizarre act of self-mutilation has yet to be discovered. But that is not the only disturbing aspect of this behaviour." Now the newswoman glanced to a point behind and to the right of the camera, as though seeking approval from one directing the outside broadcast unit. She finally received a nod of approval.

"After physically assaulting the vicar conducting the service, Callum Hayes defaced a Bible with his own blood." A deep breath. "But it's what happened after that is the subject of intense scrutiny and debate by the authorities. He-"

"He should be gutted with his own bloody knife!"

The reporter turned quickly to the voice behind, her bobbed black hair raising and falling.

"I'm sorry?" This to a woman who stepped from behind her and gesticulated to the camera.

"Never seen nothing like it," the woman growled. She was in her mid-forties, with cropped blonde hair and a heart-shaped tattoo on her left breast which peaked apologetically above the low-cut black dress, as though embarrassed by its owner's outburst. "At his own sister's funeral, an' all – and to pull that trick with the thing comin' outa his hand! Sick bastard. Hang 'im, I say!"

The newswoman glanced at her feet and then turned to the camera at a professionally trained angle, to show both speakers in full light. To the camera, with microphone held slightly too close to her lips, she said: "It is this sighting that has caused so much debate. The object that emerged from Callum Hayes's left palm has had many different descriptions.

Some said it resembled a black eel, others described it as a tentacle, while others only saw teeth and claws. Mass-hallucination brought about by group hysteria and sunstroke, or something more sinister?"

"Just a fuckin' trick," the tattooed woman hissed. "That Hayes boy was probably messing around with some chemicals."

The newswoman covered the microphone, too late to stop the swearing broadcast to the nation. She breathed a visible sigh of relief when a uniformed police officer took the woman away. Tony frowned at the sight of the yellow-suited and helmeted figure that briefly appeared with the policeman before vanishing off screen.

"The possibility of hallucination brought about by a chemical reaction has not been ruled out. It is for this reason that the village has been sealed off while experts from the Ministry of Defence conduct an investigation into a suspected biohazard…"

That explained the brief presence of the man in the yellow helmet and Hazmat suit.

"What a load of old bollocks," the old man in the corner growled. "Shows they're really clutching at straws if they gotta come out with such a crap excuse for a cover up."

Tony nodded. He noticed that Adam was silent. Then he saw why. The landlord's eyes were rooted on the glass display case above the entrance. His eyes were unfocussed, as though he was seeing something beyond the eyes of the Moray eel. The news reporter carried on speaking to the television set.

"…Callum Hayes, though, has been taken into custody in accordance with the stipulations of the recently amended

Mental Health Act. His destination is unknown at present, but members of the community I spoke to earlier believe he is headed for the new facility on the south coast, in the Dorset harbour village of Fairlight…"

Tony tore his head away from the landlord and stared at the television. His stool wobbled and a chill stroked his neck.

That nutter's going to the same hospital as my Rachel?

"You okay, Tony?" Adam's eyes focussed on Tony, knowing what was running through his mind. "Don't worry about their new patient…I'm sure he'll be kept well apart from the other kids."

Tony didn't answer. He felt the tiled floor tipping beneath him, like waves in a violent storm.

"Eels and tentacles, eh?" The old man took a gentle sip of his cider and grimaced. "Sounds familiar. History repeating itself, I reckon…"

Tony grabbed the rail on the bar just in time to steady himself. The waves died down.

"What did you say?"

There was an unhealthy gleam in the old man's eyes. He opened his mouth to speak, but the wail of approaching sirens drowned his words.

CHAPTER FIVE

When Rachel Collins came to consciousness, she was so happy she thought she had brought the Light with her.

In the past, awakening from a self-harming episode had been a struggle. She'd fight through the enveloping darkness as a free diver fights against the pressure of the waves, her lungs burning in a desire to release her screams the way the diver's lungs scream for fresh oxygen.

It had always been worth it, though. To break into consciousness with the memory of what she'd seen – and knowing that she had brought the Light one step closer – made the suffering worthwhile. After that, she only had the physical pain of her injuries to deal with.

And now I have a face to put to the Light, she thought as she took in her new surroundings. *And coming here was the right move after all.*

She felt a dull ache in her left hand. She lifted her head from the stiff pillows and wasn't surprised to see both wrists fastened securely to the metal rails of the cot. There was a little leeway in the bonds; she could rotate her wrists. The bandages that swaddled her mutilated hand were speckled with blood, and clenching her fingers within the surgical dressing did two things. Firstly, it brought fresh blood welling beneath the gauze; secondly, she could feel an empty space where her fingers used to be.

She felt woozy, and figured that whoever had placed her here had dosed her with the usual sedatives and painkillers. The cot she lay on was surrounded by dark green plastic sheeting on curved rails. She smelt disinfectant and faded odours of mass-catering meals. There was the expected bedside cabinet with a carafe of fresh water and a matching beaker moulded from the same plastic; there was the solitary plastic chair for any visitor who would be allowed entry at the specified time. Underneath would be the bedpan and the kidney-shaped cardboard trays.

The fluorescent strip lighting flickered once and darkness fell. No longer daytime…

She frowned, trying to remember what had happened before. Dad taking her to Fairlight for a "consultation". The drive from Oxfordshire to the south coast, a scorching journey through the congested motorways and A roads made almost bearable by the air conditioning of Dad's Renault. The silence of the trip, Dad's hands gripped tightly on the wheel, his eyes staring dead ahead and unable – or unwilling – to meet her own. She remembered wanting to put a comforting hand on his forearm, to reassure him that everything would be all right. She'd seen him surreptitiously place the overnight bag in the boot, knew that it contained various toiletries and spare clothes, aware it was for her in case Fairlight insisted she stay. She wanted to tell him not to feel guilty, that this was what she wanted – no, not wanted; what was *required* of her.

She'd fought the temptation to tell him last week. Even when he found the information on her laptop, realised what she was doing, she had held something back.

Even if she survived – if the war was won - she would not be the same person when all this was done.

She looked at the fresh blood welling from her wound. There was an itching in the stumps now, the promise of rapid repair. The pain of the mower blades scything into her hand was a distant memory.

She frowned at the other memory, of arriving in the harbour village, driving along the coastal path to the bay. The fishing boats and pleasure boats moored in the glittering waters, the smell of salt and fish carried by the gentle breeze that swept in from beyond the oceans. Memories of family holidays at the seaside, aromas of chips and ice cream. The scent of history, reminders of more innocent times. They'd stopped and eaten ice cream by the harbour, he trying to amuse her by throwing pieces of cornet to the ravenous gulls that flocked around them. A delaying tactic, done to put the purpose of their visit out of his mind. The sounds of waves slapping on the harbour wall and the creaking of the boat masts, the greedy cries of the seabirds were amplified, louder than they normally would be. To her, anyway. All senses had been sharpened since her visitation. And then the hands on Dad's watch ticking as loudly and ponderously as the wall clock in the funeral parlour where she had seen Mum's face for the last time. Cutting away shards of precious time, ticking inexorably to eleven o'clock and the interview with Quinn.

An interview that ended before any serious diagnosis could be made, with the Light guiding her eyes to the waters of the bay. How clear the waters had looked then. As bright and sparkling as the thing promised beneath. She'd seen hints of it before, a light that despite her attempts to see remained elusive, only appearing in the corners of her eyes when she turned away, her peripheral vision merely hinting at something that waited for her, had called her. A secret that would not be revealed until the time was right.

She'd been dimly aware of Quinn's scribbling on the pad, the noise like rats scratching on skirting boards and attic joists. What was it Quinn had asked her?

What do you see when you cut yourself?

She smiled. Yes, that was it. That was why the psychiatrist was even more nervous than her father. He must have read up on her previous medical history, knew how quickly her body could heal. Knew she was something special.

But why did he ask me what I saw? Does he know? The others who had self-harmed didn't talk about seeing anything, just told of an impulse to mutilate themselves. She knew that from the news reports and the internet forums. There was no answer in their cases, but there was a common denominator. The impulse was the same, as were the physical consequences. There was no rapid healing with their injuries. No visions.

Only *she* saw when she self-harmed. But even if she could put into words what she saw, she doubted that any medical professional would understand.

How could she put what she saw into words – even pictures? It was so far beyond human experience it was impossible to recreate.

And what she saw earlier, just beyond the sloping grounds of the hospital, the thing in the sea fading as rapidly as it had appeared…*that* was why she had to offer herself to the blades of the mower. Only the blood and pain would strengthen it.

And then, as the mower pulled away and the staff of Fairlight bandaged her and sedated her, the clearest vision yet, seen through the red mist of blood and agony.

The vision that stayed with her all through her drug-induced slumber. Parting with an unspoken promise to return and that *she was meant to be here.* Here, in the institution that shared its name with the ancient fishing village, the Light would come through – and she was essential to its birth. The itching in her stumps was accompanied by a dull, repetitive throbbing, a dull but well-timed aching that she was thankful for. The price of destiny.

The time was right. The place was right. And finally, the Light had spoken to her, with her mother's voice. Smiled at her with her mother's smile.

She luxuriated in the sense of purpose that school studies, friends and crushes could never give her. Only the memory of Dad's anguished face when he learned what his daughter had seen – the woman he loved, never stopped loving despite her death – gave her pause.

I just hope you can show him what you showed me, Mum. Show him death isn't the end, that something wonderful is coming…can you do that, Mum?

There was no reply. Her head dipped back to the pillows. They felt softer this time, more welcoming. Her eyes closed and the darkness returned.

She found herself standing on a sunless shore. She wore nothing but the hospital gown and the surgical dressing on her hand. It was difficult to tell if it was day or night; the clouds were as black and bruised as the body of water they met. The surface was a harsh, grey shingle and pebble beach that cut the bare soles of her feet when she tried to walk forwards, to the sea and the Light within.

The ebbing tide was thick and black, the breakers slopping against the shingle of the beach like old oil. She wrinkled her nose at the scent of decay brought to her by the chill sea-borne breeze that played with the hem of her gown. Rotting marine vegetation, perhaps, mingled with effluent and tidal waste. She stared at the seawater which clung possessively to the shingle like some shapeless creature from the depths, eager to reclaim the land and drag it to the deepest pits of the ocean where sunlight never penetrated.

That was when she saw what the tide was washing up onto the shore, and what gave the breakers their crimson-tinged hue.

The smell of decay was now an overpowering stench, and the fish-smell was overshadowed by that of the rotting human meat that fell from the bones of the children.

She opened her mouth to scream but the stink of decay was so powerful she could taste it in her throat. Pieces of flesh, green-black and bloated from their storage in this unnatural ocean, left on the shingle as a gift to the land.

She turned to face the land, ignoring the fresh pain in her feet from the sharp rocks. More blood soaked the shingle and dribbled down to the meat on the shoreline.

She faced what was once a prosperous coastal town. The sweep of the bay and the remains of the fishing cottages marked it as the harbour town of Fairlight, but the memory of eating ice cream on the harbour wall with her father and laughing as he threw pieces of wafer to the greedy seagulls vanished in the full horror of what Fairlight had become.

The fishing boats and yachts were burned-out hulls. Black ash coated the decks and sections of the harbour wall where the rigging and furled masts leant, nothing more than cremated skeletal limbs. The harbour master's hut was a smoking ruin, the glass of the window melted into a glassy shroud coating a shrivelled figure. The stone retirement cottages looked like bombs had exploded underneath them. The grey slate tiles were scattered along the promenade; brickwork and plaster crushed and obscured the neatly tended gardens. Beneath some of the heavier wall sections of the closest, a blood-covered hand feebly twitched once, twice, and then was as still as the rest of the bodies beneath.

The clouds were a lighter grey than those above the shore, but only because of the fresh smoke that billowed up to the sky from the warehouse units on the far side. She followed the course of the clouds, her jaw dropping in horror. They flew against the breeze, heading along the coast to the rocky headland beyond and the hospital that shared its name with the town.

The building complex was untouched by the destruction wrought upon the harbour and the sea. The single-storey villas were pristine, the cream-painted walls glowing with a green tinge as if they contained a hidden light. Behind them, the castle-like buildings of the original Victorian institution retained the colour of the redbrick materials, but now had a deeper hue, a crimson that flowed languidly like the waters of the grim sea to her right.

A solitary figure advanced from the main reception, too far for her to make out individual features but by his gait and bulk she could tell he was male. His arms were outstretched, palms facing upward. He was not alone. But what followed him was not human.

The breeze changed direction, and carried his words to her. A song, but sung in the most unmusical voice she had ever heard. Harsh, shrieking tone, which grated on her ears and sent shivers of dread through her body.

He came closer, moving impossibly fast but not running; there was no urgency in his stride. The whirling, rolling *things* that followed him now wheeled away and past him, two formations that formed an advance guard and a path for him.

Their muscled legs rotated and crunched over the shattered ruins of the townsfolk. One after another, so fast they were a blur. It was only when they came onto the beach itself that they slowed, and even then she could make nothing out of them but a trio of insectile legs, joined to a central hub of bladder-like material that pulsated with each revolution. Like some sickening incarnation of the Isle of Man symbol.

The talons on the legs crunched heavily on the shingle, and she felt the ground shake beneath her. She glanced down and cried in horror when she saw what the shingle really was, and why it was so sharp and damaging to her bare feet.

Fragments of broken ribcages, shards of exploded skulls. Ground roughly, bedded firmly down into the sand by the tides of the death sea, but unmistakably human bones.

The three-legged creatures halted and turned inwards, squatting in the ruins of humanity as though making obeisance to the young man that now faced her, less than thirty metres away. His naked torso was well-toned, the muscles so pure they looked to have been sculpted. Only the scars on his abdomen and the holes in his palms destroyed the perfection. And when his palms gave birth to creatures that stretched over the closing distance and dragged her towards him his smile was angelic.

She came to with a shriek that tore her lungs apart, as violently as the acidic touch of the appendages that had sprouted from the scarred boy's hands. She fought the restraints, rattling the metal bars. She squinted in the glare of the fluorescent strip lighting that banished only physical darkness.

The lights flickered. She heard a distant rumble of thunder and a faint spattering of rain on the tiles above her head. Then something else, almost inaudible over her screams.

She closed her lips, biting on her tongue to stifle the terror. She pulled her head free from the sweat-drenched pillows to listen. Soft footsteps on tiled floors. Trainers or soft-soled shoes squeaked on an overly cleaned and polished tiled floor. Slow, measured footsteps, no hurry in the owner's approach. Or perhaps caution, a reluctance to enter the ward and discover the source of the screams.

The figure came closer, and the plastic sheeting parted with a loud crinkling sound like a body bag being unzipped.

Bethan Appleton's tired and drawn face was pasty in the fluorescent lighting. Her bloodshot eyes struggled to emerge from the dark pits that encircled them. A faint smile escaped her tightly-drawn lips and vanished, not even a memory remaining.

"Hello, Rachel." The Cardiff accent sounded harsher, more grating than before. "What's wrong, love?"

"Night…nightmare…"

Bethan stared at her. She held a clipboard in her hand, but

the sheaf of papers was too big to be contained by the clip. The nurse struggled with them, moving the clipboard around to stop the medical notes escaping. She crossed the cubicle and sat on the hard plastic chair, placing the clipboard on the bedside cabinet.

Another flicker of a smile from the nurse, gone before it had a chance to spread to the cheeks. Under the broad strip lighting stress showed clearly in the woman's face. There were a few strands of grey in the nurse's shock of coppery curls which Rachel was certain hadn't been present during the walk in the hospital grounds earlier. The freckles fought a losing battle against the stress lines to be the most defining feature of Bethan's face.

Bethan stared at the bandages on Rachel's hand and was too late to suppress a shudder. She looked into Rachel's eyes and this time her false smile stayed.

"Must've been some nightmare."

Rachel sank down into the pillows and closed her eyes. She took deep, shuddering breaths before answering.

"I've never had nightmares before. Never…"

Bethan sat back in the chair, an attempt to look more relaxed than she was. "C'mon, love. Everyone has nightmares. Especially with what you kids are -"

"Not me!" Rachel snarled. "I'm not like the others, the Light never frightens me!" She flexed her wrists, felt the plastic straps warn her against further struggle.

"Okay, Rachel. Just calm down a minute…"

"No! You don't understand! Someone's coming here, someone who'll defy the Light! Someone who'll destroy us all!"

Bethan's face took on a contemptuous sneer. "No, Rachel.

It's *you* who doesn't understand. Everyone's got their own stories, their reasons for cutting themselves – think yours is anything special? Think *you're* special?" She leaned closer, and Rachel could smell stale cigarette smoke in her hair, the sour odour of vodka on her breath. Saw the look of hatred in the nurse's face. She paused in her struggles, forcing herself to calm down. This woman was a threat.

"I didn't say I was special. I just said that I didn't have bad dreams. Something bad…"

"Well, you've got more in common with our new arrival than you think! He doesn't have nightmares, either – although he caused his poor bloody family their fair share." The sneer vanished, became a look of anticipation. Rachel froze at that look, and the realisation that the nurse was reaching for a hypodermic. At that moment she was more terrified of Bethan Appleton than the things that had followed the singing man onto the dark beach.

"Callum Hayes is a special case, all right. Kept singing a song…" Bethan held the needle to the light and squeezed the plunger, dispelling the last traces of air in the vessel. Escaping liquid splashed onto Rachel's cheek as Bethan continued.

"Something about hospitals curing and prisons bringing pain. Preaching extinction. What d'you think that's all about, eh?"

A swab of alcohol and then the needle was in Rachel's undamaged arm. The blackness returned, and Rachel went screaming into its embrace.

CHAPTER SIX

Outside the Day Gone Down, Tony watched the rain pummel the harbour. A thick curtain of water obscured the passing cars and pedestrians running for shelter, transformed by the sudden downpour into shapeless, featureless smears of humanity.

The lights of the ambulance and the police escort reflected on the waterlogged tarmac, phantoms of unearthly blue. They too vanished as the road bent to the right, past the disused Customs House and out of the town centre.

On their way to the hospital, Tony realised. He glanced behind him, saw that the landlord and the old man were busy with glass-drying and newspaper-reading respectively. As though the TV report on Callum Hayes had never happened.

Or they're trying to forget about it, Tony thought. He hiccupped, the alcohol feeling sour in his belly.

There was a freshness in the air when the downpour finally ceased. The heavy rain on the ebb tide caused a pleasing saltwater scent to fill the air, to disperse the greasy aroma of fish, chips and cheap burgers from the harbour cafes and stalls.

Tony looked at the darkening sky, wondering if there'd be another downpour. The clouds were passing to the west, covering the sun that sank below the horizon.

He needed a walk. Air in the lungs, blood flowing through the veins; perhaps then he'd have a clearer head and be able to form a plan of action.

There was little sign of life returning to Fairlight. A few faces peered from the rain-beaded windows of the cafes, considering the possibility of a fresh downpour and deciding to stay put.

That suited Tony fine. The last thing he wanted was company.

The thunderstorm had done little to clear the air; there was an oppressive pressure. The build-up to a storm already received. To the west, the setting sun imparted an unnerving scarlet glow to the thunderheads. Like blood weeping from bruised flesh.

That image opened up the wound of his reason for being here. Another pressure built up now, this time from within, and tears became the new rain.

He quickened his stride, angrily wiping the tears away. A gull flew low over him, out to the breakwater. Its harsh squawk sounded like it was laughing at him.

Look at you, Collins! Some husband and father you are! You let the missus hack herself to pieces and now you can't stop your daughter going the same way. He watched the mocking seabird disappear briefly into the whitecaps of the sea before reappearing with a thin black fish that wriggled in the beak. The bird flew on before Tony had a chance to see what it was.

Fairlight was a dead town. The quaint lanterns of the bay had been replaced by cheaper fluorescent lights with low wattage bulbs which made no attempt to dispel the darkness. Was it only ten years ago that he, Becky and Rachel had taken family holidays here? There'd been so much to enjoy back then. The attractions of the pier; the exotic species of marine life in the aquarium; the golden sands of the beach in the bay where the shell of the old Victorian asylum had the good grace to hide from view behind the rolling meadows; the twinkling lights of fisherman's lanterns that illuminated the harbour when the sun slipped beneath the tide like it was going to bed.

Only the remains of the medieval lighthouse on the headland disturbed their peace; nothing more than a jumble of broken masonry and decayed brick, it was one midsummer night that Rachel pointed to it and screamed. Said she saw something shining "like burning oil". She slept in their bed that night, and her trembling stayed with them until dawn. Just the one time, never again; but it cast a pall over the next holidays at Fairlight. Bated breath as they drove down the coastal road and the headland came into view, expecting screams of terror from Rachel. But that had never come to pass. It was only on the second trip back that he'd plucked up the courage to ask her if she remembered anything about the lighthouse; he'd even pointed it out to her, with Becky keeping an anxious eye on their daughter in case of an extreme reaction. Nothing.

He halted. Why had he remembered that? As they drove down the coastal road this morning for the interview with Quinn the jumble of medieval masonry had greeted them, but Rachel had said nothing, not even noticed it. Neither had he.

So why now? Why am I remembering Rachel's reaction to that first night? He picked up his pace, anxious to keep moving. The longer he stayed still, the heavier and more cloying the memories.

Were there clues he'd missed? Did the lighthouse hold the key? No, that was bollocks; it was a one-off, soon forgotten by Rachel amidst the fairytale splendour of Fairlight.

The alley beside the Customs House took him to a warren of alleyways and fire exits of disused warehouses. He didn't even know where he was heading. He just knew that he couldn't face the relics of happier times. Tarnished memories.

The rain hadn't had time to disappear down the storm drains, and his shuffling feet were rapidly soaked by the lagoons of rainwater. The walls towered over him and the pathway behind the Customs House narrowed. The light from a solitary lamp post at the end of the alley only just reached him. He felt hemmed in. The air was thick and heavy and his nostrils filled with the stench of rotting fish and rusting iron.

There were piles of green slush in the gutters that may once have been vegetables. He looked up at the buckled roller-shutter door, sprayed with faded graffiti and dented with what looked like punches. He smiled thinly.

Someone else been in the same situation as me, then? Frustrated, trapped, wanting to let rip? He turned to face the door full-on, raised his right hand and let fly.

The roller-shutter door shivered and rattled in its runners. Metallic shrieks echoed down the alley and rainwater fell from the lintel. Tony snarled, drew his fist back and struck again.

That's for Rachel!

Another punch, harder this time. The skin on his knuckles split; he saw a bloody imprint on the dented metal. He felt no pain, and that angered him.

That's for Becky!

The shutter buckled, allowing him a glimpse of blackness beyond. The stink of rotting fish was more prominent. Now he felt physical pain that almost matched the emotional agony.

That's for the poor young bastards who're tearing themselves to pieces! That's for the poor sods like me who're standing by, powerless, unable to stop their kids killing themselves!

More punches, each stronger and more devastating than the

last. More dents in the roller shutter door, outlined in his blood.

His vision blurred with tears. He was aware of a shouting, screaming, and only when the roller shutter fell inwards with a last protesting shriek of parting metal was he aware that the screaming was his own.

He sank to his knees, his fist beating the sodden pavement. Filthy rain water splashed into his howling mouth and streaming eyes. Blood from his damaged knuckles accompanied the rain water on its way to the storm drains.

He stayed crouched on the ground, bleeding, panting, and weeping. The swirling rain water pulled at his trouser legs as it passed by him, as if attempting to pull him down to the depths below.

He sniffed and raised his head. His vision cleared after blinking several times, and he let out a heavy sigh.

The rage and anger had passed for now. A temporary respite; he knew it would return, just as the black storm clouds over the harbour would come back. Now he felt exhausted, drained, and just wanted to lie down and go to sleep.

What does it matter now? Just one drunken old bloke lying in the gutter, no one's going to notice.

His hand throbbed. He stared at it dumbly, noting the swelling and crusting blood forming over his damaged knuckles and wondered if anything had been broken.

It didn't matter. It was nothing compared to the pain Rachel was going through. And surely –

A movement in the corner of his eye. In the blackness beyond the dismounted roller-shutter, something white and luminous moved in a snake-like fashion along the floor of the warehouse. He had a vague impression of golden orbs, swivelling in black pits. Eyes, staring at him.

The golden discs vanished, and the white snake-like creature disappeared into the darkness.

What do you see when you cut yourself?

He stared at the ravaged knuckles of his hand, his right hand. Rachel had damaged *her* right hand this morning…

His legs gave way and he put up no resistance to the glistening tarmac that rushed towards him.

A hand fell on his shoulder. The bony fingers curled inwards, into a claw, digging painfully into the muscle. Then another hand, palm open, holding his belly. Keeping him from the ground.

"Not this way, Tony." The voice was a whisper, as though its owner was afraid to announce his presence. Tony felt himself hauled upright. He stood on shaking legs, blinking furiously.

"Self-destruction ain't the answer. You, of all people, should know that."

Tony turned slowly as the hands released him. Silhouetted in the feeble glow of the rain-misted lamp light was a small, wrinkled figure hunched in a heavy raincoat. The head had sunk so low into the upturned lapels that Tony wondered if this creature had a neck at all.

The man stepped to one side and allowed the light to illuminate his profile. A matt of greasy, grey hair was plastered to the shrivelled scalp. The nose hooked over wide lips that opened to display nicotine-stained teeth.

"It's me, Jim. From the pub, remember?" he whispered. The hooded, bloodshot eyes shifted back and forth in an uneasy appraisal of their surroundings. "Sorry to scare you, old boy. Thought you needed a bit o' support."

Tony felt no relief from this offer. The nervous flicker of the old man's eyes unsettled him, and for a brief moment he forgot about the pain in his hand, the rage and despair he had felt, even about Rachel.

Now he realised he hadn't imagined that thing in the warehouse. He took a deep breath and felt the ground shift beneath his feet like the deck of a storm-tossed fishing boat.

"Easy, Tony." Hands clutched at him again, supporting hands, concerned hands. "C'mon, we gotta get movin'."

"Why?" Tony allowed himself to be escorted back down the alleyway, past the old Customs House, and back onto the cobbles of the harbour front. In the gloom of the approaching night he saw the fishing boats' red and green mast lights swaying ponderously. The wind was stiff, turning the incoming waves into a choppy mass of silver-capped blackness. The breeze poked at his soaked polo shirt and he felt the beginnings of a chill. His hand throbbed in time to the rustling noises of the breakers on the shingle.

Jim glanced back the way they had come and breathed a rattling sigh of relief. "I didn't think you'd be heading into the Old Town. Thought you'd be heading up to the asylum."

Tony flushed. "It's not an asylum, it's a hospital."

Jim eyed him quizzically. He took out a crumpled packet of Lambert & Butler. "Asylum's what we called it in the olden days. Mad 'uns go in, locked away…and never come out again. Nowt has changed up there, I'll tell you that."

The lighter flared; the tip of Jim's cigarette glowed scarlet. Heat momentarily replaced the chill in Tony's bones.

"Don't give me that old shit, man! It's a modern treatment centre, not a prison!"

Jim coughed smoke as he chuckled. His breath steamed in the drizzle-filled air. Breath that reeked of cider and rum.

"Course it is. Modern therapy, plenty of day patients, everyone who's sectioned released after they're cured." His eyes softened. "Sorry, Tony. I'm not taking the piss. I know what you're going through."

"Really."

Jim took another drag of his cigarette. "Y'look cold, son. Let's go somewhere a bit warmer, and I'll tell you a little bit o' history."

Tony narrowed his eyes. "Tell me now."

"Thought I'd be in fer a little drinky, then. Oh well…" Jim shrugged and shuffled past him, trailing smoke.

Tony sighed. "Okay, Jim. Where do you want to go?"

The old man halted. When he turned there was a contented gleam in his eyes.

"Nice little boozer down the end, near the pier. Late licence, an' all…"

For fuck's sake. "Well, I owe you one for saving me from a night in the gutter. So I -"

"Saved you more from *that*, boy." There was fire in Jim's eyes. He gestured to the harbour as they walked. "Fairlight ain't the town it was, young Tony. Used to be one o' them rare things – a prosperous fishing centre and a family seaside resort. Summat for everyone."

Tony fell into step beside him. He kept his hand to his chest in an attempt to keep the pain tolerable. "I used to come here on holiday with my family, Jim. I remember what a great place it was."

The sounds of a harbour at night filled his ears. The creaking of timbers on dilapidated and barely used fishing vessels, as tired and as hopeless as the men who piloted them. Ahead, the slamming of a pub door and the shattering of a pint glass on the cobbles, followed by the raised voices of two angry and very drunk men who disappeared into an alley to continue their dispute.

Tony rolled his eyes. Whoever they were, they'd started early. He pushed open the creaking door and stared at the huddle of men and women staring disconsolately at pint glasses and cribbage boards. The barman glowered at them behind his prison of brass pumps and optics, but his features lightened once he saw who was accompanying the stranger.

Tony scanned the drinkers. All in the mid-fifties onwards, no one younger. Not one of them looked sober; none of them looked happy.

"Not much to do now but sit and get pissed, eh, Jim?" He didn't mean it to come across as sarcastic. After all, Fairlight wasn't the only British town whose residents indulged in heavy drinking as their main recreation. But Jim stiffened, halted his stride to the bar and straightened his back.

"'It ain't just the lack of work that drives blokes like me to drink, boy. It's history that does it, and the fear of it repeating."

Tony paid for their drinks. A double Scotch for Jim and a glass of Coke for himself. He knew that what he was about to hear he needed to be sober for. The barman grunted as he took the ten pound note and slammed the change on the counter.

Tony glared back as he scooped up the change with his

undamaged hand. He beckoned to the drinks.

"Let's find a table. You take the drinks."

It seemed that Jim felt more at home in this 'nice little boozer' than the family-friendly Day Gone Down. Not only were they in the same age group, but the drinkers all had the same shrivelled, lost demeanour and the thirst for alcohol. A hunger for oblivion, the desire to blot something from their minds.

The conversation was low and muted. Tony was aware of eyes upon them. Jim was oblivious. He took a hefty swig of his Scotch and smiled with delight.

Or relief? Tony wondered, taking a sip of his Coke. He kept his damaged hand hidden as much as possible, ignored the surly attention of the regulars and focussed on his host.

"You talked about history in the Day Gone Down…and then about it repeating. What did you mean?"

"'xactly what I said. That young 'un cutting himself up in a church and comin' to Fairlight. That new building's only been up a few years. Why d'you think they built it around the older asylum instead of a new spot?"

Tony opened his mouth to speak, then closed it. The same thought had occurred to him earlier that morning on the drive to the town, but he hadn't considered it again. Too much had happened in the space of one day to think clearly.

"Good question, Jim. What's the answer, and what's it got to do with that Callum boy?"

Jim grimaced. It might have been the weak lighting from the grimy sconce lanterns, but to Tony's eyes the old man's face was paler, his eyes more distant, as he visited the past.

"It's bad now, o'course. Never been so widespread. Before,

it were confined to Fairlight. Seems them in power think this town's the best place for them kids, think they can do 'em some good."

Tony thought back to his argument with Quinn during the initial assessment. *Drug them up, secure them and then they're unable to hurt themselves. That's not treatment.*

And then later, on the lobby. *If we can find out just what is accelerating the physical recovery – regrowth, even – we could be on our way to finding out how to stop the self-harming.*

"The answers are here, then. But how does Callum Hayes fit into it?"

Jim shook his head sadly. "That's what's got 'em all scared, and overreacting. See, what that kid done in church reminded 'em that it weren't stopped, just delayed."

"*What* wasn't stopped? And how come you know about all this?"

Jim's smile was grim. He lowered his Scotch and unbuttoned his overcoat. Underneath was a stained green sweatshirt with frayed cuffs and collar. He took a deep breath – a steadying breath, Tony noted - and then rolled up the shirt.

A flaccid belly the colour of uncooked cod poked out, the navel a solitary eye that glared at the outsider.

The hairless chest was revealed, puckered skin with goosebumps like a freshly plucked chicken. Then the scars.

Tony's glass fell to the floor.

Jim kept the shirt grasped in his hands, held to his jaw. His smile turned to a grimace.

"I been there, boy. I been through the same thing that Callum kiddie's going through. And it was Fairlight Asylum they took me to."

CHAPTER SEVEN

Callum Hayes chuckled as he took in his new surroundings. Jesus, these fuckers really *were* scared of him! A padded cell. A padded *cell*, for Christ's sake! He stroked the cushioned fabric. White vinyl, stained with the ages and inmates gone by, as well as their blood and urine.

He turned on his shoeless heels and stared at what he imagined to be the door. Yes, definitely the door. There were darker stains here, more signs of wear and tear on the padding. Funny to think this was the first section where inmates would try to damage themselves – not to cause themselves pain, but from the knowledge that as this was the way in, it must also be the way out. Head lowered, a good run-up…and when that didn't work, scratching and clawing at the vinyl in a vain attempt to find the sills, the hinges…

No, not me. I'll wait until you let me out. And that won't be long…

He sat on the floor. Just as cushioned as the walls and the door – if he'd been drugged or drunk the sensation would've been disorientating. *Imagine the room spinning when pissed up! You wouldn't know what's up and what's down! Ceiling, floor…floor, ceiling.*

Just like the little joke he'd made to the nurses when they bundled him out of the ambulance and raced him down the pristine green-painted corridor. The wheels of the gurney moved smoothly, no squeaking – no badly-oiled castors. Only the rapid thudding of soft-soled shoes behind him, pushing him further and further to his new home. One of the orderlies had leant over and glanced at him briefly. Callum had grinned at the inverted face of the nervous-looking man and would have grasped the ID tag that swung on the breast pocket of the man's short-sleeved shirt if his hands hadn't been securely fastened to the rails.

No uniform, then? Civvies, just to make us feel at ease – but without that little tag, who's to know who the staff are and who the patients are? Especially after working here for a few years. Insanity IS infectious, y'know! Staff, patient…patient, staff…

The wordless response to that had been increased speed to the cells. Callum had decided to sit quiet and enjoy the ride.

His first impression of Fairlight Hospital had been as expected. It was odd that they hadn't offloaded him at the rear of the complex, but as Fairlight's purpose was no secret they didn't need to hide the new additions. He'd caught a quick glimpse of the residential villas before the lobby of the new admin block swallowed him and his gurney. Past the unmanned reception desk, down a corridor where he heard muted female screams penetrating the closed door marked INTENSIVE CARE.

The screams had raised a snigger from him.

He examined the studs of the padding with the tip of his finger, tracing a figure-of-eight pattern when a thought struck him. He frowned, rocked back and forth on his crossed legs and stared at the holes in his palms. That girl's voice, screaming. He'd never heard it before, he was certain. And yet there was something familiar about it. If they'd put him in IC he'd find out more.

But they *hadn't* put him in IC. Shit, they hadn't even

bothered to dress his wounds.

But there had been no need. He raised his left palm and stared admiringly – and slightly nervously – at the smooth, rounded hole. The scabs of black blood had come away during the trip to Fairlight. Even he had been amazed at the result.

With the size of the gash, his hand should have required immediate surgery. The tendons should have been so damaged as to render the hand unusable. But not only could he flex his fingers and clench a fist with no restriction on movement, there was neither pain nor fresh bleeding.

The wound had healed. A fresh layer of skin, angry and sunburn-red, coated an equally fresh layer of reconstructed flesh.

And yet the hole remained. He extended his fingers, opening the hole wider. A perfect, two inch hole – not a slash, but a rounded lozenge half an inch in length that he could see through. The hole on the right hand was exactly the same.

A muffled sound from the facing wall. The door unlocking. Callum grinned and placed his palms over his face. Fingers splayed over his forehead, to enable the eyeholes in his hands to open fully. He saw perfectly. It was a fine picture frame for the opening door and the woman who came through it.

"Peek-a-boo!"

The woman froze. Her eyes narrowed; her grip on the clipboard tightened. Callum took the picture-frame palms from his eyes, to better view his visitor.

An untamed mass of red-gold curls with frizzy grey strands, and a pale, anxiety-lined face. Dark-circled eyes and tight, bloodless lips. The lower lip had half-moon indentations, and the edges of the top lip had black spots that could only be blood clotting from nervous bites.

Callum looked again at the injuries on his own bloodless palms and grinned broadly at his visitor. Like the orderlies, she too wore a laminated ID card, clipped to the strap of her vest top. He read the name.

"Bethan, eh? Come to give me the house rules?"

Bethan didn't answer, but a faint smile played at the corners of her mouth. Callum figured she was a hard bitch, but there was no doubting the warmth in her eyes. She was pleased to see him.

That was more than could be said for the man who followed her into the padded cell. Tall and painfully thin, with swept back black hair that was greying at the temples. The beard wouldn't be far behind, Callum thought. Weight loss and greyness brought about by stress, by the looks of it.

Dark grey suit and tie. Obviously a head honcho, and the name tag confirmed it. No first name, just Dr Quinn. And the look in his eyes was far from welcoming. A mixture of horror, fear and hatred. The last time Callum had been stared at like that had been in the church this afternoon, by everyone. It was a reaction he was becoming accustomed to and enjoying immensely.

"Callum Hayes." The guy spoke with a high-pitched voice, but the tone didn't hide the contempt. He took the clipboard from Bethan and flicked through the topmost pages. His eyebrows rose.

"Dr Quinn." Callum placed his hands behind him on the padded floor and sat back. His grin broadened.

Quinn lowered the clipboard and stared hard at his new charge. "No pain, then?"

"Silly question, Doc. No blood, the holes are healing up, so of course there's no pain."

"And no loss of sensation? Perfect mobility in your fingers?"

Callum stroked the white vinyl. "Slightly cool, plasticky but quality padding. No expense spared, eh? As for mobility…"

Callum brought up his hands, waggled his fingers and retracted all but two. Two middle fingers pointed to the ceiling.

"Perfect, Doc."

Quinn's mouth tightened. He turned to Bethan, who didn't return his look. Her softened eyes were fixed on Callum's hands.

"So how long am I going to be here?"

Quinn cleared his throat. "Just as long as we're sure…you're safe."

"Come again?"

Quinn unclipped a piece of paper and held it towards Callum. "I hope it *doesn't* come again, Callum. But we're taking no chances…" the paper fell to the floor.

Callum frowned, leant forwards and picked it up. It was a print-out of an emailed picture. High resolution, good lighting and crisply printed from what was an obviously expensive laser printer. Callum wondered who had taken the photo. When he'd stood behind the pulpit, impaling his palms with shards of stained glass, he hadn't noticed anyone raise a camera. But someone had obviously taken a quick snap on their phone's camera.

"Anyone else seen this?"

Quinn shook his head. "Of course not. This is being kept under wraps until we can figure out what the hell is going on."

Callum nodded thoughtfully. "Makes sense. Can't make this public, folk'll be bricking themselves. Far better to go with the story that I'm just another nutjob with a death wish. And eventually, the people who saw what came from me will be doubting their own eyes, mass hysteria…"

"You catch on quick, Callum." Quinn's hostile demeanour was betrayed by a shudder that he tried to contain by holding the clipboard to his chest. He raised his free hand and pointed a trembling finger towards the photo. "Don't suppose you'd care to explain that…that *thing,* would you?"

Callum shook his head. "What makes you think I *can* explain it?" He was aware that there was a tremor in his voice. Like Quinn, he was too late to prevent it.

It's a part of me. It's always been there…. Now he wasn't so sure. Staring at the picture, being on the opposite side of the pulpit, he had difficulty accepting the existence of this truly alien thing that emerged from his hands. His own expression disturbed him. When he had mutilated himself he had been convinced he was in full control of his actions.

But his face…God, he looked to be in some sort of rapture. The smile was one he'd associated with religious nutcases, a thousand yard stare with a beatific smile.

"We'll speak more of this tomorrow." Quinn turned on his heel and nodded to Bethan.

"Hang on a minute! I want -"

"Callum. I'm extremely tired." Quinn slowly turned his head. "You're not the first admission we've had today, and I'm not in the mood to discuss anything further tonight. If it's food or water you want, something can be arranged."

"Fuck that."

"As you wish. I'll see you tomorrow." He turned back.

"Hey, hold up, bossman! Don't you want your picture back?" Callum held the sheet of paper towards the psychiatrist. He realised he was holding it gingerly, just by thumb and forefinger at arm's length.

What the fuck's wrong with me? It's just a picture!

Now Quinn smiled. His lips drew back from his teeth in a wolfish grin. Callum didn't like that smile. Now he began to feel uneasy. Losing control.

Hatred, fear and contempt he could cope with – no, those were the things he *wanted* from the older generation. But this…this was something else. He looked briefly at the photo and reluctantly lowered his hand when it became obvious Quinn wasn't going to take it from him.

"Good night, Callum. Sleep well." He left the cell. Bethan stood aside to let him pass. She stood in the doorway for a moment, her eyes on Callum. Was that pity in her eyes? Nah, surely not. And yet…

She blew him a silent kiss, winked at him and whispered something before she followed her superior.

The door closed slowly and silently. Callum didn't notice the locking on the other side; it was Bethan's words that kept ringing in his head.

"Soon, hon. Your army is gathering."

A grin cracked on his face. Warmth and vitality surged through his body like a rush of adrenaline after a long bout of running and weight lifting. And nowhere did it feel more powerful than in the palms of his hands.

The photo didn't seem so disturbing now. He picked it up with both hands. Come to think of it, he looked pretty good in that pose. The hands raised in benediction, a priest blessing his flock. And the smile…nah, wasn't a religious nutcase smile. It was a holy smile. The preacher of extinction.

I wonder… he took one hand from the paper and stared at the hole in the palm. The vitality that surged through the hand was almost painful. Through it he could see the black denim of his jeans. And something else. He blinked.

There it was again. A glistening black film, darker than his denims, appeared in the centre of his palm. A skein that filled the hole completely. He flexed his hand, marvelling at the way the shiny film rippled like oil on seawater.

He checked his other hand. The film was there as well. He prodded it with his index finger. It felt rubbery, thin but tough, like the nitrile gloves the ambulance drivers had worn when they secured his wrists to the gurney.

It had an aroma. He raised his palm and sniffed. Pungent, sweet and cloying, like the floral tributes that had covered his sister's coffin, but with an underlying scent he couldn't quite place.

Something earthy, like freshly dug soil, and with a hint of rotting marine vegetation.

Then something else. A hint of stale crisps, pool table chalk and spilled beer. There was noise as well.

Firstly, a hissing sound, like the tide washing over a shingle beach. So low he had to bring the hands to his ears to hear it. The film-like plugs in his palms felt greasy and cold against his earlobes, like wet fish. Then the sound changed.

Voices. Male, middle-aged and speaking in low, hushed tones. Nervous, fearful.

Callum took the holed hands from his ears and stared in

wonder. There was movement within the plugs of black skin on his left palm. The darkness shifted, melting away to form shadows and silhouettes that moved.

There was little light to make out the picture completely, but Callum Hayes had the impression of two men sitting on a table. They lifted glasses and drank during gaps in their conversation.

The picture wasn't clear, but the voices were perfectly audible.

That young' un cutting himself up in a church and comin' to Fairlight. That new building's only been up a few years. Why d'you think they built it around the older asylum instead of a new spot?

Callum stared in wonder. Whoever these two men were, they were talking about him.

The answers are here, then. But how does Callum Hayes fit into it?

The mention of his name made Callum start.

That's what's got 'em all scared, and overreacting. See, what that kid done in church reminded 'em that it wasn't stopped, just delayed.

"Bloody hell," Callum whispered. His voice sounded strange, his words distant, as though spoken from somewhere else, while the words of the two men his palm transferred to his ears seemed so clear, so audible, it was as though he was sitting in between them. He heard the clunk of pocketed pool balls and the jingle of a paying-out fruit machine.

He smelled the beer, the tobacco on the older man's breath. And the stench of rotting flesh from the scars that were shown to the younger man.

I been there, boy. I been through the same thing that Callum kiddie's going through. And it was Fairlight Asylum they took me to.

Although the two speakers were nothing more than vague shadows, the scars on the withered chest stood out like bright slashes of crimson, as though they were fresh wounds only recently inflicted.

Callum brought his palm closer to his eyes. The smell of the pub was stronger, and the image cleared somewhat.

*In for a penny, in for a pound...*he closed his eyes and brought his palm to his face. His fingers curled around his temple, but apart from that he felt no sensation. He couldn't feel the bristle of his eyebrows, the protrusion of his nose. There was no pressure on his closed eyelids.

He opened them. The shock of standing in the pub, by the two talking men, was so great he gasped and took his hand away. He blinked and shook his head, struggling to take in the original surroundings of the padded cell.

The image in his palm was a shadow-show again.

I think I understand now. His palm found its way to his face once more.

Back in the pub. He kept his palm fixed firmly on his face, his fingernails digging into his temple. Clamped tight, like a facehugger from those *Alien* movies. Through the black film in his holed palm, he saw the two men perfectly.

The old man still had his jumper raised above his waist, a finger pointing inwards. But it was the younger man who caught Callum's attention.

He was in his late thirties or early forties. Average height, but with a stocky build and muscles that bulged under his polo shirt almost as much as Callum's. A manual worker, he figured. Probably a truck driver, judging by the logo on the shirt. But it wasn't his appearance that unnerved Callum; it was the atmosphere of pent-up rage and hidden strength. A strength that was not merely physical, and one that could only have been obtained through personal suffering. A strength that the man himself wasn't aware of.

This guy's dangerous. He's a threat.

"Jesus wept, Jim. What happened to you in there?"

The old man didn't respond. He frowned, lowered his jumper and turned round. His eyes met Callum's and stared right through them. Then widened in terror.

He can't see me...but he can sense something.

"Jim, what is it? What's wrong?" The younger man turned to face Callum, but his reaction was one of bafflement. He couldn't sense Callum like the old man could.

"*It's come back.*" Jim got to his feet and kicked the chair away. His hand shook as he pointed to Callum. "Jesus, it's outside the Pharos!"

Pharos. It was a word Callum had never heard of before, but Jim's utterance of it acted as a trigger to some dormant part of his mind. A part that sprang to action.

A part surely powered by the Presence. He had no control over his next steps. Like a mannequin powered by an unseen puppet master, he lunged over the table, knocking the pint glasses to the floor in an attempt to grab hold of the old man. His left palm still firmly clasped to his face, he reached with his right and stretched over, clutched at the bony flesh beneath the jumper.

Callum almost recoiled at the sensation. It was cold,

clammy like a dead snake. The ribs felt like chicken bones, but the scars that criss-crossed the old man's chest were ridges of stone. He pulled the old man towards him, pushed him onto the table and leapt up.

His knees dug into Jim's abdomen, and the old man coughed, howled and then spewed a torrent of cider and blood. Callum grinned at the scent of approaching death and pushed harder with his knees. He raised his right hand, clenched a fist, and powered it down. The table's legs gave way and they crashed to the floor, both rolling until they came to a crumpled heap at the younger man's legs.

The man called Tony cried out in alarm and took a step backwards, a disbelieving expression on his face as Callum continued the relentless assault. The chicken bones crumbled with each blow.

Blood and cider filled Callum's nostrils and he shrieked with glee, a cry that could not be heard by the stunned onlookers in the pub. The killing blows were not his own, but he relished the surrender of control. A flood of exhilaration coursed through his veins, a force more powerful and energising than mere adrenaline.

This was *power*. What he had done in the church at his sister's funeral was one thing, but he'd never imagined anything like this. He didn't know who this old man was, didn't care about his story – the Presence commanded his destruction, and had given him the means to do it. Who was he to question it?

Jim's eyes were glazed. Blood-tinged mucus dribbled from his nostrils. His screams had been replaced by dazed, punch-drunk mumblings.

One more blow, and he's finished! The thought of extinguishing a life sent a cold shiver of delight through Callum's body. He felt his cock stiffen, hard for the first time since he had begun working out, self-harming and allowing the Presence into him.

"Lights out, old ma -"

A blinding white light filled his vision. Brilliant, untainted white, so pure and clean it could have come from the sun itself. Or from another source of power not meant for human eyes. It burned right through the palm-portal, shrivelled away his closed eyelids and melted the eyeballs in their sockets.

And still it shone. Still it burned, turning his optic nerves into shrivelled twigs as it travelled directly into his frontal lobes and exploded.

The force blew him backwards. He flew through the air, only dimly sensing the world spin around and above him, lost in his private world of pain.

The fall wasn't as hard as he feared. He was on his back, but the harsh wooden floor of the pub was replaced with soft, padded cushions. His hand fell from his eyes, but he saw nothing except the same blinding white light.

Ageless seconds passed before the light condensed into a single source. An artificial light. He groped the cushions and recognised the padding of his cell.

There was a warmth in the material that hadn't been there before. The vinyl coating felt wet and slimy. There remained an aroma of stale cider, mingled with freshly-coughed blood. His vision restored, he ran his right hand along the padding and stared at what his skin collected.

The old man's sputum. Vomited alcohol and warm, black

blood.

He felt a tingling in his left palm, and heard a sound like Sellotape peeling away. Or dead, sunburnt skin.

The skein of darkness had gone. The centre of his palm was a rounded hole once more.

And with its departure, the dark energy that had flowed through every atom of his body dissipated. His shoulders slumped and his head sank on his chest, a head that still fizzed with the fireworks that had dragged him back to his cell.

His breathing returned to normal, no longer a rapid hyperventilating. His eyelids felt like they had kilogram weights nailed to them.

The Presence was no longer with him. Whatever that light was, it had been too powerful; the Presence had gone, and taken Callum's energy and strength with it.

But it'll be back. I know it. A temporary retreat while it analysed this fresh intelligence, this new power and its origins. And how to destroy it.

For now, though, it was best to give his new keepers the illusion he was still in control. That his mind wasn't whirring with unanswered questions and fears that he would lose his powers to terrify people.

He turned to the mirrored viewing window and waved smugly to the unseen watchers with his healed hand. He held his other hand to his mouth and slowly, lasciviously, licked the diseased blood from his fingers.

CHAPTER EIGHT

"So let's get this straight." The uniformed officer checked his notepad with a grim expression. He looked back to Tony with suspicious eyes. "He lifted his jumper, showed you some scars…and then collapsed on the floor."

Tony sighed. He stared at the empty space where Jim had thrashed in blood and agony. Tony could still hear the sound of cracking ribs and the air wheezing from punctured lungs.

"A pint glass fell to the floor first. Jim thought I'd knocked it over."

"And did you?" The copper's watery grey eyes narrowed; his pencil moved to his neatly trimmed beard. An accusation. *You were pissed up and had an argument. A fight in which you had him on the floor and broke his ribs.*

Tony fought the urge to retort. He knew how crazy the situation must look to this ridiculously young looking policeman, but there were plenty of witnesses who would surely vouch that he hadn't laid a finger on the old man; there were no tales of raised voices or arguments. *Stick to the facts…but don't tell him about the thing that appeared after Jim fell to the floor.*

Because then *he'd* end up in Fairlight as well. He looked to the now-deserted bar, caught the eyes of the landlord who suddenly looked away. *Yeah, you saw it as well, didn't you?*

"No, officer. As I said, he keeled over and fell to the floor. He clutched his chest…looked like he was having a heart attack."

"How d'you explain the broken ribs?" The officer's eyes

rested meaningfully on Tony's damaged hand. Tony had cleaned the crusted blood from his knuckles in the pub's washroom but there was no hiding the damage done to his hand.

"I can't. All I can tell you is what I saw." Tony's eyes bored into the policeman's.

"Nasty cuts on your hand, Mr Collins. Quite a few bruises as well. How did that happen?"

"I tripped on the harbour front. I was drunk." *I'm bloody sober now, though.*

"You tripped. I see." Another scribble in the notepad. "What brings you to Fairlight, Mr Collins?"

"I'm not on holiday here. My…my daughter was admitted to the hospital this morning. I needed a drink after that. So I decided to stay for the night. And believe me, this is *not* the way I planned on ending the evening."

"No, of course not. Where is it you're staying?" The officer jotted down the name of the Day Gone Down. The notebook was closed and returned to the policeman's pocket. A thin smile followed. "I think that'll be all for now, Mr Collins. I'd like you to come to the station tomorrow to make a full statement, obviously. Shall we say ten o'clock?"

"Fine. I'll be going to the hospital straight afterwards. Speaking of hospitals, where've they taken Jim? I'd like to pop by before I see my daughter."

"I don't think he'll be in any fit state to be allowed visitors."

"He'll see me." *And he might know what that light was — because as soon as the flash appeared, whatever was beating the shit out of him disappeared.*

"Depends on what the doctors say. I wouldn't get your

hopes up." There was irritation in the policeman's tone, and an evasiveness. Tony pressed harder.

"Perhaps I can meet the doctors, then? I'll ask again. Which hospital has he been taken to? Where's A&E?"

The copper stood up with an uneasy expression. "I'll show you where it is tomorrow, after your statement."

It hit Tony then. "My God. There is no other hospital, is there?" *Jim's in the same place as Rachel and that Callum nutter!*

"He's in good hands," was the curt reply. "They have their own Intensive Care unit. He'll be well looked after."

Tony hesitated. "Well, I'll take your word for that. I'll see you tomorrow, officer."

The policeman gave a slow, appraising nod and turned to the door. The clean-air smell of an emptied sky wafted in on the sea breeze, dispersing the smell of spilled cider and blood. He paused, a frown on his face, before turning back to Tony.

"Might be an idea to have an early night, sir." He pulled the door shut behind him.

The implication wasn't lost on Tony. *We'll be watching you.*

He didn't have any inclination to do more exploring, anyway. He felt tired, but not drained. Oddly, he felt a sense of euphoria rising within him, a feeling that had nothing to do with the alcohol and everything to do with the thing that had stopped the unseen assault on Jim.

He closed his eyes and saw again the white flash of light that had burned itself on his retinas earlier. Brilliant, unsullied and somehow...*cleansing* was the only word he could think of. It had exploded all around him, and for a moment when he had tried to free Jim the light was all around him, as though he was in the centre of a nuclear explosion.

But one that didn't burn. The light had shot through every inch of his body, but he didn't feel pained by it. He felt comforted.

Because a voice had accompanied it. A familiar, and well-loved voice.

"You saw it, didn't you?"

The barman lowered his head and stared at the drip tray. Without looking up he said: "We saw nothing. I think you'd better take the copper's advice. Go and get an early night."

Tony stood and turned to the bar. The other drinkers – the ones who hadn't vanished the moment the copper had arrived – stared sullenly at him. He faced each one with an unflinching stare. The landlord looked below the counter, hunting for something.

"What the fuck is going on here? What are you hiding?"

A slam of heavy wood rattled the empty glasses in the drainer. Tony stared in disbelief at the baseball bat the landlord had in his hand. He raised it from the bar counter and pointed it levelly at Tony.

"Take a hint, pal. Get out of here now."

Tony glared at him. His mouth tightened. "Fine. I'm gone."

He kicked the chair the copper had sat on out of his way and pulled the door open. He turned and gave the inhabitants a sardonic smile.

"Don't know where I can buy any postcards at this time of night, do you? Something with 'Warm Wishes From Fairlight', or 'Wish You Were Here?'"

The tip of the baseball bat remained pointed and

unwavering. "*Out.*"

As he closed the door behind him, he heard a dull thud and a clatter as the airborne bat struck the door and bounced on the tiled floor.

He shook his head and grinned broadly as he retraced his steps back along the harbour front and towards the Day Gone Down. A small victory, but it had lightened his mood. There was a spring in his step as he sloshed his way through the rain puddles; no longer did it feel they were sucking him down to depths of despair. The thick atmosphere didn't weigh him down anymore, and for the first time in a long while he actually felt positive.

Not even the presence on the kerb of the idling patrol car with its watchful driver dispelled his cheerful mood. He almost waved at the officer who'd grilled him earlier, but thought better of it. He walked past without making eye contact.

The hissing of the tide retreating from the shingle no longer sounded like the sea mocked him with every moment he spent in this coastal nightmare. Now, the ebb tide was almost music to his ears. He thought he detected wariness in its restless motions, as though it recognised a new presence in town. One to be feared.

In the pallid light cast by one of the rain-beaded street lights, he raised his damaged hand and stared at it in wonder. He hadn't noticed the pain while the policeman questioned him because his mind had been a whirl of emotion and bafflement.

But the moment he stepped out of the pub, when the euphoria descended on him, he was aware that the dull pounding in his knuckles and wrist had not just faded. It had gone completely.

There were still bruises, but even they showed signs of fading. Black and blue patches had eased into a mottled yellow-grey that was barely visible in the street light, and he knew they would be completely gone by morning.

The cuts had *healed.* Only faint white traces marked the former lacerations. He turned the back of his hand to and fro and noticed that there was a slight glow to the healing tracks. A pristine, white glow, like the retinal burn of the unnaturally white light that had blasted through him earlier.

And then there was the voice he'd heard. A faint echo of the words reverberated in his memory as he gazed out to the glistening blackness of the sea. The voice had sounded so similar to Becky's that he had wondered if his dead wife had been in the same room when the attack on Jim ceased.

Just one of the things Rachel's inherited from her mum. As well as her looks and her addiction to self-harming…

He stared at his healing hand as he remembered the words.

First strike, Dad. But the war's just beginning. And I can't do it on my own.

The voice had been about to say something else but the light had vanished, and with it the last trace of his daughter's words.

Whatever had powered that light and beaten off the unseen attack on Jim, it had limitations. And an adversary as yet undefined.

An enemy with human supporters. He could tell that by the reluctance of the drinkers in the pub to get involved, or even admit what had happened.

Did they just not want to take sides…or had they already chosen? The question chilled him. He glanced back towards the pub and saw the idling police car remained. The driver was a dark shadow behind the windscreen, completely motionless. But Tony knew he was being watched. He turned away and saw the glistening black edifice of the old Customs House, and the memory of what he had seen in the alleyway behind it. Slowly the euphoria drained away as the full realisation of what he was up against hit him.

Tomorrow morning, he knew he would not go to the police station. The hospital would be his first destination. Not just to see if Jim was still alive, and maybe in a position to give more answers, but to see Rachel.

To get her out. He looked once more at his palm and realised the miraculous healing no longer comforted him.

DAY TWO: TRANSITION

FINGERS AND THUMBS

He feels honoured the Presence has granted him permission to advance to the next stage. No more half-hearted scratches to his arms and legs with the old compass needle from his geometry set.

No. Now he is allowed to go further. It will mean that he can no longer hide his injuries from his parents, but that doesn't matter now. What he is about to do will send him to Fairlight, but he knows that this is part of the Plan. A war is coming, and the Presence is marshalling its troops, centralising them.

A call to arms, he thinks with a grin. He caresses the scars on his forearms as he stares out of the window. The sun has risen over the roofs of the council estate and its heat beats against the glass. Another hot day, and another day his parents will ask him why he's wearing his full sleeved shirt rather than one of his summer ones. It was easier before, they accepted that he wanted to hide as much of his obesity as possible, regardless of the weather. But it's different now.

They suspect, if they don't know already, that he's been self-harming. But they don't want to press the issue with him. They don't want their suspicions confirmed.

Too bad, Mum and Dad! Perhaps you should've listened to Granny Ulrika. Rocking back and forth in the knackered old chair in the rest home, dribbling the pureed food and pissing her knickers while mumbling random thoughts on what's happening with 'the youth of today.' You thought she was just a senile old bag, didn't you?

But she's no dummy. She gave me the look before I even started hacking away at my arms. She knew.

Perhaps old age truly was a second childhood. As the brain turns to mush and modern thinking and civilised concepts fall away, the really old see the world in a way only the really young do. They see things more clearly.

He throws the duvet cover from his sweating body and climbs out of bed. He makes his way to the desk in the corner of his bedroom, wheezing. He sits down and stares at the printed essay he is due to hand in to Miss Tyndall today. Thomas Hardy's Jude the Obscure, *and the scene in which the son hangs himself and kills his siblings.*

"Done because we are too menny," he reads, smiling at the deliberate misspelling. He remembers the doctor's speech later in the book, and the assertion that the kid's actions were "the coming desire not to live."

Well, ol' Thomas was really on to something there! But not quite accurate - there's a mistake there that Teach needs to be made aware of...

He smiles as he pushes the PC keyboard to one side and spreads the sheets of paper over the desk. I put blood, sweat and tears into this one, Miss.

Well, maybe not the tears. He pulls open the drawer beneath and takes out his grandfather's old cut-throat razor. He opens the handle, and the rising sun hits the well-honed blade, turning it into a shining arrow of pure silver. It is beautiful, it is dazzling. It is inviting.

The razor is of German manufacture. Grandad had said that his own father had used it in the trenches of the First World War, and then used it himself when stationed in France, battling the Allies. An heirloom of living history, passed from one generation to the next.

He knew about his grandfather's arrival in Britain and the years spent in the POW camp, the eventual release and waiting for Ulrika to be found and to come over to be reunited with her husband in their new homeland.

He turns the razor and watches the silver reflection flash over the textbooks and PC games on his bookshelf. Funny how his father hadn't wanted to keep the razor; he'd had to fish it out of the bin when his dad wasn't looking. Why deprive him of his birthright? Dad wouldn't say, and so he'd had to find out himself.

In one of her more lucid moments, Granny Ulrika had been very forthcoming. Told him of Grandad's true role within the German Army, his posting in Paris with the Gestapo, and how he'd deceived the Allies into identifying him as a simple country boy, recruited on the strength of Nazi lies and propaganda. He was only eighteen, how could they know?

She also told him how the razor had been used in the interrogation of Resistance members at 84 Avenue Foche.

She had begged him to rid himself of it. Said his father had done the right thing in disposing of it but should have destroyed it completely. This was living history, a secret reminder of the evil her countrymen – and her own husband – had inflicted upon the world.

They'd called him the Tailor Man. She told him of the German book by Hoffman that she had grown up with, "Der Struwwelpeter", and the story of the little boy who wouldn't stop sucking his thumbs until a journeyman tailor cut them away with a giant pair of scissors.

Scissors were too crude and required too much physical effort in the torture cellars of the Reich. A razor would cut more cleanly and efficiently.

He stares at the gleaming steel and wonders how many thumbs this tool has cut away. And what other appendages have been severed by this razor?

The Presence has a sense of irony. This is the tool he's been ordered to use on himself.

He has studied the anatomy of the human body and roughly knows whereabouts to cut. He makes a hash of it anyway. The blade parts the skin and doughy flesh from the base of the thumb smoothly and easily, but he has misjudged the position of the joint and his grandfather's razor meets the resistance of solid bone.

The agony comes in long, explosive pulses that send shockwaves up his arm. His shoulder feels as though he's touched an electrified cattle fence, while his hand is a molten ball of lava.

He persists, sawing away at the bone. He could have moved the blade to its correct, intended position but why bother? This is more painful, prolonging the agony, just as the Presence desires. Surely he will please the Presence with this additional, bonus pain?

Something else stirs, this time in his abdomen. He frowns, the agony of his hand momentarily forgotten with this new sensation. It is not painful, but it is unpleasant. As though his belly is filled with worms, writhing, thrashing. Pressing against the walls of his stomach...

Then the agony returns, and he focuses on the job in hand. Quite literally, he thinks, and despite the pain a small snigger of self-amusement escapes his lips.

The pudgy thumb twitches on the soaked pages of his essay

as it is freed from his hand. Like a finger, beckoning. The ragged section of bone is grey and honeycombed beneath the coating of blood. Fragile, delicate.

Bad bone structure. He was warned by the family doctor of the onset of osteoporosis, another incentive to lose weight and get fit. He stares at the severed digit for a moment, and then wonders how he's going to cut off his other thumb.

The Presence has a comforting answer. He listens thoughtfully and smiles. Of course, that makes perfect sense. But in order to make it happen, the other digits must come away.

It takes him a while to cut away the four fingers from his hand, despite the ease with which the fatty flesh parts. A red mist has descended over his eyes and blackness lurks at the sides, threatening to take him to a state of unconsciousness. He must pause, allow his body time to recover between each amputation. Not too long, though. Shock and blood loss will make him pass out before the operation is complete.

There. The final finger lies with its fellows on his essay. "Done because we are too menny," he croaks.

His hand is a mass of swollen, bleeding meat. Pieces of bone peek through the holes where his fingers and thumb have come away. Yet when he moves his hand he can still feel the presence of fingers and thumb through the curtain of pain as though they're still here.

Phantom injury, he tells himself. And then realises that is not the case, and the reason he can feel digits on his hand is because they have been replaced.

He watches in awe as the long and sinuous black appendages appear from the holes, writhing like tapeworms in rotting meat.

There is another stirring in his belly. Sharper now, as though the worms within have teeth. He ignores it, captivated by his new fingers.

The glistening he first takes to be slime that coats these eel-like digits. But no. The glistening is the reflection of sunlight on hard carapaces, a chitinous, shell-like armour. Only the diamond-shaped nail at the end of these new fingers glitters more brightly than the shell.

He won't need the razor for the fingers and thumb on his other hand. His new appendages will do the tearing, slicing and hacking.

His grandfather's razor, the interrogation tool of the Tailor Man, lies forgotten amongst the growing pile of severed fingers and thumbs.

CHAPTER NINE

Sleep was the last thing on Tony Collins's mind when he returned to his room at The Day Gone Down. But the stress brought on by the day's events had begun to take their toll.

The euphoria had diminished with each step back to the pub, until the feeling was nothing more than a pleasant - but distant - memory. Exhaustion threatened him like the storm clouds over the town. His eyelids were heavy curtains which kept obscuring his vision as he dragged his drained body up the carpeted staircase. He stared at his healed palm before inserting the key to his room.

First strike, Dad. But the war's just beginning. And I can't do it on my own.

"Neither can I, Rache," he whispered. Whatever power had passed onto him, it had gone now. As if whatever had granted it to him had deemed it no longer necessary since his wound healed...

It's a finite resource then, he thought as he closed the door behind him. *Something that's being guarded...but by what?*

He pressed the light switch and rubbed his eyes. The bed was a single divan with an over-flowery pattern on the duvet and pillow covers, but to Tony's eyes it was the most inviting thing he had ever seen. And yet...

He placed the key on the bedside cabinet and stared at the curtains that covered the window. They were the same hideous floral pattern as the bed coverings, but it was the two bags on the stiff chair that caught his attention.

Rachel's bags. Adam must've taken them out of the

Renault. Tony had a dim recollection of having to leave the car key with the landlord because of the restricted parking; Adam had said he'd move the Renault into a spot as soon as the contractor vans had gone.

Christ, I forgot to leave the overnight bag with her...

The second bag and its contents he knew wouldn't have been accepted within Fairlight. Rachel's laptop. He stared at the Post-It note attached.

Tony,

Thought I'd bring these in for you as they were sitting in full view.

Too tempting for the light-fingers around here!

I'll give you a buzz at eight, see if you want breakfast.

Cheers,

Adam

PS: WiFi code is DaG0nD0wn15

Tony stared at the laptop bag. The stickers of Jensen Ackles had been torn away – it was a crush she'd grown out of. Attached to the zipper was a kcy fob with a picture of a grinning cartoon squirrel. She'd outgrown Jensen Ackles but kept her love for her favourite animal.

What would Quinn make of this? No nihilism, no sense of despair causing her to self-harm. She had the same interests, the same teenage crushes, tastes and silliness that all girls her age have.

The squirrel was smiling too broadly for his liking, mocking him. The note crumpled in his hand and his palm tingled. He dropped the note and held his hand up to the light. A disc of newly healed skin glowed red under the lamp light.

"First strike. The war's just beginning," he said in a whisper. He lowered his hand and stared at the laptop bag.

I can't do it on my own, Dad.

He opened the bag and took out Rachel's computer. The laptop he had bought her for Christmas. The laptop she had been glued to for most of the year…

He felt a twinge of guilt; it was like snooping through someone's diary, a complete no-no. Especially for a concerned parent; you never knew what you'd find.

But he had to know.

He placed the machine on the bedside dresser and lifted the screen. The keyboard and screen were immaculate, testimony to Rachel's almost-clinical attention to hygiene. The chemical scent of screen and keyboard wipes filled his nostrils as he pressed the power button. While the machine hummed into life, he caressed the keys. He imagined Rachel's fingers gliding over them, performing their usual light and graceful dance as she typed out her school essays, her Tweets, her emails to her friends –

"What the hell?" The power indicator light should have glowed bright blue. Instead, a tiny ruby eye glared at him.

Bile rose in his throat, tears in his eyes, when he realised what the red light was.

Rachel had slipped up with her cleaning. A single, tiny drop coated the power indicator light. Minuscule, nothing compared to the copious amounts he'd seen her lose over the year…

But that tiny drop of dried blood crushed him. Even when she was on her computer, self-mutilation was a part of her life.

He stared at his fingertip. Under the lamp light the dried blood that had settled into the grooves looked like rust. He swallowed the bile in his mouth, lowered his hands and forced himself to concentrate on the screen.

The loading screen faded, replaced by the image Rachel had used as her wallpaper. At the sight of that, the dried blood on his finger was forgotten. He took a step back from the dresser.

Even when his legs gave way and he sank onto the edge of the bed, he couldn't take his eyes from Rachel's computer. Her lifeline, her gateway to the world of social media, networking, information. Image manipulation…

It had to have been done with Photoshop. An image like that couldn't exist anywhere.

But why? Why would Rachel do that to a picture of her own mother?

It wasn't even a picture he thought Rachel had access to. The image of Becky was taken during her student days. Fresher's Week at the University of East Anglia back in the 1990s. Doc Martens and tie-dye skirt, PWEI T shirt, henna tattoos and spiky blonde hair.

The same golden colour as her daughter's. The same cerulean eyes. Even the way she stared at the camera had been inherited by Rachel. The head inclined, tilted to the left, staring at the world with an incongruous combination of child-like wonder and world-weary cynicism. A pint of snakebite and black in one hand, a Marlboro Light in the other.

On each wrist were fresh bandages, the left spotted with red. The action of lifting the pint had caused the wound to open again.

Mummy hurt herself, he remembered saying to the

inquisitive toddler who'd jabbed a curious finger at the picture. *She fell on a gravel path and scratched her arms.*

And then vowing to hide the picture – and any more like it – from Rachel's disbelieving eyes. Even at two years old she'd been captivated by the image. What was it she'd said?

Mummy did it on purpose. Said with contempt, not for what Becky had done as a student, but for her father's attempt to deceive her.

The memory of that chilled him far more than the additional imagery. Even at such a young age, Rachel had shown she could not be lied to. Had known instinctively that her mother had deliberately harmed herself. Becky did everything she could to hide the photos of her bearing marks of self-harming, and Rachel had eventually forgotten about it, as new delights and mysteries came into her world.

But she never really forgot, did she? Tony pondered, keeping his eyes fixed on the face of Becky and not the monstrosity coming from her. *Was it coincidence that she began to self-harm at exactly the same age as Becky?*

Where would it end? Would Rachel have continued along the same path, eventually going too far, just as her mother did? Surely Fairlight was the best place for her, would prevent her going down that path?

And if Quinn was to be believed, her unique ability to heal could only be beneficial for all.

Yeah well, if it wasn't for what Jim told me, maybe I could accept that.

Even if he hadn't met Jim, what he saw on the picture changed everything. It confirmed that Fairlight hospital was the last place Rachel Collins should be in.

The black shapes coming from Becky's mouth and groin were sinuous and snakelike, like coils of tentacles formed from shadows – or ink. They snaked around her head, following the path of smoke laid down by the smouldering Marlboro, to form a sickening halo of corruption.

Tony blinked. Like the lenticular image on a 3D postcard, the halo continued to writhe with each movement of his head. Some patches of darkness were blacker than others, shaped in a different way. Curved and jagged, smooth and bulbous. They spoke of eyes, teeth and claws. As had the congregation for the girl's funeral earlier today. What was it the reporter had said?

"The object that emerged from Callum Hayes's left palm has had many different descriptions. Some said it resembled a black eel-like creature, others described it as a tentacle, while others only saw teeth and claws. Mass-hallucination brought about by group hysteria and sunstroke, or something more sinister?"

"Definitely the second one," Tony said with a snarl. The healed circle of his palm tingled, and he wondered why he wasn't scared of the image. He told himself it was anger that kept the fear at bay. Anger that something had forced his daughter to digitally mock his dead wife. Anger that losing his daughter wasn't enough for God, or the fates, or destiny or *whatever.*

But he knew, deep within himself, that the healing of his palm and the lack of fear were connected somehow. Perhaps it meant that the image *wasn't* Rachel's doing?

He hoped so. Because the feeling that rose within him was anger. A righteous anger, one he knew would be necessary for the battle to come.

He tapped the documents folder with a sense of relief, justification. Now he didn't feel so guilty about looking through his daughter's private files.

"All's fair in love and war…" he muttered. A quick scroll through the picture gallery revealed nothing. Some snaps of a school trip to the Ashmolean Museum, more pictures of her and her friends larking about on the streets of Oxford than studious pictures of the historical treasures within.

How long ago was this? Last year, year before? He wondered how many of the smiling girls in the pictures were undergoing the self-harm epidemic.

A few Word files of her essays. Like the photos, nothing was dated earlier than last summer. He scanned through them, found nothing of interest.

Perhaps the emails…he tapped the Chrome icon, looked at the Post-It and carefully tapped the code in with one finger.

Facebook was the homepage. Like so many kids her age, Rachel couldn't be bothered to memorise passwords and had set it to automatic log-in. With another pang of guilt, he clicked on the Messenger tab.

Callum Hayes has sent you a message…
"What?"
He opened the message in disbelief.

Rachel.

If you don't wanna contribute to the group, that's fine. But DON'T tell us what's right and what's wrong. You sound just like my sister and where is she now eh? Dead, that's where. Food for the worms – not much, seeing how fucking skinny she was.

Like her, you've chosen the wrong side and you'll be sorry when the time comes.

We're evolving. We'll be the new masters of the world. Bitches like you will be out in the cold, food for the worms. Like my sister. Like your mum.

Oh yeah – your mum. Here's a pic I found. Won't tell you how I got it…

Enjoy.

Callum Hayes.

"Well, I'm fucked," Tony said in a strangled voice. The picture attached was identical to Rachel's wallpaper. So Callum Hayes had manipulated the image, not Rachel. But why had she used it as her background?

The date of the message was one week ago. Tony searched his mind, trying to remember what Rachel had been doing at that time.

She'd told him it was preparation for her project on Shakespeare's plays, *A Midsummer Night's Dream* or something…

Not a word to him about this.

He scrolled through the remainder of the messages but couldn't find anything of note. He tried the Facebook group Children of the Evolution only to find that had been taken down. The same for Callum Hayes's profile page.

Back to the files, perhaps I've missed something. Music? Worth a shot. See what's -

"Jesus Christ!" The volume of his words shocked even him, so that he found himself jumping on the side of the bed. The laptop threatened to slide off his lap and fall to the floor. He clutched it with trembling, sweating palms.

Children of the Evolution. The folder's name could have been a simple typo, but Tony knew Rachel had never heard of Marc Bolan's T Rex. And there was only one Children of the Evolution.

Callum Hayes's self-help, self-mutilation group. So what was in the folder? His hand shook as it hovered over the mousepad, knowing that these weren't music files. Knowing that Rachel had been aware that Callum Hayes's web presence would be deleted within time.

"What have you got in here, Rache, darling?" His voice was hoarse now. His mouth dry and sour from the drinks earlier. He opened the folder.

PDFs, downloaded from the website before it went offline. Poems, sonnets…shit, even plays! Dedicated to the 'joy of despair.' Quotes on darkness, as a physical entity or a scientific explanation.

Then photographs. Step-by-step guides on how to self-harm, to cut oneself and inflict the maximum amount of pain and damage without causing death that were so clinical, so detached and precise, they could have come from a medical manual.

Diagrams showing the most sensitive areas of the human body. Treatment for shock, techniques on applying ligatures and tourniquets. Bandaging and dressing of wounds, and most sickeningly of all, methods of hiding the wounds from parents and guardians. Things to say to distract elders from asking about the self-harm until the time was right for the faithful to be called.

The site of the battleground has yet to be decided; I don't know when or where the war will be declared. But be assured, chaps and chappesses: the Presence will call me soon. I feel it. I sense it. I know it will be in High Summer, the time most precious to the Light. And when I'm summoned, you'll also be called.

Some of you will be with me when it occurs. Others will be called upon to wage war in their own towns and cities, to widen the struggle and further our cause.

Be patient. Be strong. Inflict the pain and destruction on yourselves, but make sure you hide it from your parents as best you can. They'll try to stop us, prevent us changing the world, just as old ones and 'know betters' have always done.

We are the future. We are the Children of the Evolution. Our true Father will call us, and through Him we will make the Dark shine!

Keep the faith, brothers and sisters.

Callum Hayes.

Tony's eyes narrowed. He no longer felt chilled by Callum Hayes's words. A wry smile played at the corners of his mouth at the realisation of Rachel's hoarding of these documents.

Her self-harming was still a mystery, but it was so similar to her mother's – with the same reaction to the pain, the same areas of cutting, as well – that there was a connection he found oddly comforting. There was none of the nihilism or despair that powered the self-harm of the Children of the Evolution.

His nascent smile died. "But what *is* powering it? What needs you to hurt yourself so badly? It destroyed Becky…will it destroy you too, Rache?"

*A war is coming…High Summer…*he frowned. *Strange*

choice of words for a kid, even one as twisted as the Hayes lad. But then, it is midsummer –

He froze. The memory of a recent folder name hit him. He went back to the folder containing Rachel's school work.

A Midsummer Night's Dream.

He held his breath as he double-clicked; the breath exploded when the folder revealed its secrets to him.

It wasn't a collection of essays or school project work on a Shakespeare play. There was a PDF named 'Theatre' and an MP4 titled 'Dad.' The thumbnail showed Rachel staring back at him. His finger shook so much on the mousepad the thumbnail shot across the screen, almost into the recycle bin; he took a deep breath before double clicking.

Rachel's face filled the screen. She was pale, drawn; she wiped her nose with the back of her hand and sniffed loudly, blinked back tears. Her smile was forced.

"Hey Dad…if you're watching this, you'll know why I wanted the laptop down here with us. I knew I was going into Fairlight, I knew I wouldn't be allowed my laptop – but I also knew that you'd need what's in it. Because I – I may not come out alive…"

He pressed his fingers to the screen, to Rachel's face. She threw her head back, her hair shining in the soft glow cast from the Anglepoise lamp on her desk. A lump blocked his throat as Rachel fought back a sob.

"Okay. It's okay. Look, you've seen the files I cribbed from Callum Hayes's website – if you haven't, dig them out. Study them, Dad. Learn as much as you can, because he's the enemy. It's through him that this…this darkness, the *Presence* he calls it, will work. I said a war is coming and I can't fight it on my own. I don't know if there are others like me in Fairlight, or if it'll be purely Callum's domain. Time will tell, I guess."

He saw the rest of her room. The books neatly stacked to one side, the plush squirrel sitting upright with a grin and an acorn on the pillowcase behind her. The framed pictures of cornflowers, the print of John Tenniel's illustration of the White Rabbit from *Alice in Wonderland,* staring anxiously at his pocket watch. *Time will tell.*

"But I know I'm going to need your help. I'm going to be very limited in what I can do inside…and that's why the folder contains a map of the hospital. It's a blueprint of the original plans when the NHS trust took over the old asylum and converted it into what it is now.

"The Light that reveals itself to me – it only does so when I harm myself. I can't explain it, and I know how much it hurts you. But please believe me when I say that it's for the greater good. I don't know why, it just *feels* right. It's not the same thing that's working Callum Hayes. This I know." She glanced behind her, to the blank space next to the White Rabbit print, and Tony saw the bare nail and remembered the other Tenniel print that had once accompanied it.

"Something is working through me, the same way it tried to work through Mum…it needs blood and pain, but I don't know why. It isn't able to communicate with words…it just shows me things. Beautiful things, unexplainable things. But they're good things. Total opposite to the monsters Callum's trying to bring through."

Monsters. He remembered the other print now – the Jabberwock. A monster about to be overpowered by a child…

"You'll need help, Dad. I tried to find out about the old

asylum that came before Fairlight, but nothing's available. A big black hole in cyberspace where its history should be. Something happened in the past, something that caused the closure of the asylum, and it's been covered up. If you can find someone from that period, their knowledge of it may help us defeat what's coming."

*I can't fight it on my own…*was that why she'd taken down the picture of the Jabberwock? Hiding the image of a solitary child engaged in battle with an all-powerful, all-consuming monster?

"I…I know you've booked my consultation with Dr Quinn on the 20th of June. That's a week away – it's also the day before midsummer's eve, the time when the light is at its strongest. I think Callum Hayes's darkness will try and strike then. Something else is going to happen, but I don't know what. And I…" she broke off, turned her head from the screen and wept.

Her face was a blur; Tony couldn't see it clearly through his own veil of tears.

"The hardest thing about this, Dad, is that I have to keep this from you until I'm in Fairlight. They have to be convinced I'm suffering the same delusions, the same sickness that Callum's gang are suffering. I…I'm no actor; I have to convince myself if I'm going to convince the Fairlight guardians to let me in. Please understand if you feel I'm distant the next couple of days. I have to…well, get into character."

"No, Rachel." His voice cracked. "You didn't have to – you *could've* told me. You *should've* told me…"

He tried to deny it, but he understood. He would never have allowed her within a hundred miles of Fairlight if he'd known what he knew now.

"I don't know when I'll speak to you again after you've seen this. I hope you can get into Fairlight, with friends. With people who can help us beat back the darkness.

"And will hopefully give us some answers. I don't know why this is happening, and I don't know why it's using us to wage war. I'm frightened, Dad. But I know this is where I have to be. We may not win. We may never see each other again. But we have to try..." She wiped her eyes, forced a smile. "Hey. Don't give up the day job, okay? I love you, Dad."

He couldn't bear to see her reach for the screen to end the recording. It felt like a door slamming in his face.

He curled up on the bed and buried his face in the pillows. The sobs racked his body, and the pillowcase was soon soaked with his tears.

Birdsong woke him. He blinked dried tears away and wiped his nose. No sunlight poked through the gap in the curtains, but the dawn chorus told him sunlight wasn't far away. The thought of light gave him hope. Strength. He looked at the laptop screen, now dying with low power.

"Midsummer. Twenty-first of June." *I think the darkness will try and strike then. Something else is going to happen, but I don't know what it is.*

"Yeah. Callum's sister's funeral. That's what happened. That's why he's in there now...with you, Rachel. Oh, dear God..."

The birdsong was louder. Mocking him with its cheerful sound, and promise of light.

Something happened in the past, something that caused the closure of the asylum, and it's been covered up. If you can find someone from that period, their knowledge of it may help us defeat what's coming.

"Jim," he whispered. "Jim knew. And he survived…"

With a new sense of purpose – and a rekindling of hope – he opened the PDF and stared hard at the plans of Fairlight hospital.

Going to have to print this out. Find a printer somewhere…maybe in the town's library. He looked in the laptop bag and found Rachel's ancient 16GB memory stick, smiled faintly at the plastic covering: a moulded squirrel, its jaws spread wide around a greenish acorn head. He took the head off, pushed the decapitated rodent into the USB port and waited for the files to transfer.

It's outside the Pharos.

"What did you mean by that, Jim? What *is* a Pharos?"

The curtains lightened with the pink glow of sunrise. A stream of liquid butter transformed the dust motes into flecks of gold. It was time to make a move.

That was when he heard footsteps on the staircase.

Ascending, creeping. As though the owner was quietly crawling up to his room after a heavy night on the tiles, not wanting to disturb anyone.

The twisting of a key into the Yale lock – the lock on *his* door – changed all that.

CHAPTER TEN

Karen Tyndall blinked in the glare of the tube lighting. It seemed brighter than usual, harsh and penetrating, adding to her headache. Perhaps it was the blackness of the previous, sleepless night and the gloom of the pre-dawn.

Nothing to do with the two bottles of Merlot, then? She sighed and felt her shoulders slump under the weight of guilt. No, that was too hard on herself. It wasn't a problem, just her way of letting off steam, to deal with recent events. No sign of alcohol dependency.

Not yet, anyway. But you're going that way, you mark my words, girl. Jesus Christ, it felt like Mum was right behind her, admonishments thrown at the back and—once upon a time— bouncing off harmlessly.

But the warnings and nagging of twelve years ago were more insistent, and more effective. She knew she'd lost weight. Knew the stress was finally telling – she only had to look in the mirror to see that. The grey hairs were winning, no matter how much of the blonde colouring she used. How pallid her skin was, the lines around her sunken eyes walking the line between laughter lines and wrinkles, just as she walked the line between habitual drinking and alcohol abuse. The offers of counselling were all very well, but…Karen could just imagine her mother lying in her coffin, a smug look on her decomposed features. *See, Karen? I was right after all. Mother DOES know best!*

*No, Mother. You're a part of it, and if I was a bit less charitable I'd say you were the cause…*she caught her ankle on a tube chair that had been left carelessly in the aisle. She stumbled, put out a hand to halt her fall and felt rough pine scrape her palm. Her bag slipped from her shoulder, but the books within cushioned her fall.

She lay for a moment, dazed and conscious of the dull pain in her hand. The tube lighting spun above her like neon-lit helicopter blades, slicing into her head.

She closed her eyes and got to her feet. She dropped the bag and dusted herself off before realising the desk had drawn blood. Thin streaks of crimson striped the leg of her beige trouser suit.

"Oh, for God's sake." The words echoed around the empty classroom. A few of the hand-painted posters from class 4T fluttered in answer, and she realised the caretaker had left one of the top windows opened. The breeze stiffened, as if trying to enter and bring the darkness inside. Stupid bloody thought, she told herself. Get a grip…

The poster of Thomas Hardy rippled behind her desk, his moustache bristling and his eyes crinkling in disapproval.

"You can piss off as well," she muttered, relishing the freedom of swearing in the classroom. Wouldn't be able to do it with the kids around– certainly not after the last disciplinary she'd had– but that wasn't the reason she had come into the school buildings early.

She examined the wound on her palm. She fished out a tissue from her bag and clenched her fist around it. The paper was soaked within seconds, but the blood seemed to ease up. There was a sharper pain in her palm; she realised there would be splinters buried in the flesh.

She glanced at the desk she'd tripped onto, took in the gouges inflicted by years of compass needles and graffiti from generations of bored doodling. She frowned at the newest words gouged and etched in red ink. Its execution and content were markedly different to the football team slogans and puerile drawings of ejaculating penises.

Children of the Evolution!

The Dark will shine!

Her lips tightened. After all she had done, it was for *nothing*. The inroads she'd made into the town, the hope she'd brought to the working-class kids of a dying community. Despite the parents' contempt and her fellow teachers' cynical amusement of her efforts, the madness had now come to Fairlight School.

She heard a muffled dripping, and felt warmth running through her fingers. She raised her hand, saw the fresh blood dripping from it. The tissue was nothing more than a walnut-sized ball of scarlet. She hadn't known she'd been holding it so hard.

She felt sickness rise within. The blood-soaked tissue had the faint aroma of stale wine – or was she imagining it?

And to injure herself on a desk that had been defaced by one of the group who *deliberately* harmed themselves…she looked back to Hardy and wondered if he would've appreciated the irony.

"Hardly one of life's *little* ironies," she muttered and emptied her bag onto her desk, trawling through the exercise books and paperbacks with her good hand until she found a packet of travel tissues.

Blood welled from her gashed palm, greedily drank up by the fresh tissue. She studied the wound, wondered if she should get some medical attention. The nurse wouldn't be in until half-eight. Three hours…

"I'll survive." Her words were muted, sounding faint and distant to her. From the corridor she heard the door swing open and bang against the rubber door stop. She started, jerked her head around and saw the door to the classroom shiver in the jamb. A scent of fresh rainwater and sea air permeated the room.

She turned back to her desk and leafed through the Norton text notes on Hardy's *Jude the Obscure*, and the assignment she'd set her class.

Poor old Thomas. They never forgave you for this, did they? She could understand why Hardy had given up writing novels after the critical and popular backlash. One of her favourite books of all time, and one she enjoyed teaching and discussing. The themes of frustrated ambition and unalterable destiny were, to her, timeless. It was also refreshing to remember that the spirit of the working class was one of self-improvement and education. She saw disturbing parallels between Jude Fawley's plight and the new generation of working class scholars, unable to pay for their higher education…

Her hangover was forgotten for a moment as she considered the empty desks in front of her. Bright kids, just disadvantaged. But how many of them actually wanted to increase their education? How many of them would fall into the same trap their parents did?

There were a couple who had real potential. Who weren't prepared to settle for the half-life their classmates were heading for. And yet…she stared at the exercise book on top of her pile. At the name.

Stephen Fleischer…the lonely fat boy. Serious and morose,

and shy with it. She'd assumed his interest in 19th century literature was faked, a way to get to know her better. But what she had taken to be a harmless schoolboy crush was turning into something more disturbing.

And he'd taken a little *too* much interest in the pivotal scene in *Jude the Obscure*: the murder of Sue Bridehead's children by Jude the younger - 'Little Father Time' - and his suicide. '*Done because we are too menny.*'

Youthful despair and its consequences. Ofsted will have this book banned one day, because of that scene – way too topical.

She tapped the exercise book thoughtfully, frowning at the line drawn through the Christian name, and the scrawled Germanic replacement above it. *Fleischer*...yes, his grandfather was German, a prisoner in one of England's POW camps. She'd asked him about it a few years ago, but he'd been reluctant to say anything. A family embarrassment, by the sounds of it.

Or is it something more? No, that was ridiculous. The crap spouted by the Children of the Evolution was colouring her judgement, making her see things in her pupils that weren't there...

But it is there with Stephen, isn't it? her inner voice argued. *How he's insisted on being called Stefan rather than the Anglicised version of his name – even though he was born in England and christened Stephen!*

More noise from the corridor. The door banging open and rattling on its hinges made her jerk her head away from the desk again.

"For fuck's *sake!*" She stood slowly, making sure the dizziness didn't return. The hangover was staying all day, so she had to make some allowances. *But I'm not going to put up with the bloody elements shaking the remains of this bloody school to the ground when I'm trying to bloody work!*

She paused at the new sound that accompanied the rattling of the window panes and the banging of the exterior door. She cocked her aching head, frowned.

Footsteps. Heavy and plodding. So who would be here at this time? She had a vision of the stranger in the Day Gone Down from last evening – the one who'd recognised the Orwell quote. A man she knew instantly had lost his child to the hospital. They all had the same look, those parents, but there was something else about this guy…

Physically fit, not a professional type judging by the sound of his voice and choice of clothes. A work-issue polo shirt revealing well-toned, tattooed arms that bore the tan of an outdoors worker. Sharp and watchful eyes that had seemed dulled by the stress he'd been under - and held a deep-rooted pain that went beyond his current situation. She knew he'd wanted to talk to her but hadn't been in the mood to be picked up.

There was something dangerous about him. A danger that had nothing to do with physical strength. He was lean and fit, but not a muscle man. No, something else, she decided. Something within, an anger born of grief and frustration. Loss.

Footsteps again. Fear took hold, crept up her bruised spine and caressed the throbbing base of her skull. She opened her mouth, forced a commanding tone of voice.

"Who – who's there?"

The footsteps were more of a light shuffling than the heavy footfall of a mature man. As though they belonged to a frail, injured child or…

The door opened with a gentle push from a bandaged hand. At least she hoped it was bandaged. There was so little resemblance to a human hand that yards of surgical dressings could be the only explanation for the strange, blood-soaked limb that preceded the entry of the lonely fat boy.

"Stephen!"

"*Stefan*," he said with a grin. "It's *Stefan* Fleischer, Miss. Not Stephen."

Karen's vocal cords refused to work. Too much was happening for her to respond. Relief that no menacing stranger had entered gave way to the realisation that the pupil in front of her was a stranger.

The second bandaged hand came into view as Stefan Fleischer stepped forward and nudged the door closed with his back, keeping both arms raised and in full view.

He was always a pale-skinned child, but the whiteness shocked her into silence; it spoke of massive shock and blood loss…and the dripping fluid from his shapeless hands confirmed it. *He shouldn't even be conscious,* she thought, *let alone grinning like the Cheshire Cat!*

"What happened to you, Stefan? You need an ambulance. Let me call -"

"Not yet, Miss." He waved a dismissive hand which spat flecks of blood onto the poster of Shakespeare to his right. Karen blinked. Stefan glanced at the poster and chuckled. "The Bard's suffering from measles. Perhaps he needs the ambulance, not me."

Through the windows, dawn sunlight caressed the nape of her neck but did nothing to dispel the gooseflesh. She'd never felt so cold in her life.

His blazer was buttoned up, despite the warmth. The lapels were folded forwards in an attempt to hide as much of his shirt front as possible. She saw the distinctive school tie, loosely knotted around a blood-soaked collar that had once been white. And his belly seemed bigger than before: no longer merely fat, but swollen.

What the hell is he hiding?

"You're in early, Miss. Why's that?"

She didn't answer. Her heart beat rapidly, in time with the pulsing of blood from the wound in her palm. She swallowed, tasted sour wine and bile. Her toes tensed, creeping back as though on the brink of a precipice. Her mind filled with images of the news report of Callum Hayes's funeral attendance. She knew now she was in the presence of one who had fallen to whatever it was that possessed the Children of the Evolution.

"Same reason as me, I guess." Stefan inclined his head towards the exercise book and the copy of *Jude.* "Bit of extra learning...or teaching?"

"What?"

"Education's a wonderful thing, Miss. I know you despaired at times, thought none of us were listening, giving a toss about dead old writers. I was different, though. You knew that."

"Yes, you were – *are*, Stefan..." her voice wavered and hated herself for it. Her eyes were drawn to his bandaged hands. The blood had coloured the bandages pure scarlet, and her grip on her sodden tissue tightened. Was it her hangover, the poor light – or were those shapeless appendages *pulsing*, inflating and deflating like party balloons?

"You really inspired me, Miss." He held the shifting hands to his face. He turned them over, smiled lovingly at the tearing sound and held them outwards towards Karen. "I know you've got your problems, just like the rest of us in this town. I could smell the booze from the doorway! That's why you come in early, isn't it? You can't discipline yourself at home to stay off the wine. The crushing loneliness, the despair…"

"Now just *wait* a minute…"

"It's nothing to be ashamed of, Miss. In fact, you're to be admired because you're determined not to let your problems get the better of you or your career…you know you can do your best marking and class prep here, where there's no alcohol and a time limit. Three hours to get everything done and be sober before the kids turn up, and it works.

"To a point. You were wrong about the killing scene in *Jude.* I think you slipped up by trying to draw parallels between Jude the younger and what's been happening to my generation. Last night I got thinking about it, and I knew you were wrong. *Everything* is wrong. That's why I came in early. I wanted to show you my new essay."

Karen shrank in her chair. The vinyl covering squeaked like a frightened mouse. Her eyes flicked from the pulsing globes at the end of Stefan's arms to the essay on her desk.

"I – I don't think there's anything you need to change, Stefan." She forced a smile. "It's fine as it is."

"No!" Stefan's smile vanished. His hands dropped, and the bulges in his arms told her he was clenching whatever passed for fists. There was a tearing sound, like that of wet newspaper shredding. Fresh blood splattered on the carpet tiles.

"What was it the doctor said about the killings? Let me

remind you… 'The doctor says there are such boys springing up amongst us – boys of a sort unknown in the last generation – the outcome of new views of life. They seem to see all its terrors before they are old enough to have staying power to resist them. He says it is the beginning of the coming universal wish not to live.'" He gave a smug smile. "Good recall, eh, Miss? Shame it's all bollocks."

He stepped closer, into the spreading rays of light, and Karen knew her eyes hadn't deceived her. Those *mitts* were indeed pulsating, each bladder-like movement squirting blood down Stefan's grey school trousers and into his trainers. Each footstep was accompanied with a marshy, squelching sound that turned Karen's already-curdled stomach.

"Why has the message been ignored? The Children of the Evolution aren't self-harming through despair. 'The coming universal wish not to live' – rubbish! It's not that we don't *want* to live, it's that we know the next stage in our evolution means we'll have to get used to a different *form* of life. One we'll embrace!"

His hands were outstretched, bandaged palms upwards. The squelching sound gave way to more tearing, more tearing of flesh. Something black and vaguely metallic poked through the bandages like oil-coated rose thorns. They glinted in the dawn rays, serrated and yet sinuous. *Insectile* was the image that sprang to Karen's mind.

No, she thought when the bandages fell to the ground in sodden clumps. The appendages that sprouted from the ragged, still-bleeding knuckles where Stefan Fleischer's fingers had once been couldn't be described as anything else than *alien*.

And lethal.

"The message came to me this morning." Stefan's voice was now as far away as his gaze. He was looking past her, through the cracked window panes and into the rising light. "For too long we've hidden our injuries, our portals to the greater ones who will come through…for fear of being imprisoned by our elders. For our own 'protection.'" He spat the last word; his eyes filled with fury and hatred for a moment before glazing and becoming distant once more.

Karen slowly reached for her bag, and her mobile phone.

"Callum Hayes was the first to realise it was time to come out of hiding." There was a louder sound now, of cracking and popping. Karen kept her eyes averted, but in her peripheral vision she saw the black, serrated appendages extend, fold outwards…

Her fingers trembled as they reached the handles of her bag.

"He's the first…our leader. The one who the Greater Ones will speak through, who will marshal their forces…their battalions."

Golden dawn light caught one of the angular sections of Stefan's alien fingers. A blinding light reflected from one of the diamond-shaped talons, causing her to cry out and the bag to slip from her fingers.

The mobile spilled out, along with her purse and keys, onto the carpet tiles. Stefan glanced downwards and smiled. He stepped backwards and indicated her fallen possessions with a razor-edged finger that curled and twisted like a charmed serpent.

"Go ahead, Miss. Call them. I'm not here to harm you." He took a further step back.

Karen warily crouched down, her eyes never leaving Stefan's as she reached out for her Samsung. The eyes were chilling, as inhuman and detached as his manner…but marginally more bearable than those nightmarish things that came from his hands.

Her fingers touched her phone's screen. She almost recoiled in horror at the warm, sticky feeling of blood but took a deep breath and forced herself not to flinch. Her knees trembled and the ground swayed once more, but this time through fear rather than alcohol.

"You're not going to hurt me, Stefan?" She winced at her plaintive tones. "Why am I not convinced?"

"Why would I *want* to hurt you?" His ravaged palms were outstretched, the alien fingers splayed. There was genuine surprise in his tones, not a mocking preparation to her death. She exhaled, forced her knees to stop shaking, and got to her feet. The phone's glass threatened to break under her grip.

"The Children of the Evolution predict death and war against the old," she said while unlocking the Samsung. "You're on their side now. Of course you're going to kill me."

Stefan stared at her as she keyed the 9 icon three times. "Not me. The orders are clear. We each have our roles to play in this war. Mine is not to harm you…but to educate you."

He traced a line down the lapel of his blazer. The material parted, exposing the white shirt beneath, which in turn was cut in two by the alien talon. Her eyes widened at the healed scars and scratches that spoke of months of self-harm.

Oh, Stefan…no, Stephen, damn it! They got you a long time ago, didn't they?

"The young replace the old. It's a natural and unalterable

law of nature. The pupil becomes the teacher and the teacher becomes the pupil. Now your education *really* begins, Miss. Once upon a time, the word became flesh."

The talons flexed, the nails pointed inwards, and Stefan Fleischer began to write his new essay. The flesh became word.

The dialling tone lasted an age. By the time the operator answered and asked which service she required, Karen Tyndall had dropped the handset and sank to the floor, her screams echoing around the classroom and joining with the fresh howls of joyful agony from her former pupil.

Her education had begun.

CHAPTER ELEVEN

Rachel woke to half-remembered, unfamiliar words soughing in her ears like retreating waves on an ebb tide. She blinked, stared dumbly at the green canvas that rippled in front of her.

Sea's extra green today…why's that? Her head was full of candy floss. Her mouth was dry, and her throat swollen; swallowing was impossible. She opened her mouth and a dry cracking noise emerged. She tried to speak again and gave up. All she could do was watch the pleasant rippling of the green sea in front of her.

*No smell of sea water or candy floss. No ice cream. I can't hear the sea gulls, either. They always come for my hot dog…*the canvas rippled again and allowed a faint ray of sunlight to touch her clammy brow.

The imparted warmth made her realise just how cold the rest of her body was. She shivered, tried to cross her arms over her chest; frowned when she found them immobile.

She managed to lift her head from the pillow for a brief moment before fatigue forced it back down. A more audible groan escaped her lips. One of despair and fear. For in that moment she had seen the ligatures that bound her wrists to the rails of the bed, and the memory of yesterday's events came back to her.

Fairlight. I'm here at last. She pulled feebly against the ligatures, grimly noting that although they weren't tight enough to restrict circulation, she wasn't getting out of bed until someone allowed her to.

She closed her eyes, and snatches of the dream-vision

dispersed the candy floss in her head and played on the back of her eyelids. Her fear increased and her alertness began to return.

Now she was frightened. Callum Hayes was here already. Whatever force powered him was one step ahead. And the Light had been silent. Was that because of the drugs she'd had pumped into her? Or was Callum's power too great?

Her breath quickened with the full realisation of the danger she faced. The face of that nurse – Bethan somebody? – filled her vision, the words spoken the last thing she had heard before despatched to a chemical sleep that contained no dreams.

No dreams…and no messages from the Light! Whatever was in that sedative had blocked it from communicating to her. She tried to swallow the ball of fear that rose from her gut, but still no fluid came to her aid. She closed her eyes and moaned.

Sensation returned to the rest of her body, slowly replacing the chill. With it came pain. Pain from the wounds on her wrists.

She jerked her head up once more, managed to keep it off the pillows and her eyes firmly locked on to the surgical dressings of her injuries. They must have been white, once. Now they were scarlet, soaked with fresh flowing blood. She smelt a sour, metallic odour that told her the bleeding must have happened some hours ago. She held her breath: did that mean the wounds had begun to heal, as they normally would after an offering to the Light?

Only one way to find out. She released her breath and gently clenched her fists. At first she felt nothing but an impenetrable barrier of plastic and cotton; then her fingers obeyed the brain's commands and curled inwards. Flex, relax, flex again…until she felt fingernails make contact with the heels of her palms. Pressed harder, then relaxed. Flex, relax. Flex, relax.

She eyed the dressings, felt nauseous at the sight of their bladder-like pulsing, as though alien creatures had taken root in her hands…

The pain was there. Not the itchy, repetitive pain of healing flesh, but the sharp, dagger-like sting of a fresh wound opening once more. Fresh blood pushed through the clotted mess and dribbled onto the rails.

Her heart beat rapidly and moisture beaded her brow. She sank back into the pillows and stared at the ceiling. The lights were cold and artificial, and she wished she could feel the warmth of natural sunlight on her face. But to do that involved pulling her weakened body up from a supine position, and that meant seeing the unhealed hands again.

The curtains bellied once more with fresh breeze, and she detected the sweet aroma of cut grass and roses. Even that mocked her, reminding her of the self-harming she had enacted with the groundskeeper's lawnmower.

The sounds and smells of summer…they felt sour and distasteful when experienced from the cot of an acute ward in a mental hospital. She forced a grim smile of self-reproach.

She'd brought it on herself, hadn't she?

Or had she? She saw how confused Quinn had been with her attempts of a description of her self-harming. How could she explain this communication – of sorts – when she didn't even understand it herself?

Feeling the rubber bonds on her arms, the fresh and

unhealed pain in her wrists, and the scents of summer and childhood happiness now giving way to the sterile aromas of disinfectant and medical supplies, all cruelly reminded her that she was alone and helpless. Even the Light, with its soothing and ecstatic healing that came with the dream-visions, was no longer here. Now she felt anger.

Perhaps the ever-comforting presence of this…this *thing* had blinded her to what was really going on. So other kids were self-harming. So what? That they were experiencing different things probably confirmed that they were all loopy! Perhaps the psychiatrists were right, that it *was* an epidemic with a discoverable catalyst! Chemical rather than…what was hers, anyway? Religious? Spiritual?

The fact that they doped me up and the Light isn't here shows something, at least!

The anger boiled inside. Strength flowed through her veins; power coursed through her body. She heard the increasing drip-drip-drip of blood on floor tiles due to her increased pulse rate. Felt fresh pain as her wound gaped deeper and greedily swallowed up the cotton wadding.

*Daddy. I want my daddy…*the sob rose more easily in her throat now, and the tears flowed. The ceiling lights blurred and swam in her vision, then swung crazily as she rocked her head back and forth on the pillow.

She heard footsteps rapidly approaching, soft-toed shoes or trainers like the Bethan woman's, and realised she'd found her voice and had begun to scream.

The curtains parted, framing a spiked mess of blonde hair that the sunlight behind turned into an explosion of golden light. It was dazzling enough to make Rachel stop crying for a moment, but she couldn't make out the figure's face. She noted the bulky silhouette, knew then it was a stocky woman recruited to Fairlight for physical strength rather than a bedside manner. That brought memories of Bethan back to her, further hammering home her predicament.

Not here to help, but to subdue and control.

"Hey now… and there was me thinking you were a vampire, scared of the light! Well, you've not burned up to a frazzle, so I guess sommat else is upsettin' you."

The voice was different from the others she'd heard: younger, more light-hearted. A Northern accent, Yorkshire probably. Rachel imagined the words were spoken with a smile – a smile that was *meant.* The figure pulled the curtains aside and turned to face her.

The face was just as pleasing as the voice. Pudgy with a squat nose, it reminded Rachel of a relaxed Boxer she used to dog-sit for a neighbour. The large eyes were just as warm and affectionate. The nose chain and the lower lip ring would have brought cries of disgust from older patients in an NHS ward, but Rachel realised the girl's youth and penchant for body modification made her a good choice for the young charges of Fairlight.

Early twenties, looking like everyone's favourite big sister. A far cry from that Bethan bitch…even thinking that name brought a grimace to her face, one the nurse picked up on.

She may have been young, but she was nothing less than professional. She made no comment on Rachel's grimace, but opened her mouth to reveal a wide, lop-sided grin that fit well with the sculptured spikes of her hair.

"I'm Gillian." She pointed to her name tag. "The kids call

me Gilly, so you can, too. You're Rachel Collins, yeah?"

Despite herself, Rachel smiled. "Yes, I'm Rachel." The hoarseness of her voice scared her, but she forced herself to continue. "And I guess your career as a children's entertainer didn't stop when the magician sacked you for bursting the balloon-animals with your hair."

Gillian stared at her for a moment, and then her smile broadened. "Aye, not bad." The smile faded when she glanced at the bonds holding Rachel to the bed rails. It vanished completely when she saw the fresh blood dripping from the dressings.

"Let's get you cleaned up, and then get you some breakfast. You can meet the gang there."

The wounds were cleaned and expertly dressed by Gillian – and the young nurse's face was expressionless while she performed the task, giving Rachel no clue as to the severity and extent of her condition – and then she helped her to the shower unit. Gillian tactfully stayed out of sight while Rachel washed herself, delighting in the fresh, hot water blasting away the sweat and despair of the last twenty-four hours, but Rachel sensed her presence, knew she was not far away. Close enough to assist if she collapsed from blood loss.

Or prevent any self-harming, Rachel thought.

"Didn't see an overnight bag, so I had to scrounge clothes from the other kids. Hope they fit."

Green T-shirt and grey combat trousers. Too big for her, probably male, but the looseness pleased her; she felt she could lose herself in them. She stared at herself in the mirror, saw the drawn cheeks and sunken eyes. There was none of the sapphire glow Dad always said shone from her eyes. They looked – to her, at least – cold and lifeless. And *older*, somehow.

She thought back to her initial impressions on waking, the self-doubt and feeling of abandonment.

No, she told herself, glancing at her bandaged wrists. *I was wrong.* The lack of fresh blood and the fading pain of newly healed flesh told her that.

But the Light isn't here, she reminded herself as she followed Gillian down brightly painted corridors to an area that smelled of fresh grapefruit juice, bacon and eggs. *There's something else, though.* It felt like a sickness, a palpable aura of physical unease that deepened on their way to the refectory. Her pulse quickened and her heart raced. She felt the wounds begin to reopen, as if the healing was going into *reverse…*she thought she heard the dripping of blood from her wrists on the tiled floor of the corridor. She forced herself to blank out the feeling, to concentrate on following the nurse. Not to show any fear.

It was hard. Because she knew that somewhere in the institute, Callum Hayes was aware of her presence, and was waiting for her.

She cast a glance at the corridor they'd both traversed. Like the rest of the hospital she'd seen so far, it almost gleamed with freshness. Everything was new. Under the glare of strip lighting, fresh paint on the walls gleamed with pastel shades of green and blue and the tiled floor glistened with polish that made hers and Gillian's trainers squeak. Prints of colourful seascapes complimented the oceanic atmosphere; some still had the remnants of their price labels on the glass.

The double doors they now faced smelled of pine and fresh varnish, as well as the appetising scent of breakfast. Despite her unease, she realised she was hungry — but the tempting smells and the freshness of the corridor couldn't dispel the feeling of antiquity that followed her through the corridor of Fairlight Hospital. The choice of décor seemed forced somehow, as though the owners of Fairlight were trying too hard to dispel the antiquity.

No, not antiquity, she realised when the doors swung open. The original hospital buildings had Victorian origins, she knew that; yet the sensation was one that suggested something far older than a nineteenth century institution.

Something ancient. She swallowed, realised her throat was dry once more, and glanced at Gillian. The young nurse glanced back and gave her a smile that didn't reach her eyes.

"The grub here's bloody good, Rachel." The nurse held the doors open and beckoned her inside with a quick toss of her head. The nose chain swung gently, a further invitation. "Forget all the jokes about hospital food. Even the staff eat here."

The attempt at forced modernity and youth was even more obvious here. The leather sofas, the unmarked pool table, the massive TV and three gaming consoles on the far left were no surprise, but what took her attention was the floor to ceiling glass – Perspex, more likely – that opened onto the south facing lawns and made the spacious living-cum-dining room seem even larger than it already was. This was slightly higher than Quinn's office, so there was a better view of the sloping cliff tops and the bay. It looked beautiful.

Too beautiful, she thought. The sky was an iridescent blue,

and the rising sun imparted the calm waters and swaying grasses with a luminescence that seemed too *real,* somehow, as though even the view of the outside world was forced. Perhaps the glass was tinted with something? The spotlights in the ceiling were switched off, so they weren't adding to the effect.

Before her was another set of double doors that swung open to allow a smiling male orderly – also young but not quite as 'nonconformist' as Gillian – entry bearing a tray laden with four plates. He looked up, grinned at Gillian, and went to the breakfast bar and its three inhabitants. A solitary silver earring sparkled in the strange light that passed through the bay windows. He distributed the plates and sat down on the bench, began to talk quietly with his companions. His black box alarm and ID pass were hidden; he looked just like any other member of a teenage group.

"As I said, everyone likes the food." Gillian winked as she approached the breakfast bar, a sisterly arm draped over Rachel's shoulders. "Glyn here likes it a little *too* much. You ask me, I'd say he only got the job so that he could pig out every day."

"Button it, you gobby Northern tart." Glyn lifted a skewered sausage in an "up yours" gesture. "You're just jealous 'cos what I eat don't go to me hips."

"It'll catch up with you one day, you soft Southern shite."

The banter seemed forced. Rachel just smiled and said: "Nice to meet you, Glyn."

"Likewise, Rachel," he said with his mouth full. He swallowed, pierced a grilled mushroom and nodded to his companions. "Julia, Ant and Iain. The Gleesome Threesome."

Three young faces turned from their untouched plates to

face her. Eyes glazed with sedation regarded her blankly, lips twitched upwards into shy smiles of welcome because it was expected, not because they genuinely wished her to be here.

Julia was the youngest one, with dark brown hair held back from an equine face in a greasy ponytail. Her eyes met Rachel's before dulling again and returning to stare blankly at her uneaten food.

Iain's eyes were small dots behind thick-lensed glasses that may have been fashionable a few years back; they reminded Rachel of the sort of glasses worn by one of her father's favourite science fiction writers. Another Iain. Perhaps this Iain's parents couldn't afford new specs for him, or he liked the look it gave him, combining it with tousled black hair and uneven beard for full geek chic. He grunted in acknowledgement and turned back to his plate. Like Julia, he just stared at his food without eating. Unlike Julia, he glowered at it, as if blaming the breakfast for his woes. There were no bacon or sausages on his plate; a watery omelette and pureed baked beans sat cold and congealed on the porcelain. His cheeks were oddly sunken, as if the lower part of his face was collapsing in on itself.

Pureed beans, and he won't smile or talk, she realised. *He doesn't want anyone to see how few teeth he has left.*

Ant was short for Antoinette, Rachel figured. The girl looked like she'd come from a posh background. Delicate features that may once have been haughty, contemptuous of children her age who didn't come from the same social standing. No signs of distancing herself now, though. What brought them all to Fairlight was a great leveller…and yet, she still seemed *distant* from the other two, somehow. Not class consciousness, though. Something else.

Something that called to Rachel herself. Ant's cold grey eyes gave nothing away, yet Rachel had the strange impression that beyond them lay a power the girl was unaware – or terrified of. Ant's eyes remained fixed on Rachel's, and a knowing look passed between them before the fog of sedation clouded the grey orbs once more.

Rachel sensed a kinship, a connection with this girl. Then she saw Ant's hands and the plastic, toothless cutlery held in them. They resumed cutting into the piece of fish before her. Rachel saw the edges of bandages beneath the cuffs of the girl's long-sleeved T shirt. She glanced at the others' wrists.

No bandages covered Julie's bare arms. Faint white ridges of scar tissue trailed over her wrists and forearms like fossilised snakes. It had been some time since she'd cut herself – or perhaps she'd started somewhere else on her body?

Iain's pullover was an odd choice for what was to be such a warm day, but Rachel guessed that meant he was more self-conscious of his wounds. The sleeves dangled from thin wrists, and she caught a glimpse of white surgical padding. Iain shot her a cold glare that had her looking away. Back to Ant's hands, busy cutting the fish with surgical precision.

"Kippers, eh?" Rachel smiled, anxious to break the tense atmosphere. "My dad likes them. Tried to get me eating them, but they're the wrong thing for breakfast, I found…"

Ant's fork paused in mid-air. Her head swivelled to stare coolly at Rachel.

"Brain food," Ant said in a voice that was almost musical, that spoke not of gymkhanas, private schools and garden parties but something ethereal, something beyond a rich girl's experience. "Food for the brain…and maybe the brain will feed the little fishies when I'm gone." The fork went to her lips and the grey flesh slipped into her mouth. She closed her eyes as she chewed, and Rachel felt that it was not enjoyment of the food's taste, but reflection, as though Ant was contemplating the very nature of the thing she ate.

"Fuckin' nutty bitch," Iain muttered. He glanced at Julia, and Rachel caught the look of understanding –agreement – between them and wondered if either of them realised the irony of the insult.

She glanced at Glyn, noted how his eyes were rooted to his own food as though he wished to remain apart from the scene, not getting involved. Not wanting to be here.

Not wanting to take sides, Rachel realised with a shudder. She turned and looked at Gillian, her heart sinking at the sight of the female nurse's head turned towards the window.

Another one, not wanting to take sides.

War is coming, Daddy. And I can't fight it on my own. She realised then that she was truly without allies.

Ant swallowed the chewed fish and took another bite. Her eyes glinted before they closed once more.

Rachel knew then. That glint was of the same nature as the unearthly Light that communed with her. Rather than feel encouraged by it, Rachel Collins was scared. Because behind that glint lurked something else. Something not quite human.

Something that was within her as well.

CHAPTER TWELVE

The key completed its turn in the Yale lock to Tony Collins's room. It turned smoothly, swiftly: accompanied with the sound of another set of footsteps pounding up the stairs. The intruder had company and obviously didn't care about stealth.

Easy target, am I? We'll see about that!

His fist closed over Rachel's flash drive. Like a talisman, a defence against dark powers. And the only weapon he had in the war waged upon his daughter. Knuckles whitened under newly healed skin. For a brief moment, before his hand dipped into his pocket and secreted the flash drive, he had the impression that they glowed.

Tony lifted the laptop's power pack and threw it towards the open window while he moved to the opposite side of the room. He held the laptop close to his chest, wishing his heart would stop hammering, wishing he could breathe, as he crouched behind the door.

The door had begun to swing back as the first uniformed officer moved to the source of the disturbance, and what he had assumed to be Tony's exit.

"What the hell…"

The policeman's confusion at the dangling power pack, with its cord wrapped in the twisted net curtains, didn't last long. He saw the window wasn't opened widely enough to allow the exit of a fully grown man.

Tony momentarily froze at the sight of the bulky officer's massive hands drumming on the windowsill. *Big bastard.* Instinct for self-preservation broke his fear.

He pushed past the door, grabbed the key by its wooden fob, slammed the door closed on the approaching back-up officer and lifted the laptop.

The first officer turned slowly. Too slowly. His eyes widened at the sight of the slab held aloft in his quarry's hands. His jaw dropped.

Tony brought his daughter's computer crashing down on the copper's face in a devastating side swipe that sent shock waves rippling through his arms. The crack of plastic and dental enamel filled his ears. The curtains twisted as the burly copper collapsed into the bay window. His peaked cap fell to his knees before rolling to the floor. Blood dribbled down the cracks in his teeth as he sat, dazed and uncomprehending. Tony lifted the laptop once more; this time he jabbed it directly under the copper's chin.

The head snapped backwards, and another cracking sound filled the room. Glass fell in heavy shards to the courtyard below.

Tony dropped the shattered laptop and put his hands on the officer's chest and felt the hardness of the stab vest beneath his palms. The copper was out cold, a dead weight. It would be no effort to push him through the remains of the window…

What the hell am I thinking? Hot blood drooled on his knuckles from the unconscious policeman. He shuddered at the thought of what he had been about to do.

He pulled the copper away from the bay window, grunting with exertion. He dragged the dead weight over to the pounding door. A natural door stop, he thought with satisfaction. The door shook violently in the frame, dirty flakes of once-white gloss paint falling to the frayed carpet and showering the unconscious officer.

His heart pounding, adrenaline racing through his system, and sweat pouring down his face, Tony Collins knew his time was short. He could let the second copper in and risk taking him on, but the only reason he'd overpowered the first had been the element of surprise. He doubted his luck would hold a second time.

He eyed the key. The room number was blazoned in gold foil on the wooden fob. That bastard Adam must've given it to the coppers without alerting him. That made him an enemy as well.

Christ, is anyone *on my side now?* The only exit available to him was the shattered bay window. He took a deep breath and pulled the bloodstained curtains aside. Below he saw pieces of glass scattered on the cobbles, and the wooden bench that had broken the pane. Beside it Adam stared quizzically up at him.

"Shit," Tony breathed. He turned back to the hammering door. *What now? Think, think...*

"Hold your horses! I'm coming out."

The hammering halted. A muffled voice called out: "Frank?"

Tony glanced at the natural door stop. Frank began to stir; he let out a thin growl, snorted wetly and raised his head to spit out the blood. Tony started at the motion of the copper's lower jaw with this action. It moved in two directions.

Clean break. Christ, he looks like the Predator!

"Frank'll be okay. Eventually." With that, Tony could almost feel the hostility burning through the door. The voice continued, tight with unsuppressed anger.

"You fucker...*Right.* Once you've opened the door, step away. Make sure you're by the window."

Yeah. And what then? He glanced out the window again. Adam had gone.

Frank's eyes turned in Tony's direction, stared blankly for a moment before recognition filtered through. A snarl. Tony picked up the laptop once more.

Now.

Tony lunged for the door, flipped the catch and slammed the door back into the rising Frank. The edge of the jamb caught him on the jelly-like gap of flesh between the sections of his broken jaw; his cheeks bulged like a hamster's and his eyes screwed tightly shut in agony.

Tony saw Frank's companion behind the door and felt relieved to see the copper was younger and slighter in build. An easier opponent.

That momentary relief vanished as the policeman ducked his head to avoid the laptop which went flying into the lobby, missing its intended target. Tony pushed on the door, attempted to slam it back into the approaching copper's face, but his opponent was too swift – and despite his diminutive size, too damn strong.

The hammering in Tony's chest was joined by a sudden pain as the second policeman crashed into him, forcing him back from the door and onto the bed. His head struck the wooden headboard with a sickening crack that filled him with dizziness and nausea. His body slumped and the world changed to a mottled white surface of cracked plaster and yellow-stained Artex that spun before his eyes. He felt like a space traveller approaching the surface of an alien, hostile planet. He heard growls from the approaching policeman, animalistic snarls of fury and hatred. Hands grabbed at him, like sharp talons clawing at his face, accompanied by bony knees that pressed into his abdomen.

The hands bunched into fists and ploughed into him with a fury and impact that belied the young copper's build. Tony's head lifted from the headboard and thrust back into it, this time sending huge, shivering cracks through the ancient wood. Tony's vision exploded in a shower of red and black, and his assailant's face turned to that of the monster he imagined him to be.

Waves lapped at his ears. Warm, syrupy fluid that caused him to frown and shift his position. His head no longer felt comfortable lying on the sandy beach; the angle he'd fallen asleep on meant he'd have a nasty crick in his neck for the rest of the day, just like the time Rachel and Becky had left him sleeping off the after-effects of too many beers in the sun, his head fallen at a ridiculous angle on the sun lounger.

Where are they? Why have they left me again? Perhaps he'd fallen asleep again and tipped the lounger over, too pissed to realise he'd crashed to the sandy ground. Too pissed to even feel any pain. He began to open his eyes, but the sun was too bright. Nuclear explosions blasted his sight, burned his eyes back into darkness. Then came the pain.

A rhythmic pounding in his temples and a constant burning from the fire that had been lit behind his head. The syrup that warmed his earlobes was static; he couldn't hear the soothing sound of the sea that brought the liquid.

Instead he heard the smooth purr of a car's engine. He felt the rhythmic bounce and sway as the vehicle turned a corner. He felt the sun's radiated warmth behind him. He opened his eyes more slowly this time.

A monster faced him. A uniformed beast that had once been a man, its shirt soaked in crimson, its hands gripping the headrest of the passenger seat in front of it. Its face turned to him, and its jaws parted, a snarl of hatred accompanied by fresh blood dripping down its broken teeth.

Tony held his breath; he forced his head away from the vinyl covered headrest and tried to push backwards. His cheek made a sticky, Velcro-like sound and he saw black blood smeared on the vinyl. Fresh pain flared in his mouth, and then his head as it made contact with the hot glass of the window.

The pain was forgotten briefly, replaced by terror and the grim realisation of the trouble he was in. The hostility from the broken-jawed policeman was a physical hatred that had him writhing in his seat, placing further stress upon hands bound behind his back by rigid handcuffs.

Now he felt a chill seep into his battered body. He tried telling himself it was from the patrol car's air conditioning unit.

"You're dead, Collins." The voice was softly spoken; it came from the driver whose eyes burned into his via the rear-view mirror. "Frank would like to kill you himself, but he's going to be out of action for a bit. As soon as we get to Fairlight we're going to get *him* fixed up and *you* torn to pieces."

Tony snorted; clotted blood rattled in his nostrils. He cleared his throat, ran his tongue around his mouth and felt several loose teeth.

"Why?" He didn't recognise his voice. It sounded weary and distant, an old man's voice; an old man who realised death was approaching and although he feared it, he was determined to fight it. "What've you got to gain by this?"

He heard a wet gurgling from Frank, a sound that might have been a laugh. Behind him, through the window, Tony saw the rain-sodden streets of Fairlight glimmer with light from the rising sun. The vehicle slowed as it reached the lights, then increased speed when amber changed to green. The dilapidated warehouse buildings and harbour frontage glistened like ancient vessels risen from the sea.

He thought back to his visit and his assault on one of the units; the damage to his hand, the meeting of Jim…and the appearance of that sinuous, snakelike creature lurking in the darkness beyond the warehouse doors. Golden orbs surrounded by blackness that was darker than the night.

What do you see when you cut yourself? He glanced down at his healed hand, the only part of his body that felt completely whole and healthy. Even the redness had gone.

But the memory of that thing remains, doesn't it? If that's what I saw when I harmed myself…what the hell do the poor kids in Fairlight see? What monsters are driving them insane?

"Orders, Collins," the driver continued. "That's all. Too much is at stake to let you fuck around. Of course, if you'd come quietly we'd have given you a quick way out. Your choice, pal. You chose the hard way."

"What the fuck *for?* I'm just trying to find out what my daughter –"

Jim. *That young' un cutting himself up in a church and*

comin' to Fairlight. That new building's only been up a few years. Why d'you think they built it around the older asylum instead of a new spot?

Jim was in Fairlight as well. What was it he'd said before that… that assault?

It's come back. Jesus, it's outside the Pharos!

"Pharos," Tony said softly. He saw the shoulders of the driving officer stiffen. The eyes burned once more in the rear-view mirror. A hiss of trepidation came from his fellow passenger. "What's a Pharos?"

"Doesn't matter," the driver said quickly, changing up a gear.

"Mattered to Jim, though, didn't it?" Tony pressed the attack. He leaned forward, thrust his face into the gap between the two front seats. The harbour was far behind them. Ahead lay the road that would take them past the dark cliffs that hid the bay – and the institution – from view. "He's been there before. Whatever he went through, he survived. Now you fuckers have taken him back there – same place you're taking me! You might as well tell me, because he sure as fuck will!"

The gearstick moved backward, and the police driver's elbow carried on, powering into Tony's jaw.

His head snapped up and back, the loosened teeth protesting with new shooting pains. He fell back.

He heard the congealed coating of blood on the vinyl upholstery crack beneath his skull, smelled fresh blood that dribbled through his throbbing mouth. Stars filled his vision and static clouded his ears.

He turned to the window and rested his head on the cooling glass. Eventually the stars faded to reveal a choppy, murky sea beyond the headland. The sunlight made the still, syrupy waters of the shallow bay beneath Fairlight glisten with the same sickly appearance of rotting vegetation that had coated the storage units on the quayside.

He glanced at Frank's jaw, swollen and bulging but still causing the man considerable pain with every intake of breath or movement the vehicle made. Despite the pain and the terror that filled him, Tony Collins smiled. At least he'd made that bastard suffer. Frank glowered at him, but made no attempt to speak.

The static grew louder, more piercing. White noise. Human voices.

The shriek of brakes and the skidding of tyres on gravel replaced the static. Tony narrowly avoided smacking his head on the driver's seat.

Now what? Even Frank looked puzzled. Tony made out the word 'school' and a woman's name, but little else.

"You're fucking joking." The police driver stared at the two-way radio console. His knuckles tightened on the handset as he glanced behind him. "We can't piss around; let's drop Collins off first and…what? Well, at least let's get Frank checked over…for fuck's *sake!*"

The car spun round and the blues and twos came into play. Frank looked puzzled, his pain forgotten. Tony stared hard at the panicked expression on the younger officer's face. They went back the way they came, the lights splashing sapphire onto the slimy walls of the quayside.

There was urgency in the policeman's driving, one that seemed at odds with whatever professional training he had received. Sweat beaded the man's unlined forehead. His eyes flicked once more into the rear-view mirror but there was little hostility when they met Tony's eyes. Now there was anxiety, trepidation.

He's wondering how much of a threat I'm going to be. Wherever we're going, he's going to have to leave me on my own for a bit – or with Predator-face here.

Tony felt a brief surge of hope. It wasn't much – he didn't know where they were heading, and if the coppers were worried, by rights he should be as well. To be sent without even giving Frank medical attention meant this was a real emergency.

One I can take advantage of.

The eyes flashed at him in the rear-view mirror once more, as if reading his thoughts.

"Don't get any ideas, Collins. Other units will be at the school soon."

"School?"

The driver didn't reply. His mouth was a thin, bloodless line. Tony sank back into the seat, pushing his belly forward to prevent extra pressure on his cuffed wrists. They overtook a stationary brewery truck by the Day Gone Down. Tony saw Adam chatting with the two draymen, his arms folded, leisurely leaning against the raised hatch of the drop cellar. Their eyes met, and Adam looked away quickly.

"You'll get yours sunshine," Tony muttered. Rage flared in his chest; he forced himself to hold on to it. *Harness it. That fucker just admitted they'll be the first unit there. Take 'em by surprise…*

Adrenaline coursed through his body at the prospect of further action. He closed his eyes and breathed slowly, deeply.

School. Thoughts of Rachel's homework, courses and extra-curricular activities flooded his mind. The files on her laptop – now on the flash drive in his pocket.

School. Dear God, what had happened all over the country must have begun in Fairlight by now. The dashboard clock told him it wasn't even eight o'clock yet.

"Too early for lessons, surely? So what's going on there?"

No reply.

"You don't even know, do you?"

Tony noticed the driver turn off the air conditioning; despite the sweat trickling down his neck, the officer was chilled to the core.

The Civic raced towards its destination, but the journey felt agonisingly slow to Tony. The dilapidated storage units of the harbour gave way to retirement bungalows and the brief glimpse of green fields. The rising sun beat down on the side windows as it passed the playing fields of the school, imparting light and warmth.

Yet the chill remained.

CHAPTER THIRTEEN

Through the closed doors of the staff room Karen Tyndall heard the police car's sirens but took no comfort in them. The roar of the Honda's engine and the squeal of tyres on the tarmac may have relieved her twenty minutes ago, but what she had seen emerge from the ruins of Stefan Fleischer would take more than the presence of mere police officers to wipe from her memory.

The blue lights splashed through the half-drawn blinds, imparting an ethereal sapphire-ruby glow to the dripping blood that coated the frosted and fluted glass pane of the staffroom door: an alien life fluid.

Alien. She clasped her hands to her knees, upper body bent forward and shuddering uncontrollably. The sofa shook with her.

Alien. Nothing like it could have originated on Earth. No way could a creature like that evolve naturally – and no way would a Creator or intelligent designer construct such a monstrosity.

A knocking on the glass. A scratchy, scraping sound rather than the fleshy thud of chubby schoolboy knuckles. There was nothing left of his hands. He had to be pounding with bare bone.

"Miss! The cavalry's here."

Stefan's words chilled her further. The voice was weak and distant, barely audible over the solid barrier of the locked door and the dying sirens. The voice belonged to a young man who should not be alive, who had lost too much blood to remain conscious, let alone be able to follow her around the school and bang on the doors she closed behind her.

"C'mon, Miss! You've got to tell them what you've learned!" Now there was amusement in the child's voice, barely suppressed laughter. "Education's gotta be shared!"

She clamped her hands over her mouth, but not fast enough to prevent the escape of a whimper. Fresh blood welled in her damaged palm as her teeth inadvertently bit into the lacerated flesh. Sweet, metallic tastes filled her mouth, and she remembered the stench of the hot blood that had erupted from Stefan's throat and painted the classroom windows. Bile rose in her throat, and she tasted sour Merlot once more, but the taste of blood remained; an underlying accompaniment to the liquid that had her dry heaving. The creature outside the staffroom door heard her retching. She heard it giggle.

Why aren't you dead, you fucking monster? She wiped away the strings of saliva and forced herself to her feet. As soon as the coppers saw the coating of scarlet on the windows, the pieces of child flesh that littered the classroom, they'd go into action. What they would do she had no idea, but at least she would no longer be alone against this *thing.*

The thought gave her a small amount of comfort; just enough to raise a spark of defiance in her.

"Fuck off, *Stephen.*" Her voice was calm and more forceful than she'd expected. The decision to rile the boy by refusing to call him by his chosen, Germanic name gave her strength. She even felt the trembling in her legs dissipate. The displeased hiss from behind the door sent a chill down her back, but despite that, she felt the beginning of a smile on her lips.

"I'm not impressed with your little show-and-tell. All

you've done is earn yourself a one way ticket to the institute. See how much you and your friends can cut each other up in *there!*"

The hiss grew louder, turned into an alien laugh. She was thankful the frosted glass obscured his shape.

"Miss, you have no idea! You really think they've come to save you?"

What? The slamming of doors and the squeak of rubber-soled feet on linoleum filtered through the alien laughter. Sounds of rescue that were no longer welcome.

She heard him move – or rather, *slither* – away from the door. The smell of blood was stronger, and she saw thin rivulets creep under the door and soak into the floor tiles. The slithering sound grew fainter, and she guessed Stefan was going to greet the policemen.

She swallowed thickly, felt her heart pounding. She moved to the window and pulled the blinds across. In the playground, the police car sat on the hopscotch grid, the engine purring, the lights revolving. She blinked. Was that someone in the back seat?

It looked like some contortionist act. A man trying to free hands that had been cuffed behind his back by dragging his legs through...now his hands were in front of him. He began to pound on the window, then lay backwards in the seat and lifted his legs. His feet drew back, and then powered into the window. Again. And again, the car rocking on its springs with the force; the glass cracked.

The police hadn't had time to take this prisoner – whoever he was – to the station before coming here. He looked dangerous; there was blood on his scalp and shirt but whatever injuries he'd suffered hadn't incapacitated him, and that meant her rescuers would need her help. She glanced at the staffroom door, saw the misshapen figure had gone. She took a deep breath and made her decision.

Key in the lock. Turn. Exhale. Hand on the doorknob…another deep breath, and then in.

The deep breath she'd taken violently left her lungs as though she'd been punched in the gut. The two policemen stood in the open doorway leading to the lobby, frozen rigid in disbelief and horror at the sight confronting them. Rising sunlight shone through the streaks of scarlet on the upper windows, misting the classroom with a fog of blood.

The sight of the bigger officer's face briefly caught her attention; the shattered jaw and the agony in his eyes made her question just what sort of a police force Fairlight had that would demand its officers face a razor-wielding teenager in this condition. Then she saw what had frozen them, and everything else left her.

Stefan Fleischer had sat down at the teacher's desk, underneath the blood-dotted poster of Thomas Hardy. His expressionless face was pale, and his skin had an odd sheen that made him look like a waxwork dummy.

The slow, rhythmic, rise and fall of his chest was one indicator that he was still alive. Or was that the motion of the creature hidden inside him?

His elbows were on the desk, the remains of his arms hidden in a pile of clotted blood and sodden bandages. They twitched.

His eyes were glazed with a faraway expression. They flickered momentarily as the door closed behind the policemen. Realisation.

Then the lips parted. Stefan's normally gleaming white teeth did not reveal themselves. Instead, there was a patterned blackness that gleamed like gunmetal. The hissing returned, harsher and more threatening now there was no barrier between the teacher and her former pupil.

The lips parted wider, gave definition to the blackness within. A grin of serrated, diamond-shaped teeth welcomed them. Something just as black and jagged stirred in the ruined folds of the scarlet bandages, something Karen was all too familiar with. The limbs of the creature that had tried to take her.

"Stay back," she croaked to the policemen, trying not to gag on the stink of decayed flesh that filled the sunlight-warm room. The policemen didn't respond, were seemingly oblivious of her presence. The younger one had begun to back away, his cold grey eyes rooted on the jellied lumps of flesh and pools of blood that paved the way to the teacher's desk. He made heaving noises.

Karen held a hand to her nose, realised she'd raised her injured palm and quickly switched hands. She pressed her back to the wall and slowly began to edge her way leftward. She kept her eyes fixed on the doorway behind the bulky, injured policeman, who seemed to have forgotten the pain of his broken jaw. Like his younger comrade, his eyes were rooted on the thing sat at the teacher's desk; the thing Karen kept her eyes from.

She heard rapid breathing from the young officer and nasal snorts from the other; accompanied by the slow, unearthly hiss that reached neither peak nor trough but remained constant, like an airline inflating a tyre.

Whatever that hissing was, it was not breathing. In her peripheral vision, she saw the chest of Stefan Fleischer rise – or rather, inflate. The hiss continued. Karen's skin rippled with gooseflesh. She pressed onwards, reaching the corner. The open doorway was ten yards away.

The younger officer had his radio out, slowly raised it to his lips. "*Where's my back up?*" Nothing but static answered him. The white noise attracted the attention of the thing sitting at the teacher's desk. The hissing paused, and the waxy head swivelled in the policeman's direction. A wet, pulpy tearing sound now joined the hiss.

Without taking his eyes off the pupil, he said, in a lower voice: "Frank. I'm going to try and raise them on the car's R/T. Look after the bird. Make sure she doesn't go *anywhere.*"

Karen froze. She shrank back into the corner when Frank's eyes bored into hers, his expression of fear replaced with a look that was incompatible with the man's role as protector and saviour. In that instant she knew something was terribly wrong with the Fairlight police force.

They're not going to help me.

Instinct for survival overrode her terror. She was no longer paralysed by fear; adrenaline kicked in and she launched herself from the corner. She swung her bag into the bulky copper's face; more of a distraction than a plan to cause any serious harm. But the extra weight of the books within the heavy canvas meant more than that to the officer with the shattered jaw. His cry was barely human.

Karen Tyndall felt an almost euphoric sense of satisfaction as the bulky policeman sank to the floor and revealed the unbarred doorway to her. *Escape.*

She hopped over the policeman's thrashing legs, her bag swinging back onto her shoulder. A heel snapped off her shoe as she landed awkwardly, and sharp pain shot up her calf, but the sound of the beast's hissing and tearing kept her legs powering onwards, ignoring the signs of a potential sprained ankle.

She pulled the door towards her and almost smiled at the terrified expression of the younger copper. The nascent smile vanished with her final sight of the thing on her desk and its last act.

In the moment before the Stefan-thing tore itself to pieces, she could swear that the thing had smiled at her - or rather, smiled *through* Stefan; it pulled the human child's lips back in a grotesque parody of what it thought to be human amusement.

Its insectile claws folded inwards, tore away the remains of the school shirt to reveal the bloated, gyrating mass of flesh that was once a fifteen year old boy's chest and stomach. The old scars from previous self-harming thrashed like worms in grave soil. Then the head dropped backwards, the eyes staring sightlessly at the ceiling, the rippling tube of his jugular exposed to the light. The right claw rose, then rested on the Adam's apple. Whatever was within pressed violently against the prison of skin, as if sensing its freedom was at hand. The claw vibrated, then sliced inwards, just as the left claw tore into the writhing nest of the belly.

The explosion filled the room with impenetrable blackness and pushed the door against her, slamming it into the jamb more forcibly than she could have managed herself. She fell to the ground, her ears ringing with the shriek of shattering glass and the rapid *thud-thud-thud* of sharpened metal striking the masonry and the door in front of her.

Even in her dazed state she thought the latter sound strange. It was almost like machine gunfire…no, not gunfire. *Shuriken,* she thought dumbly.

Ninja throwing stars? Why …then she saw the outer edges of the things that had exploded into the door.

Saw the dozens of black, jagged edges protruding on her side of the barrier. But unlike shuriken, they *moved* in the door; pulsating and writhing, creatures attempting to escape their wooden prison. They weren't shards of metal. They were living things: tiny limbs that made sawing motions, spitting splinters of wood into the hallway.

*Limbs…*she swallowed and slowly got to her feet. Limbs that were miniature versions of the lethal, alien cutting tools that had replaced the hands and lower arms of Stefan Fleischer. Now she knew what the swelling in his belly had been.

Babies! My God, it's given birth!

The sprained ankle protested and she let out a sharp cry. The tiny beings in the door paused, the sawing limbs frozen. She had the sensation of dozens of invisible eyes watching her from within the chitinous limbs. Appraising her.

Then the sawing continued, became stronger. The limbs whirled, became miniature circular saws that tore through the wood like paper.

Sawdust filled the air, had her coughing and her eyes streaming. She turned, kicked away her shoes and hobbled down the lobby. The varnished wood felt cold beneath her bare feet. She increased her pace, her lips clenched into a thin line to stifle her screams. Twenty yards to the double doors.

Fifteen.

She didn't dare look back.

Splinters of wood tore into her and she knew she'd be no match for the speed and ferocity of those things. *If that's what they can do to wood, how quickly will they tear through me?*

Ten yards.

Five.

The remains of the door fell away with a shriek of rusted hinges. Then a hideous, scuttling, *scrabbling* sound, like thousands of crabs racing along a wooden promenade. Chitinous legs and sharpened claws...

The mental image spurred her onwards. The door handles were in her sweat-drenched palms. She pulled the doors towards her, felt her grip loosen on the brass knobs momentarily. Sunlight shone through the opening, and she felt warm rays on her face, scented the salt tang of sea air, before the doors swung to and blocked the light.

She heard the cry of a lone seagull, drowned out by an unearthly cry of agony from far behind her - behind the hastily slammed doors of the classroom. It died, and the sounds of scrabbling, clicking and *cutting* sounds grew louder. She grabbed the handles once more.

This time there was help. The doors were forced inwards and the sunlight blotted out by a silhouette. A man, with his arms raised and joined at the wrists, frozen on the door.

"What the bloody *hell*..."

As she pushed past him, she saw sunlight fall on the silver link that bound his wrists together.

The guy in the police car. But right now, the company of an escaped felon didn't disturb her – not just because of the arresting officers' behaviour to her. There were more pressing matters to be concerned by.

"*Close the fucking door, for Christ's sake!*"

He didn't respond. His entire body had gone rigid, his eyes bulging in disbelief at what he saw in the lobby.

She yanked his bound hands from the door and grabbed the handles, pulling the doors to. They shuddered in the frame, the bolts rattling.

She held onto the handles, her knuckles whitening and her eyes clenched shut with the vision of horror she had seen in the lobby before slamming the doors. A vision that would never leave her.

The sight of Stefan Fleischer cutting himself with alien appendages was one thing. The sight of his swollen, glistening belly that writhed with unseen creatures was another.

But to see what had come from him – what had chased her, what had sawn their way through the solid wooden barrier of fire doors – that was far worse.

She shuddered violently, feeling each new vibration as the creatures buried themselves in the door like an electric shock riding her spine, but she couldn't release the door handles. Her hands felt like they were glued to the brass.

Crabs along a wooden promenade. Spider-like creatures, with chitinous legs and sharpened claws. None of those mental images had prepared her for the horror of what she had seen before the doors closed.

Creatures with only three limbs. How the hell could they exist, let alone move so quickly? She saw the deep grooves they'd made in the wooden floorboards on their spinning approach toward her.

Spinning. Like a vertical starfish, travelling on the tips of its limbs…but unlike any starfish she could imagine. More like the emblem of the Isle of Man, a three-legged creature but with far from human legs. The speed – the *velocity* – of these black, shining three-limbed cartwheels was more like the shuriken she had imagined. Just as lethal.

"Come on now, lady. Ease up." Her hands were pulled slowly, gently, from the handles. She tensed, barely comprehending the words.

"I saw them too. I don't understand them…but we can't hang around."

She faced the doors one last time. The sound of sawing and tearing began again. She allowed herself to be pulled from the door and into the line of vision - and then the arms - of her rescuer.

He held her awkwardly with cuffed arms, allowing her sobs and shudders to be absorbed into his body. When the wood-chipping sound got too loud, he raised his arms and said: "Come on, let's go. It's not just those things we have to worry about."

She stared blankly at him. He inclined his bloody head, nodding towards the road that disappeared in a gap of the cliffs.

Blue and amber lights flashed; sirens wailed. She thought back to the agonised howls of the policemen within the school and the call the younger officer had made on his radio.

She looked at the felon. She recognised his face now: he was the man in the Day Gone Down yesterday, who'd held her bag when she dropped it. There was a flash of recognition in his eyes, replaced by urgency when he spoke. "We've got to go, now. They're not coming to rescue us."

She shuddered violently, nodded, and allowed herself to be led away from the school building. Towards the playing fields and the hedgerows that surrounded them.

The pain in her ankle returned, and she had to lean on her companion for assistance. The sirens grew louder. A glance over her shoulder revealed the first vehicle to enter the school grounds: a police patrol car, identical to the one with the broken rear window that had held her rescuer. Then the next one: military trucks with olive coloured canvas, bulging with soldiers like Stefan's stomach had bulged with the monsters. Swollen with death-dealers.

"Jesus," she heard him mutter. "They've brought the fucking army in!"

"They'll need more than soldiers," she said stiffly, trying to ignore the pain in her ankle as the hedgerow swallowed them up. "Did you see those…" she couldn't bring herself to finish the sentence. She wanted to focus on the greenery and the blue sky, the clouds and the sea. Anything but allow her mind's eye to re-imagine those things…

"Yeah," he said grimly. "I saw them. Jesus, those *eyes*…"

She swallowed and sank to the ground. Eyes. As terrifying as the alien creatures had been, with their scythe-like appendages and ferocious speed, it was the eyes that had made both of them freeze.

Tiny, bulb-like projections that ran on the exterior side of each leg — she'd originally thought they were just raised indentations, markings like those on a crab shell, until the lids had parted and revealed pale, golden orbs. Orbs with black pupils that burned like the darkest pits of hell, that saw them.

And hungered.

Through the gaps in the hedgerow they watched the first rank of soldiers surround the building, L85A2 rifles raised. Then the next, carrying black tube-like things connected to heavy black canisters strapped to their backs. Flamethrowers.

"You're local, Miss? I hope you know somewhere safe we can go."

She held her breath as the school doors were torched. Burning wood and spent fuel assailed her nostrils.

"Somewhere with tools…and a printer."

She looked at him. He indicated his cuffed wrists, and then opened a clenched palm. Inside he held a small, plastic squirrel. Its head was missing. A bushy plastic tail gleamed in the sun.

"My daughter's flash drive," he said quietly. "It's got answers."

"Answers…or more questions?"

He didn't reply. They both watched the flames rise and spread to the roof of the school. Before long smoke obscured the clock tower, hiding the hands that pointed to nine and ten.

"I know it's early," she whispered. "But I *really* need a drink."

CHAPTER FOURTEEN

"At first, I thought they were starfish. Black, slimy starfish. But when they got closer, I saw they definitely only had three legs. And…" she swallowed and tasted the black pudding she had eaten earlier. It tasted more of blood than oatmeal, fat and herbs now. Her bile rose. "Every step they took…well, every spin of the wheel, anyway…they soaked up the blood on the shore. They carved a path through the bones, like a bike through snow. They'd…God, they'd eaten the bones. But how, I don't know. They didn't have any mouths. They-"

"Quinn will have a field day with that one," Julia said with a knowing smirk that Rachel was beginning to find irritating. "Lots of symbolism and imagery to play with. Three-legged symbol, feasting on death. Land and sea. Not that he knows bugger all, of course. Clutching at straws if you ask me."

"But what *are* they?" Rachel pushed her plate away, blanching at the sight of the ketchup smears. The shell of Julia's boiled egg looked as fragile and brittle as the bones crushed underfoot - under *wheel* - by her nightmare creatures.

Julia looked down at her notes again, the premature lines in her forehead crinkling. Rachel wondered if they were lines caused by the stress of her illness, or a natural consequence of too many hours spent frowning at school text books and academic websites.

Just like me. And yet…I don't feel a kindred spirit here. This girl is just way too distant.

"Triskelion," Julia said finally. She underlined the word on her notepad with a deliberate flourish to show her satisfaction.

She looked up at Rachel with that irritating smirk again.

"Triskelion?"

Julia nodded. "It's a Greek word, means literally 'three-legged.' Like the symbol on the flag of the Isle of Man. Three human legs, bent at the knee and conjoined at the hip. Sicily has a similar motif, but the legs are naked. The Isle of Man's triskelion has armoured legs."

Rachel watched Julia draw a rough image of the Manx symbol on the paper. The tip of the felt pen was split and worn, and the ink bled into the paper, but the image took shape in a familiar form thanks to the hands of a gifted artist.

Too familiar. Rachel swallowed.

"Armoured..." Julia raised the pen to her lips and tapped it against her teeth, a thoughtful expression on her face. "That may be significant."

The tapping sound echoed throughout the dining room. Rachel stared, fascinated, at the girl's teeth. They were yellowed with tartar on the bottom row, the hallmark of a smoker; but Rachel hadn't seen the girl light a single cigarette. She didn't smell of tobacco, either.

The thought made her think of Dad, and her heart sank. She took a deep breath and forced herself to stare at the image on the paper. A black, spider-like creature that could not possibly exist, yet felt so real in her dream. Even the way it traversed the shore of skulls had looked so natural, an alien presence perfectly at home in a place it had no evolutionary right to be a part of.

"And you've never dreamt of it before?"

Rachel shook her head. "How come you're so...familiar with these things?"

"I'm not." The felt tip pen continued rattling, and Rachel felt her own teeth itch. It sounded like the tapping of naked tree branches on her bedroom window when the winter winds grew strong. *Let me in, let me in!* Dad would say with a mock-sinister laugh as he turned the light off and closed the door on her. *The tree beasts are hungry for little girls tonight!*

That stopped when she used the shards of broken window on herself. To this day he still believed she had smashed the window herself.

"Have a closer look at Gillian's tattoos when you get a chance. She's got a triskelion on the base of her spine. No, no, nothing like this thing here! It's more of a Celtic symbol than the Manx symbol; the legs are curved rather than angular."

Rachel glanced over Julia's head to the double doors leading to the kitchen. She felt uneasy. Julia saw her worried expression and smiled.

"Nothing to worry about, Rachel. I asked her about it when I got here and she gave me the full history of the triskelion: bored me to tears, if I'm honest. It's not an evil symbol like the swastika, so those things you dreamed about…"

"Wonder if Callum Hayes dreamed about them?"

Julia stiffened. The smirk froze on her face.

"He was there. Singing a song as the things approached. He seemed to be…well, not in control of them as such. But definitely on the same team."

Now the pen-on-teeth tapping had halted, Rachel heard the sounds from the kitchen. The rattle of crockery and jingle of cutlery placed in a dishwasher rack; the hiss of hot water blasting onto frying pans and saucepans too big or too grimy for the dishwasher; the tuneless whistling of Gillian, pretending not to overhear the conversation between her two charges.

Ant and Iain had left to clean their teeth, for which Rachel had been grateful; she tried not to wonder what teeth Iain had left to clean. Glyn had accompanied them, and that had hammered home the realisation she was a prisoner.

Constant surveillance and observation, accompanied everywhere…for our own protection, of course. Rachel glanced at the window while Julia busied herself with her drawing. She wondered what Gillian's reaction would be if she decided to throw herself at the Perspex. Had she seen that sort of thing before? Would Rachel be impeded before she got anywhere near the window?

And what about Callum Hayes? Would he try to escape when the medication wore off? No, of course not. She remembered the last email from him.

You sound just like my sister and where is she now eh? Dead, that's where. Food for the worms – not much food at that, seeing as how fucking skinny she was. Like her, you've chosen the wrong side and you'll be sorry when the time comes. We're evolving. We'll be the new masters of the world. Bitches like you will be out in the cold, food for the worms. Like my sister. Like your mum.

She ground her teeth with anger. No, he wasn't going to escape. Whatever force was compelling him wanted him here in Fairlight. She glanced back to the double doors, knew Gillian was listening.

"What do you know about him? Were you part of the Children of the Evolution?" She resisted the pressure to whisper her question but felt her heart in her mouth. The smiling, whistling Gillian remained in the kitchen, but no sounds of kitchen duties could be heard. The nurse now felt like an unseen threat.

She's got a triskelion on the base of her spine. Rubbish, that meant nothing. No connection. She focussed on Julia.

Rachel had been irritated by the other girl's smugness, but now she wished the smirk would return. Anything to replace the look of sheer, white-faced terror. Julia hunched over the table, rubbing her thumbs together.

Rachel glanced at the faded scars on the girl's wrists, saw how white they were in contrast to the reddened fingers and arms. Perhaps she hadn't cut herself recently? Perhaps her self-harming was history.

Then why is she here?

"Julia?" Rachel leant closer. Her forehead almost touched the greasy bangs of Julia's hair. She ignored the smell of the girl's breath and spoke quietly. "Personal question, I know. But...when did you last self-harm?"

Julia rubbed her thumbs harder, her eyes riveted to the digits, unable to meet Rachel's gaze. She waited for Gillian's whistling to resume before answering.

"Last night. I cut myself last night...when I heard Callum Hayes had been admitted to Fairlight." Her head rose, and Rachel started. The cold grey eyes were no longer full of disdain and supercilious arrogance, but pools of despair in which hope had long since departed. "I was scared, Rachel. More than scared. I left the Children of the Evolution months ago...I thought he was coming for me."

The chill passed between Julia and Rachel. Rachel swallowed, no longer felt the warmth of the summer sun beating through the window.

"I tried to end it. I found a chisel from Site Services and tried to open my wrists…" A sob broke free as she stopped rubbing her thumbs and held her hands to Rachel, palms upwards. They shook. Her carefully-constructed charade of self-satisfied superiority had fragmented like the shell of her breakfast egg.

Rachel's eyes widened. The faded white worms of Julia's scars looked old. And yet…

"Yes, Rachel. These *are* the wounds. They healed. They *healed!*"

Rachel unconsciously picked at the dressings on her own wounds. She flexed her fingers, hoping to feel pain from healing flesh. There was nothing.

Julia saw her movements and frowned. She looked at the bandages, then into Rachel's eyes. Julia's eyes widened; she opened her mouth to speak but Rachel shook her head.

Their eyes remained locked. A silent understanding passed between them. Rachel moved her hand over the table and gently took Julia's fingers. Their hands clasped, resting on the hand drawn image of the triskelion. This time, there was no trembling.

"How are you today, Rachel?"

Better than you, she almost said. The overcast sky may have darkened his face, but even without the thicker shadows around his sunken eyes Quinn looked terrible. As though he had lost weight and aged ten years in the space of one night. The fear that had greeted Rachel on her first appointment with the clinical psychiatrist was still there, but muted; as though he had something far worse to be scared of.

"I'm okay, Mr Quinn." Noncommittal, her expression as blank as possible. She turned back to stare at the sundial. She could have sworn the blade had moved, but that must have been caused by the shadows cast by the sycamores.

"That's good," he answered with a weak smile. "I appreciate your awakening wasn't the most welcoming, but you'll be relieved to know you'll have your own room tonight. No dormitories or shared rooms, obviously. And no restraints…"

What about meds? She kept that to herself. Whatever pills Gillian had given her before breakfast had no effect, but Rachel recognised the sedative that kept the others doped up. It made sense to play along for now, act like a zombie.

"I think Gillian has explained all the ground rules, but if you're not certain of anything, please don't hesitate to ask her or one of her colleagues. Or even myself. My door's always open." Another weak smile.

"When's Dad coming to see me?"

Quinn's eyes dropped to the ground. He pushed a clump of soggy grass cuttings with his toe. "I'm sure he'll be along at some point today. But you must understand, Rachel…the times he will be allowed to visit are restricted."

Monitored as well, I bet. She allowed her lip to tremble, and then bit it. The worried expression that must surely have passed over her features was not forced.

She thought back to the laptop and the folder she had secreted within. Would Dad have gone through the PC after all? Or would he have respected her privacy, seen it as the equivalent of flicking through a private diary, and left well enough alone?

"Didn't you fancy the film?" Quinn asked, casting a glance behind him to the sun room. The glance looked uneasy, more the look of a man scared someone is creeping up on him. The heads of Iain, Ant and Julia were just visible, as motionless as the armchairs they slumped on.

No. Can't sit with the zombies. She remained motionless as Quinn took a seat on the picnic table. He sat not directly opposite her but at an angle, so that the sun shone behind him and she had to blink and shield her eyes with a quickly raised hand. Too quickly, she realised. Quinn visibly relaxed. He placed his briefcase on the slatted surface and flipped the catches, raised the lid and allowed it to rest against the pole of the folded parasol.

"Or is it because you don't want to be confined? That you feel a very real and very disturbing atmosphere within Fairlight? There's no need to pretend, Rachel. I know the medication doesn't affect you. You're a good actor, I'll give you that." Although he had caught her out, there was still fear in his voice. She took comfort in that, but remained silent.

Quinn looked up. "Aren't you curious as to how I know?"

Rachel shifted, positioned herself directly opposite the doctor. The sunlight no longer blinded her; he no longer held the advantage. "Do you want me to be?"

Quinn's smile vanished. He withdrew a manila folder from the briefcase and placed it before her.

"It's not a game, Rachel. I won't beat about the bush, nor will I insult your intelligence. You know very well we have no answers to what is affecting the children in Fairlight. When your father brought you here I expected you to be just like the others -”

“What others?” Rachel flushed. If Quinn was through playing games, so was she. “There's only three kids here! And none of them look...”

“Yes, there *are* only three. If you'd asked how many there *have* been...do you understand now?”

Rachel thought of the Intensive Care unit. The restraints on her slashed wrists and the cold steel of the cot's rails. The closed curtains of her cubicle, and the realisation hers had not been the only occupied unit in a corridor full of identical cubicles. All with closed curtains.

“How many?” she asked in a voice that was no longer her own. “How many were here?”

Quinn sighed. “Since last summer – when Fairlight reopened - we have taken in a total of twenty-three patients.” His eyes locked on hers, and she saw how much he fought to keep the tears from forming. Tears of frustration and shame; the grief of a professional healer unable to help his charges. Unable to even understand what was happening to them, desperate enough to confide in a young girl, his latest patient –

Why me, Quinn? That could wait. She had to absorb the full significance - the full horror - of the number he had uttered first. “Twenty-three ... Where are they? They can't all be...”

Dead, his eyes said. His lips parted, as bloodless as his face. Rachel didn't hear what he said next. She felt the ground shift and thought the picnic table had given way. She grabbed the parasol pole with numb fingers, heard the liquid roar of something racing to her head.

Her vision cleared as quickly as it had clouded. She stared

dumbly at the parasol, saw fingers other than hers clasped around it. Long and thin, almost skeletal, which belied the strength with which they grasped hers.

She threw Quinn's hands away from her, and despite her light-headedness swung her legs over the table's bench and stood up. In her cheeks she felt the heat of her rage. *What am I, a magnet for people who need comforting?*

Quinn stared at his hands with a bewildered and hurt expression. He looked up. "Did you hear what I said, Rachel? They're not physically dead. They're still here." He indicated the open manila folder, took out a photo and held it aloft. It trembled, as though the summer breeze wanted to tear it away from her and throw it in the sea, keep it hidden along with the ocean's other secrets.

"Why are you telling me this?" She folded her arms over her breasts, deliberately ignored the photo.

Quinn stared sadly at the photo. "Because we almost lost Julia the night before last. She returned at the very same moment you had your…*incident* with the mower."

Despite her anger, she was puzzled by his choice of words. *Returned? Not 'regained consciousness'?* Her eyes flicked over the photo, and she saw the girl she had discussed triskelions with less than two hours ago.

Her arms dropped from her chest, all defences gone. All rage evaporated, replaced with curiosity and the desire to help a friend she had formed an unspoken bond with. She regained her seat and took the photo from Quinn's fingers. He relinquished it almost reluctantly; she felt as though a vestige of his professional pride refused to admit his powerlessness.

The image filled her vision. She was no longer aware of her

surroundings: the damp clumps of grass beneath her feet; the hard pine of the picnic table; the smell of sea air and Quinn's failing deodorant; even the golden sunlight failed to register.

One solitary photograph opened up a fresh Hell before her. Despite the clinical setting and the modern machinery of twenty-first century intensive, life-saving care, the figures in the centre of the photograph belonged to a darker, older world: one of almost medieval anguish and pain. She saw now why Quinn had said 'return' rather than 'regain consciousness'. Even that word failed to explain how the girl had survived.

Julia was the only conscious patient in the unit. It could have been a ward, but it bore little resemblance to a hospital wing. More clinical, less humane; more a laboratory than a hospital ward. The four beds looked similar to the cot Rachel had been restrained to upon her arrival, but the resemblance ended there. The blood didn't just soak the sheets and pillows, it *swam* across them; a deluge too fast and too powerful for mere cotton to absorb. The four occupants should not have been smiling so much, and not in that manner: beatific, rapturous. Ecstasy that went beyond the human capacity for orgasm, ecstasy that belonged to the carved stone and painted faces of saints and martyrs, touched by the Divine and immortalised by artists on a similar quest for the holy.

The floor was streaked with blood and discarded pieces of flesh and skin. A pair of arms lay on the foot of the nearest bed, joined by grasping fingers that had dug into the muscle of each forearm.

How had their owner torn them away? Rachel screamed to herself. There must have been some assistance, and yet…

Julia's smile was the most ecstatic, the most inhuman of

them all. Her eyes were glazed, dead, and yet they still saw the photographer. The arms were held aloft, in supplication and welcome; but to all who viewed the photograph, not just the white coated attendants in the unit.

If they *were* arms, of course. Rachel saw now how the discarded, entwined limbs on the foot of Julia's bed had been replaced with the angular, chitinous formations that terminated in diamond-shaped digits and glistened with the sheen of toxic oil.

Rachel looked again at the discarded human arms. The arms she had held in the breakfast room less than three hours ago, arms that bore scars of wounds that spoke of infliction months ago, not hours.

She returned at the very same moment you had your incident with the mower.

"Returned," Rachel muttered.

"Your presence - your pain and self-mutilation - halted this. For the others it was too late."

"The others," Rachel said sharply. "The ones in the photo. What happened to them? Are they dead? Why didn't they survive?"

"That's just it. We don't know if they're dead."

"What?" She looked at the three girls in the picture, saw how their stages of self-destruction were on a par with Julia's. But no alien appendages replaced the missing pieces of their bodies. "How can you *not* know, Quinn? They're either dead or they're not!"

"No, Rachel." There was calmness in his words, a sense of inevitability. Perhaps relief at confessing, she didn't know. Or care. "It's no longer that simple. Dead or alive is neither here nor there. After the light struck, only Julia remained. The other three vanished.”

“Vanished. What is this, a bloody magic act? People don’t just vanish!”

“No,” Quinn said quietly. “*People* don’t.”

It took a while for the meaning to sink in. Rachel looked at the alien appendages of Julia again, and then the remains of Julia’s bed fellows. Then she saw it: what she had taken to be the splayed intestines resulting from the worst of the self-induced atrocities was something else. Something that made her forget the impossibility of Julia’s recovery and healing, the sickening things that had temporarily replaced Julia’s arms.

“That was all that was left of her. Does it look familiar?”

Black, slimy starfish...

She wanted to stay silent. She didn’t want to admit anything. Not to Quinn, but least of all, to herself.

The intestine-like creature was formed by three curling tubes that glinted in the light of the camera’s flash. She saw beyond the blood and gastric juices and the torn intestines that enrobed the creature.

Smaller than the things that had infiltrated her dreams and accompanied Callum Hayes, but there was no mistake.

Triskelion.

CHAPTER FIFTEEN

"Started early, Bethan. Why's that?"

She halted before Callum's prone form, her lips tightened. There was no clock in the cell, her watch remained on the kitchen drainer from last night's washing up, and he'd had no contact with anyone since she sealed the door last night. There was no way he could know what time it was, nor what time her shift was due to start.

"Doesn't do to show off, Callum."

A soft chuckle from the prone figure. His hands were folded leisurely in his lap; his eyes remained closed. "Nothing psychic about that deduction, m'dear. I did my research on Fairlight. I know the shift patterns, and it was purely the smell of soup wafting in from the corridor that told me it's not long past lunchtime, which the unit always serves between noon and one. You've come in two hours early, and your first port of call is me."

She took a deep breath, inhaled, and smelled the aromas Callum referred to. *Okay. Perhaps a spiteful little dig because he's not been fed for almost twenty-four hours.* She crouched before him to inspect his wounds.

With his eyes still closed, Callum unfolded his hands and held them out to her, palms upward. The holes in those palms were still covered by the oil-like skeins. They glistened as they caught the light from the corridor beyond the viewing pane, rainbows swirling in the unnatural blackness caused by the movement beneath. Bethan started, and felt the heels of her trainers dig into her buttocks as she rocked backwards. She put out a hand to steady herself, and recoiled when she felt the lukewarm crust of blood on the white vinyl.

"Shit!" She jumped to her feet, wiping her hand on the thigh of her jeans. Frowned when she realised there was nothing there. The floor was clean.

Now his eyes opened. The smile was fixed, frozen, complimenting the glazed, exhausted look in his gaze.

No, not exhausted, she realised. Lifeless. The kid looked on the verge of death! She reached for her buzzer, about to call for assistance when Callum's hand slapped the unit from her trembling grasp.

"*No!*" His smile had vanished, replaced with an expression that looked totally alien on the boy. *Fear.* Fear he tried to cover with a quick, insincere smile.

"I'll be fine. Just need rest..."

She swallowed, felt the buzzer grow warm and heavy in her grip. Wondered what earthly medication would have helped him anyway. And why the fear?

"Where's Quinn?" he asked suddenly.

"Haven't seen him. Why d'you ask? Don't tell me you're scared of him?"

His eyes flashed. "No, of course I'm not *scared*. But I'm not stupid, either. He's still the guv'nor of Fairlight, still in a position to make life difficult. He won't leave me alone for long, not with what I showed him."

She frowned. "What can he do? He still has to answer to the Clinical Commissioning Group."

"It's not just him. It's what the Collins bitch can do...what she'll *make* him do."

Bethan exhaled. *That* was it. That was what he was afraid

of. "She's an...unknown quantity, Callum. Like you, they don't know what to do with her."

His eyes saw straight through her. Or was that the dilation of the pupils? "She doesn't know what she has, what she's capable of. That girl, Julia? Translocation was halted. I felt it, Bethan. I felt the girl's pain, felt her ecstasy as her arms came off...but the Presence couldn't come through. *She* stopped it, Bethan. The Collins bitch prevented Julia's evolution. But how?"

Bethan stood on trembling legs. "The timings indicate it happened the moment Rachel Collins offered her wrists to the mower. The CCTV shows nothing but white noise after that moment, as though an EMP had hit the cameras."

"Electromagnetic pulse...a *pulse*," Callum said in a distant voice. "Was there a flash of light beforehand?"

"Difficult to say. We're not getting much out of the patients, as you can imagine."

His eyes still saw through her, not recognising her. The faraway look that made her wonder if he was seeing through the walls as well. Or beyond, through to another place. This time she couldn't prevent the shudder.

He blinked, his eyes focussing on his immediate surroundings. The pupils contracted.

"She doesn't know, Bethan. She doesn't know what she has. But she must suspect. I bet the meds didn't knock her out, did they?"

Her eyes widened. "Of course they did! I gave her the dose mysel-" Realisation hit her.

"Thought not." He sighed. "Quinn kept that from you, didn't he? He's not stupid, Bethan. He knows he can't trust you."

The professional, detached side of her said that was no surprise. The chief clinical psychiatrist was not duty bound to share all aspects of his patients' conditions and treatments with the staff nurse.

Her other side – the side that dominated more and overrode her professionalism – felt hurt and betrayed. She knew how childish that was, and yet…

"It doesn't matter…much." A glint came into Callum's dead eyes. "There's not much he can do with the Collins girl, anyway; there's certainly not enough time before midsummer. The problem is: how much of what you've kept – or rather, *think* you've kept - from him does he know?"

She snorted, tried to feign contempt. "Quinn's an idiot, and under too much pressure to realise." With those words, she felt doubt trickle into her like the intravenous drips she had put on the patients in the Acute Ward. Callum said nothing, but the glint in his eyes brightened. His gaze was steady, focussed. Appraising, and saying: *how can you be so sure?*

She couldn't. She'd been unaware of Rachel Collins's immunity to the tranquiliser – enough to drop a horse – and something like that would have been one of the first things Quinn would have told her about. But he hadn't, had barely acknowledged her when she signed in and asked for a status report.

Quinn, you bastard. She took a deep breath, steeled herself and stared back at Callum, challenging him. But the fear in his eyes had gone. Self-control and arrogance had returned. Her eyes dipped to the floor and she hated herself for it.

"You still have full access to all parts of the complex?"

The question surprised her, made her drag her eyes back to his. "Of course I do. Even if he suspected anything, Quinn wouldn't put any restrictions on my keycard."

Would he? Her hand went to the lanyard holding her card. Her fingers closed around it, protective and possessive, as if fearing Callum's stare would wrench it from her. Identity card and access key, all in one piece of plastic the size of the credit card the supermarket had declined last night.

All I have left. My identity and the key to…to what, exactly? My future?

"I'd check if I were you, Bethan. Check all parts – even beyond the Acute Ward. Just to be certain."

Her legs trembled, but she fought the urge to sink to the floor; didn't want to be any closer to Callum. Beyond the Acute Ward. She knew what he meant. *Who* he meant. It was ironic Quinn made every excuse not to visit there; she enjoyed the sense of superiority she felt whenever she returned from that area, relished the disgust in his eyes and the sweat on his brow as she gave full reports on the status of the subjects. And now she herself feared to go there.

"It won't do to be denied access on midsummer, will it?"

"That wouldn't stop *you*, though, surely?" She forced a laugh. "Locked doors are nothing to someone with your…"

He glanced at his palms. She thought she saw wariness in his inspection of the black skeins, but like the fear earlier it was gone in a flash, as though she had imagined it.

"My powers? My abilities? Don't overestimate me, Bethan. I'm only human." He grinned. "For now, anyway."

"You need food, Callum. I'll get Glyn to bring some down. Don't worry, he can be trusted." She didn't add what Glyn had told her about the exchange between Rachel and the three patients in the sun room at breakfast. The Collins girl had not only recovered her bearings unnaturally quickly, she had managed to break the reserve of the girl who should have translocated - and was making headway with Antoinette. A natural leader, one who would be more than a worthy opponent to Callum Hayes and the Children of the Evolution. No, that was not to be permitted; Rachel Collins would have to be stopped.

But first things first. Check the access areas, see if Quinn ordered Site Services to shut me out of anywhere. "If I have been denied access, I can get Jon Rogers to override the system -"

"But he'll tell Quinn. No, don't do that yet." Callum closed his eyes. His shoulders slumped, and his head dropped onto his chest. Deep breaths, fighting to stay awake – or conscious. A puppet with the strings cut, she thought. Lifeless, unable to move or operate of its own volition. Yet the sense of power – the unearthly presence that powered his evolution – remained. It felt more vibrant, more baleful; an alien force angered by its inability to keep its host moving and obeying its will.

I'm only human. For now, anyway. She backed away from her patient and reached for the door.

His head rose slowly. His eyes were glazed and unfocussed, his jaw slack. It was an effort for him to speak, and the words seemed to come from someone else. Not the leader of the Children of the Evolution, but a small, frightened boy.

"Bethan…are you sure you want this?"

Was this a trap? Testing her resolve? She gripped the handle. Or was it a chance to back off, leave the battle? *And what?*

Accept the lot of humanity and perish with them? "Yes. More than anything."

A cloud passed over his features. The eyes closed and the mouth tightened. "Okay…" Still the frightened boy's voice. "But remember…everything has a price. This fountain of youth is made with blood. It'll need replenishing."

She left the room without a response, set the lock on the cell door's keypad with shaking fingers. The buzzer sounded, indicating successful lockdown, and only then did she release her breath.

The words hammered into her with every slow, reluctant step she took to the end of the corridor.

Everything has a price. *Yes, but it's a price I'm glad to pay.*

This fountain of youth is made of blood. *Better others' blood than mine. The adult human race is doomed, anyway.* Far better to join the victors.

It'll need replenishing. That made her pause. It hadn't been the frightened little boy who said that. It had been the arrogant, confident teenage leader of a doomsday cult who was in control of everything around him, who had engineered his own incarceration in preparation for a war and mocked the adults who guarded him – whether they were on his side or not.

He mocked you. Now her mother's voice. *That thing about replenishment – that's a warning, Bethan. When the blood has run out, what's to stop him taking yours?*

"Piss off, Mum!" she hissed as she swiped her card through the mounted reader. A click and a buzz, and she was through.

With thoughts of blood and replenishment, she entered the Acute Ward.

CHAPTER SIXTEEN

Karen Tyndall's home was in just as poor a state as its owner, Tony thought. The terraced two-bedroom starter homes would probably have looked clean, fresh and inviting when they were first built; now the shoddy building work showed their true colours. Crumbling plasterwork peeled away in sections and revealed leprous yellow masonry; the lawns of postage stamp-sized gardens were fat with rain but anaemic with lack of sunlight. Curtains twitched, almost imperceptibly, in the houses they'd passed, and Tony felt eyes burning into the back of his skull; the small-minded village mentality of old people, hostile and suspicious towards outsiders. With memories of the pub goers in Jim's local the previous night, he could imagine the whispered words spoken. *That drunken furriner, she be bringin' a man home with her. Ain't she got no schoolin' to be doin'?*

Karen's house was an end terrace, as though the other houses were determined to push her away.

Two recycling boxes overfilled with empty wine bottles reached up to the doorbell. Remnants of last night's rainfall beaded the green glass, sparkling in the morning sun. An angry buzzing came from the crates when Karen's bag knocked against them, and Tony shuddered with the memory of the saw-like noise the creatures in the school had made.

Karen looked even paler than she had coming from the school, and slumped against the doorframe. Even when the bluebottle flew past them, noisily protesting against the disturbance to its feeding, it took a while for their breathing to return to normal.

They hadn't been pursued, but Tony had insisted they take no chances. His jeans and her trouser suit were coated with grass stains and mud smears from the shortcut they'd taken through the school bushes, the unused allotments and the fields beyond the church. Not a soul had been seen, but the distant hum of heavy traffic had echoed through the fields and bushes, rolling over the lanes and alleyways, following their every footstep. Military vehicles.

Now they'd reached their destination, but no sense of relief came with the achievement. His heart pounded and adrenaline raced through his veins, maintaining the anxiety and sense of being hunted. This was only a temporary sanctuary. And perhaps his companion knew that as well.

The keys shook in Karen's hand as she pushed the door open, the wood swollen with damp protesting at her entry.

She glanced once – guiltily, Tony realised – at the stacked recycling crates and offered him a weak smile.

I know it's early, but I really need a drink, she'd said. Tony couldn't blame her – he needed one himself – but knew he had to keep a clear head for what was to come. *Then again, what is to come? How the hell do you cope with starfish-like monsters exploding from a child and attacking you?* It put the human enemy into perspective. He could only hope that the town's police force was now too wrapped up with army liaison and the events in the school to concentrate its forces on him.

He thought back to the twitching curtains of Karen's neighbours, wondered if they were the type to phone the local Plod over the slightest little thing. *That man the furriner brought over...yes, he matches yer description, officer. 36*

Ditton Street, you know where that is. Yes, I'll watch 'em fer ye...

Another thought struck him: to get the army in this quickly, the powers that be must have been expecting something the local Plod couldn't handle. The news report on the Day Gone Down's TV, the lockdown of Haverton - Callum Hayes's town.

Fairlight will be next, that's obvious. Shit. As if the prospect of breaking into a psychiatric institute to rescue his daughter wasn't challenge enough, he'd have to figure out what to do when they got out.

If we get out...no, scrub that. Stay positive. His fingers tightened on the memory stick within his pocket, felt the comforting plastic squirrel body dig into his palm. Not just a container of valuable information – the key to accessing Fairlight – but also a talisman, he thought. Video footage of his daughter, with what might be her last message to him. If he kept that with him, promised himself it *wouldn't* be the last vision of her, the last words he heard...

Karen looked so small, so frail on the sofa, but that was only to be expected due to her surroundings. On each wall, huge bookcases towered over their owner; their contents threatening to burst free of their pine surroundings and swamp her with reams of literature, travel, history and imagination. Stained paperbacks from charity shops that time forgot, laminated ex-library books with the catalogue numbers peeling from the spine, and on one section a pile of new hardbacks with mint, crisp dust jackets. More books than he had read – or could be bothered to read - in a lifetime. He suspected that very few of these books had not been read or reread at some point.

"How's the ankle?"

"A bit sore, but not as bad as I thought."

That was good. He'd seen her limping, and worried about the prospect of a sprain and an incapacitated companion.

Karen's nails dug into the knees of her trousers, scratching. Her eyes were fixed on the plastic carrier bag in the corner of the room, the shiny white plastic at odds with the flat, dull grey of the carpet. Two black bottle tops protruded from the carrier.

He leaned over and pulled the first bottle out, noted the way her eyes glittered with strained longing at what he held. His shoulders slumped with sadness. No, he wouldn't ask her for any more assistance. Just the chance to print out the maps from the flash drive, ask for some directions, then he'd leave her to it…

On the coffee table was a dish with a half-finished lasagne and an empty wine glass. She picked it up and held it to him.

He broke the seal, twisted the cap off and poured slowly. The liquid sloshed in the goblet-sized glass, and he realised his hand was shaking as well as hers. Their eyes met and a sheepish grin shared.

She eased back into the sofa, slowly, as though crippled with chronic back ache. The glass was held in both hands, the fingers pale worms that slithered restlessly.

Tony raised the bottle in salute. "Here's to further education."

The laugh that broke from her was shrill, high pitched, but soon gave way to deep chuckles of mirth. Like the cork of a champagne bottle giving way to the pressures within.

He grinned and took a swig of the wine. He grimaced. Red, strong. Probably a Merlot, not that he was an expert; would probably have tasted better if it was drunk at a more civilised time. His eyes watched her carefully, waiting for the laughter to turn to sobbing, the tears of mirth to change to those of shock and terror.

And what about you, Collins? How long before you crumble and fail, like you failed Becky? Like you're going to fail Rachel? His fingers tightened on the bottle, and he fought the urge to thrown it. *I won't fail! Rachel's coming home with me!*

Karen's laughter drained away, but there was little sign of shock or stress replacing her mirth. Now her eyes filled with concern.

"And what's your story, Tony?"

He was surprised how easily the words came out, the full story flowing freely and unhindered into the room with its millions of words frozen in time, trapped in paper prisons.

With each pouring of wine into Karen's glass the history flowed. He tried not to dwell on Becky's alcoholism, the way she would reach for the Chardonnay at the time he would reach for the kettle; the inevitable descent into stronger drinks, longer stupors and harsher hangovers, and the physical toll it took on her health.

He tried. But he saw the same signs of alcohol abuse on Karen's features. The lines around her eyes and lips more deeply etched than they should be for a woman in her thirties;

the bloodshot eyes coloured only by the dark circles around them; the way her skin took on a jaundiced aspect in the dim light. He saw the guilt and self-loathing on Karen Tyndall's face when he recounted Becky's story.

"Amazing how similar people's stories are," she said quietly. She took a smaller, self-conscious sip of her wine. "Becky loved her booze and books…just like me."

Tony shook his head. "It wasn't the booze that killed her, though. Alcohol wasn't a crutch, it was her way of escaping the…the condition."

The second bottle had been opened but was not poured. An unspoken admittance from him – and understanding from her – that Becky Collins didn't escape, couldn't escape. The alcohol had failed to release her. The relief it gave was temporary.

"D'you think she was one of the first?"

"No. Her self-harming is – *was* - totally different to what these bloody kids are doing." Bitterness coloured his voice, made it harsh. "And it feels like…I don't know, a slur on her memory, y'know? When Rachel started with the knife, I thought she was taking the piss…and then I saw her face when she did it; I knew this wasn't any copycat bollocks. That look of…*ecstasy* couldn't be faked, couldn't be simulated. That came from her alone, from her cutting.

"Becky once told me that cutting herself eased her…her inner suffering. 'Hurt myself to get pain out,' she put it. As long as we could moderate it, use clean dressings and hygienic blades, she had it under control – sort of. We'd know the times when she was ready for another cutting session. Jesus Christ, once a week and we thought she was doing well! Until…"

Until they started. The Children of the Evolution. He shuddered. "Pain gave way to despair. The cutting released her pain – but it couldn't, could never, stop her from despairing. Post-natal depression led to full-blown clinical depression, and nothing worked. I would see Becky holding Rachel with a strange look in her eyes, and I wondered if she was thinking of turning the knife on our own daughter – as if Rachel was the cause of her despair."

Karen's glass rattled as she placed it on the table. The bottle remained full.

"Plenty of sleepless nights followed, I can tell you. I got used to being woken at all hours in the first six months after Rachel's birth, but now my sleep was broken by silence. I'd hear Becky leave the bed in the early hours, hear her tiptoe across the landing to Rachel's room…hear all this and imagine the worst.

"We argued. Why was I spying on her? Why was she keeping her midnight visits to our daughter's cot a secret? I put locks on all the cupboards, made sure she had no access to sharp objects…should've seen the hatred on her face. 'You really think I'm going to kill our daughter? If I was, d'you think locks'll stop me? Why wouldn't I just smother her or drop her from the balcony?'"

He saw the shock on Karen's face.

"She calmed down when I told her what she was doing with Rachel. But how could I describe the look she gave her? It wasn't normal, for Christ's sake! It went beyond the loving gaze of a mother for her child –there was *some* of that, but it was more the love that comes from…awe, I guess. Like she had something miraculous in her hands, something more than a child. Something superhuman."

"Was there fear as well?"

Tony nodded. "Fear and awe, love and hatred. This from the woman I loved, the mother of my child…but also a woman who was mentally ill. What was I supposed to do? Shit, what was I supposed to think? I'm no psychiatrist, I'm a bloody truck driver!"

He hadn't gone into details of the start of their relationship, how he'd met Becky when working the UEA bar in Norwich; nor how he'd followed her like a lovesick puppy from one part of the country to the other while she collected degrees like other people would collect beer mats.

Lovesick puppy? That was what his dad called him, but how could he explain to the old man it wasn't just love, it was fear? Fear of what she would do to herself. Fear of how far she could go.

Fear of others finding out. "I was the first person she told. The first person she trusted. I'd never heard of self-harming, until that bloke from some rock group carved "4 Real" in his arm."

"I think I remember them. I also remember how some of the group's fans became fascinated by his self-harming." Her shoulders hunched; she stared through the window. Her gaze was distant. "Some imitated it. That must've shocked him, being a poster boy for a mental illness. Becky was a fan, I assume?"

Tony hesitated. "Yeah, she idolised him, said she felt alone until he came on the scene."

"Lot of self-harmers do. And when they find a spokesperson, or a group who they feel speaks for them, there's an awful lot of responsibility to be borne by that person or group. A lot of power, also…"

"The Children of the Evolution. Not my first choice of spokespeople." His jaw tightened and he felt once again for the plastic squirrel. The warmth he'd felt it imbibed with had vanished. Now it felt cold and slimy, as if coated in the venom from Callum Hayes's messages to Rachel. "Have you got a computer and printer I can use?"

Karen's eyebrows rose at the sight of the flash drive. "Yeah. I've got a mouse your squirrel can play with as well."

"It's Rachel's. She loves squirrels." The pain within must have been visible on his face, must have looked harrowing, because Karen stood and put her arms around him. He was astonished at how powerful her arms were, how strong and supportive the embrace felt. Or was it because his own physical stamina had drained and he was ready to collapse? He didn't know. He returned the hug, lowered his head onto hers. He smelled flowers and freshly-mown grass; the salt tang of the sea; inhaled the moisture of rain and ocean. It took him a long time to realise the dampness of her hair was caused by his tears.

CHAPTER SEVENTEEN

As the aging printer coughed out hard copies of the maps, Tony wasn't quite certain what chilled him the most: that the iron fist of the military was closing tighter, even to the extent of knocking out the local internet signal – it wasn't Karen's ISP, nor her router, because the 5G on his iPhone wasn't responding either – or that his daughter had unusual foresight in preparing this groundwork. And yet...

She'd seemed unaware of the messages secreted in the memory stick during their conversations over the last few days. Even during her interview with Quinn...no one could be that good an actor, surely? And why go to such lengths?

What if I'm wrong? What if this is a trap? But how likely was that? There were enough traps in Fairlight waiting for him: Adam at the Day Gone Down, the local police force, the monsters in the school: all these should have been sufficient to stop him getting near Rachel. He turned from the printer and stared out the window. Here on the first floor he had a better view of the street, and could see above the line of hedgerow that separated the terraced houses from the damp fields beyond. Karen stood motionless, her hair shimmering in the sunlight. The printer wheezed out another sheet with a grinding noise that cut through him. He wished he hadn't touched that wine now.

He walked over to the window, and then frowned at the sight of two rows of footprints in the marsh-like grass. He looked past the fields to the school and shook his head. Where there had been plumes of smoke there was nothing but blue sky and wisps of delicate cirrus cloud. Karen passed a tiny pair of binoculars to him.

"Complete clean-up. See that truck on the left, by the gates? That's a modern Green Goddess. They even brought their own fire engine with them."

He widened the bridge, stared through and blinked. At first all he saw was blurred green and brown, and only when he raised the lenses and controlled his trembling hands did he see the school yard and the vehicles within the locked gates. Patches of foam spilled from the lobby and coated the hopscotch grid. It was already dispersing; he saw the yellow numbers on the top part of the grid appear. Nothing else moved.

"D'you see any movement?"

"None from the school," he replied. "Whatever else they've done, they did it when we were running away." He frowned. Now that was odd – he could have sworn the troops had come from a Bedford truck. But where was it? Apart from the Green Goddess and a Land Rover-style vehicle - probably a brass hat's - there was no other military presence.

"So what are they waiting for?"

"I don't think they *are* waiting," he said in a grim tone. "By the looks of things, they've finished with the school. Just left the clean-up boys there and one of their guv'nors." He lowered the binoculars and rubbed his eyes.

"Which means..." she stared at the router and its lack of green lights.

"Which means Fairlight will be locked down pretty bloody quickly." He tapped the windowsill thoughtfully. "That may work for us. If they know they've got all exits sealed, they'll take their time hunting us. I think they've got other priorities at the moment. Then again..."

The sun was warming the grass of the fields, but the tracks remained. He remembered the twitching curtains of Karen's neighbours.

"I don't think we should take any chances. Let's get the paperwork and clear out. Anywhere in the town we can hole up for a bit?"

"I'd say the Day Gone Down, but after what you said about Adam... I don't think anyone can be trusted. Doesn't take much for a small community to collaborate with its occupiers..."

"Strange set of standards: gang up on 'foreigners' just because their great-great grandparents weren't born here, and don't tug the forelock to those in power?"

"It's more common than you'd think, and Britain has a far from noble history about such things. People would accuse their own neighbours of witchcraft purely to settle a score, and if you want a more recent example look at Jersey. When the Channel Islands were occupied by the Nazis there were quite a few people who willingly collaborated, gave the names and addresses of Jewish neighbours to the Gestapo."

"I thought we'd moved on from things like that. Guess not." He frowned. "I'd like to know what Adam's getting out of this. His place sure as hell isn't getting a five star rating from me on Tripadvisor."

She smiled grimly. "That pub is symptomatic of the town's decline. I often wondered why he was so cheery when he must have been losing money."

"Wouldn't surprise me if he's on the payroll somewhere. Or

offered relocation to somewhere decent." He sighed. "Okay, let's see what Rachel's left us..."

He flicked through the sheaf of printouts as Karen turned to the window with her binoculars again. "Still like to know how she got hold of these. I couldn't find anything about Fairlight on the web." He held up the first pages. "These look familiar to you?"

She put the binoculars on the windowsill and took the paper. She held the first two up to the light, squinting at the faded lines. She shook her head. "I've never been inside the hospital, but I can tell you now these won't be of much use."

"Why not?"

"They're *old*, Tony. Layouts from the original building, nothing from the recent build."

He frowned. The scans were low resolution and hadn't looked that clear on Rachel's laptop; he'd hoped the clarity of print would show him something the screen had not. The ink cartridges in Karen's aging printer had other ideas. "Look again, Karen. There's gotta be something."

She peered at the bottom. "There's a date here. 1952, must be relating to modifications made to the Victorian structure. As to what that modification is..." She shrugged. "No idea."

Tony sighed and took the next section of map from the printer's output tray. Without looking at it, he passed the sheet to her. "Try this one." He checked his watch, felt the ever-growing sense of urgency increase his breathing. There was no sign of life on the streets. Surely word would have blazed like wildfire through the town by now? And if not, surely he'd have seen some sign of children leaving for school...

"Now that *is* interesting." She looked up. "Nothing to do

with the hospital, though. This is a sketch of the Oratory."

"The what?"

"The Oratory - sorry, you'd know it as the lighthouse. Or what's left of it." Now Karen sounded puzzled. "Why would she send you a sketch of the lighthouse?"

He thought of the nightmares he'd endured: nightmares of his daughter running from his outstretched hands, leaping over the wooden fence and running the last ten metres to the edge of the headland, her legs powering her off the cliff and thrusting her into the roseate sky before gravity claimed her and pulled her down to the jagged rocks below…

He shuddered. When Rachel had run to the hospital's mower yesterday, he had initially thought she was making his nightmare a daytime reality. She had been facing east when that look descended on her…

No, wait a minute…what was to the east of the hospital grounds? The cliffs, surely. The remnants of the lighthouse…

What will you see when you cut yourself?

He swallowed the lump of apprehension in his throat and faced Karen. "Let's have a look."

Now where the hell had Rachel got this from? Maybe the same source as the blueprints and plans of the Victorian institution that was still the core of the modern psychiatric unit. But what was the connection?

Perhaps it was a scan of a photocopy; the alignment was off centre and there were irregular light patches on the farthest ends of the sketch. Combined with the low ink in Karen's printer it made the sketch difficult to study, but the artist had done a good job of bringing the ruined building to life. If Karen hadn't mentioned the lighthouse, he would never have associated it with the ruins Rachel had been obsessed by. The steel information plate on the site had a rough rendering of what the original lighthouse had looked like, but the elements had worn the etching away.

He peered closely, squinting at the plan. The centre illustration was a top-down plan of the oratory as it must have appeared in the Middle Ages: a squat, church-like structure angled to face east and the rising sun. The tower on the west side was shown more fully in the next sketching, marked "side elevation facing S.E." A medieval, ecclesiastical structure unlike anything he had seen before: further elevations showed the tower to be a six-sided affair with a conical roof and thick, wedge-like buttresses that anchored it against the elements yet gave the impression of an ancient forerunner of a space rocket. Something Leonardo da Vinci could've knocked up in his spare time.

The sixth elevation showed an ugly gash where the monastery would have been: never sealed, open to the elements.

"When was this made?" he asked.

"I'd say the sketches are Victorian. The handwriting certainly looks from that time."

"Christ, you can make out the words? All I can see is scratches and blobs."

She smiled. "Practiced eye, Tony. You think this is bad, try reading an original Folio of Shakespeare. Some of Thomas Hardy's handwritten poems aren't so easy on the eyes, either."

Tony held it to the light, then lowered it. He looked at Karen. "You asked me why Rachel would send this. What I'd like to know is how come I've never seen this before? I've been to Fairlight quite a few times, but I've never come across a detailed picture of the lighthouse."

"I don't think many people have, Tony." Her voice was low, her eyes distant. He realised she was looking beyond the picture, past the fields and the schoolyard, to where the clouds rolled away to the sea. "The Oratory was taken apart during Henry VIII's reign; this wasn't the only religious institution to suffer dissolution. But the tower remained standing until the eighteenth century, still performing its function as a lighthouse. The chantry priest would tend the light as well as run the Oratory, but after the Dissolution it was left to volunteers to guide ships away from the rocks.

"Gradual wear and tear did for the tower what Mr Tudor did for the chantry, but there was no desire to rebuild it when it collapsed. This wasn't the best spot for a lighthouse, anyway; lots of sea mist lingers on the down."

"Britain's oldest lighthouse. Surprised there wasn't any effort to restore it – this would be one hell of an impressive structure."

"The stones were used elsewhere, as was the custom. But no one knows where they were taken."

"The hospital?"

Karen shook her head. "The oldest part of that building dates to the 1870s, and it's all pure red brick. Nothing of the lighthouse went there."

And yet Rachel sent me this. What's the connection? He held it to the light again, struggled to decipher the words. It was hopeless. "Okay, I'm gonna need your translation skills, Ms. Tyndall. Let's start with this word here. What is it?"

"That's the nickname the older villagers gave to the

lighthouse. Pharos."

Tony's blood froze. Ice water churned in his guts and his fingers curled inwards, crumpling the paper. "What did you say?"

Karen frowned at his reaction. "Pharos. It's an old name from the third century BCE, given to the lighthouse the Ptolemaic kings built at Alexandria. Well, technically the name of the island it was built on, but… Tony, what's wrong?"

Pharos. "I've heard it before, Karen. Last night…and the two pigs that tried to nick me earlier were a bit worried when I repeated it to them." And then there was Jim's cry from the night before: *It's come back. Jesus, it's outside the Pharos!*

"There's a connection, Karen. Between Fairlight and the lighthouse – the hospital *and* the town. Rachel knew of it, but not what it fully is." *She knew it was something to be scared of, though.*

"So where does that leave us?"

"We've got to dig deeper. This looks to be a photocopy from a book. You got any books on local history?"

"No. The library's our best bet." She blinked in the sunlight; the sun was stronger, and the temperature was rising. "But I don't think you want to be walking the streets, not after what you've done to Fairlight's finest."

He smiled. "I'd quite happily do it again."

"I'm sure you would. But let's take it slowly, okay? We'll take my car, and you stay in the back. Hide under the blankets I've got in there while I hit the library. I'll also be able to see what's happening in the town and can tell you as I'm driving."

He nodded slowly. "Sounds like a plan. As long as we stay away from major roads I don't think we'll get any grief. And then?"

"Then, Mr Collins, you can buy me a drink."

CHAPTER EIGHTEEN

Rachel stared at the sundial. With the break in the clouds, the sunlight had returned and the line of darkness cast by the pointer moved, coming to face her. She looked away, back to the door that led into the hallway. The door Quinn had taken.

She blinked in the harsh sunlight reflected from the mirror-like panes of glass. She didn't need a watch to know it was midday; the sundial told her that.

It was comforting in a way, disturbing in others. The pedestal was a block of granite, carved to form a tree-like structure with squirrels darting around the trunk. A closer inspection had shown the small fruits to be acorns, which the stone squirrels were chasing. Her smile had turned to one of sadness, though, at the overall effect. Woodland animals frozen in the act of hunting for food, forever hungry, forever denied. The dial itself was made of some shining black metal, too dark for untreated metal, although the material did not look as though it had been painted. The Roman numerals on the dial were raised and highlighted in gold, and the gnomon was a gleaming silver crescent, like a scimitar. The whole piece looked Arabic, middle-eastern, and incongruous with the carved squirrels.

The sundial was the first thing she had noticed in the Sun Garden, as Quinn called the enclosure formed by three of the hospital buildings. The south-facing part was the only side not blocked off by red brick or gleaming glass, and its lawn sloped gently, welcoming the sun. In time, after Quinn left, she had noticed other things: the grass here was long and unkempt, well over ankle length, and the stamens of daisies and dandelions bent to follow the direction of the sun. Yellow eyeballs, she thought with a shudder, staring balefully at the life giver.

The sun continued to burn the ground, leeching the moisture from the grass and the angry weeds as if trying to deprive them of energy rather than aid their growth. The heat of the noon sun soaking into her neck and shoulders didn't energise her; now she was alone with her thoughts she felt exhausted, drained with the recent turn of events and the knowledge imparted to her.

She stood slowly, wincing at the sudden light-headedness that took her. The sunlight bounced around the grass and the sundial spun crazily, the squirrels scampering backwards. She clutched the wooden slats of the picnic table to steady herself, and a part of her marvelled at the smooth, laminated finish, made even slicker by the dampness of her sweaty fingertips. No splinters, no chance of harming yourself…

What was Quinn playing at? *"Your self-harm saved Julia from turning into a monster"… trying to instil in me a Messiah complex?* She eased away from the picnic table and stared at the discarded bandages in the centre. There had been no point pretending she needed them, but the psychiatrist had looked more disturbed than entranced by the healing.

She caressed the slats again, frowning. Yes, there was more sensation than before. But wasn't freshly healed skin more sensitive?

The dizziness subsided. She took a step forward, away from the table and the surgical dressings and past the sundial. The lawns sloped more sharply here where the ground led toward the sea, and she had images of her not so long ago, lying face down and rolling down the hills of the Wittenham Clumps, the passage a blur as speed increased and the bottom of the hill rose to meet her. She smiled at the prospect of doing that here: even if there'd been no barrier between the hospital grounds and the cliff edge, the staff would no doubt be on her like a ton of bricks before she rolled over the edge and went down to meet the sea…

Her smile faded. Quinn had left in a hurry after the call from someone in Site Services, but she was certain she hadn't been left here unsupervised. Gillian had called out to her from the sunroom, telling her lunch was almost ready, and Rachel knew her attendance would be mandatory, regardless of her appetite. She could feel eyes sweeping over her from all directions: human eyes from behind, where the smells of tomato soup and pizza emanated from the kitchen vents, and mechanical, impartial eyes from the CCTV cameras on the higher points of the building. The sunlight glinting on the white metal hoods told her every point of access and egress from Fairlight Hospital was watched, 24/7. She wondered where the feeds went, who was watching.

Last night's rain was a distant memory. The grass was dry and crisp beneath her feet, and the line where land and sky met was blurred with a heat haze. She walked a little further until the chalk cliffs of the headland beyond the bay rose from the haze. She froze, remembering this was the exact same path she had taken on the morning of her interview. Then, another barrier had presented itself: the ride-on lawnmower, which turned out to be not so much a barrier as a means of self-harm…

…which brought Julia back…

…and now there was nothing to obstruct her view of the bay and the stone remains that surmounted the headland.

The heat haze blurred the outlines of the Oratory, softening the ruined stone tower into a barely visible clump of grey smeared on the cliff top. She felt a sudden pang, a yearning in her heart to be at one with the tower. It felt like home. Only now that she was imprisoned, and a barrier forcibly erected between her and the Oratory, did she feel the aching that first time prisoners must feel when they stare through the bars of their cells towards the open sky. The sudden awareness of what you've lost, brought on by the sight of something you take for granted.

The pain was a physical one, a burning in her chest that stifled her lungs. She couldn't breathe, couldn't move, could only feel the agony of incarceration and the desperate cry for freedom that demanded to be voiced. The dizziness returned, accompanied by a pounding at the base of her skull. Her vision clouded; the diaphanous wisps of heat haze that garlanded the cliffs became thick, coiled serpents of fog that expanded, blotting out the sun and replacing the blue sky with the empty greyness of limbo. More movement from the fog that was surely a living thing, a frenzied writhing and tumbling as if trying to squeeze the life out of the very cliffs themselves, drag them down into the depths of the cold water below.

Serpents of mist that turned their attention to the observer on the shore opposite, aware of the scrutiny upon them, now reached out to her, coiling around her arms and breasts, soaking the legs of her combats with cold sea water. Her mouth opened in an attempt to draw breath, to scream, but the air was beaten by the mist which greedily filled her lungs with water mixed from the sea and the sky, which tasted of brine and pollution, of diesel engine oil and putrefying fish. Icy tendrils of rotting marine vegetation choked her air passages, and the sea mist that filled her vision so completely was now imbibed with red. Ripples of pure, incandescent scarlet flickered in the mist; lightning from Hell.

Grey and scarlet suddenly merged, became less distinct: like the blending of old bones and fresh meat, a thick, grainy porridge that clogged her airways and her throat, oozed over her eyeballs and congealed, preventing the lids closing. She remained upright, rigid, and unable to move. Her eyes became two bulbs of agony, burning with chilled, stale air and the diseased remains of ancient sea life. She tried to see beyond the veil, to reach out with her mind's eye towards the object that had brought on this attack, the ruined Oratory she had hoped was home to the Light.

Nothing shone. No illumination came from the ancient lighthouse. No summoning from distant planets or alien dimensions; no sense of power or healing. No *light*, she realised with despair.

Grey-pink gave way to darkness, then nothing.

Quinn almost smiled at the display from the CCTV monitor. Almost, but not quite; any relief Bethan felt that her keycard had not been compromised vanished the moment the door swung open.

She's terrified. But still she goes in. Rather you than me, m'dear.

A sneeze from behind caught his attention, but his eyes remained fixed to the screen.

"Nasty cold you've got there, Jon."

"Not a cold. Bloody hay fever that's -" Another sneeze ended the Dorset-accented words and had Quinn turning in disgust at the sensation of a fine mist spray caressing his neck.

"For God's *sake,* Rogers!"

"Sorry, boss." The site services manager-cum-handyman rubbed his nose with a crumpled piece of kitchen roll stained yellow – hopefully from the man's lunch, Quinn thought with a shudder.

Jon Rogers squeezed the sodden paper into the top pocket of his checked shirt and rubbed the flecks of dried snot from his greying moustache. He indicated the screen. "Why the cloak and dagger? If you don't want her going in, all you have to do is say the word and I'll block her card."

Quinn sighed. "It's about catching her in the act, Jon. How long ago was this?"

"Five minutes ago." Rogers retrieved his snot rag and opened it, peering closely at the contents as if thinking *yep, room for another blow in there.* Quinn averted his eyes but there was nowhere in this grubby little office that didn't offend his senses. If the relatives of the patients had seen this before the glossy reception and Quinn's own pristine centre of command they'd turn back, and the children wouldn't be seen for dust.

Scratch beneath the surface and the filth always shows, he thought sourly. The Pirelli calendar was still on May, but Quinn imagined the top-heavy "model" emerging from a swimming pool was Rogers's favourite – or perhaps he really couldn't be bothered to turn the page? That would explain why the list of maintenance tasks had stacked up.

The dust on the monitor casings was almost as bad as that on the windowsills; Quinn had remarked it was deep enough to grow potatoes in, and it was even thicker now, as though Rogers had taken him up on the remark and seen it as an invitation. Not that there was much of a view. The site services office was on the northwest wing of the compound, adjoining the stores and facing the service yard. The green wheelie bins had company, small black bodies buzzing happily in the gap between the ill-fitting plastic lids and feasting on the rotting food within. It would appear there had been few takers for the meal today; Quinn could almost smell the pizza rotting away in the late afternoon heat. One of the fat flies flew past the window, and Quinn knew now why Rogers kept the windows closed.

"Shoulda set a camera up in the Acute Ward." Rogers sat back in his chair and wiped his fingers on the gas lift pedal before cradling his hands on his beergut. "Would love to know what she's seeing in there."

No, Jon. You wouldn't. Believe me. Quinn checked his watch, surprised he hadn't broken into a sweat on the dash from Rachel in the Sun Garden to Jon Rogers's office. He felt the exertion catching up with him now, though; the fine mist of Rogers's nasal clearance was joined by the familiar beads of dampness on the nape of his neck.

Five minutes. And still she hadn't come out. Maybe it wasn't enough time for her to do anything, but every second she was out of sight was as irritating and unnerving as those flies buzzing about the window.

Rogers raised his legs and plonked his feet on the desk. Grass stains from his work boots smeared the requisition slips and purchase orders yellow-green, matching the rag shoved in his pocket. Quinn felt a flush of anger at the man's insouciance.

"You haven't asked how the girl is," he said in as icy a tone as he could muster. "I would have thought you'd at least have felt some responsibility."

Rogers swivelled in his chair, his head cocked. The paperwork beneath his boot heels dragged across the desk. There was mild contempt in his eyes, but no anger; Quinn was no threat to him. "Don't lay the guilt trip on me, son. That were self-inflicted, and you know it."

Quinn's jaw dropped. "I'm not talking about blame; I'm talking about your lack of concern! You didn't even ask if she was alive!"

"Does it matter?" Rogers reached for the Beconase nasal spray and popped the cap. "I know how many kids have died. She wouldn't be the first, or the last." Two squeezes of the nozzle into each nostril followed.

Quinn felt pressure in his temples. The anger – partly borne of powerlessness, he admitted to himself – combined with his tension, and he knew it was going to be one hell of a headache. This old bastard's attitude wasn't helping. He gritted his teeth.

Perhaps the repetitive nature of the self-harming had desensitised the man. Rogers had actually whistled while he unclogged the wash basin yesterday morning, thinking nothing of the collection of pubescent teeth that clogged up the pipe with blood and shattered enamel. Or was it gallows humour, a way of dealing with the horror?

Rogers rubbed the bridge of his nose and snorted loudly. "Besides, I knew she were all right. I saw the way she were looking at the Pharos."

"What?"

Rogers turned and faced him. He sighed at Quinn's expression. "You ain't been here long, but I thought you'd at least find out a bit about your placement. Never read up on Fairlight? Not the asylum, the town."

"Of course not," Quinn snapped. "I'm here -"

"You're here to make the little kiddies better with pills and chit-chat. Not got time to be a part of the local community, take an interest in your surroundings."

Quinn took a deep breath. "What I do or do not do outside my professional duties is hardly relevant, Rogers." *And why would I involve myself in this grotty little community, anyway? Six months and I'm gone, that's what I was promised.*

"Everything's relevant, *Doctor* Quinn." The title was sneered, a deliberate insult, and there was more than just mild contempt on Rogers's features now. "As I said, that girl were staring at the Pharos – that's the old lighthouse ruins on the headland, to you outsiders – when she hurt herself. None of the others done that, did they?"

"Lighthouse?" Quinn's anger and tension was quickly replaced with bafflement. "What the hell's that got to do with anything?"

"Maybe nothing. Maybe everything." A shrug. "No one knows. You don't, I don't, and I bet a pound to a pinch of pigshit *she* don't." He tapped the monitor; Bethan still had not made an appearance. "But she's got her orders, ain't she? And not from you, or *your* guv'nors." He reached for the joystick and brought up another screen. "That nasty little bastard's the one you should be worried about."

Quinn's anger and bafflement faded. His shoulders tensed and the hot flushes of anger were replaced with cold shivers of fear.

On the other side of the camera, Callum Hayes grinned at him. He didn't need Jon Rogers to turn the sound on to hear the words; the boy was mouthing them slowly, as if speaking to a child.

Quinn. Hell is coming.

Even Rogers took a sharp intake of breath. He didn't need to lip-read, though. Callum Hayes had thoughtfully painted the words on the floor in his own blood.

CHAPTER NINETEEN

Antoinette Penner stared thoughtfully at the body on the lawn. The sea breeze ruffled the unconscious girl's hair and sent ripples down her baggy T shirt, so Ant had to peer closely to see if there were any signs of breathing.

There it was: a slight rise and fall of the chest. But very slight. Ant kicked off her trainers and stood over the body, enjoying the cooling sensation of moist grass beneath her bare, toeless feet and the fresh breeze ruffling her hair as she decided what to do. She belched, giggling at the unexpected attack of wind, and put her hand over her mouth, tasting again her lunchtime tuna salad as well as the breakfast kippers.

Food for the brain…and maybe the brain will feed the little fishies when I'm gone. That was what she'd said to the girl on the ground - Rachel, wasn't it? Yes, Rachel Collins – this morning. Rachel hadn't eaten much then, and Ant doubted she'd eaten anything since.

Maybe that was why she'd passed out, Ant thought: low blood sugar; emotional stress from being sectioned; not to mention the debt she owed her body from the self-harm. Everyone forgot that, how much energy was sapped from the cutting. Mental energy, as well as physical. That's why it was so important to eat well, quantity *and* quality. She would tell Rachel that when she came to. If only the doctors realised how simple things were. They always had to confuse things, make them more complicated than they really were.

The breeze lightened, and Ant felt the heat of the afternoon sun. *Soon be teatime.* She closed her eyes and smiled at the thought. The warmth of the sun bathed her face and the darkness behind her eyelids became a warm, fuzzy screen of beige. Except for a small patch of darkness…

A patch that grew like a spreading inkblot. A liquid darkness that contaminated all it touched.

She frowned, opened her eyes too quickly, blinking in the light. That was preferable to the darkness, but now she saw where it had come from. And why Rachel Collins had passed out.

"Well, well, well. There *is* something special about you after all." She sighed and resisted the temptation to stamp her feet. That would be childish, and surely she should be pleased she was no longer on her own in her ability to sense the Light.

But it's unfair! Why should anyone else have this sight? It's mine! She pouted and looked down at Rachel.

The older girl remained motionless. Ant's right foot moved closer, the nubs that were once her toes caressing the soft hair that sparkled like spun gold in the sunlight. A natural blonde, Ant reckoned, and felt another pang of jealousy: this time for Rachel's golden mane, much more attractive than her own mousy locks.

A thought struck her: *press down on the bimbo's neck. Crush the windpipe, strangle her. No one else will have the sight then.*

Ant froze, and it was a huge effort to keep her foot pressed to the ground. That thought…it was more like a voice; not the first time she'd experienced it. A voice that tried to make her do Bad Things, but she'd always resisted, always knew it was wrong – because it was only in the grounds of Fairlight Hospital that it spoke to her. And killing a fellow patient – that was beyond Bad. That was *evil.*

And it was almost desperate. But why? What had changed here?

Her heart thudded against her ribs and sweat began to bead her forehead. Her palms were moist, and the pleasant taste of kippers and tuna salad turned sour in her mouth. She pressed both feet firmly onto the ground, digging into the grass with the stumps of her toes, as though trying to root herself on the lawn before trusting herself to look at Rachel Collins once more. Her eyes settled on the headland beyond the bay, and the ruins of the old lighthouse. She shuddered at the sight of the seemingly innocuous stones. Who would know what evil that collection of rubble and stone contained?

After all, she thought, *who else can see it?*

That was close. She'd almost done it, almost killed the one person who could be her ally. She remembered all too well her first sight of the Shadow Pharos. No wonder the darkness had acted so quickly, tried to get her to murder the girl.

It's getting desperate – or is it getting stronger? To summon itself in daylight like that! And why can't the Light just speak to me, like the darkness does?

Perhaps the older girl had some answers. It was doubtful; she looked just as confused, bewildered and upset as the rest of them had been. But that was only to be expected on the first night.

Ant stared at the girl's inverted face. The full lips were parted slightly and the strong jaw was slack. Peaceful, as though she'd just decided to lay down for a summer snooze and overslept. No signs of bleeding or concussion from her fall – Ant assumed Rachel had fallen, she'd seen other inmates fall like a sack of potatoes when they passed out – but just because she couldn't see any damage didn't mean there was none.

Or maybe there really was no damage. The girl's scars were barely noticeable, but hadn't she run her hands underneath Rogers's lawnmower? Yes, her wrists had been swathed in bandages at breakfast, dressings that hadn't remained white for long. And now she was free of them.

That made Ant remember Julia's scars. Julia said she'd had no memory of inflicting the wounds upon herself, which Ant had thought odd. The self-harming was many things: terrifying, thrilling, agonising, liberating, but it was never *forgettable.* You always remembered cutting yourself. *Always.*

"Hey."

Rachel's eyelids flickered and a brief frown passed over her face, but she didn't wake up. Ant crouched down and took the older girl's head in her hands.

Snap it. Go on: break the neck, crush –

"Fuck you!" Ant bellowed. Rachel's eyes shot open and Ant laughed at the bewildered expression that greeted her. "Sorry, not you. Glad you're up, though. This isn't the best place to take a nap. They'll be cutting the grass again soon."

The older girl's face darkened. She tried to speak, her lips parted to say *very funny* or the equivalent, Ant assumed, but Rachel could only manage a dry croak.

"Dehydrated as well as low on blood sugar," Ant continued, hoping she didn't sound *too* smug and Little-Miss-Know-It-All; Heaven knew her cut-glass accent put enough people's backs up as it was. "If you're going to cut yourself, you really need to learn to look after yourself."

Rachel held a hand up to keep the sun out of her eyes. When she found her voice, she said in a hoarse voice: "Do you have *any* idea how bonkers that sounds?"

Ant grinned by way of response. "Well, they call me the nutty one. Which is a bit rich, when you think about it. We're all mad here. I'm mad. You're mad. How do I *know* you're mad?"

Rachel smiled. "I must be. Or I wouldn't have come here." She put her hands on the grass and began to push herself up as Ant clapped delightedly. "Been a long time since I heard Lewis Carroll quoted at me."

"'I wonder if I've been changed in the night? Let me think. Was I the same when I got up this morning? I almost think I can remember feeling a little different. But if I'm not the same, the next question is: "Who in the world am I?"'"

Rachel stared at her then turned away. Ant saw the gooseflesh rise on the girl's shoulders, and realised she'd gone too far.

Must control myself. No one else sees it as a game. "Sorry, didn't mean to freak you out."

Rachel waved a dismissive hand. "It's okay. I think…" Her attention was on the bay as Ant helped her to her feet. The shudder that ripped through Rachel's body came as no surprise to Ant, who planted her feet firmly on the drying grass and braced herself for the fall.

"You can see it as well, can't you?" Ant slowly released the older girl and affectionately patted her shoulders. "Funny how the others can't."

The look on the older girl's face made Ant sigh. "Oh, my. I've got a lot to teach you, haven't I?" Ant couldn't prevent a giggle, and mentally cursed herself. *Little-Miss-Know-It-All, getting too smug again.*

Rachel looked over Ant's shoulders, scanning the building behind her. Ant watched her eyes closely, noting how they flicked between the doorway to the dining room and the CCTV cameras above.

"Yes, it is odd no one's come, isn't it? We're supposed to be under constant observation – you may think you're alone, but Big Mental Brother is watching our every move." Ant waved cheerfully to the camera. The glinting black lens beneath the metal hood seemed to wink back at her, and she grinned. "And any faints or falls, someone'll come running to help."

Rachel rubbed the back of her neck, then froze. Her eyes were no longer on the doors or the cameras. They were fixed on the remains of Ant's feet. "And they sent you?"

"Not quite," Ant said, and stretched her feet, balancing on the nubs like a ballerina. She chuckled at the soft slurping sound they made as they dug into the moist ground; it sounded just like the gurgling sound coming from Rachel's throat. She hopped out of the small burrow her ravaged feet made and performed a neat forward roll that ended in a handstand. From her inverted view of the world, through the curtain of frayed brown hair, she saw Rachel Collins's vomit spray into the air and soak into the sky-grass. *Need to learn how to hold on to your food, girl.* She tottered aimlessly on her hands for a while, then got bored and righted herself. She retrieved her trainers and slipped them on.

"They don't like me doing that. All the blood rushing to my head, affects the meds or something. I think they're full of *shit.*" She giggled, relishing the sound of the swear word, then side-stepped around Rachel's vomit and waited patiently for the older girl to get to her feet. She folded her arms across her breasts and drummed her fingers on her upper arms.

"What was Quinn talking to you about?"

Rachel wiped the back of her hand across her mouth and stared blearily at Ant. "Nothing much."

Ant caught the narrowed eyes and the too-quick reply. She raised an admonishing finger and waved it. "No need for that, we're all friends here – but not the adults. They're *not* our friends." She stamped her feet in emphasis but the effect was lost on the soft ground.

Rachel pushed her hair over her ear and smiled faintly. "Anger doesn't suit you, Ant. Tell me why I shouldn't trust them."

"Because they lie. You saw what was on Gilly's shoulder, didn't you? The tattoo?"

Rachel stood and put her hand to her mouth again. She winced, tensed, and Ant waited for the stomach cramps to pass before continuing.

"The Isle of Man symbol? Yeah, what about it?" She eased past Ant, making for the picnic table.

"That's proof she can't be trusted. She's at one with the Manxome Foe." Ant hopped onto the same side as Rachel, making the picnic table lurch. Rachel pressed her hands on the laminated pine, winced again, and then frowned.

"Manxome *what?*"

Ant felt the breeze turn chill, and the gulls were no longer crying over the bay. It was always like this when she mentioned the enemy that hid behind the Light.

Even the older girl sensed it. Rachel rubbed the gooseflesh of her forearms and wrapped her arms over her shoulders, but her expression was more of confusion than fear.

She'd learn, Ant decided. She'd have to, if she wanted to survive. "Manxome Foe. Just what I call it. You and Julie called it something else – triskelion, or something. Whatever it is, Gillian knows more about them than she's letting on."

Now it was Rachel's turn to be suspicious. "Gillian. Thought something wasn't right there. Too keen to be seen as 'one of the girls'. And Quinn…Quinn was telling me something. Showed me pictures of…who's the other girl? Juliette?"

"Julia."

"Yeah, Julia. Showed me some snaps of her…" her face whitened, and Ant knew then what Rachel Collins had been shown. "He was going to take me there as well, show me…"

Now Ant's jaw dropped. "He was going to take you to the Acute Ward?"

Rachel smiled faintly and rubbed again at the gooseflesh. The thin white lines of her scars were even paler. "Does that make me special? He went on his own in the end. Call on his mobile, couldn't get there quick enough…"

Ant drummed her fingers on the table. "Wonder what's happened?"

Rachel didn't answer. She stared at the lines on her wrists, and for a moment the entire world centred on the older girl's wounds.

Everything was forgotten: the coldness creeping in on the afternoon sun; the silence of the gulls, now disappearing out to sea and away from Fairlight; even the sudden mystery presented within the hospital and the absence of adult staff.

The only thing Ant and Rachel were aware of was the fresh blood on the older girl's wrists. Seeping from newly opened skin and flesh. Where once had been scar tissue and impossibly healed flesh was a sheet of blood that failed to mask the opened wounds in Rachel Collins's wrists, opening and closing with each shudder of her body, like the mouths of monstrous fish.

Tony slumped in the passenger seat of Karen's Volvo, impervious to the jolts and shudders of the aging suspension on the potholed road surface. He was overcome with the desire to close his eyes, to slip into something darker and more permanent than sleep. And strangely, more welcoming.

Exhaustion, he wondered, or something else? It was a bone-weariness, a feeling of being completely drained, like at the end of each shift when he'd dragged himself in to work before being completely recovered from flu a few years ago.

Coming home, after ensuring Rachel was okay, he'd been powerless to resist, and he sank into a death-like slumber, undisturbed until the alarm clock heralded a new day. This was a similar feeling, no doubt aided by the heat of the day that had built up in the Volvo. A knackered air conditioning unit, and only when the car built up speed, leaving the estate for the cliff road and its freshening breeze, did the heat within the vehicle dissipate, but it didn't refresh him enough to keep the tiredness at bay.

Hide under the blankets, with heat like this? No chance.

He dared not close his eyes, not even for a second. Too much was at stake. Fear – not for him, but for Rachel - kept him awake. But only just.

He wound the window down further, grateful for the fresh

breeze that cooled the sweat on his face. The air smelled sweet with the scents of ocean freshness and summer meadows, but all that changed when Karen turned off the cliff road and into the harbour.

Diesel and hot metal, fish and seaweed filled the car's interior, the stink of a working dockside. Tony shrank back into the tattered vinyl upholstery, reluctant to meet the eyes of the harbour workers. Paranoia, that was all; they didn't know who he was. Did they?

Still, best not to take chances. He wouldn't be much good to Rachel if his presence was made known to the authorities. Karen seemed to share his unease as she downshifted, missing the correct gear and filling the car with the noise of metallic crunching. She glanced in the rear-view mirror as the dock workers paused in their actions to stare at her with expressions that said *typical bird behind the wheel. Can't find it, grind it* and gave them a weak smile. The sunlight caught on the frame of her sunglasses, and the light dazzled Tony's weary eyes. "Thought this was the best way in," she murmured. "The dockside will be the last place on their list of priorities."

"We hope." Tony pulled the baseball cap's visor further down, until the frayed cotton covering touched his nose. Even then he felt conspicuous. "I walked this stretch of the town last night. Didn't exactly get a warm welcome." He shuddered as the Volvo passed the pub Jim had taken him into, then the streetlight the cop car had been parked by. Sunlight glinted on the dusty white bodywork and headlight clusters of a Vauxhall, and for a moment he thought he saw police livery on the door; then the rust patches became more visible, and the POLICE sign changed to PORTCO. An Astra van: an ancient delivery vehicle with the boot lid raised and a man struggling with an icebox.

"Lobsters," Karen said, catching his eye. "There's a restaurant down here that advertises shellfish, 'freshly caught from the coast'. They don't say *which* coast, though. Bloody idiot tourists go for it, not knowing Fairlight hasn't had any decent fish for years."

Tony felt his cheeks redden, remembering the times he had taken Becky for a romantic meal at the restaurant the Volvo now passed; the buttered lobster and chilled champagne they'd enjoyed. Expensive but worth it, they'd told themselves; can't get better than local shellfish. *God, what a bloody fool they took me for!* Bad enough that his and Becky's holiday resort was now a prison for their daughter, but that was not insult enough, obviously. One by one, all his perceptions and memories of their favourite holiday resort were being broken apart like rotten oyster shells, revealing the putrid reality within. Anger rose, and he embraced it. It would energise him, fuel his mission to take Rachel back from Fairlight – and maybe help him find out what was going on beneath the surface.

"Fairlight stinks," he muttered. "What brought you here, Karen? And why d'you stay?"

Karen gave a dry chuckle. "Needed a change of scenery after a shitty relationship turned shittier. It was too good to be true. Quiet little comprehensive on the coast, a complete change from the inner city pits I taught in. And on the Dorset coast - ideal for a Thomas Hardy nut like me!" She shook her head and changed down a gear for the traffic lights. "Oh, it was great for a bit, don't get me wrong. Parents were arseholes, but some of the kids were great – I even got some of them reading outside of class."

The harbour and its transforming memories were forgotten. He didn't notice the dockside workers trundle sack barrows along the hardstand, the creaking of masts and the squawking of seagulls fighting over scraps of last night's kebabs and battered fish. He stared at Karen Tyndall, and the tears that ran from the lenses of her sunglasses.

"Doesn't sound much, I know. Kids reading in their spare time. But…if you'd seen what I'd had to deal with when I came out of teacher-training. Yes, I was green, full of…well, what you might call 'a middle-class passion to bring enlightenment to the inner cities'." She gave a humorous laugh. "I felt I was up to the challenge. I was warned I'd be ripped to shreds if I took up the post in Hackney. I thought I knew it all at that age."

What graduate doesn't? Tony thought of Becky and forced the image away. He thought back to the overflowing bookshelves in Karen's house, the copies of the *Morning Star*, the recycling boxes. A liberal who read too much, thought too much, and despaired at being unable to change the world. Just like Becky.

"I could never come to terms with the fact that kids just didn't want to read anymore…" Her words poured out, tumbling, and he knew then the loneliness and isolation she had endured. *How long has it been since someone actually listened to you?* She talked of the passion for teaching that had long deserted her, but she didn't say why the desire had gone. She would, in time. He knew that. Perhaps an affair that shouldn't have happened, a more senior teacher or a married one, and she'd drawn the short straw.

"Some do, Karen." It felt good to say her name. "They just take their time. Hell, I was a slow burner with the written word, but in my day the teachers weren't exactly…encouraging. What books did you get them to read?"

"What was on the syllabus, to start with." She snorted. "Some kids just aren't ready for Shakespeare or Dickens, and it doesn't matter how much passion you have, no matter how good a communicator – and believe me Tony, I knew my limitations – if they don't want it, they won't take it." She sniffed, and Tony looked away, remembering all too well the grief he'd given his own teachers as a kid. He wished the lights would hurry up and change.

"I tried genre fiction then. Science fiction, sword and sorcery, and straight-up thrillers."

"Good move. That's how I got into reading as well."

She fingered the worn vinyl covering of the steering wheel and cocked her head. There was a smile on her lips; a warm, affectionate one. "Who was it who got you into the classics?"

"What makes you think I got into literature?"

"When we met in the Day Gone Down, you made the Orwell reference. 'We shall meet in the place where there is no darkness.' *Nineteen Eighty-Four.*"

"My missus. It was one of her favourite books."

The lights changed. Karen engaged first and moved her foot off the brake. "A lady with taste. One of my favourites as well. Orwell was wrong, though."

He didn't answer. He saw the Day Gone Down at the far end of the road, and realised just how close it was to the town centre. The dray had long gone and the doors were open to the sunlight.

"'Hope lies in the proles.' That was my mantra for a long time. Three years teaching in Hackney told me that was wrong."

Two men in rolled shirtsleeves and loosened ties smoked furiously, sweat patches under their arms and quick glances at their wristwatches telling Tony these were not the usual lunchtime drinkers escaping from the office to enjoy a quick pint.

"Don't underestimate us," Tony replied, his eyes rooted on the white collar men. "We're not all beerguts and England away T shirts."

Their suit jackets were draped over the wooden chairs. Uneaten salad baguettes and drained glasses of juice, the melting ice retaining a sickly orange colour, accompanied a pair of briefcases and what looked like a laptop bag. These items were much closer to the two men, and their eyes darted from their wristwatches to the baggage, unwilling to allow them out of sight for a second.

"We'll talk class war later," Tony said. "Any idea who that pair are?"

Karen followed his pointed finger. She squinted, raised her sunglasses, and then lowered them. "I don't recognise them. They're not local, that's for sure."

"They're not tourists, either. They're waiting for someone."

The lights changed to green. Karen ground the gears again, then pulled the Volvo around and down the side street. The two men turned sharply at the sound and their eyes narrowed. Tony held his breath, fearing they'd recognised him, but then each raised a hand to shield their eyes from the sun's glare. In that brief moment before their hands covered their eyes and the Volvo shot past them, Tony got a clearer look at their faces.

Youngish, maybe early thirties. Short-cropped hair and clean-shaven. He wondered if they were military or plain clothes coppers. *But since when does Plod look that nervy?*

The pub disappeared, and the beer garden gave way to the older, taller buildings of the quayside. The sunlight stayed behind, as though reluctant to follow them. Tony saw the battered roller shutter door he had attacked the night before and shuddered at the memory of the pale, luminous thing he'd glimpsed in the gap.

"Karen. Pull over for a moment, will you?"

"Why?"

"Please. I just need to check something."

She glanced in the rear-view mirror, then indicated and bumped the nearside wheels up the kerb. "Can't stay here for long, Tony. Even a pushbike would struggle to get past me."

"No problem." He opened the door and climbed out. The heat of the day had not penetrated this part of the town; the cold, dank feeling of his night-time exploration of the alley remained. He sniffed, smelled again the rotten odour of decayed maritime vegetation and shellfish, and thought back to the restaurant and their "local coastal" dishes. More lies and bullshit. He snorted, felt the anger rise, and held on to it. His fists clenched. The few rays of sunlight that made it this far down the backstreet caught the angled indentations on the steel roller shutter, made the traces of his blood sparkle like rubies.

Didn't I knock this fucker down? Who the hell put it back up?

He exhaled slowly. He no longer felt angry. Now he felt scared.

"What are you looking for, Tony?"

"This place." He tapped the roller door gently and started at the almost musical echo the shutter made, as though it danced in its ratchets. Mocking him. "What's it used for?"

He heard her close her door and felt her presence behind him. "That's…I think that's part of the old Customs House. Yes, hasn't been used since the '50s."

"Modern shutter door, though."

She ran her fingers over the dents, shuddering at the dried blood that flaked away. "A fish wholesaler took it over at one point, tried to make a go of it. They didn't last long."

"So it's unoccupied?" He frowned, convinced that they were being watched by someone. He felt – or rather, sensed – a presence behind the roller shutter. Had to be a warehouse worker or someone.

Had to be. The alternative was that pale-skinned, luminous eyed thing that…*no, that's bullshit.*

"As far as I know. I don't come down to this part of town very often."

So why had the door been repaired?

Tony glanced over his shoulder. At the entrance to the backstreet, just past the one-way sign, he saw two silhouettes against the raging sun. He blinked and held his hand up to blot out the sun. Just as the two smoking, nervy figures outside the Day Gone Down had done earlier.

"We got company," he muttered. Karen took a sharp breath. Then he froze, heart racing, when the two men entered the backstreet and walked towards them.

CHAPTER TWENTY

Callum Hayes stared at the holes in his palms and smiled. The oily black pools rippled with life, energy and strength flowing through and turning the skeins into waves that seemed to crash and thunder like the storm. And with that energy came a return of vitality for him; strength pulsed through his vessels, energising him in a way adrenaline – or, he imagined, cocaine – would. He looked down at the words he'd scrawled in his blood, drawn by puncturing the skeins. It had been hard work; the alien material that covered his stigmata had coarsened overnight, become hard as sail canvas. Fingernails had been ripped and torn in the attempt to open the wounds anew, and the material had evidently fused to his flesh – or replaced it, he wasn't sure which – because his nerve endings screamed a new hymn of agony with each probing slice.

Finally, the skeins had parted, but he suspected they'd done so of their own volition rather than a result of his self-harming. The Presence was happy with the pain he had inflicted upon himself, and he thought the wave-like motions of the skeins had uttered a reptilian growl of approval and pleasure. Even more so when he painted the words HELL IS COMING on the vinyl padding of the floor.

Power is restored, he thought happily. He didn't know why the Presence had been so weak before, but he knew not to question it; just to accept and be grateful. He sank into the padded floor with a contented sigh, his palms raised to the ceiling. Perhaps the creatures would return? The more he thought of his sister's funeral, the more he wondered why the eel-like creatures that emerged from his palms had not returned. Had they disappeared back into his body, like a snail's eyestalks? Had they detached from his palms in the church and secreted themselves in the holy building – and if so, what would they do next?

"The mysteries of evolution," he said, surprised to hear a waver in his voice. Almost as though he doubted…

No! There is no doubt, and no reason to doubt. Look into the pools for proof, if you need it. See how they've sealed, preventing further blood loss. See how they sparkle with energy, like forked lightning in storm clouds. The power of the Presence, and it's within you!

Was that his thought, or the voice of the Presence? It was hard to tell, they sounded so similar…but what the fuck was he questioning this for, anyway?

"Power is restored. The battleground is prepared. The war is inevitable." There, that was better. Not a single quaver in his voice, each word enunciated to perfection; the masterful, disciplined voice of a natural leader ordering his charges to fight for assured victory.

He hadn't seen any of them yet, but during the conversations between Quinn and Bethan he'd overheard hushed references to something called the Acute Ward. The tones in which it had been spoken of made it sound like a special level of Hell, and he had known then where his army were bivouacked.

And there must have been one hell of a commotion going on there if no one was coming to check on his wounds. Quinn and Bethan in the Acute Ward, Rogers watching disinterestedly from the Site Services office like the fish-like simpleton he was, and the others…

He frowned. He didn't know what threat the others posed; it was early days yet. Still, they couldn't be much of a danger.

Except the Collins bitch. He felt a sharp, jolting pain in his palms and was alarmed to see the ripples freeze, the sail canvas of the alien material turn slack and lifeless, like the skin of a blister that has just been lanced. Shit, even the thought of her name had caused a cessation of the power. Was the Presence scared of her? Or was it merely a manifestation of his concerns and self-doubt that caused a blockage of the power?

The latter would be even worse, he decided. Who would bother to follow him into the next stage of human evolution if he was scared of a *girl*?

His face darkened when he remembered what Bethan had said to him before leaving. *How far back did you go in your research? To what Fairlight was, before the hospital…before the lighthouse. That's the trouble with you kids: no sense of the past.*

That was worrying as well. Defiance like that wasn't usual for Bethan, but it mustn't be allowed to continue. When she came back from the Acute Ward they would have…words.

The lighthouse. That jumble of rocks on the headland – what possible importance could that have on anything? He hissed, felt another jolt in his palms shoot up his arms and force his shoulders back with the strength of an electric shock. His vision blurred and panic gripped him. *What is this?* He stood on trembling legs and the dizziness increased. He stumbled forward and tripped, fell heavily, his knees and palms smearing the blood words on the floor into incomprehensible hieroglyphs. He moaned when another shock pulsed along his arms; this time it was a pleasurable one, as the blood beneath his palms disappeared, sucked into the skeins.

More energy. More vitality. More *power*. He giggled, remembering his words to Bethan. *I'm only human. For now, anyway.*

His translocation would be earth-shattering, would show up the so-called "wonders" of the universe as mere shadow plays in comparison. The deaths of stars, the births of galaxies; explosions of light and dying in the void of eternal blackness, none of these would match his own evolution! Godhood, elevation to the spheres of existence beyond the stars and to become one with the puppet-masters who rule the universes.

But patience. You must show us what you are capable of, prove your worth. He sighed at the memory, despite the pleasure coursing through his veins. When the Presence chose to speak to him in words, it sounded like a nagging old woman at times. *Just the age gap*, he told himself. *Like most kids, I don't like admitting my elders know better.* When he communicated with his followers on social media, he had been astonished at the realisation of just how inane the conversations were, how distanced he felt, and that was *before* the Presence graced him.

He hadn't used the same words, the same symbols and punctuation marks in place of words. He hadn't celebrated every tiny, insignificant celebrity and fame-hungry airhead. No, he had used his time and youth wisely: *study*. Such a dirty word to the chavs and chavettes of his generation, but no longer!

"Know your enemy." Three words from *The Art of War*, a phrase since used for song titles by countless rock bands. Pure gold for the Children of the Evolution: Sun Tzu's saying adopted by younger warriors who fought with bass guitar and drums, a declaration of war from a new generation who would sing their victory over burning buildings and the wasted corpses of the old. No wonder the elders had pulled them off every social network going!

And it was proof they were the natural successors to humanity. If the so-called "know-betters" couldn't even be bothered to work out the hint in their manifesto's slogan, they were more stupid than he first thought, and deserved oblivion. *Know your enemy, Mummies and Daddies! You didn't bother knowing us, though, did you? The threat we pose to the order, the talents and savvy we have at our disposal!*

Proxy servers, VPNs, dark web, hidden networks…as one site went down, another went up, and the messages were sent, redirecting the faithful to the next website. Only by forcing the ISPs to block all pages associated with the Children of the Evolution could their online presence be nullified. By then, it was too late.

The information had already gone out. The manifesto, the declaration of war and the weapons to wage it, all downloaded onto laptops, tablets, smartphones in the form of PDFs and MP4s.

Study materials: the ultimate weapon. Knowledge is power. How to cut yourself without succumbing to shock; how to minimise blood loss and maximise pain; how to hide the damage and disguise the flesh, to keep the parents unsuspecting and unaware until the time of muster.

But the time was now, surely? Tomorrow was midsummer, and that was the time set for invasion. So why had he received no summons, no orders?

The Acute Ward. Bethan. *Why is she taking so long?* Perhaps it was terror; perhaps her mind was unable to cope with the evolution. No, that was bollocks. She'd described the state of her charges in a dispassionate, emotionless manner. Nothing would shock her into inaction. Would it?

I'm only human. For now, anyway.

But Bethan Appleton was human. And all flesh has its weak points, especially one who was too old for the Children of the Evolution. Perhaps the Presence had deemed her unnecessary? Perhaps she had seen through his lies, realised she would be one of the first to be destroyed despite her service?

He swallowed, angry at himself for feeling fear. For doubting. He pulled his body from the floor and shook his head in wonderment at the clean, bloodless vinyl. He glanced at the rippling blackness of his stigmata, grinned, and then sat.

"Grace me with your Presence. Show me what lies beyond."

He crossed his legs, wincing at the effort it took to fold them; the sessions in the gym had improved his strength, stamina and muscle tone, but he'd neglected the exercises required to make his body supple. Still, no matter. After tomorrow, any discomfort would be forgotten. Pain would be pleasure. Death would be life. Mutilation would be evolution.

He closed his eyes and held his palms outwards, facing the door. He engaged his mind's eye, the third eye through which the Presence would grace him. And, just as he'd done with Jim and the bitch's father, he let the portals within his hands do the seeking.

CHAPTER TWENTY-ONE

Quinn raised his keycard and hesitated. Before him, the doorway to the Acute Ward looked formidable: twenty-first century materials and locking mechanisms could not make it appear any less a door to a dungeon, a solid barrier to keep horrors at bay.

Horrors we created, he reminded himself. He checked his watch again, calculating how much time had passed since Bethan had gone through. Over twenty minutes now.

But why was he worried? Fears for her safety? Her Man-Down alarm hadn't sent warnings racing through Site Services and Reception; there'd been no sign of calls made on her mobile, according to the MoD's thoughtfully supplied receiver – he prided himself on keeping that little fact from her – so she wasn't in danger.

Yet. Even if she was, it couldn't happen to a nicer person. No, he knew all too well why he was worried: suspecting Bethan Appleton of aiding and abetting the service users in self-mutilation was one thing, and he'd been looking forward to catching the bitch in the act. Now, he wasn't so certain. With the arrival of Rachel Collins and the still-unexplained healing powers she had brought with her, things were no longer as simple as he'd thought. Bethan was going to make a serious mistake, and Quinn knew the Callum boy would be pushing for it.

Not as smart as you think you are, kid, he thought. Arrogance and over-confidence couldn't hide the moments of self-doubt that flickered in the boy's eyes during his interrogation. Both he and Bethan were worried about Rachel Collins's admission to Fairlight; that should work to his advantage, but Quinn knew all too well the opposite was more likely. Panic led to all sorts of fuck-ups, and he shuddered to think what Bethan Appleton had felt compelled to do since Julia's "return".

He pressed the keycard against the panel, heard the familiar click, and retreated a few paces to allow the door to swing back. He stared at the glistening white steel of the corridor and hesitated. He glanced at the CCTV camera, knew Rogers was watching him. It was too much of a coincidence that the CCTV cameras in the Acute Ward hadn't been wired into the main network yet.

"Fucking Rogers pretends it's a maintenance issue," he muttered, running the edge of the card along his beard. "'Ceilings are too old, boss – all need rewiring.' Lying bastard."

If I go in, what's to stop him manually overriding the locking system and trapping me inside? Now where the hell had that thought come from? Rogers had no reason to do that! What was it he'd said about Bethan? *But she's got her orders, ain't she? And not from you, or your guv'nors.*

The Beconase-snorting bastard knew more than was necessary, that was true, but Quinn didn't suspect the Site Services manager of wanting to put anyone else at risk. After all, he'd been vetted by the security services.

But then, so had Bethan…Quinn stared again at the white corridor and the door sealing it from the older, red brick corridor beyond. It was the twin of the dungeon door he'd just opened, but it seemed so far away, so insignificant. *First portal opens, the rest follow too easily…*

"Portals? Dungeons?" he said quietly. *Christ, what's happening to me? This is a modern psychiatric laboratory, not a medieval torture chamber!* Guilt flared at the use of the word "laboratory". Experimentation first, care and compassion afterwards – if at all. No one was fooled; everyone knew Fairlight was the last chance saloon for the self-destructive new breed of teenagers.

But what's in the Acute Ward goes beyond "experimentation". You know that! His self-loathing made grim company during his slow walk. Each accusation hammered into his brain, ringing as sharply as his shoes on the metal tiles; each rebuttal a poor defence smashed to pieces, like the rocks of the old lighthouse.

Desperate, Quinn! Confiding in the Collins girl, even offering to show her the Acute Ward! Why was that? Because you think she can help you? He resisted the urge to look over his shoulder and face the sight of the outer door closing. He heard it, though; a metallic thud and a double-click that made him start.

Relax, the keycard works this side. You're not trapped. Unless Rogers had something planned.

His footsteps were louder, the echoes piercing in the sealed corridor. Almost like knife blades, sharpening on a whetstone. Now his legs shuddered with each step. By the time he got to the other door he felt he was walking on jelly.

He fumbled the card into the panel, and had to repeat the process as the sensor didn't detect the chip due to his shaking hand. Just as well there were no cameras operational in the corridor, he thought. Rogers would piss himself laughing at his lack of control. He was certain this door swung open slower than the first: as if it was sentient, malevolent, imbibed with the horrors it kept secret from the twenty-first century part of Fairlight.

The impression was reinforced by the smell. At first the scents of modern laboratory equipment and chemicals assailed him, but the odours gave way to something much older, familiar and sickening. Sweet and metallic. Pungent, meaty and rancid. Blood and decay.

He stood still for a few moments, his eyes squeezed shut, until his imagination imbibed the odours with more horror than he could stand. It was almost always a relief to open his eyes and see the source of the stench wasn't quite as bad as he'd imagined, but that was only because the process hadn't reached the final stage. It would, soon.

He breathed a sigh of relief to see nothing had changed since Julia's return yesterday. The overhead lights glared, harsh against the eyes; but the decision had been bright light was preferable to dim. It made the horror more visible, but easier to deal with - shadows made the transforming children far, far worse. The bed sheets had been replaced with rubber sheeting of course, and the visible remnants of the hidden patients' bodies were more bandages and surgical dressing than exposed flesh. Some of the limbless ones twitched on the rubber sheeting, like slugs writhing in salt, and Quinn heard faint moans of ecstasy. Fresh blood stained the tiled floor; no matter how often the dressings were changed or the wounds sealed, the blood always found new ways to escape. There was nothing out of the ordinary here; no new developments.

His confidence slightly restored, he walked the central aisle and glanced at each bed as he passed. Once, he would have recognised them, known their names, shaken the hands of their fathers and mothers with sympathetic smiles as they were committed to his care. Now there was little to remember them by. They were alive only in the way haunches of meat are: writhing with maggots, worms and parasites whose feeding animated the flesh and gave the illusion of life.

It was a fair analogy, he thought. What these children had done to themselves should have been fatal; nothing human could survive such bodily trauma. Only the things within powered their ravaged carcases, parasites making the flesh their own.

It eased his conscience somewhat, knowing there was nothing he could do for them, and nothing human remained of them to grieve for. Where once bright eyes, shining with agony, pleasure and bewilderment had gazed beseechingly at him from bandaged faces, there were now dull, pink-hued orbs: milk-white, opaque and unseeing. Where once young voices had sung hymns of agony and whispered unintelligible prayers, now there was silence save the occasional reptilian hiss – and that was surely from the medical ventilators.

Even the movements were unrecognisable. The twitching of torsos was no longer that of confused, agonised adolescents operating phantom limbs; rather it was the sinuous, sideways motion of snakes, creatures at home with their environment and this new method of locomotion.

As always, fear and disgust initially overcame his guilt at failing his charges. These children were no longer human, and the seeds of their inhumanity had been sown long before they came to Fairlight. What happened to the patients was beyond comprehension: all he could do was watch, observe, try to find a pattern and a cause. Maybe then – and *only* maybe – a cure would come.

Containment, that's all this place was. He was doing the best he could. At least there were signs of hope now, with Rachel Collins. Whatever that power of hers was, it held the key to the future. But how to harness it? To tap into it, without Rachel destroying herself?

Did they dare use it? A power that would only be released by the girl who carried it cutting herself…what sort of cure was that?

Quinn hesitated at the first empty cot. The pristine white bed sheets, crisp and unused, should have given him hope. A single bed that wasn't a rubber-sheeted receptacle for shedding blood and pieces of flesh but was the site of salvation of a sort. Julia had been on her way to becoming one of the bandaged, hissing things surrounding him. And Rachel Collins had stopped that.

But how? And how the hell am I supposed to put that in my report? Christ, the consequences of that chilled him to the bone. Observation would go out the window if Rawlings and company were let loose on her. They'd go in with their own idea of "laboratory conditions", and Julia – and then Rachel - would be little different to the pieces of meat in the cots surrounding him.

He caressed the starched bed sheets, felt the plump firmness of the double pillows as the MoD man's high-pitched voice continued, its weasel-like face reddening in disapproval.

Remember your brief, Quinn. Remember why you're here. This is no time for weakness!

"Shit," he muttered. He sat on the end of the cot. The pillows felt cold and clammy beneath his hands, and it was a while before he realised the dampness was from his own palms. He lifted his hands gently, rubbed them on his knees and stood. He glanced across the aisle at the opposite bed and frowned. Something had changed. That cot had been occupied. Now it was empty.

It was the only other bed with cotton bed linen rather than rubber sheeting; bed sheets that lay strewn on the tiled floor and wrapped around the bed posts. It was also the only bed in the Acute Ward that had restraints. Rubber-lined wrist and ankle cuffs that now dangled, empty and unused, from the cot's rails.

His mouth was dry; he had difficulty swallowing as he approached. Each step was an ordeal, each inch closer to the bed a hammer blow to his gut. The restraints mocked him with their emptiness. Now he knew why Bethan had been so long, and why she was no longer in the Acute Ward.

The only adult inmate of Fairlight, one who had been admitted for the damage that someone else had inflicted upon his body. Quinn lifted the nearest restraint and inspected it. No signs of damage, no forcing apart of the material. The restraints had been undone deliberately, and the prisoner taken elsewhere.

But that prisoner had not gone willingly. Quinn saw flecks of blood and small clumps of hair on the exposed mattress. He crouched and inspected the railing fixed to the floor, noted the plastering of matted grey hair and blood. The old man had put up a fight, and Quinn marvelled at the desire of a man who preferred to stay in this chamber of mutilation and death rather than accompany his liberator.

Following the trail of blood to the third and final door – the portal beyond the Acute Ward – Quinn understood why. This wasn't the first time Jim had been inside Fairlight, and the old man would rather die fighting than return to the scene of his first mutilation.

But Bethan surprised you, didn't she? Hell, she surprised all of us. Quinn stared at the sealed door, over a five metre gap that felt like an immeasurable distance.

"What are you doing to him, Bethan? Why is he such a threat?" He stepped forcefully towards the final door, stifling his fear as best he could. He swiped the card and heard the familiar double-click. Like a pistol cocked before being placed against a prisoner's head, he thought. He had no time to go back and get help – it was unlikely he could count on any of the staff, anyway – and there was nothing he could use as a weapon to defend himself.

If I go in, I'm probably going to my death. The thought didn't alarm him; instead, he felt a strange elation at his decision. He'd been at the crossroads for too long. At last, he had been shown the way.

Alone, unarmed and defenceless, he felt his fear evaporate. A smile broadened his face as he went beyond the Acute Ward.

CHAPTER TWENTY-TWO

Tony Collins pressed his body hard against the intersection of the two buildings and pulled the wheelie bin closer. Even with the slimy plastic hard against his shins and forehead he felt hideously exposed. The roller shutter door rattled in its ratchets, as if calling out to the two approaching men: *Here he is! Hiding!*

He watched the exhaust plumes of Karen's Volvo dissipate and the car vanish into the intersection ahead. The sounds of her engine faded, replaced with the faint cries of the ever-hungry seagulls and the slowing footsteps of the two men.

Slowing…did that mean they were after Karen or him? He closed his eyes, shut out all visual stimulation to focus on the sounds, waited for speech. The smell of last night was stronger now he was crouched on the floor, the stink of fish and seaweed from the bin making him nauseous. He strained to make out the words above the clatter of the roller shutter and the squawk of the gulls, but as the two men came closer he heard them more clearly.

"Shit! Was that them?"

"Dunno, couldn't tell. Had to be though, yeah?"

A sharp intake of breath, then a pregnant pause. Tony frowned at the voices: they confirmed the youth of their owners, the accent undeniably local, and told him hiding was the right idea after all.

"Call it in? They'll twig otherwise, no matter what he says."

"Nah, leave it." A brief pause, while tobacco was imbibed ferociously. "In a few hours' time it won't make much difference, anyway." The tone was nervy. Tony could picture them now, puffing away on their cigarettes, the case clutched tightly between them, convincing themselves they didn't need to do anything.

But they sure as hell aren't coppers – neither civilian nor military Plod. So who the hell were they, and what did they want with him and Karen? And why were they so bloody *scared?*

"Not sure about that, chap. Orders are orders, yeah?"

"Fuck. Okay. Radio in the reg number, tell 'em to pick her up."

Ice prickled Tony's spine. There was another pause, and then the static of a two-way radio. *Shit, what have I done?* It had seemed the best idea; split up and meet later. After all, it was just him they were after…

Obviously not. Then the white noise ceased, and the following words were a punch in the gut.

"Hang on. How can we be sure Collins is still with her?"

"You shitting me? Where else is he gonna go?"

There was anger in the other's voice now. "Ask yerself why they stopped here. Now we know who punched seven shades of fuck out the roller door yesterday. It were him, weren't it? Trying to get in." There was a hiss and sizzle of a cigarette butt thrown to the soggy pavement.

Tony held his breath. In this dank corner of Fairlight, untouched by the sun, he fancied his breath would mist and give away his position.

"Y'reckon he's got in there now?" The crunch of boot heels on the litter and the rattle of the shutter filled Tony's ears. *Fuck off, you bastards. Let me breathe. Just fuck off back to the pub and...*

Another rattle. "Nah. He'll be more worried 'bout his little girl, won't he? It's Fairlight he'll be headin' for, not 'ere." There was relief in his tone; he sounded reluctant to investigate what lay behind the roller shutter.

"Yeah, must be still in Missy's motor. He's hardly gonna walk to the unit, is he?" Another voice of relief that ended with the pair walking away – fast.

Tony waited until his breathing returned to normal, until the cramping aches in his thighs became unbearable, before pushing the wheelie bin aside and rising to his feet. The alley was darker now, and Tony looked to the sky, frowning at the sudden blackness of the clouds above. Blotting the sun and turning the skies the same grey as the roller shutter, the afternoon heat replaced with a chill breeze that threatened cold rain. The roller shutter rippled in the breeze like a metallic wave, and Tony smelled rotting fish again. He knew then it didn't come from the wheelie bin; this was stronger, ranker, and it came from behind the roller shutter door.

"You can stop hidin' now, Mr Collins."

The whispered voice was like a policeman's firm hand on his shoulder; the shock initially froze him, tensing his body but still allowing the sense of despair to flood his mind with the message: *You're nicked, sunshine!* His eyes closed and his shoulders slumped.

To Karen Tyndall, the town of Fairlight was no longer recognisable. The warren of back alleys and side streets no longer felt like the familiar, crumbling parts of an unfriendly, dying coastal town; the hostility was more pronounced, no longer latent. Every street and alley entrance she drove past harboured a monster; behind every set of curtained windows and partially opened doors was a hostile observer, muttering words into a telephone handset or texting her location to…

She bit her lip and pushed her sunglasses further up her nose. Stupid, really: no disguise and certainly no protection, but at least they wouldn't see how nervous she was.

She ground the gears again at the next junction. "For Christ's sake," she muttered, and imagined hordes of eyes turning to stare at her, mentally noting the make, model and registration of her car as she engaged first and kangarooed down the next side street … *Stop it!*

She hoped Tony knew what he was doing. It made no sense, splitting up like this. What was he going to do, jump one of those men and beat some answers out of him? He could handle himself, that was certain, but she hoped he wouldn't do anything stupid. Then again, who'd blame him?

Okay, he said he'd meet her at the library in one hour. He said he'd text her if he got into any trouble. That didn't inspire confidence. With his daughter's life at stake, anything could happen…

And what was the fascination with that roller shutter door? She tried to think when Ocean Wave Direct had left the premises. It may have been a year ago, she couldn't be sure. They'd not left much of an impact, that was certain.

She saw the sign for Silver Street, and the long-stay car park. No multi-storey in Fairlight, not that the town attracted many out-of-towners these days. She had her pick of bays but chose one closest to the stone archway that led to the green. Open spaces, plenty of witnesses in case…

In case what? Who's going to help you?

With shaking hands, she fumbled twenty-pence pieces into the meter's slot, each coin swallowed greedily by the rusting machine. It took its time in printing out her ticket, the grinding and clunking echoing around the stone walls of the car park, and finally spat out the square piece of paper almost as an afterthought.

Ocean Wave Direct. Why had they come here? She'd had no thoughts on their departure until she'd seen the whitewash-spiralled windows and the locked doors of the old Customs House, and then had tried to think who exactly *had* been there. Only the fliers in the gutter with the firm's logo had reminded her. And seeing Tony's bemused examination of the roller shutter door brought home the strangeness of the company's occupation. Tony worked in transport and logistics, he understood warehouses. And he was right: for a Goods-In entrance, it was totally insufficient.

But that wasn't why they'd vacated. She knew that much. God, if only she could remember anyone who worked there.

She emerged from the stone archway like a rabbit warily exiting its burrow - on edge, all muscles taut and ready for flight at the first sign of a predator. The sun touched the low arch of the Methodist Chapel and the elongated shadows from the surrounding sycamores joined the gathering clouds in darkening the green, blanching the colour from the flowerbeds and leeching any warmth from what should be a perfect summer afternoon's resting spot. Karen removed her sunglasses and tucked them into her bag's side pocket. She blinked once. It wasn't her imagination, nor the glasses; the sky had darkened. The clouds were black, pregnant with thunder, and the sun was giving up without a fight; skulking behind the Methodist Chapel as though the House of God would protect it from the coming storm.

An elderly couple, arm in arm and wrapped in beige, walked past without acknowledging her. Two girls with slumped shoulders sat on the park bench at the far end, hunched over a shared cigarette. She recognised them as Connie and Tina; failed GCSEs and a future in the town's bakery all but assured last summer. Now she saw the name tags on their tabards and knew their destiny had been fulfilled. They looked up as she passed, eyes flashing in recognition and hostility, but also embarrassment. *Yeah, you were right, Miss. Happy now?*

Karen felt less self-conscious as she passed them. Her paranoia on the car journey had been just that: paranoia. All the same…as she stepped over the gravel path and past the flower clock, she looked behind her. No, Connie and Tina hadn't bothered to give her a second look. But were they hunched over their cigarettes and smartphones, alerting someone to her presence…

Get a grip, Karen! She adjusted the shoulder strap of her bag and glared at the chapel. Not much of a library, but at least the disused church had come in useful when the council cuts hit the education services of Fairlight.

God, we're going back in time. Relying on the Victorian zeal for "self-improvement" to house books and be a centre of learning outside the school. Now the only place of learning, she thought with a shudder. She knew she would never set foot in the school again. No one would.

She checked her watch, ensured her mobile was switched on and receiving a signal, and then made her way to the chapel. The doors were open; they welcomed her into new darkness.

The hand didn't come. There was no twisting of his wrists into a set of handcuffs; no shoving against the wall; no squawk of a two-radio as a partner radioed for back-up.

These aren't cops. He opened his eyes, then slowly turned his head. The figure held his hands up, palms showing. Tony turned to get a better look.

He looked even younger at this distance. Blond cropped hair that seemed more of a style statement than a military necessity; a single earring in the right lobe that was dull and grey in the failing light and definitely not police issue; and a thin, pinched expression matched with wide, fear-stricken eyes the colour of storm clouds. A blocky razor cut above the bridge of the nose an attempt to prevent the thick black eyebrows becoming a monobrow.

He had replaced his suit jacket and buttoned it, and Tony suspected it wasn't the threat of rain or the cold breeze that made the young man shiver. No smile of welcome accompanied the man's words; instead, he glanced nervously to the entrance, back where he and Karen had passed the Day Gone Down. Tony remained still, watching him for any sudden movements.

"We ain't got much time, Mr Collins – can I call you Tony?"

"Tell me who you are and what you're up to." Tony was surprised at how smoothly his words came. "Then we can be on first name terms."

Another nervous glance to the left. "Please, Ton – Mr Collins. He'll be wondering where I've got to. I said I was just going to get some fags."

"Your mate?" Tony's eyes narrowed. There was no mistaking the young man's anxiety, or his fear. He really didn't want to be where he was, or a part of…whatever it was. And the time to call his mate and say "I've found Collins!" had long passed.

The suit's Adam's apple went up and down his thin throat like he was attempting to swallow a knife.

"Okay. They'll be after the teacher, but only because they think you're still with her." He stepped into the alcove and pressed his back against the wall. Tony involuntarily shifted away. "Listen! They know she witnessed the assault on the school, but it'll be an open secret soon anyway; they're not bothered with her. She'll be safe – trust me."

"What assault?"

The suit pressed his head against the wall and sighed. "The assault you witnessed. Them things that came out of that kid's body, remember? Them little starfish monsters?" He turned and leant forward, his forehead almost touching Tony's. "It's no isolated incident; there'll be more. You know this, don't you?"

Despite his reservations, Tony nodded. "Fairlight'll be under military lockdown, won't it? And the presence of you and your…*comrade* over there tells me it's already underway…"

The man gave a grim smile. "Got it in one, Mr Collins."

"So why are you willing to help me?"

The monobrow rose. "Because you're the only one who can stop it. If you don't get into the unit and find your daughter, what you saw in the school will be a playground fight in comparison."

"What d'you know about Rachel?" Tony's fingers snapped around the suit's neck. The Adam's apple protruded. "What's happening to her?"

He didn't see the blow coming, or the keys bunched in the left hand. His belly exploded and his vision clouded with red mist. The roller shutter rattled in its ratchets again as the suit threw him against it. A forearm pressed against his neck, and the face before him was calm, implacable. No longer anxious or frightened. Emotionless.

"What's happening to her will happen to all of us before long, *Mister* Collins." The voice was flat; only the intonation of Mister betrayed any anger in the man. "She's in Hell. And Hell is coming to us all."

The forearm snapped back, and Tony was free. He rubbed his chin, gingerly touched his windpipe, and winced at what was sure to be a bruise. "Hell? Bit melodramatic, pal. I don't think Quinn's much of a Satan, somehow."

"Quinn?" A humourless laugh. "That twat? He's in charge of *nothing*, mate! And as for Satan..." Now the smile became a grimace. "What's running that thing is worse than Satan. Much worse."

Tony thought the elbow was at his throat again, because he couldn't breathe.

"The military's sealing off all routes into the town now. Communications will be cut as soon as they've got their own comms links up and running."

"Haverton," Tony said, rubbing his throat. "Just like Haverton."

The suit nodded. "Just like Haverton. Because of Callum Hayes."

Tony's throat was forgotten as another, deeper pain struck him. Realisation was agony. "The Hayes kid is in the hospital, isn't he? And…"

"Yeah." The word was a snarl. "And it ain't enough to hold him. Bodily? Maybe. But that ain't good enough. You know what I'm talking about, don'tcha?"

Tony shook his head.

"That old boy you had a drink with last night. Jim." There was anger on the kid's face, and now Tony realised why the face looked familiar.

"What he did to my old man is just the start. The little fucker don't know what powers he's got – or rather, what power's using him."

And now Tony knew why he was being aided. He wondered if the kid would have offered help if his father wasn't in Fairlight. "Where's Jim being held?"

"I dunno. He told me about a place they held 'im in when he were young. Said he always had nightmares o' going back there."

Fear returned to the kid's eyes; fear not for himself, but his father, and the unknown horrors he was enduring. A fear Tony understood all too well. "I'll do what I can, mate. If I can get my daughter out, I'll try and get your old man as well. But…he looked in a pretty bad way."

The kid smiled faintly, understanding the implication. "I know. Do what you can, yeah?"

A place they held him in when he was young. Tony remembered the cod-like skin and the ancient scars of Jim's childhood stay and shuddered. "Where will he be? The original unit isn't there anymore, is it?"

"Oh, it's there all right! It's just been hidden."

"Hidden where?" Tony knew his voice had risen, but he didn't care. *"What the fuck is that place?"*

Jim's son reached into his pocket and retrieved a laminated plastic card with a lanyard. He held it out to Tony by the canvas strap and said, "That'll get you access to the Acute Ward. And beyond."

Tony snatched the card and untwisted the lanyard. Beneath the name and rank of the counter-terrorism officer the unsmiling features of Jim's son stared back at him. Tony's jaw went slack.

"You've gotta be shitting me." He almost handed it back. "You're gonna need this, aren't you?"

"No. The squad I'm in will be the last one into the unit; and we'll only be there once the town is pacified."

"Pacified? What the fuck does that mean?"

The face was impassive. "It means that come dawn the town of Fairlight will no longer exist."

Tony stared at him. He couldn't speak. Now he knew what was in that case the two suits had carried. Why they were so nervous.

"Protocol 15," the young officer said in a sickened tone of voice. "The final answer to the Orpheus Project. Just in case they couldn't be contained, destruction: destroy the host before the invader gets a firm grip." He glanced to the left once more, then. "Hidden under the guise of a terrorist attack.

Justifies the lockdown, see. I really gotta go now, Mr Collins. Get to the hospital as soon as y'can, 'cos before nightfall no one's leaving Fairlight town. *No one.*"

"You said they were going to pick up the teacher," Tony managed. "Where will they take her?"

"Forget her, Mr Collins. Just think o' yourself, and your little girl." He turned on his heel, was about to walk away when he halted.

"You should prioritise, but you wanna know what's behind the door, don'tcha? Fair do's." He reached in his pocket and pulled out a key ring. He rifled through the keys, selected one, and peeled it away from the ring. He tossed it to Tony and without a further word, turned and walked briskly away.

Only when the noise of the explosion reached the side street did Jim Dawson's son break into a run.

CHAPTER TWENTY-THREE

Rachel Collins felt the darkness press on her eyelids; it was a physical presence now. The sight of blood no longer alarmed her, nor did the pulsating of the open wounds in her arms. Weariness descended on her, as cloying and oppressive as the black clouds gathered above the Oratory on the headland. The unconsciousness promised would not be that of chemically induced sleep, but the oblivion of darkness triumphant.

The memory of her dream on the hellish shoreline with Callum Hayes and his Triskelions told her this.

*Must resist. Keep eyes open...*she slumped, felt nothing beneath her feet. Concrete or grass, she didn't know. Darkness tunnelled her vision; two ever-decreasing circles on the outside world. A flash of blue-grey, then green. Water and earth, she thought. Her remaining vision turned green, and freshly-mown grass, damp from last night's rain, filled her nostrils. She inhaled, determined to take this last pleasant taste of earth with her before she woke to the Hell of Callum Hayes's nightmare shores.

But why am I moving? There was something holding her, pushing her upright. A smell of tuna and kippers, then a flash of mousy brown hair and white T-shirt came into her diminished view. *Who is this? Gillian?*

Gillian. Had to be; no one else was strong enough to hold her, surely? *Okay, in good hands now. Patch me up, blood transfusion, right as rain...then you can take me to Daddy. Daddy is here, isn't he?*

She heard Callum Hayes's voice now, singing that song

about hospitals curing while prisons bring the pain. She whimpered, and her mind's eye hinted at the black seashore with its harvest of bone shards. She sensed the hunger of those three-limbed creatures, an alien longing that went beyond desire for proteins and carbohydrates; a hunger for her very essence, her being.

*Dad…*She pictured his face: the strong, concerned features that masked his own pain and anguish; the smile at her achievements and pleasures in school; the tears in his eyes when he buried Mum; the anger in those same eyes when she'd been threatened by a gang of lads on her way home from a party. It was that anger that stayed with her – the look of pure rage and almost unnatural fury that rarely showed above his surface calm.

A hiss. The darkness retreated. Callum Hayes's singing faltered, and a strange keening like the hissing of tyres and plaintive call of a vixen for her mate marked the frustration of the Triskelions when they sensed her essence was denied them.

Fat blobs of liquid splashed her face. The smell of salt water and rain mingled with copper. Strange. Where was she? Must be at the seaside. That metallic smell – rusty railings on the breakwater, maybe.

Pressure on her cheeks. She winced as the pressure became a pinch, then a tug. Her vision cleared, and the two penny-sized discs of sight expanded. A girl's face stared down at her, impassive. Roaring filled Rachel's ears, so she couldn't hear the words, but she saw the girl's lips mouth *Rachel. Come back.*

Come back? That was odd. She wasn't going anyway, was she? And who was this girl? Behind her were steel-grey clouds, blurring the division between sky and sea, save for a cloud black as night that roiled and gyrated in the motionless sky.

The aroma of sea air was accompanied by the unmistakeable smell of smoke. But Rachel, coming slowly to consciousness, had something else to consider. The blobs of liquid she had taken for rain hadn't fallen from the sky. The clouds threatened rain, but they had yet to break.

With each second that passed, Rachel felt stronger, more focussed. Sensation returned, but there was no pain in her forearms. She felt calm, clear-headed. Her senses were enhanced; the moist grass against the nape of her neck felt like living creatures caressing her skin with sensuous, silky tentacles; the breeze brought the usual scents of salt water and grass, but they were much richer, enhanced odours than before. She didn't have time to enjoy them, though – the smell of blood, burning fuel and smoke overpowered them all.

She suspected her eyesight would be enhanced, and that's why she was scared to open her eyes further. The blood smelled strongest, because it was closest. *What will I see?* She knew what had happened, knew what Ant had done. How did she know it would bring her back? And how had she managed to cut herself?

She sat up, opened her eyes, and kept them focussed on her forearms before taking in anything else. The smoke was a dark background to the incredible horror before her eyes.

Blood trickled down her forehead and onto her cheeks; the blood Ant had spilled on her first attempt. Perhaps the younger girl had misjudged the angle or her target had moved.

No, not target...transfusion point? The fish mouth-like opening and closing of her wounds looked just as obscene as before she passed out. Yellow and white streaks of fat and tissue, black clots and red trickles – all as before. But this time, with something worse.

The wounds were fed by *Ant's* blood, dribbling from ragged gashes in her wrists. Rachel's mouth opened and closed, in time with the gulping motions of her wrists wounds. In time with the opening and closing of Ant's mouth. Ant's eyes were closed, a frown of concentration creasing her small features, as though this barbaric transfusion was taking all her mental energy.

Rachel moaned in disbelief, watching the blood – *feeling* the blood – fill the holes in her wrists; each dribble a burst of pleasure, like a splash of rainwater on the tongue of one dying of thirst. Each drop of the precious fluid not so much feeding Rachel's veins so much as *absorbed* by her flesh.

And with the absorption, the power. The heightened senses, the vitality, the strength. Every cell of her body cried out for more, hungering for this wondrous, ecstatic essence. With more she could take on the world. She could escape, if she wished. She could *fight!* Callum Hayes and his darkness would be nothing against her and this power…

Her heightened hearing amplified Ant's moan, turned it from a soft whimper of discomfort to a wail of despair. She gritted her teeth and fought against the desire to drain the girl, knew the energy she received had a price to be paid: knew the cost was Ant's life.

She thrust her arms against Ant's, forcing the girl to open her eyes and lose her concentration. Their eyes met, glacial blue and Atlantic grey becoming one as their bloods mingled.

Mingled. Rachel pressed harder, forcing her wrists against

Ant's. Now the blood was no longer given or received. It was *shared*. And their eyes – the soul windows – stared and reflected each other, like mirrors angled against the other and showing an infinite reflection of the energy that burned between them. An energy that commingled, fused, became visible to them alone. A light flared: a light brighter than the sun, yet whose burn was colder than ice. Colder than the darkness that threatened to rise from the shadow world Callum Hayes heralded.

Both girls screamed, but not with pain. It was the scream of knowledge and despair, for both knew then the price of their power. The self-harm, the pain of mutilation, was only the beginning. Behind Ant's thrashing ponytail, Rachel saw the smoke on the headland with heightened vision, knew the darkness it hid. A darkness that saw them, recognised them and the power they held.

A darkness that rushed towards them like a moth to a flame, but not with self-destruction on its mind. Blackness painted the sky, the grey of the clouds a mere primer for the darkness that drenched sea, land and sky in its hunger for the bearers of the Light. The darkness enveloped them, stifled their breathing; then swallowed them, and the Light was extinguished.

I'm back. The scarlet of the shadow world's ocean was deeper, more intense; a sea fret of human blood added a dark energy to the waves that sucked hungrily on the broken skulls and shards of bone that comprised the shore, using the marine ossuary as a foothold to encroach further.

The hissing was louder, more of a shriek, when the waves came in contact with her feet. A cry of pain, of being burned. She saw the scarlet trails recoil from her, retreat into the mass, and smiled.

For steam rose from her trainers with each contact. It filled her nostrils with a scent of crematoria, of butchery, but it was sweet because it was the smell of victory over the darkness. *It can be harmed, so it can be defeated!*

Light-headedness took her and she stared into the puckered, burned edge wound of what passed for a sun and grinned. The red hole in the sky no longer had the power to dismay her. She could smell, hear, feel more strongly than before, and the energy from Ant still flooded her veins –

Ant! What's happened to her? The realisation took some of the triumphant spirit from her, and she twisted, searching the shoreline for her companion. The waves hissed again, triumphantly, as she turned back and waded through the bones, heading inland; grateful for her departure, so they could advance unimpeded.

Rachel didn't care. Knowing she had the power to banish the waters of darkness was enough for now; whether she could stem the entire tide was another matter.

Whatever power she had, she knew it was finite. *And temporary,* another thought said with a hiss. She ignored it, dismissed it with contempt. Nothing lasts forever, but the power coursing her veins had the potential for...

"Something wonderful. Something *forever*," she yelled over her shoulder. The ocean's hiss became a scream and Rachel shouted in triumph.

The mystery wasn't resolved, and she suspected it never

would be. Her powers of healing were not confined to her own body; Quinn had said Julia was "cured" or "returned" when Rachel had fed the mower – but this was something else. Had Ant been waiting for her, or did she not even know herself what happened when their bloods mingled?

Ant was the key. But where the hell was she? "Ant! Can you hear me?"

Her voice was loud, carried across the ossuary shore like thunder, and the dark ocean appeared to hesitate in its advance. But the sea wall soaked her words and she knew they carried no further. This was the barrier, and Ant was beyond it. She hesitated, remembering what came from that direction the last time she was here. *I have to climb it, regardless of what's on the other side.*

The bones were less tightly-packed, the footing more treacherous: a scree slope that shifted like quicksand beneath her feet and threatened to send her plummeting to the depths. She tripped several times, felt cruel lacerations on her bare thighs from the skeletal fragments; but when she fell forward and put her bleeding hands out to protect herself from the fall even the bones screeched and became still.

She suspected it was more than blood that leaked from her palms – and like blood, this power was finite, could be drained and render her lifeless if she lost more. The dark sea roared in her ears, the ocean of blood advancing on a flood tide that now suspected her weakness and advanced more confidently. The blood slopped in the wells created by her stumbling, creating rock pools which filled with a multitude of minute creatures that chittered and crooned in alien tongues.

The sea wall was soft, made of damp earth that stank of the

grave and, when she disturbed the lower section, wriggled with worms that had not fed in ages. The carved steps were femurs, the same length of her own, and she tried not to think how many thighs of long-dead girls her own age she would have to climb over to get to the other side.

They provided poor footholds: with each downward step they cracked and splintered, her trainers' soles tearing and lacerating as they traversed the razor pieces. She felt blood well in her footwear, and only when it spilled onto the grave soil did the earth harden and allow her purchase.

The wind was hot, filling her nostrils with the smell of crematoria and her hair with bodily ashes, but she refused to curse her enhanced senses that enabled her to smell every atom of human flesh that had gone to the fires while its owner screamed in agony, sense the life that had once inhabited every fragment of scorching tissue that burned her neck.

She focussed on her ascent. *One step at a time. Each step, you rise out of the pit of Hell. Each step, you're closer to Ant. One step more –*

The last step made a concerted effort to halt her, to freeze around her ankle like cement and hold her immobile until the crimson tide could take her. She sensed the grave worms penetrate the holes in her trainer, felt their cold, greasy questing in her torn flesh. Her palms tightened on the parapet of the wall, which hardened and turned to clay and crumbled in her hands. Her balance shifted; the black skyline jumped and she fell backward, the clay grip on her leg impassive, her ankle about to twist and break and release her tumbling to the ossuary shore, the one living piece of bone in the shale graveyard…

The clay of the parapet became dust, and her hands clutched empty air.

CHAPTER TWENTY-FOUR

Callum Hayes cried out at the jerking agony in both palms. It forced his eyes open, made him abandon the vision granted to his mind's eye by the Grace of the Presence. Where he had seen Quinn's trembling shoulders hunched before the open portal that exited the Acute Ward, he saw the padded vinyl of his own cell door. Where he had seen the darkness beyond the Acute Ward – and the blessed things it held – he now saw blinding fluorescent lighting that seared his eyes like a cauterising wound. Burning to heal. Burning to seal and blind.

Burning to deny me! "I'm not afraid of the light!" he screamed, and forced his eyelids to remain open, unblinking, to prove the point. But it wasn't the glare of clinical, artificial white light that had his eyes watering, blinking, drenching his cheeks. It was the agony in his palms.

It was the reverse of the sweet agony he had experienced in the church; the dark stigmata had brought as much pleasure as pain, whereas the agony he suffered now was beyond endurance. He crossed his arms over his chest – keeping his palms free - and rolled forward, his forehead dipping into the pool of black liquid cast from his hands.

He smelled it before he felt it. Rank, nauseating, like putrefied roadkill, but there was nothing in his stomach to vomit. *It's my blood!* his now-terrified mind screamed above the pain, and that realisation chilled him as much as the separation pained him.

He rocked back and forth, keening with self-pity and pain. He tried to brace himself and surf each wave of pain as it approached, but it overwhelmed him, had him gasping for breath with each successive battering. When it began to abate, to become shallower and more bearable, he steeled himself to look at his hands.

The black skeins had gone, save for a few torn shreds that clung to the meatier parts of his palms. They were stiff and unyielding, all life gone. The black holes of his self-induced stigmata stared back at him, and with eyes recovering from the retina-flash, each ragged circle of yellow-white fat and mottled pink flesh seemed to be an eye that burned into his own with a light – and judgement - that surely came from God Himse-

NO! Callum ground the heels of his palms into his eyelids in a circular motion, just like when he had suffered hay fever and the itching became unbearable. Just like then, the sense of relief was instantaneous, pleasurable, even knowing that relief would be paid for by hours of burning pain afterwards.

But it was something else. For Callum Hayes, it was an act of faith. He refused to believe the herald-creatures had gone, even though the sudden, wrenching agony told him they had been severed from his physical body just as surely as if surgical steel had sliced them away from flesh.

Concentrate. Feed them with your tears. They'll come back, surely. He sobbed with the thought, terrified his doubt would prevent their return. He wept, feeling his eyeballs itch with each tear shed. He ground the heels of the palms into his eyeballs harder, countering the itching with more furious rubbing.

*More rubbing, more pain later. That's the price...*oh, the relief. The beautiful, ecstatic feeling of relief. His eyeballs continued to water, and his vision was a rippling stage curtain of heavy velvet, a scarlet veil that would surely lift again soon, and allow the show to resume…

Oh yes! Further rubbing, more violent, more strenuous; his tears mingled with sweat from his palms, and another fluid.

Now the skin around his eye sockets burned with friction: the pain of sunburn, and the grinding of hot, slippery flesh against rough, exposed bone. He didn't hear the tearing and shredding of his eyeballs, pulled along the optical orbit and popped and smeared against his cheekbones, but he felt it. It was an explosion of light and darkness, the scarlet curtain torn to shreds by a cast of claws and weeping blood and entrails onto the stage.

Oh yes! The blackness, shifting and so erotically sinuous, emerged from stage left and stage right in the familiar shapes he knew so well. He opened his mind's eye and allowed the creatures to return.

Quinn's fingers froze on the keycard. Like a totem, a talisman – or maybe even a comfort blanket – if he held on to it tightly enough and wished really hard, he would be home, and none of what he saw before him would be real.

But his fingers refused to obey. Like the rest of his body, they were frozen, rigid, with the sight before him. The resignation and sense of relief that came with the self-righteous knowledge earlier evaporated like superheated blood. The question remained, however. *What are you doing to him, Bethan? Why is he such a threat?* Whatever it was, nothing could justify this.

The earth tremor scattered fresh dust and sandstone, and the door shook in its frame. The handle vibrated painfully in his other hand, and his head spun. Behind him, the lights flickered in their ceiling mounts, and he heard shattering sounds: beakers and chemicals shaken in their secure cabinets, their vessels broken. Metal scratched tiles, and something told him the cots had come free from their floor mountings. A groan of relief came from one of the occupants, a cackle from another, and then a mixture of the two from something else.

Something. The word throbbed in his mind, ceased to have any meaning. *Something* couldn't describe the horror before him. *Something* meant nothing when his eyes took in the sight of Bethan and what she had done to Jim.

Jim Dawson. The reports Quinn had managed to pull from the database were sketchy at best. Scans of the man's admission records and doctor notes from the 1950s. Cursory, blunt, and incomplete, yet so obvious in the omissions. *Data Unavailable*, and *Incomplete File* were the slogans on the blank pages.

He had almost smiled at the blatant censorship, and was looking forward to finally meeting the man in question, one of the first self-harmers Fairlight had taken in. Of course, with all the other crises on his watch, Quinn hadn't pressed too hard to discover the identity and history of Fairlight's newest admission; he had even believed the assurances that Dawson would be sent to an outside, civilian hospital once the emergency wounds had been treated.

He'd forgotten. It was only Bethan's evasiveness that had reminded him. That and her early visits to Callum's cell and whatever instructions she had received from him. Now Quinn saw why she had been so evasive.

The eyes were the only things remaining of Jim Dawson that could be described as human. The despair and suffering within surely belonged to no other creature that walked this earth. There was a child-like innocence in them, a *why me?* combined with a soul-drained look that spoke of one who had been reunited with a nightmare he had long thought he'd escaped.

The lights flickered and dimmed, sparing Quinn the full sight of Jim Dawson's body; beyond the Acute Ward, inhabitants were reliant on the old 1950s electrics amid the Victorian red brick walls and chipped floor tiles. Nothing was stored here; no one was treated here. That was the given reason not to update the facilities.

Shadows leapt from the corners and joined the darkness that danced from beneath the soul-drained eyes of Jim Dawson. The lights returned and the shadows retreated, but the darkness of Fairlight's newest – and oldest – inmate remained.

There was no more blood to come from the abdominal wound. To Quinn's eyes, struggling to cope with the varying light, the gash in the pale flesh looked like a mouth, the neat, surgically-sliced edges a pair of puckered lips that opened and closed in a jerky, spastic fashion, a landed fish gasping for oxygen.

But instead of taking in air, this mouth was *feeding*. The lights flared with a fresh burst of electricity before the overhead light bulb shattered, plunging Quinn and Jim's obscene living corpse into further darkness.

Quinn was thankful. Even though the darkness left him

exposed to the woman who had reduced Jim to this, he was spared the sight of the further feeding of Jim's abdomen.

Now he could believe that what he saw were merely intestines spilling from a wound Bethan had inflicted, rather than pieces of meat cut disappearing into the hole.

Much better, he thought. There was a flash of reflected light – darker, grimier light from further down the corridor - as Bethan raised the dripping bone saw and ran towards him.

CHAPTER TWENTY-FIVE

To the Lighthouse. The battered copy of Virginia Woolf's book faced Karen from the recent-returns trolley. She had pushed the trolley from the aisle that led to the Local Studies section when the title caught her eye. She shuddered and pushed the trolley harder. With squeaking castors protesting at their lack of oil, the front of the trolley collided with the unattended PC station. The flat screen vibrated and the screen saver disappeared, revealing the Dorset County Council logo and the smaller Fairlight Library Services icon beneath. A mouse cursor jerked to the left, then the right. Karen stared at it silently, then glanced at the trolley. Woolf's novel had slipped and fallen open and now hung on the shelf. She felt a disapproving glare from Sally Adams, the sole librarian on duty and turned to stare her out. For once, the old cow averted her eyes and continued tapping on her keyboard instead of giving Karen the usual disapproving glare she had come to expect from the Fairlight locals.

There's a connection, Karen. Between Fairlight and the lighthouse – the hospital and the town. Rachel knew of it, but not what it fully is.

The scans of the Oratory. The Pharos. She looked at the desultory selection of mouldering books in the Local Studies bay. On the lower shelf were a series of plastic magazine holders, from which faded pamphlets drooped their open leaves like wilting plants. There was nothing recent there, she recalled, but checked anyway. *Cold Harbour – the Secret History of Fairlight* by Philip Lotson was pretty much the only comprehensive study of the town and not a very good one; a small press publication whose shoddy production values was complimented by its appalling editing. Still, beggars and choosers…

Gone. *Shit.* Who the hell would've taken that out? She remembered his book signing at the library a few years back. The man had looked embarrassed, distinctly uncomfortable with the hostile reaction from the locals and his would-be customers. He couldn't wait to get back to Cambridge, even left his unsold copies behind. Karen couldn't remember what happened to them, because the publisher had gone bust soon after. *And what I'd give for a copy now.* She glanced at the monitor once more.

She thought of Tony Collins, his fascination with the roller shutter door down Silver Street – the back of the Old Customs House. Ocean Wave Direct…yeah, what had happened to them? The library was served by the council's ISP, so maybe, just maybe, their link was still operational…

Sod it. Won't hurt to check. She pushed the trolley away once more, wincing as the Woolf book fell to the floor with a dull thud and a cloud of dust. She picked it up and tossed it back onto the trolley while seating herself at the PC.

Okay, Ocean Wave Direct. Let's see what you're up to these days…

Tony Collins fumbled the key in the lock. Christ, this was an old one. The Yale was thin and bent, threatening to snap in the lock if he twisted too hard or too quickly – which, given the recalcitrance of the roller shutter, was all too tempting...

Take your time. The explosion on the harbour front had diverted all attention, had the few sightseers and locals running towards the spectacle. Tony smelled powder and smoke, felt the oppression in the air, but knew, just knew, his focus had to be here and what he saw the night he had punched the door and Rachel had been committed to Fairlight.

What do you see when you cut yourself? "I don't know. What *do* you see when you cut yourself?" He gritted his teeth and gently shook the key in the lock.

Protocol 15. The final answer to the Orpheus Project. "Yeah, well. That's just not making any sense." God, surely this lock had to give. Or would that be pacified along with the town?

Time's running out. And more quickly than Jim's kid expected, Tony thought, grunting with satisfaction as the lock gave. Flakes of rust fell like Chernobyl snow, and he brushed them off with a grimace.

The roller shutter slid up its ratchets remarkably smoothly considering the pounding he'd given it last night; then he remembered the clean, gleaming metal and realised only the lock had not been replaced. Every muscle in his body tensed, ready to flee from the snake-like apparition with its luminous eyes which would surely be within...

Gloom greeted him, and nothing more. There was little in the way of darkness or threatening shadows. That'll change when night falls, he thought with a shudder. He took a step forward; his boots made no sound on the concrete floor slab. He took a deep breath, puzzled as to the lack of scent. At the very least, there should have been –

Dust. He'd been in enough warehouses – working and unmanned – to know dust was a constant companion. There was no stale smell of an unaired warehouse, either. When the roller shutter was replaced, the floor had been swept clean. As his eyes adjusted to the gloom, he saw the raised lids of chest freezers, open to the roof and inviting him to peer within.

Each was empty, save for a few puddles of meltwater. He dipped a finger and held it to his nose. Nothing, just a faint scent of shellfish. It triggered a memory, a distant recall of him and Becky, eating somewhere…He turned and stared through the doorway into the side street beyond, and tried to remember where the seafood restaurant had been.

Tony stroked the keys absent-mindedly. *Dawson.* So why the hell were military police interested in a disused fish market? Or rather, what were they covering up?

"And why," he whispered, "did you give me the keys? What're you expecting me to find?" The silent gaping chest freezers swallowed his words.

Ocean Wave Direct, he thought. That was what Karen had called the company who'd last occupied the building. What was the connection?

He sniffed his finger again. Shellfish. *C'mon, something else. What is it?* He turned on his heel and caught his elbow on the corner of the chest freezer.

"Ah, *fuck!*" Pain swamped him; his vision clouded. He was aware of something moving, a huge open jaw closing: the lid of the chest freezer slammed down on his arm as a shark or crocodile would, pulling him down into the depths where only darkness and death waited…and two shining lights.

Glowing spheres that stared impassively, just as they had

done last night.

"Good God," Karen said, oblivious to the *shh!* noises from the library users. Her eyes were locked on the screen, her jaw slack with horror at what she read. Now she knew why Ocean Wave Direct had closed so quickly. Bankrupt after one too many lawsuits.

Food poisoning. Not fatal, but potentially as dangerous as salmonella or lysteria – Ocean Wave Direct were fortunate that their oldest customer had been in his forties, and none of the affected had weak immune systems – a dead OAP and there would have been hell to pay. As it was, forty-eight cases – twelve of them resulting in hospitalisation – were all linked within a seven-day period and the same geographical location.

She scanned the names, noted the scattered areas of the UK they had come from and took the infection back to. *The restaurant came very highly recommended; we thought it a perfect way to round off a romantic weekend.*

At the time, I thought it was the best shellfish I'd ever tasted. Guess some things are too good to be true. Never again.

I never liked fish, but the missus can't get enough. No, I had a steak, so I guess that's why I was okay.

It was heaven going down, but hell coming back up. What I spewed up stank like a dead crab.

Where the hell did they get these things from, anyway? Local delicacy, my arse! Do they dump plutonium on the shores of Fairlight?

The restaurant and fish market in the picture were the same

ones Tony had spoken of earlier. And yet…that was odd. She checked the dates again.

The cases had come to light fifteen years ago. The seven day period peaked on the twenty-first of June.

Midsummer, she thought. *Now why's that significant?* Something else had happened on that date, something that had – eventually – made national headlines. Something forgotten and erased from the town's history long before she had come to live in Fairlight; only now did faint recollections of the matter attempt to reveal themselves in the ebb tide of her memory.

God, the bloody connection was slow. She tapped the elderly mouse on the desk irritably, waiting for the image of the shellfish to load. The trackball made a rattling sound. She sighed, opened another tab and typed into the search engine once more.

Nothing else came up on the Ocean Wave Direct front, but the image of Tony Collins standing alone in the backstreets awaiting the approach of those two strange men wouldn't leave her. She pulled her mobile from her bag and checked for messages. Half an hour had passed, and he had not texted or rang. She glanced at the phone's screen again, and her eyes narrowed.

No signal bar showed. *Don't come for me unless I call you. I'll be at the library as soon as I can: just sit tight.*

"Yeah, right." She replaced her phone and stood, shouldering her bag. There was nothing she could do here. Just retrace her steps and head back down to Silver Street. If all was well, she'd meet him coming in the opposite direction. If not…

She was about to close the browser down when the picture

she had waited for filled the screen. She froze, and the bag slipped from her shoulder.

Local delicacy. New shellfish. *How the hell could anyone eat that?*

Its shell was peeled away, inverted, and placed next to the exposed meat. Pink-white flesh threaded with a fine tracery of scarlet reflected in the glossy black underside of the mollusc's carapace. At least the legs had been removed. No one would eat it if they knew how closely it was related to the things that had burst from Stefan Fleischer this morning.

She closed her eyes and was back in the classroom: the razor-sharp tips of the creatures' limbs scraping like butcher hooks on the floor; the impossible speed with which they spun down the corridor; the relentless, destructive fury with which they broke through the door.

She opened her eyes to see the room spinning; she waited for the bookshelves to come crashing down on her and slam her to the ground, holding her prisoner until those *things* could claim her…

The crack of thunder brought her back to reality. She started, staggered and fell onto the PC station, her fingernails snagging on the keyboard, her elbows knocking the monitor with its hateful image over. She staggered back, thankful she could no longer see the image of the larger shuriken-type creature – an adult? – and then something else claimed her attention.

That wasn't thunder. The dark grey plume visible in the west-facing window was too animated, too energetic, to be storm clouds. She walked slowly, everything else forgotten, and placed her trembling hands on the chipped wooden frame.

The column of grey smoke thickened, darkened, and she saw orange flames licking the base, stretching to the roof finials of the old Customs House. It reminded her briefly of the flames that wiped out the alien creatures birthed from Stefan Fleischer, until the smell hit her: along with the aroma of burning concrete and wood, there was the unmistakeable stench of cooking meat. Burning flesh. The direction from which she and Tony had come in her Volvo…

The orange flames reflected against a sheet of corrugated metal, like a roller shutter door-

Silver Street!

"Tony!" she cried, and the black plume thickened, darkened the skies with early night; the only illumination came from the tongues of fire that greedily consumed the last place she had seen Tony Collins.

CHAPTER TWENTY-SIX

Tom Dawson saw the flames spewing from the beer garden of the Day Gone Down and felt the weight of the world on his shoulders. His ears rang with the explosion, his eyes streaming with grey smoke that swirled into his face.

There was only one other man besides himself who could have activated the explosive device in the briefcase – and only one reason why he would.

Rawlings knows. He's on to us.

Tom's hand fell to his side, the mobile phone now worse than useless. The call was cut, the signal destroyed, and it was now too late to warn Tony Collins not to meet him in the town centre. It would also lead Rawlings to his own location.

He had the back open and the battery disconnected when a figure emerged from the wrecked pub, shrouded in wreaths of grey, swirling smoke. It staggered, its centre of gravity upset, and the widened, shocked eyes met Tom's. There was no recognition of his partner, just a continued, vacant stare that slowly moved to the scorched stump where his arm used to be. The arm that held the briefcase containing the bomb.

The smell of melted fat and burnt meat ravaged Tom's nostrils and forced a scream from his throat. His partner's eyes flickered in recognition before glazing.

Tom turned and ran before the body hit the floor. The sun blinded him, made the thronged passers-by a blurred mass of something that approached humanity. He pushed past them blindly, ignoring the hisses of reproach and mumbled curses. The seagulls, momentarily shocked by the bomb blast, resumed their screeching and took to the streets once more, following the source of the smell, its promise of food.

Burnt meat remained in Tom's nostrils; not even the stink of decayed marine growth and old diesel shifted it, and by the time he reached the end of the harbour and hit the sloping road leading out of Fairlight, the fresh tang of salt air and roadside flowers made themselves known.

He crouched by the hedgerow to catch his breath. Sweat trickled down his forehead.

With that came a decision. The urge to leave Fairlight harbour was an instinctive one, born of panic, but now the realisation Rawlings would have listened to his conversation with Collins hit home. Hard.

He loosened his tie and slid it over his head, pocketed it, and glanced up, following the hedgerow that curved and ascended with the pitted road leading out of the town. He didn't dare look back. The sound of sirens and roaring diesel engines had joined the screams, but they weren't just those of the emergency services.

Rawlings started early. This was fucking planned!

Hoping the ash from the bomb blast had sufficiently darkened his white shirt, he got to his feet and continued running, away from the military lockdown. He spared a brief thought for the man investigating the Old Customs House. *Hope my keycard comes in handy, pal. I gotta feeling I won't be needing it again...*

The darkness surrounding Tony Collins was a physical entity.

He felt it caress his hair with cloying fingers, slide over his skin with reptilian grace; smelled the stink of the grave in his nostrils, tasted death and crematoria ash on his tongue.

What filled his vision was not so cloying or oppressive. The dark flickered in diagonal bands, alternating layers of shadow. Dark grey, then purple-blue, then pure black.

Waves, like an incoming tide at night, accompanied by a wind that carried the physical darkness.

Neither was part of the four walls of the storeroom. The sloping concrete slab had gone; he lay on brittle, dead grass that stung his cheek and rock-hard sand, twenty paces from the shifting tides of the impossibly black sea under a scarlet sky.

A twin flash of light in his peripheral vision, like a close-set pair of headlamps, reflected on the sea, and the dark waters paused in mid-roil, as though sentient and hesitant of the source of the light. Tony pushed against the dead ground, wincing in pain at the sharp detritus that dug into his palms. He turned his head to follow the illumination but saw nothing.

It's gone.

He looked at his bleeding palms and jolted from his semi-prone position when he saw what drew the blood, all thoughts of the mysterious light momentarily forgotten.

The cause wasn't brittle, dried husks of grass stems. He pulled the sharp thorns from his palms and stared in horror at the white bone beneath his blood.

Shards of bones, blackened by the ash and grey sand. They crunched under his shifting body and he stared out to sea, his jaw dropping at the sight of the shingle. Not a stone or pebble amongst them – everything was bone. Broken bones, crushed, shattered, pulverised, but a fragment of cranium here, a section of jawbone there, informed him they were human remains.

He got to his feet in a haze of nausea, plucking the tiny shards from his palms and wiping his hands on his jeans. He took a deep breath – filled his lungs with noxious fumes of crematoria and scorched flesh – and released it in a shudder. The black tide ebbed, revealing more shattered bones, coated in liquid darkness.

He turned in disgust, fighting the urge to vomit. A dull ache throbbed in his skull, and he remembered the chest freezer's lid that crashed on his skull.

Unconscious. This had to be a dream. But why did he still feel pain?

Behind him the shore sloped, became a sharp incline whose shadows reluctantly revealed larger, less broken bones in its centre - like a crude staircase made of thighbones - and terminated in what appeared to be a man-made wall.

All thoughts of climbing it to escape the dark shore left him the moment he realised the thicker shadows at the base of the incline formed the outline of a person. Someone had been here before him, someone who had tried to climb the grisly incline, failed and fell back. Unconscious, or dead? Was there any difference in this terrible place?

The torso and head was hidden by a tumbled heap of bone fragments. Grey combat trouser legs were visible, covered in dried blood from scratches, and the trainers on the feet were disturbingly familiar. The desire to vomit was replaced with a sinking feeling in his stomach, roiling like the black sea behind him. He walked toward the prone figure.

"Rachel?"

There was no reaction, no movement.

"Rachel!" He broke into a run, the ossuary shore shifting noisily beneath him, as though he ran in a quarry of pottery fragments. They felt alive; grasping carpals attempting to trip him, to stop him getting to his daughter. He trod harder, stamping with grim determination, until he reached Rachel.

Tears blurred his vision, made the bones coating his daughter's face and chest squirm with new life. He sobbed as he threw them to one side, stared at the unconscious girl.

There was a gash on her right temple, and the bone shard that caused the cut glistened in its scarlet coat. He plucked it with shaking fingers and caressed her matted blonde hair with his free hand.

"Rachel…can you hear me, darling?"

A soft murmur answered him. Closed eyes squinted, a frown causing the blood to flow more freely. He reached into his pocket, searching for a tissue. His fingers found the hard laminated plastic and lanyard of the access card the blond kid had given him.

No tissue. He wiped his fingers clean as best he could on his polo shirt and reached for her temple. Her skin was cold and clammy, the dried blood hardened into a scab. He left it. The freshly flowing blood, however, he could do something about. His fingers made contact, felt the warmth, the *life*, and his vision exploded with light.

Rachel's eyes opened, her frown replaced with a bewildered expression that momentarily turned to joy, recognition, then horror as the light shattered around both father and daughter.

Flame sheathed Tony's fingers, golden fire that burned, scorched, and shrivelled his fingers to charred stumps of bone. Behind him, bone shards littering the beach erupted into life, shining white and pure in the light. Even the black sea lightened, the oil-like waters momentarily translucent and allowing a brief glimpse of the horrors that dwelled within. Two saucer-shaped eyes stared at him, glowing with intensity - even stronger than the golden fire that had erupted from his daughter.

Tony felt hands on his shoulders, pulling or pushing - he wasn't sure which - and twisting his body. A female voice screamed at him.

Pain fired his skull, and the golden light faded, paled, took on the pallid gloom of the storeroom. Scarlet misted his vision, and warm liquid dribbled into his left eye. The pressure under his armpits intensified, dragging his body towards a different light, and he felt long nails digging into him.

A woman's nails. A woman's voice.

Not Rachel's.

"Tony," Karen Tyndall said.

Tony looked up, dazed. The golden light - sunlight, he realised — imparted an angular halo to the teacher crouched over him, but thin tendrils of smoke drifted past the doorway to Silver Street, and he knew he'd woken from one nightmare only to return to another.

But...Rachel. Is she alive? What the hell just happened? Then pain returned; this time to his head. He welcomed it, stared in disbelief at his fingers clenched on the lid of the chest freezer. Unburned. Undamaged. *Whole.* Blood marred the dirty white enamel, and his hand went to his forehead. His fingers came away damp and sticky.

Karen frowned at the gash. "I'll fix that later. Tony, that explosion...it had to be a bomb. We've got to get out of here."

"Damn right." He glanced at his surroundings. Just as they were before the explosion: faded white and green paint on the walls, cracked concrete floor slab with a myriad cracks and fissures – *were they all there, or did that explosion add a few more?* – and a battered door. "But not yet."

"The roads are filled with soldiers, for God's sake! They're putting up roadblocks – it's like bloody Ukraine out there!"

He stood, clutching her shoulder for support. He waited for the dizziness to pass before saying, "Exactly. How far will we get? We lay low, wait for nightfall."

Karen glanced over her shoulder. She took a deep breath, hesitated as though making a decision. Then she turned from him and strode to the roller shutter door's control panel. Agonised, eternal seconds passed before the corrugated metal descended and shut out the light. She leant against the door and began to shudder. Tony went to her. Hesitantly, he put a hand on her shoulder.

She stiffened, and Tony took his hand away. Now the daylight had been blocked out, the dank chill of the disused Customs House settled on them, but to Tony it was nothing compared to what he'd experienced moments before. The sounds of sirens and boots pounding concrete were muffled, felt distant.

"Karen, something happened when I clicked out. Something terrible, but…it gave me hope." He took the keycard from his pocket. The lanyard was cold and greasy with sweat, just as it had been on that black shore. He shuddered. "Something's happened to Rachel, but not in the way I feared."

She turned and fixed him with a raised, quizzical eyebrow. She listened in silence as he related his experiences.

"That light…I've never felt anything like it before. It didn't feel like any light I've known. Not sunlight, torchlight, fire…" he examined his unburned fingers and remembered the scorched, shrivelled stumps. "It burned and yet…it didn't. Does that make any sense?"

Karen sank to the floor. "No. But what does today?"

Tony nodded and sank to the floor. He rested his back against the shutter, which responded with a warning clatter. He put a hand around her shoulder. This time she didn't pull away.

"It was when I touched her blood…that was the moment the light flared." He stared at the cracks in the concrete. "But it was the fact that *my* blood was on my fingers when I did that… I don't know why that's significant, but it's the first solid piece of hope I've had since I landed in Fairlight." He passed her the keycard. "This is the second."

She studied the photograph and read the name on the laminated plastic. She passed it back to him. "That's one of the guys who carried the briefcase."

He nodded. "Jim Dawson's son. Seems like he's had a crisis of conscience."

"So why did he give you this? Won't he need it?" She shook her head. "Sounds like a trap."

"All he had to do was call in our position from here. No, my guess is he has a back-up card – or, if he was bluffing his employers, he'd planned to take a comrade's card and get access that way. It explains the explosion – it was a bomb. He said something about a protocol, closure for the Orpheus Project." He pocketed the card and pressed the heel of his hand against his temple.

"Hurting?"

"Not too bad now." He cocked his head, listening for sounds from the street. It was quiet. For now.

"Orpheus Project?" Karen said.

"He was a Greek god, wasn't he?"

"A prophet and a musician. And….best known for going into the Underworld to retrieve his dead wife. Here." She passed a Wet Wipe from her bag. "After what I read about the seafood stored here, I don't want you getting infected."

His eyebrows rose. "You found something?"

She pressed the wipe against his forehead and rubbed gently. She inspected the cotton, threw it away, and reached for another one. "There's a link between what attacked us this morning and what caused the food poisoning fifteen years ago."

He winced at the harsher action on his forehead. "Go on."

"The shellfish and the starfish-things from Stefan." She leaned back, inspected his cleaned wound, and then gazed into his eyes. Dread settled in his stomach at the sight of her hollow eyes. He knew what was coming.

"They're one and the same, Tony. Those things were being sold by Ocean Wave Direct fifteen years ago. Food."

The room spun. The concrete floor turned a ninety-degree angle and threatened to send him plummeting. A rhythmic pounding beat the air, like a helicopter's rotor blades. He gasped, and clutched Karen's hand.

Fifteen years ago. The night he and Becky had made love, right after consuming…

"Fifteen, Tony. That's the same age as all the kids who are…"

Who are in Fairlight. The pounding was louder. Wind rattled the roller shutter, and Karen started. He kept his hand clasped over hers. "Go on. Tell me."

She hesitated, then squeezed his hand. There was more than concern there. "People came from all over the country, when Fairlight was a holiday town. Ate here, went back to whichever parts of the UK they had homes in…

"I'm certain every child who has been admitted to Fairlight Hospital, every teenager who has self-harmed, have parents who ate the shellfish."

He raised his head and stared at the door leading to the office. There wouldn't be anything there. Whoever was behind all this would have ensured all aspects of the Ocean Wave Direct incident were hidden or destroyed.

But what if…

He stood, his hand still in hers. The pounding was louder, the wind stronger.

Karen's grip was equally tight. She turned, pulling them both from the roller shutter, and he realised the pounding wasn't in his head – she heard it as well. The draught rattling the corrugated steel wasn't wind.

Helicopter.

"Don't panic. It's obvious they'd bring in air support, to cover the fields and keep an eye on people escaping that way…"

He had to shout to make himself heard. The helicopter engines drowned his voice.

No point in taking chances, though. He pointed to the office door, motioned her towards it. She nodded, white-faced, and clutched her bag tightly to her shoulder.

*Keys...*he searched the ground by the chest freezer. *That's where I dropped them, isn't it? So where the bloody hell are they?*

He froze when the shaft of fluorescent light spilled over him. He wouldn't need the keys after all.

The office door opened fully, spilling more light into the stockroom. The figure sat on the swivel chair dangled the key fob mockingly with his left hand. The right held a SIG-Sauer automatic pistol, aimed at Tony Collins's face.

The roller shutter clattered into life once more. Rotor wash swept litter and sand into the stockroom, accompanied by the rapid movement of booted feet.

CHAPTER TWENTY-SEVEN

Rachel Collins felt a mixture of despair and hope. The blood-red tide was in a state of flux, roiling and churning but no longer advancing – or indeed, retreating.

Neither ebb nor flow, she thought, inspecting the blood on her fingers. It was dry and caked, crumbling; the gash on her right temple, from the now-shattered skulls she had landed on, was healed, painless. The flakes of blood crumbled and vanished like autumn leaves in a winter storm.

The blood-sea no longer held any fear for her. The water had actually *recoiled* from her, not ebbed, and now it remained undecided. It wanted to flood the shore, to consume her, but the power she held kept it in check: a wild beast confronted by fire.

And that's what this light is, she decided. *Fire.* She shuddered at the memory of how it had burnt her father's hand, and her heart sunk at the realisation of how close Dad had been to rescuing her. The joy she'd felt on seeing his face had been tempered with shock, fear for his safety – and anxiety at his expression upon seeing her.

Do I look that bad? Or was it anguish at knowing he can't rescue me from here?

The gash on his forehead – a fresh cut, but not self-inflicted. Attacked, knocked out – unconscious…

She closed her eyes, remembering the exact moment the Light had struck and banished him. *Our blood mingled. Father's and daughter's…*

She stared into the sky. Even that seemed lighter, less

oppressive; maybe remnants of the Light had lessened the darkness, or was it a sense of hope?

She smiled as she turned to face the seawall. It no longer seemed an impossible obstacle, and she relished the prospect of attempting the ascent once more. If Dad could reach her here, in this dimension, there was more hope than she'd realised. Her smile faltered as she stepped on the incline, thinking about the gash on his forehead.

Had he been attacked? If so, would he be able to get into Fairlight before midsummer?

Perhaps, she thought as skull shards crumbled underfoot, *he's already in. Perhaps he was attacked as he made his attempt. If so, does his vanishing mean he's regained consciousness? And who has him?*

Grim-faced, she bent forward as the incline deepened. Fresh cuts on her palms no longer concerned her; indeed, she hardly felt the pain. The incline was less unstable; the bones and skeletal fragments were firmer, more compact.

The blood tide hissed behind her, a further spur to victory.

"Ant!" she called. "I'm coming for you!"

Hot wind no longer blew crematoria ash into her face. The ascent tore air from her lungs, her muscles shrieked with the effort demanded from them, but adrenaline and confidence flooded her system.

She wiped sweat from her brow, pleased to feel the gash from her tumble had gone. Healed.

She stood atop the incline, resisting the temptation to cast a backward glance of contempt towards the dark shore. A small victory, but the battle hadn't been won yet. Instead, she took in the new vista.

If the nightmarish cove below represented Fairlight Bay – or *was* Fairlight Bay, in this strange dimension – the buildings before her were to be approached cautiously.

Not one was intact. All the seafront cottages were a jumble of broken stones and shattered roof tiles. Window panes were replaced by swirls of some sparkling liquid, now solid, where the molten glass had cooled and retained its new melted structures. Some of the masonry slabs smouldered and the cobbles of the pathway glowed red like hot coals. The dark sky crackled with red lightning, adding a momentary scarlet glow to the wrecked town. The air reeked of burning stone and smouldering rubber from the soles of her trainers.

Whatever had blasted this version of Fairlight into oblivion had left not only its unnatural heat but a presence, a palpable sense of otherworldly fury and destruction. The view may have resembled one of nuclear Armageddon, but Rachel Collins sensed the destruction was not of man-made origin.

The survival of the lighthouse was proof of that. Turning back to the blood-tide, the ancient Oratory on the opposing stretch of headland now looked more imposing, more ominous; the only manmade structure that had survived the mysterious apocalypse.

She turned back and made her way into the centre of the dead settlement, keeping to the less-smouldering paving slabs.

The absence of Callum Hayes and his weird monsters added to her sense of hope.

The layout of this Fairlight was the same; despite the ruined buildings she recognised the streets and alleys they had formed prior to their devastation. It felt like walking through a war zone; she half-expected to be taken down by an enemy sniper.

She smiled grimly at the thought. This enemy wouldn't use stealth, or even bullets.

"Ant?" Silence swallowed her call. No echoes.

She headed inland, to what she imagined to be the centre of the town. It felt cooler, and the damage was slightly less severe. Not a single building remained intact, and the lampposts and road signs were twisted and molten strands of linguini, but it was clear the holocaust's primary objective had been the seafront. Perhaps the lighthouse itself -

She halted. The Old Customs House had come into view and was intact. Not a single piece of scorched masonry, no fallen roof tiles. The wooden shutters over the windows bore no signs of fire. The drop kerb leading to the double doors was unmarked, and when she pressed a finger to it discovered it was cool to the touch. She suspected that if windows had remained prior to its closure, the glass would have stayed intact.

"So what makes you so special?" She laid a hand on the ornate doorknob. Again, cool to the touch. It twisted easily and the door slid open on oiled hinges. Too easily. Too welcoming.

Ant. Are you here?

The lobby was cooler than the drop kerb and the door handle; the chill of a well-maintained air conditioning unit filled the hall, but not its sound.

Like the heat outside, the cool air was not of human manufacture. She paused at the threshold, debating her decision to go forward. Nothing sinister met her eyes. The reception desk, ornate and Victorian, gleamed with recent varnish and polish. There was a leather-bound ledger, open to the centre. The last time she'd seen a book like that was in a museum, but the leather shone brand-new and apart from the writing and hand-drawn columns the pages were crisp, clean and white.

She leant over the desk – cold red oak, the varnish slippery like an eel – and rotated the ledger. It smelled of broken ballpoints. A blotter stood nearby, smeared with fresh red ink.

Copperplate handwriting filled the narrow columns. Names filled one column, dates of birth and home addresses the next two. She peered closely. This was a nineteenth century log of admissions for Fairlight Asylum for the year 1848.

The next two columns made her clutch the slippery edges of the desk. Her stomach lurched and the air left her lungs as though she'd been punched in the stomach. Her breath misted when it left her lips.

Dates of admission. Details of "malady". Curative procedure followed…then dates of death.

She flipped through the pages, desperately searching for variations, only to find the same entries in all columns. All teenaged children, all dead within a year of admission, all before their sixteenth birthdays.

The same cause of death: self-applied exsanguination. Suicide by self-harm.

She lifted the cover, her throat dry, and read the inscription. Fairlight Admissions, 1848.

Volume One.

The ledger slipped from her frozen fingers. She stared into the closed doorway beyond, and the glimmer of light between the door and frame. The book fell from the desk and took the blotter with it.

The double-thud and the disappearance of the impossible ledger shook her into action. She walked around the reception desk and towards the door.

The light halo of the door was soft, golden, and alive. It was the light she knew.

Was this the source, then? Here, in the old Customs House? The brass door handle turned with a click; the door opened gracefully, and in the centre of the golden light Rachel Collins found Ant.

The younger girl was kneeling on the tiled floor, her back towards Rachel, leaning over something. The Light wasn't the overpowering, blinding burst of energy Rachel had experienced so many times before; it was softer, suffusing the laboratory equipment with a golden glow that pulsed, like the living thing it undoubtedly was.

But as before, she couldn't see its source. It should be easier now, as it wasn't an immediate flash or burst that dazzled the eyes and fired the soul. It was everywhere; it was in everything.

Glass beakers and flasks on brass retort stands shone like diamonds; their liquid contents glowed. Rubber tubes glistened like tropical snakes, leading from gleaming bronze gas taps on the wooden work surfaces to equidistant steel tubes, hollow save for the gas that burned bright blue. Bunsen burners, Rachel realised, recognising them from pictures of her father's schooldays. But the newness of these instruments was at odds with the rusted, antique-looking gas burners of Tony Collins's school. Everything in the laboratory was an antique, the room a treasure trove of scientific Victoriana, but new, freshly supplied.

Is it the Light that's done this, or have I stepped back in time? But how did that account for the future – or possible future – Fairlight outside?

She shook her head. That wasn't important right now. The only thing that mattered was the girl who had led her - or enabled her journey - here.

"Ant?"

The younger girl didn't reply. She rocked back and forth, each motion allowing Rachel a partial glimpse of the creature in Ant's arms. She was singing softly to it, crooning, and Rachel realised the creature was weeping.

Silent, tearless, but weeping nonetheless. Rachel advanced, veering to the left. Now she saw why the Light pulsed.

It followed the rhythm of the creature's weeping. Intensification of the Light followed each drawn-out sob; each sigh of despair momentarily strengthened the illumination in the room, then faded. It had the same effect as a torchlight shining in morning fog: the Light was diffused, the droplets of moisture retaining the illumination like a memory of light.

Ant raised her head, turned and faced her. There was none of that otherworldly, bizarre playfulness in her grey eyes. The sadness was deep, profound and keenly felt, and not even the arrival of her friend could lessen the effect. Ant sniffed, wiped her nose with a long sleeve of her T-shirt – already damp with tears – and shuffled to allow Rachel a better view of the object of her pity.

Callum Hayes and his Triskelions were bad enough. Their alien appearance and lethal intent were terrifying, but she knew where she stood with them. This creature didn't offer that comfort.

Rachel backed away. Her hand struck the desk and rattled

a beaker in its retort stand. She continued to back away until the door she'd passed through was in her reach.

The frame was hunched, folded over, belying its true form. Only when the hands unfolded from the six forearms - which in turn unfolded from the shoulders like the claws of a mantis – and extended towards her did she have an idea of the beast's true form. She prayed the thrice-folded lower limbs didn't extend as well, because once that thing gave chase nothing on Earth would be able to escape.

The skin was bare, hairless, and sparkled with scales that shone with iridescent rainbows. These too pulsed, the minute folds between each scale a gleaming light that enhanced the disturbingly beautiful hide of the creature and took attention from the multitude of stalk-like appendages that stiffened to attention with each arm's unfolding, their diamond-shaped tips vibrating.

And the head…dear God, the *head…*

Ant's confused frown turned to one of disapproval. "What's wrong with you, Rachel? She needs help."

She needs help? Rachel wanted to scream, to break through Ant's self-contained and bizarre world, but the angular yet serpentine shape of the monster's head and the twitching black lips of the twin, circular mouths, tongue-less and toothless, denied her breath.

The eyes were the worst. Huge, saucer-sized spheres that swivelled on snail-like stalks, bloodshot with grey irises, and despite their abnormal size shockingly familiar.

There was humanity there. The alien body and impossible head contained a spirit that felt sorrow and despair – indeed, showed signs of human grief.

Something human. No, it can't be…I know this – this thing!

And the monster knew Rachel Collins. The alien appendages were no longer threatening, but imploring, wanting human contact. Comfort.

But to give, not receive.

Rachel found her voice and screamed. Her hand searched for the door handle, clutched it and pushed the door open behind her.

The double-mouths drooped then contracted, the lips becoming pallid, self-consuming worms before irising open and uttering a word in a crystal-clear, note-perfect human voice. A woman's voice, one that Rachel knew all too well and thought she would never hear again. A voice as full of warmth and humanity as that revealed by the monster's eyes, alien windows to a human soul that wept human tears.

"Rachel, my darling." The Light pulsed faster, more intense – an indication of the creature's excitement, emotional high at what she – *no, not she: IT*, Rachel screamed to herself - had found.

"It's all right, Rachel. Mummy's here."

CHAPTER TWENTY-EIGHT

This must be how they see, Callum Hayes thought happily. *What a gift I've been granted – and all because I kept my faith!*

The miracle of human sight, with its depth perception, stereoscopic vision, ability to differentiate between hundreds, thousands of shades of the spectrum, was nothing. His human eyeballs lay on the cell floor like squashed grapes, the juice dried and hardened. He didn't miss them. The frayed ends of his optical nerves still screamed to his brain the message of agony, this ultimate in self-mutilation, but that pain - that blissful, beautiful, *pure* pain - was what powered his new vision.

Purity through pain had been promised him, a covenant he had passed to his own followers. This, surely, was the next stage. Excitement fuelled him, and the stalks of his new optical instruments squirmed within their new homes, sending electric thrills of pleasure coursing through his body that were almost sexual.

But the visual information his new eyes fed his brain was too much. Even viewing the plain white padding of his cell was sensory overload; the white split into its constituent colours, each piece of the spectrum standing proud and true while simultaneously blending, merging into the white like a living, writhing entity. He dared not look at the recessed spotlights, but even their weak beams added a new dimension to his vision. The creases and folds in the vinyl were gaping fissures into the depths of space.

It was temporary. His mind would adapt eventually, he was

certain. But for now, he needed to rest his mind, rein in his youthful exuberance and not wear out his new toys.

These eyes wouldn't behave like his human ones, though. They would not sit obediently behind wearied, closed eyelids. They had life of their own, feeding on his own energy as he fed on their power.

They were newborn. They wanted to explore. He felt the stalks thicken, extend, and more pain flooded his skull. The door loomed, sped towards him.

My own organic telescopes. Despite their extendable stalks, they didn't move in opposing directions, like a snail's. Whatever patterns their mounts drew, they rode in the same direction as each other.

"What else can you do, my babies? What sights can you show me? Can you take us to see the Collins bitch?"

The stalks halted. He felt them quiver with new tension, and his vision tilted, rotated, inverted. He briefly saw his own pallid face, the cheeks glistening with slime that shone a thousand shades of red, the eyeless sockets fathomless caverns from which translucent, glimmering tentacles struck out, the alien sight riders striking the air like moray eels. Questing.

Sightriders, he thought with a chuckle. His face and its twin cavities, birthing beautiful abominations, vanished.

He raised his hands, palms upwards, knowing what his Sightriders sought. The vision filled with his healed stigmata, black oil slicks shining with unearthly rainbows. Within, a new vision waited.

The pain filled his hands once more and his sight returned to the familiar vision he witnessed through his skeins earlier. His cock bulged, swelling as thickly as the stalks upon which his new eyes rode. The pulsing of all three was simultaneous, beating to the same rhythm.

This time he was an outsider. He viewed the other Fairlight as the Sightriders erupted from the blood tide, raced along the ossuary beach and into the hellfire-razed buildings, but he was no longer *within* the scene. He was acutely aware of his present location, felt the sweaty warm vinyl of his cell's padding under his knuckles. There was hesitation on the part of the Sightriders.

"What's wrong?"

He felt it. The building they had halted before was not like the others. It was intact, with no burned stone or breached wall or holed window. The hanging sign read CUSTOMS HOUSE, in words of electric blue fire. The building shone, a luminescence that promised – threatened – to be a mere taste of the light within.

The light burned. He felt the Sightriders' pain, shared it, but refused to let them succumb.

"Go on!" He took their agony as his own burden, howling with the acid burn that had none of the sexual pleasure of his self-inflicted wounds; the feeling of dread, of fear, accompanied it.

Terror. The Sightriders, the heralds of the Presence, were actually *afraid* of what lay within.

How could this be? "Fear nothing! Go on! *Fear nothing!*"

Momentarily freed from their agony, their terror momentarily diminished, the double doors raced into view and shattered under their assault. An old reception desk was the next barrier, just as easily destroyed. Wooden shards passed through his eyes, but the pain they brought was nothing to what he was enduring.

Another set of doors, but these didn't require forcing down. They opened of their own accord, and Rachel Collins came running out.

Rachel Collins didn't care where she headed. She would rather burn in the holocaust of the shadow-Fairlight, take her chances with the blood-tide – even succumb to Callum Hayes and his monstrous Triskelions – than face the abomination Ant Penner had befriended.

"Rachel! Don't leave me, my darling!"

Its howls of loss – of despair at its rejection - rang in Rachel's ears as she fled, cut into her back like knives. Tears blinded her.

Of all the horrors she had endured, all the dangers to her health and sanity, this was the worst. This was the ultimate obscenity.

It had to be a trick of the force commanded by Callum Hayes. Just like the photo of her mother he had digitally manipulated. Had to be.

But the Light…this is one of the sources of that Light, the very same one that Callum fears. Ant may be nutty as squirrel shit, but she's not stupid; she wouldn't be taken in by this.

And the girl didn't even *know* Rachel's mother.

"Rachel! Stop! It's not what you think!"

This from Ant. Rachel hesitated, her hand on the door to the vestibule. She clenched her fist around the handle, felt the maddening cooling sensation that was part of the Light. An oasis of otherworldly purity in an apocalyptic wasteland. Wasn't that how the Light felt when she cut herself?

The Light here, weak and pulsating in time with organic grief and suffering, brightened. Stronger, more consistent.

Two voices called her name once more. Both female, both familiar, both human…both *genuine.*

I can't deal with this. Dad, where are you?

How would he handle this? This thing claimed to be her mother – would she make similar claims to Tony Collins? That she was his wife, the love of his life?

"Rachel, let me explain…only you can help me now." More pleading from the creature. Rachel's heart snapped, and she fell to the floor, sobs wracking her body. She heard a muffled sound of breaking wood from beyond the door, then footsteps in this room approaching her, and felt a hand on her shoulder. She stiffened, imagining one of that creature's awful limbs with its feathery appendages caressing her cheek in a motherly manner.

"Your mum's here to help, Rache," Ant said. Her voice lacked compassion, her tone one of bewildered frustration. "She's the only one who can."

A skittering sound, of talons skating over cold stone tiles, followed, and Rachel stiffened once more.

"NO!" She leapt to her feet, regained the doorknob, twisted it and pushed the door open. The Light spilled into the lobby and washed over the shattered remnants of the reception desk. It fell onto the figure before her and new screams filled the Customs House.

Callum Hayes stood framed in the apocalyptic wasteland of this Fairlight, orange flames forming a satanic halo above his greasy black hair. His hands were raised, palms outwards, towards her.

His Triskelions were not here; something else had accompanied him. A new nightmare burned the tears from Rachel's eyes.

The centres of Callum's palms were black, ragged holes — like stigmata wounds. From each fleshy chasm, a tube-like structure the width of the palm hole emerged, glistening black and dripping with slime. They weren't completely rigid; these *vibrated,* like intestines uncoiled on the anatomist's bench, resisting the scientist's eager fingers, but at the sight of Rachel Collins they grew, extending and flexing and looming towards her.

They terminated in bulbous growths with serrated fringes of rust-coloured muscle, and Rachel found herself inches away from these obscene polyps. Within the swelling black rosebuds she saw pale, milky pools centred with a glistening red marble, glinting in the backwash of the Light.

Staring at her, with alien and malevolent intent. Just for a second, though; the Light generated from the creature that claimed to be Rachel's mother had a devastating effect on these eyes.

They exploded. A cloud of milky fluid took their place, and this dissipated, vaporised. The glistening red marbles liquefied, became momentary lava that fell to the ground as piles of smouldering clinker. The appendages upon which they rode snapped backwards, a fine mist of black slime droplets marking their passage.

Back to Callum Hayes's palms, and through the stigmata wounds, and into the empty caverns of his eye sockets. The leader of the Children of the Evolution staggered backwards with the force of the impact, his holed hands clasped to his head.

Rachel stared, too stunned by the physical reaction to the Light from the alien eyestalks, and Callum Hayes's agonised expression, to grasp the enormity of what she had witnessed. Callum sank to his knees, fingers clutching at the remnants of the stalks in his eye sockets.

He was trying to pull them back from his skull. "Please...please don't leave me..."

The sound of tearing flesh – new, freshly healed tissue – and dripping blood accompanied his pleas. Rachel turned away, bile rising, to find Ant and the creature staring at her.

Rachel fixed her eyes fully on Ant, not daring to see the obscenity that used her mother's eyes and voice, but the expression on Ant's face made her start.

"What?" she said.

Ant wasn't looking at her, but beyond her, to Callum Hayes. She raised a finger. "That. Did you see what you've done?"

Rachel glanced back to the Hayes boy, who now writhed on the floor, painting it scarlet with the blood from his fresh wounds. It combined with the black droplets cast from the eyestalks, both steaming and bubbling where it caught the light.

The Light...

"Wasn't me, Ant. It's the Light from..."

Now she dared face the creature. The expression in those oversized, luminescent eyes stunned her.

There was love, there was maternal pride, and there was

something else. Rachel stared in disbelief, realising the Light that had devastated Callum's creatures had not emanated from this thing.

Shaking her head in bewilderment, Rachel raised her hands and stared at them. Ant took them in hers.

"But…I didn't do anything."

"It's not from your hands, Rachel," Ant said in an awestruck tone. "Your eyes. The light came from your eyes."

Rachel turned from Ant and stared hard at the creature claiming to be her mother. Its expression was one of fear.

And pride. Maternal love and approval shone in those alien eyes.

CHAPTER TWENTY-NINE

For the second time that day Karen Tyndall found herself facing an armed assault. This time the soldiers had come for her, not the creatures borne of her student.

Three of the six soldiers quickly surrounded her, their yellow Hazmat suits and the setting sun casting a sickly luminescence to the tiled walls and stone floor of the stockroom that she found even more disturbing than the glistening black barrels of the MP5 submachine guns pointed at her. Their breathing was steady, assured, and amplified by their mechanical respirators. Robotic and inhuman.

"Hands behind your heads. On the floor, now!" The voice was just as alien.

She cradled the back of her head and slowly squatted. She glanced to the doorway, saw the other two soldiers take backward-facing positions to her and Tony, their weapons aimed towards Silver Street, while the sixth entered and strode to the open office door. He executed a salute, encumbered by the protective clothing, and didn't seem concerned that the seated man – obviously a superior officer – was not similarly attired; his camouflage fatigues were pressed and clean, his boots glistened.

The suited soldier bent forward and momentarily hid the older man's face from her view. She couldn't hear what they said to each other, but the nodding of the Hazmat helmet told her they were discussing strategy. The SIG-Sauer didn't move from its position, still pointed directly at Tony, despite the presence of more armed men.

The sixth man turned, speaking electronically to the inside of his helmet. She was surprised to hear the helicopter rotors and engines fade, and the detritus of Silver Street resumed its stillness when the rotor wash disappeared with the ascending helicopter.

Karen cried out as her hands were roughly pulled behind her back and secured with a thin plastic strip. The soldier then pulled her to her feet and thrust her forward.

Silence filled the stockroom, broken only by the rhythmic electronic aspiration of the six soldiers. Then by the slap of booted feet hitting the concrete floor; the older man stood and pushed the chair from him.

He waited until Tony's hands were securely bound with Plasticuffs. Tony gritted his teeth but said nothing. Only then did the man flick the safety on his sidearm and holster the weapon.

"Tony Collins." The man's approach was wary, as if he expected Tony to strike him at any moment, despite his restrictions. The narrow eyes, as steel-grey as his cropped hair, widened momentarily. A tongue flicked out and licked dry lips.

He's scared of Tony, Karen realised. She regarded the stranger steadily when he turned his eyes upon her.

"And Ms Tyndall. You've both had quite a day, have you not?"

"Day's not over yet, mate," Tony snarled.

The grey-eyed stranger smiled thinly. "Tell me: why did you come here, rather than straight to the institute?"

Tony sneered. "Institute, eh? Not a hospital? Finally, you lot are coming clean."

"Clean..." the stranger murmured. Aware of Karen's

attention, he turned to her. "No one's coming out clean. You must realise now how much is at stake here. You, Ms Tyndall, witnessed the next stage of the condition these children suffer from."

"It's not about treatment, is it?" Karen said. The fear slowly faded. Her legs no longer shook. Anger flared. "It's *containment*. That's all Fairlight has been about: containing the kids, preventing those things from coming out of them!"

The stranger sighed and checked his watch. "It's much more than that, Ms Tyndall. Much more. The admission of Mr Collins's daughter marked a new phase in the project."

"The Orpheus Project, yeah?" Tony's biceps swelled. Veins stood on his forehead. "Christ. You were here all along. You heard what me and Karen were talking about."

"Indeed. Dawson did you - and himself - no favours. He'll be apprehended shortly." The grey-haired soldier glanced up; the beating of the helicopter rotors faded completely.

"Who the hell are you, anyway?" Karen said. "And what the hell were *you* looking for here?"

The stranger didn't reply. He inclined his head towards the roller shutter door. Karen's and Tony's guards took the cue and pushed them towards the exit. An olive-green Range Rover had drawn up. Its engine idled quietly while two soldiers opened the rear doors.

"I wasn't looking for anything, Ms Tyndall," the superior officer said behind them. She glanced back to see him lower the roller shutter door before the muzzle of her guard's MP5 pressed into her kidney. She groaned.

"I was clearing up." He indicated an archive storage box filled with stuffed lever arch files, overflowing ring binders, and banded advertising flyers. "And waiting for a visitor."

They were pushed into the rear seats. The door slammed behind Karen and she jerked around, trying to find the handle with her bound wrists. There was none.

One of the soldiers took the box from the leader, raised the rear door, and placed it in the back. Karen snarled and tried to summon enough saliva to spit at him. The door slammed down before she could do so. She turned to face front.

The soldier in the driver's seat held his sidearm casually, but she had no doubt he would draw it on them in a moment at the slightest provocation. She couldn't read his face through the tinted face mask, but the calm, rhythmic breathing told her all she needed to know.

It was a stark contrast to the rapid, panting breaths of Tony. Rage had flushed his face and his lips were drawn back.

"Relax, Mr Collins," the older man said as he held the passenger door. He gave a quick salute to the two soldiers who now stood guard at either side of the roller shutter door. She watched the others form pairs and stride off in opposite directions. "You'll see your daughter shortly."

The Rover moved off, and their captor turned in his seat. The setting sun shone through the windscreen of the vehicle and turned his hair sparkling silver. His even teeth were too white; they gleamed. He seemed relaxed, almost happy, to be leaving the Customs House.

The number of Hazmat-suited soldiers on the quayside now outnumbered the civilians. Karen froze at the sight of two armed men pushing an old woman to the ground while a third pulled back the slide on his weapon and pointed it at the younger man who rushed towards him in anger.

Jesus. Poor Mrs Stephens. Gunfire filled the air and the man – her son, Richard, Karen remembered – sank to the floor, arms around his head. They hadn't shot him, she realised; a warning volley, nothing more. But there was blood on the quayside. Mrs Stephens had landed headfirst. Hard.

"A little excessive, maybe," their captor said. "But essential to the pretence. Rest assured, there'll be none of this at the institute."

"Rachel had better be all right, you bastard," Tony said through gritted teeth. "If one hair on her head is harmed, I'll make you fuckers pay."

The quayside was behind them. The driver downshifted and took the ascending road out of the village.

"If she is harmed, Mr Collins," the older man said softly, "it won't be by our hands. It'll be by hers. Or yours."

"What?"

Their captor smiled. "I saw what happened in the Customs House. 'Translocation' is the word. Oh, so brief, so very brief. But it proves you and your daughter have something in common. Now we have to work out how that connection works." He reached for the handset on the dash-mounted radio transmitter.

Karen stared at Tony. His face had paled, and his jaw was slack. *Translocation.* His hallucination when he blacked out: *It was when I touched her blood...that was the moment the light flared...but it was the fact that* my *blood -*

It hadn't been the alcohol or stress that made her imagine him flickering in and out of existence upon her entry into the stockroom. She stared at the bristle-scalp of their captor and wondered what he had seen before she had got to Tony.

The grey-eyed soldier held the R/T handset to his mouth and pressed the transmit button. "This is General Rawlings. The two have been apprehended. New tango: Tom Dawson…yes. *Our* Tom Dawson. He's been compromised; you will eliminate him on sight. Alert Quinn at the institute; ensure access swipe points are reprogrammed."

"Understood, sir."

Rawlings hesitated, lost in thought. Then he pressed the talk button. "Protocol 15 has been initiated. Repeat, Protocol 15 has been initiated."

The lack of static ensured the receiver's sharp intake of breath was perfectly audible. Rawlings didn't wait for his listener to catch up. "Fairlight is now under lockdown. Ensure press release appropriate to the protocol is issued to all media. Apart from local law enforcement, I want nothing coming within thirty miles of the village, is that understood?"

Rawlings replaced the handset. Without looking back to his prisoners, he said, "Don't look at me like that, Mr Collins. It is now up to you and your daughter to ensure we all see the dawn."

"What's Project Orpheus, shitbag?"

The general's cold smile didn't reach his eyes.

"A failure, Mr Collins. Project Orpheus is a failure. But what happened to your daughter proves it has some…fringe benefits. The rapid healing has military and civilian applications you can only dream of."

Tony snorted. "Only works if you cut yourself."

"Leave that to us. But I'll be asking the questions from now on, Collins." The "Mr" was dropped, and now the steel in the general's eyes was as cold as the Rover's air conditioning. He pointed a rigid finger at the laceration on Tony's temple, inflicted by the stockroom's chest freezer. "For starters: what did you see when you cut yourself?"

The rear-view mirror reflected the setting sun and filled the car's interior with scarlet and gold. The rhythmic thumping of helicopter rotors assaulted Karen's eardrums and made her head ache. Now her whole body ached. The Plasticuffs were too tight; pins and needles danced in her fingers. Nevertheless, she strained to see what was behind her.

The road swung to the left and descended. The dying sun disappeared under the black silhouette of the Merlin HC3 helicopter.

Nightfall.

DAY THREE: INCORPORATION

REVISITATIONS AND REMEMBRANCES

He is back in Fairlight Asylum, but this doesn't alarm him. He'd expected the new powers behind Fairlight to take him if the Presence returned. Mentally, he's been preparing for it, knowing what was banished would surely find a new way to break through to our world once more.

Wheeled into the Acute Ward, he'd been shocked to see the original fittings and equipment from his sojourn in the 1950s are still here. The Victorian heart of Fairlight Asylum remains beating, and the newer buildings are just a glossy façade to hide the reality of the hospital's treatment methods.

Between periods of oblivion, he's fifteen years old again. He feels the flesh of his belly part, smells the tang of blood as it drips from his gurney and splashes into the runnels of the tiled floor. He hears the despairing howls from his mother and sees the anguished, tear-filled eyes of his father – the last sight he has of them as the doors close on him. Custody is taken from his parents and given to the Superintendent of Fairlight Asylum.

He doesn't know this yet; he can't see the scribbling of notes on medical forms, the letters to his parents and doctor typed, carbon copied, and signed in triplicate. Only as the seasons change and his Christmases and birthdays pass with no visits or cards from his parents does he become accustomed, even resigned, to the realisation they have disowned him.

Every day that passes, he thinks about them. He wonders if Dad still runs the fish market, or if Ocean Wave Direct bought him out; if Mum still cleans the museum exhibits in the Old Customs House.

Do they miss him, or are they secretly relieved they no longer have to watch his every move, attend to him with bandages and iodine when the call to cut is too powerful to resist?

Does the fish market have customers, despite his warnings

to Dad about the new shellfish?

He can't worry about that now. That's another world, another life. Maybe one day, when he's older, cured, they'll listen to him…but for now, the pain of loss, of separation, is hard for a lonely, mentally ill fifteen-year old boy to deal with.

The pain passes. He's young and has a new family now. The other teenagers receive no seasonal or anniversary visits or gifts, either. But that's all they have in common.

For unlike them, the impulse to self-harm, to cut himself, has gone. But the authorities will not release him. They know it's not their "curative solutions" that has banished the call to open skin and flesh – the screams and zombified, slack-jawed, glazed expressions of the other children as they take their turns in the electroconvulsive therapy chamber soon give way to the beatific, rapturous smiles as the imperative to self-harm returns.

No. He's different. They wish to keep him, to study him, and the time to his twenty-first birthday - and with it, the legal obligation to release him - draws near. He resists; they have taken too much blood, sent too many samples of his mysteriously healed flesh to laboratories across the globe, and still they want more. It's only a matter of time before an "accident" is arranged and his corpse is given freely to the anatomists' knives.

There's precious little reading material in their wards, but he's glanced at the medical texts during the recovery periods after ECT before the books are hastily snapped shut, recognises the phrases "longitudinal section" and "frontal lobe removal", along with the diagrams, and he knows this is his fate.

They'd thought he would be institutionalised, would be so used to the captivity of the Victorian brain zoo and its petty rules, its regulations, and the keepers with their painted smiles, with his fellow charges and their zombie grins, that returning to the outside world – indeed, beginning an adult life – would be unthinkable to him. They are wrong.

They can't allow him to leave. Not with what he knows of their "treatments". He pretends he's oblivious, sits slack-jawed in the Sun Garden with the others, staring at the ruined lighthouse across the bay, but he's no actor and his pretence doesn't fool them.

Something stirs within. The Presence he fought so hard to deny physical access, that he'd thought gone for good, has returned. He clutches his healed abdomen and feels something kick within. This time he's not afraid. It has sensed his approaching death, and will not allow the keepers of Fairlight to extinguish his life.

I'm a vessel, nothing more.

He watches the midsummer sunset illuminate the ancient Oratory, wonders what secrets the Pharos holds. A beacon that's older than the town itself, one whose history is shrouded in mystery. The medieval monks who lit the torch did so from a genuine, altruistic desire to guard ships from wrecking on the treacherous coastline, but they were unwittingly maintaining a link to another world. That's all he knows – all anyone who grew up in Fairlight knows. The last recorded entry in its history was during the Civil War, when it was destroyed by an explosion. Even that is sketchy information; there were no recorded battles between the Royalists and the Parliamentarians here.

The sundial's elaborate gnomon with its Damascus steel and curious engravings always points towards this ruin, and the shadow that falls across it holds some secret, he's certain; the ability to tell the time is a secondary purpose.

His fellow inmates gather around him, glazed eyes staring with devotion. Drooling lips mutter strange words to him – foreign-sounding names, or maybe titles of respect from long-dead languages.

What has he done to inspire such reverence? He's no leader, no liberator; these are not God's Chosen People, and he can't deliver them from this Egypt. There is no Promised Land. The only certain destination on their map is the dark country, death itself. And yet…

He caresses the scars on his abdomen. They pulse, writhe like serpents, and it won't be long before the wound demands to be reopened. Perhaps that's what they're waiting for. The voice of the leader won't come from his lips, but from that alien Presence that speaks through his mutilated flesh.

The sun bleeds its last into the ocean. The Oratory flares scarlet with the backlight and the shadow falls across the sundial's plane. The gnomon flashes scarlet in reply to the light from the Oratory; the engravings glitter.

It is time, the Presence commands wordlessly. He stands, pulls his shirt over his shoulders and tosses it to the ground. His abdominal scars writhe in excitement within his concave belly, puckering in the thin flesh like alien lips.

The final cut. His last self-mutilation. He holds the sundial's pedestal firmly between his knees, grasps the octagonal plane with trembling, sweating palms, and leans forward. He rests his belly on the diagonally sloping gnomon, gasping at the heat it has absorbed from the midsummer's day.

It's all he remembers. It's only later, amongst the blood-spattered bodies of the disciples without a leader, their bodies smouldering from the machine gun fire that tore them to pieces, that he's brought back to consciousness. He's questioned by men in khaki uniform, their eyes harsh and their interrogations as forceful as their weaponry, and this time he doesn't need to pretend. He simply doesn't know what happened.

His abdominal scars are ancient and withered. There's no life there now.

And there's no life for him within Fairlight Asylum. The fire brought the townsfolk to the hospital long before the police and army. Amongst them, his parents.

Guilt and joy merge when they see how old his wounds are, how long it's been since he self-harmed. How…normal he looks.

Happy Birthday, Son.

Six years inside Fairlight. No longer a child – and the Presence couldn't use me…

And now, sixty years later, it still can't. Despite the pain wracking what remains of his body, he smiles.

New owners, same techniques. Same desperation. Although the Welsh woman applying the blade is taking a personal pleasure in the mutilation. She bears the smug smile of one pleased with the homework essay she's prepared for school, the self-satisfied smirk of a student who knows her teacher will approve her work and reward her.

I's too old to give a shit, you silly bitch. I don't belong here, and your "teacher" will soon realise that. No gold stars for you, Missy.

She started on his old wounds, and that initially worried him. What if the Presence answered the call of the knife, send its seed scuttling through the dimensions using the old scars as their passageway?

No. The scars resisted as old, toughened flesh will, but no portals opened. He remembers her hiss of anger, and steeled himself for the pain that would surely follow. Petulant, spiteful; the petty acts of vengeance from a thwarted child.

Child…he wonders about his son. Death is coming for him, and in the brief respites from agony, he has the chance to look back on his life. It isn't pretty viewing.

But he won't blame himself. What chance did he have, anyway, to make something of his life? His son couldn't wait to get away from Fairlight, seeing what a local upbringing did to the old man.

But now Jim wishes Tom was here. To tell him why he drank every night, why he couldn't hold down any of the scarce jobs in Fairlight when Ocean Wave Direct closed down following the food poisoning scandal.

To tell him why he had to remain in Fairlight, despite Jeanie's tentative offer of remarrying. Move to York, with me and the boy. Perhaps we can make a fresh start.

Sorry, love. Nothing doing.

Now tears fall from his eyes. All his adult life, he played the part well: a drunken old fool, thick as pigshit and with no recollection or understanding of the events up to his twenty-first birthday, just counting down the days to each benefit payment and the bottles it bought.

It was the only way to keep their eyes off him, while he kept a vigil. The last watchman, awaiting the return of the Presence. Fooled you all, didn't I?

Fooled meself, as well. What I missed out on…what can I do now? Shoulda read up more on the Pharos. That bloke from Cambridge, Phillotson? Phil Lotson? Sommat like that…he knew more o' that lighthouse thing. Wish I'd kept a copy of his book, now. There was a list of extra reading in there…

Scarlet floods his vision, a crimson tide raging under a storm. Black waves follow, bearing gingery fronds of seaweed. They wave like jellyfish tendrils, the nematocysts promising more pain as they part.

A face revealed. A cold smile, rejoicing in his tears. The eyes are as black as the waves of despair she rides in on, and the familiar knife glitters once more.

He succumbs, forces a smile of triumph he no longer feels. I can manage that, at least…give the Welsh bitch no fuckin' satisfaction…

It can't be long now, before the final cut. Before too much blood flows and he passes on.

Just hope that Collins bloke'll be able to do sommat…his

little girl is special, and them here knows it! I ain't seen fear in Fairlight Asylum since…since I were first here.

There are sounds. Male screaming, the slamming of security doors. The muffled but unmistakable rhythmic thump-thump-thump of a helicopter's rotor blades.

The Welsh witch freezes, panic on her sharp features.

His smile is genuine now. He manages to snort back blood from his flooded sinuses, feels fresh blood flow from the stump of his severed tongue, and rolls it in his mouth like a thick plug of chewing tobacco.

May not make much o' my life, but I'll sure as shit make sommat o' my death. Take this, y'bitch.

He spits it into her face.

CHAPTER THIRTY

Quinn crashed to the floor under the onslaught of Bethan Appleton's charge. One meaty forearm locked itself in place between his chin and sternum and pressed hard. He choked, struggled in vain to ward her off while her free arm raised the murderous bone saw. Blood from its serrated blade dribbled onto her bare skin, covering her liver spots, before trickling into his gasping mouth. The taste of blood galvanised him, shook his body from inaction.

The sight and smell of the things in the Acute Ward were bad enough, but the taste of another man's blood in his mouth acted like an electric shock. He thrashed wildly, jerked from side to side, but the arm crushing his throat didn't shift. Her eyes gleamed with a maniacal light, her lips parted and drooling with anticipation and delight at the slaughter to come.

"Come on, love," she said with a laugh. "Put up a good fight, why don't you?"

Red mist filled his eyes. Hers multiplied in his vision, became a sea of glistening brown orbs above an undulating wave of stained teeth. The overhead strip lights flickered, adding a stroboscopic effect so that the frizzy mass of hair writhed slowly like the serpentine locks of Medusa. The bone saw came closer, its blade pressed under the strip of cartilage that separated his nostrils. More pressure; the teeth of the blade bit.

His thrashing aided its journey. More blood, no longer a trickle and no longer second-hand, but his own, flowed into his mouth. Liquid fire filled his nostrils and agony raced through him.

The tip of his nose curled and rose to the centre of his vision. The bridge followed it, and Bethan grunted with the exertion. He no longer smelt the slaughter odours of the Acute Ward.

The bone saw slipped from view, and all he saw through a scarlet curtain was a triangular lump of flesh that flopped from side to side; his body continued its thrashing.

The pressure from his throat lifted, but it took an age to draw breath again. Each inhalation was agony to his bruised – or crushed, he didn't know which – oesophagus. Then the pressure returned, but this time to his arms. Talons dug into his armpits and he was pulled to his feet to face his attacker. Bethan cracked a smile at the sight of his almost-severed nose. She transferred her grip to his loosened tie and dragged him closer.

His words were a sequence of guttural snorts and snuffling, an alien language to his own ears, but he was satisfied to realise there was no pleading in them.

Bethan's grin widened and she threw the bone saw to the ground. Its clatters echoed throughout the Acute Ward. Her free hand reached for the bleeding flap of flesh and cartilage.

Quinn reacted before her fingers landed. His right fist balled and powered into her belly. Bethan grunted but it was only the second blow – delivered with more force and extended fingers rather than a fist, powering up into her diaphragm – that made her release his tie. She staggered back, curled over, and Quinn brought his knee up into her face.

You sick Welsh bitch! He pushed her back, his pain briefly forgotten. Rage fuelled him, and the red curtains, twitching at each side of his vision, became diaphanous sheets that unfurled, a red mist of fury. Each blow he struck her barely registered. The skin on his knuckles scraped and tore with each contact. She raised her hands to cover her face, a weak plea barely audible. He hesitated, and with a cry of disgust pushed her, open-handed, away from him. She landed on the side of the bed, the railings striking her back, and she grunted before sliding to the floor in a crumpled heap.

Thunder rumbled through the ward and the ground shook.

Again, he took no notice. Only when the bone saw took a life of its own and moved, rattling towards him to rest against his shoe, was he aware of the vibrations shaking the secret chamber within Fairlight.

He knelt, picked up the instrument. He examined his knuckles briefly. Blood. So much blood. Bethan's, his…and the patient's. Every inhalation was agony, each exhalation torture to his exposed nasal passages. He tried to swallow, but the bruising to his windpipe was too severe. He spat instead, and the exertion made his head swim. The taste of blood was overpowering, but there was an addition to the flavour that startled him. The familiar tang failed to hide something that resembled some sort of shellfish his father had tried to make him eat as a child – cockles, mussels, something along those lines – and something else.

I must be in shock. It tastes like…like light.

Light. He looked up.

Bethan's head was tilted against the headboard, a thin mixture of drool and blood dribbling down her cheek. Her eyes were half-closed, and her left hand clutched feebly at the sheets covering the patient. She pulled them to her, wrapping her body in the rubber and revealing the full extent of the damage inflicted upon Jim Dawson.

There was none. Where, less than five minutes ago, Quinn had seen multiple lacerations and incisions on the old man, all he saw was fresh scar tissue. Pink, healthy – a contrast to the grey, puckered skin that had been tortured. A patchwork quilt, whose stitching faded, became barely visible.

The eyes opened. They were glazed, dead eyes; the mirrors to a soul passed on. Then the opacity slowly cleared, like ice melting beneath hot water, and life returned. He stirred; first, one shrivelled wrist shook the rubber strap securing it to the railing. Then his leg twitched. Toes curled and uncurled, and the rest of the sheet fell away.

Bethan whimpered and buried herself in Jim Dawson's bloodstained bedsheets. She seemed to shrivel.

Quinn got to his feet. Then he started, took a step backwards, when Jim Dawson stared at him. He thought of the other inmate who had shown superhuman powers of recovery.

The old man's lips parted, and his chest shuddered with each intake of breath. Fists clenched and fought against rubber bonds. Then, wheezing, he said, "You gonna stand there all day, sonny, or are you gonna let me go?"

Quinn's red mist faded. Light-headedness overcame him and the ground lurched beneath his feet. Another rumble, this one more rhythmic and pounding. Repeating.

Helicopter…

Quinn forced his body onwards. He moved to the opposite side of the bed, away from the sobbing, broken Bethan, and with numbed fingers tackled the first of Jim Dawson's restraints. His fingers felt like they were encased in iced gloves; the buckles fought back.

"I sees the asylum's treatments ain't changed in the last fifty years." There was disgust on Jim's face. He glanced at Quinn. "You the guv'nor here, then?"

Quinn nodded, not trusting himself to speak. The pain wasn't worth it – but even if his face and throat hadn't been so damaged, he doubted his ability to reply.

"Not fer much longer, by the sounds o' it." Jim stared at the ceiling. "That there helicopter's comin' closer. Army boys, aye?"

Quinn nodded as he unbuckled the ankle strap. Now there were the right-hand restraints to undo — and the thought of reaching over that unnaturally healed body, and whatever power flowed through it, terrified him as much as the prospect of undoing the straps from Bethan's side of the bed.

"Don't worry yerself, boy. I can manage." Jim's left hand

pulled the strap and flicked out the metal tongue from the hole. He sat up and reached for his right ankle. "Where's me clothes?"

Quinn stepped back. He glanced around the Acute Ward, dumbly wondering where patients' clothes would be stored. There were no bedside cabinets, no wardrobes; patients admitted here never needed clothes again.

Jim rubbed his wrists and ankles. He shook his head. "Figured as much. Gimme a sheet, then. I's bloody freezing." He swung his legs off the bed, his foot catching on the huddled Bethan. "Unless you wanna gimme yer clothes, bitch? I knows they's too big, but I'll grow into them."

A strange mewling answered him. Jim pulled the sheet from the nurse's head and laughed at the sight. Quinn's eyes widened.

"She'll be no more 'arm to anyone, boy. Her mind's snapped – but I's not taking no chances. Gimme a hand."

Despite the pain, Quinn began to feel less incapacitated. He felt less light-headed, and breathing was painful but not impossibly so. He followed the emaciated old man's orders, helping to lift the unresisting woman from the floor and throw her to the bed face-down. The patient's restraints became those of his torturer.

Jim picked up the bone saw and stared at the serrated edges. Then stared at the trembling body of Bethan. There was a gleam in his eyes that made Quinn uneasy.

"Nope," Jim muttered as he threw the instrument to the ground. "I ain't descendin' to their standards. Yer guv'nors will have to deal with her."

Quinn nodded, relieved. Then he was nervous. The helicopter noise had faded which meant the aircraft had passed by or had landed. He rubbed his swollen throat and managed, "They'll deal with us at the same time. Let's go."

While Jim tore off a sheet from an empty bed and wrapped

it around his midriff, Quinn felt for his keycard, breathing a sigh of relief to find it still in his pocket. Clutching it like the totem against evil – as he had done upon entering the Acute Ward – he pointed towards the exit.

Jim Dawson turned once to spit on the prone body of Bethan Appleton before following.

CHAPTER THIRTY-ONE

With the third rumble beneath her body, Rachel Collins stirred. Cut grass, crusted with her blood, bristled against her face while the sea breeze caressed her matted hair. The wind was colder, and when she raised her head she saw the sun had set.

She rolled over and pulled herself up into a sitting position. She shivered, rubbed the gooseflesh of her forearms with both hands. As on her previous visits to the shadow Fairlight, she felt shaken, traumatised, but this was worse. Looking around her she was relieved and grief-stricken to see her mother wasn't with her.

"Mum…" she whispered. The breeze took her words, whipped them behind her to the bay and the ruined lighthouse on the headland beyond. Now she remembered the physical darkness that rushed towards her and Ant from the Oratory during their blood-sharing.

Rachel stared at her wrists. The wounds had healed, felt like they'd been cauterised during that bizarre blood transfusion. Now the scar tissue had returned; raised pink veins of flesh itched intolerably, the pins and needles of healing.

But for how long? She rubbed her forearms again, realising she wasn't getting any warmer. Was that blood loss or the effects of her visit to the other Fairlight? She stared at the patches of grass where her blood had spilled.

"Ant!" she called. "Ant, where are you?"

The Sun Garden was deserted and silent. There was no sign of movement through the darkened windows of the hospital, and it took her befuddled mind a moment to realise what else was wrong.

No lights in the Sun Lounge. The television was off. Rachel walked forward; her arms crossed over her chest. Her legs trembled and her head spun. She grasped the handle on the door and shook it.

Locked. No surprise there. But why had no one come out to get them? Wasn't Gillian supposed to be keeping an eye out for them?

And Quinn? Where was he? She looked over her shoulder towards the car park, saw the same three vehicles that had been there earlier. No one had left, then. In the distance she heard a helicopter's rotor blades beating the thick, humid air, and wondered if that had caused the rumbling. It seemed to be coming from the town itself, but the acoustics of the bay magnified and distorted the chopper's sounds, so that the aircraft appeared to be coming from all directions. Coastguard, she wondered, or police?

And where the hell is Ant?

She faced the bay and the distant Oratory. There she saw Ant.

The younger girl stood rigid, her ponytail whipping back and forth in the stiffening sea breeze. Her hands clutched the low wall and Rachel saw blood oozing from Ant's fingernails, painting the white masonry.

Rachel hurried towards her, the harsh sea breeze biting and bringing tears streaming down her face. The younger girl was trembling – or was that the blurriness of her vision? Rachel stood behind Ant and placed a hand on her shoulder. Ant didn't turn, didn't even appear to register the contact. Her shoulder was stiff and rigid.

"Ant?"

The ponytail whipped back and forth, even more forcefully, as Ant's head shook.

"Ant."

Finally, the shoulder relaxed, but the trembling continued. Rachel started at the violence of the girl's shaking. She opened her mouth, about to utter meaningless but comforting words, but realised she had nothing to say.

Ant had relished her visitation to the Plutonian Shore – and the new friend she had made. Was that it?

"Tell me something, Ant. Was that the first time you've…you've been to the place I've been?"

The girl spoke, but didn't turn to face Rachel. "No, not the first. But it was the first time I climbed the seawall. The first time I went into that…that place."

Now she turned. Rachel tore her hand from Ant's shoulder, horrified by the bleakness in the younger girl's eyes.

"I followed the call. Thought the source of the Light was just beyond the seawall. But everything there is death. There's no escape. Your mum…do you realise what happened to her?"

Rachel closed her eyes. The tears that trickled down her cheeks were no longer caused by the biting wind.

"She's trapped, Rachel. Caught between the two worlds. I don't know how, and I don't know how she can be freed…but she told me time's running out. That we must escape from here, and get to the other side of the bay." She raised a trembling finger. Through Rachel's tear-blurred vision the darkness surrounding the Oratory was thick, shifting – just like the black fog that had spat from it towards the two girls earlier in the afternoon.

"The answer's there."

Rachel nodded. "I guessed as much. But how -"

"No! You don't understand!" Terror forced the girl's voice to a higher pitch. "Not in the lighthouse, but the Shadow Pharos. We have to cross again!"

Rachel's stomach turned to ice at what Ant meant. *We have to cut ourselves within the lighthouse… and hope the Triskelions don't get us.* She glanced back to the Sun Room. There was a figure at the door, a silhouette backlit by the lights that flickered into life. The fluorescent glow spilled onto the grass of the Sun Garden and the black metal face of the sundial. The gnomon glimmered, as did the nose chain on the woman's squat features.

"It'll have to wait, Ant. Gillian's here."

"So's Callum." Ant stared at the black waters. "And he'll be in *both* places."

Rachel squeezed Ant's shoulder. "Here, he can't do anything. We're more at risk in that...that shadow-world. He's got powerful friends there."

Gillian walked towards them. There was a curious expression on the assistant nurse's face, and hesitancy in her approach.

Ant turned and wrapped her arms around Rachel. She buried her head in the crook of Rachel's arm. "We're no safer here, Rachel."

"Maybe not." Rachel caressed Ant's head. "But they don't know what we can do. That's in our favour."

"No, they *do* know. Why d'you think Gilly's so wary?"

Rachel raised a hand towards the nurse. Gillian didn't acknowledge her. Instead, she licked her lips – a nervous gesture – and glanced back to the open door. She raised her walkie-talkie and spoke quietly into it. Rachel swallowed.

"Why d'you think they locked up without getting us back in? They looked for us, Rachel, but they couldn't see us. *We weren't here, that's why!*"

Rachel's head spun. It couldn't be. Everything on the dark shore and the shadow-Fairlight felt so real: the smells, the physical sensations, the sounds – but that was all part of the hallucination, surely? There was no way they could...

"Translocation," Ant whispered.

Now Rachel knew why Gillian was so wary, so nervous of approaching the two. "She watched us vanish," Rachel whispered back. "Or the cameras picked up on us coming back here." She pressed Ant closer to her chest, felt the girl's racing heartbeat. She didn't know if she was holding Ant to comfort her – or if she was trying to derive comfort and reassurance for herself.

I want my mum. For so long she had seen Dad as the one to rely on, the strength in the remaining family, but the vision of her mother – or what her mother had become – threw that certainty out the window.

And where are you now, Dad? The thought of him meeting the thing that pretended to be her mum chilled her. How would he cope with that?

Gillian looked up. Rachel followed her gaze, saw the helicopter's running lights flash in the gloom. It hovered over the ruined lighthouse like a dragonfly.

"We ain't got much time, girls." Gillian's Yorkshire-accented voice, so warming and comforting before, lost its soothing quality with the quaver in her tone. Her eyes were wide in the gloom, but Rachel knew it was the sight of her and Ant – and the approaching military – that alarmed her more. From the road leading out of the hospital grounds came the noise of an approaching vehicle. Headlights crept around the bend and splashed the glass frontage.

"Quick!" Gillian hissed, grabbing Rachel's arm. Rachel pulled back. "For God's sake, Rachel! If they find you now, you're both dead!"

Two vehicles crested the rise. Rachel had a brief glimpse of drab olive livery on the first, followed by police markings on the second, before Gillian pulled her and Ant from view and the vehicles disappeared into the car park.

"The bloody military," Gillian muttered. "They're the ones running the show here, not Quinn, not the NHS."

"Okay," Rachel said. "Come on, Ant."

Ant resisted, seeing where Rachel was leading her. "No! I'm not going back in there!" She dug her bare heels into the grass.

Gillian turned, her hand on the door. "Ant, only reason t'bloody soldiers are coming is to shut Fairlight down for good. Our only chance is to hide, get into t'deeper areas."

"And then?" Rachel heard the thumping of boots on tarmac, the slamming of doors and the squawk of radio-transmitters. There was also a chorus of metallic sounds: magazines slotted, and slides pulled back on automatic weapons.

"That's your answer. *Come on.*"

The police car joined the Rover just after Rawlings's Rover left the main road. Tony Collins twisted in the back seat to stare at the approaching Civic and groaned at the familiar sight of its occupants. The cop Tony had smashed in the face sat in the passenger seat. There was an unhealthy gleam in his eyes.

"I gather you've already met our local constabulary," Rawlings said as he replaced the handset on the R/T. "Impressive work, Mr Collins, but quite pointless. I'll do my best to ensure Frank doesn't act on any harsh feelings he may have towards you."

The neo-Gothic turrets of the older Victorian building rose above the line of trees as the Rover crested the hill. For a brief moment the ruined lighthouse beyond joined them, centred between the two, and Tony blinked, the coppers behind him forgotten.

Then the tree line sank, and the newer structures of the old asylum came into view. Courtyard lights sprang into life when the Rover swung into the parking area, its headlights sweeping through the glass frontage and illuminating the modern trappings of a twenty-first century building: the vase of orchids and slim monitor on the beech reception desk; the twin fire extinguishers by the entrance door; the plush reclining chairs to the right of the reception desk; and the metal plaque that announced the travellers they had reached Fairlight Hospital.

But the sense of ancient habitation remained with Tony

when the gunmen dragged he and Karen out into the courtyard. He looked up, saw the darkness pooled around the turrets' finials. The lighthouse was beyond sight now.

He glanced at Karen. "You okay?"

She gave him a brief, tight smile as Rawlings helped her out – *helping her, like he's a fucking valet* – and nodded. "Been better."

"When we get out of this the first two rounds are on me."

"No talking," his own guard snapped, and pushed him between the shoulders. Tony stumbled, almost lost his footing on the loose gravel, and the PlastiCuffs dug into his wrists. He glared at the soldier.

"No need for that, Private," Rawlings said and closed the Rover's door. He reached into his breast pocket and retrieved a plastic keycard on a canvas lanyard which he placed around his neck. He nodded to the two policemen exiting their vehicle and passed Karen's handbag to the battered Frank.

"Gentlemen. Escort our guests to the nearest…" he smiled at Tony. "Forgive me, Mr Collins. I almost said 'cell'. Not politically correct terminology to describe the rooms Fairlight's guests live in."

"Containment, Rawlings. Your word, not mine. Cell is as good a word as any." Tony grimaced as the PlastiCuffs bit tighter. The bonds had an upside, though. The back pocket of his work trousers was accessible to his fingers, even with bound wrists.

Frank stared at the handbag, not sure how to hold it. Only the swelling of his jaw prevented him from gritting his teeth.

"Suits you, cop. Just your colour."

Frank snarled. His companion raised a finger and said, "You'll get yours, Collins!"

"That's enough, Napier!" The amiable air Rawlings had put on slipped away like the mask it was. "One moment…"

Tony took a step back, his eyes narrowed, as the general

advanced on him. Rawlings quickly slipped his thin fingers into Tony's left trouser pocket and pulled on the lanyard, retrieving the keycard Jim's son had given him.

Tony held his breath. He'd forgotten about that. *Thank Christ I hadn't put it in my back pocket...*

Rawlings tossed the keycard to the driver. "Young Dawson's card. Access all areas. Take Ms Tyndall and Mr Collins to level two."

The general used his own card on the access panel and the twin doors slid aside with a soft hiss. He inclined his head, gesturing for the two policemen to enter first. Napier grabbed Tony's shoulder and spun him around, then pushed him into the vestibule. Tony pretended to be hurt by the push; he cried out, deliberately stumbled, and fell against the reception desk. The vase of orchids rocked on the desk as Tony's shoulder pushed the Visitors' Book against it. He turned, sliding down to the floor.

His captors couldn't see his hands now.

Rawlings shook his head. "Dear me. Not so tough after all. Or perhaps you wanted to smell the flowers?"

Tony looked up. "No, I'm good. Could do with a fag, though."

Rawlings smiled and wagged a finger. "Sorry, Mr Collins. This is a no-smoking facility." He turned to Frank and Napier. "As soon as they're secured, report to the Site Services office. Second stage of Protocol 15 will be initiated at midnight."

Napier nodded. "Sir." He prodded Tony with his boot. "On your feet, bastard."

"Gimme a moment." He put on a pretence of breathing heavily, tried to look exhausted, drained of energy and hope.

The Zippo was in his right hand.

Karen stared at him, her eyes wide with concern. Tony closed his eyes. He heard the hiss of interior doors open, the footsteps of Rawlings and his armed escort fade behind the closing doors…*okay. Time to move.* He winced as the Zippo ignited, and as it burned hairs from his knuckles he wished he'd had a disposable Clipper instead.

Frank to the left, Karen in the middle, and that other one – Napier, is it? – on the right. Behind them, the door.

He scraped his boot heels on the carpeted floor and clicked his head on the modesty panel of the reception desk, trying to hide the noise of melting plastic, but it was only a matter of seconds before the two coppers smelled the burning PlastiCuffs.

Hot plastic dribbled down the inside of his wrist. He had visions of veins melting under scorched, torn skin, and…

…translocation…

…and an image of Rachel on a nightmarish seashore. *No! Keep it together!*

"Come on, Collins. Don't make me boot your arse down to - what the fuck's that? Burning?"

Now!

He opened his eyes and launched to his feet. His hands, no longer bound, were balls of fire. A serpent of lava coiled around his right wrist. That was the one to use.

Frank was the harder one; he had to be taken out first. Tony sprang on him and whipped the burning remains of the PlastiCuffs into Frank's face. The molten plastic clung to his broken jaw like a leech and burned into his flesh.

Tony didn't wait for a reaction. He ducked around Frank, passed a stunned, immobile Karen, and rabbit-punched the younger policeman with his left fist. The pain in Tony's wrists – from the burning and the trapped circulation – prevented too much damage; the blow stunned Napier rather than incapacitated him, but that was all Tony needed. He grabbed Napier's stabvest, extended his left leg and hooked his ankle around the back of the cop's right foot, then simultaneously twisted, crouched, and threw Napier into the thrashing arms of his comrade.

The doors were before Tony, but it wasn't an exit he was looking for. On a red plastic stand was a pair of fire extinguishers. He went for the smaller one with the plastic funnel.

He snapped the seal and extended the funnel, but Frank was too quick for him. The heavy-set policeman had already pushed Napier aside and now crashed into Tony. Tony grunted as he went down, his grip loosened on the carbon dioxide extinguisher, and his hands were now occupied in preventing Frank from throttling him.

Fat fingers closed around his throat and a knee powered into his groin. Fire spread through him and vomit filled his throat, but the policeman's fingers tightened and the spew had no way to go but down, into his lungs.

Frank lifted Tony by the throat and slammed his head down onto the floor. The thick-pile carpet did little to cushion the blow. Scarlet-tinged blackness filled Tony's vision.

CHAPTER THIRTY-TWO

The beating of the helicopter's rotor blades was an omnipresent background noise to their flight from the Sun Garden. It had to be hovering over the institute, but why wouldn't its pilot try to land?

"This way they can keep an eye on all exits," Gillian said as they entered the lounge. She held a hand out when Ant tried to turn the main lights on. "No. You'll alert 'em." She took out her iPhone and activated the flashlight app. On its lowest setting, she shone it in the direction of the dining room. "Slowly."

The lounge and the dining room weren't just deserted; they were lifeless. To Rachel, both rooms felt cold and empty, as though no human presence had graced them. Had it only been six hours since she met Iain, Julia, and Gilly's co-worker Glyn?

"Where are the others?" Rachel's voice echoed in the kitchen, where Ant was drinking her second glass of water. Gillian passed a plastic tumbler to her. "Drink," she said. "You can heal, but you can't replace blood so quick. You need fluids."

Rachel took a sip, then the full force of her thirst hit her. She gulped the cold water down, wordlessly passed it to Gillian for a refill. She took her time with the second glass.

Ant's bare feet made light, slapping sounds on the tiled flooring as she went to open the refrigerator. The interior light turned her face wan and ghostly.

Rachel swallowed the salt tablets Gillian handed her, then took the proffered Snickers bar from Ant. She didn't feel hungry, faint or nauseous, but knew adrenaline was fooling her body into maintaining its state of alertness, so hadn't protested Gillian's insistence on a trip to the kitchens for sustenance first. She'd crash otherwise. *And there's a lot to face now.*

"Julia you know about." Gillian's face was grim. "Iain…Iain went into Acute Ward an hour ago."

Ant's hand froze on the bottle of Lucozade Sport. Rachel stopped chewing; the peanuts felt like marbles stuck in her throat.

"I don't need to tell you why. Glyn went with him, but I bet that southern bastard gave him the knife and the pliers beforehand."

Rachel closed her eyes. A vision of Iain pulling the rest of his teeth out and smiling with agony filled her mind and she dropped the Snickers bar. Gillian checked her watch.

"All this at same time t'shit happened downtown," she said. "News report on telly said some shite about a terrorist attack. Soldiers in yellow boiler suits and helmets walking down seafront with guns. All roads leading out o' Fairlight shut down, curfew in place, and phone lines are down. No interweb, no communications. Nowt."

Rachel forced herself to swallow her mouthful of chocolate and looked at Ant. "When we…when we went under, we both saw something from the lighthouse. Like a black searchlight. Was that reported?"

"Aye." Gillian took a swig from a milk carton. She wiped the milk moustache away with the back of her hand. "Plenty witnesses. Army spokesman said sommat about mass-hallucination, which no bugger's buying. They said same thing about Callum Hayes's little stunt at his sister's funeral."

Rachel's eyebrows rose, questioning. Gillian shook her head. The nose ring and chain flapped against her cheek.

"Aye, you don't know 'bout that, do you? He came in same time as you did – but his entry were a lot more showy. His hometown's been shut down and sealed off an' all."

"Okay." Rachel took a deep breath. "Iain's in the Acute Ward. Glyn's not come back yet, so I'm guessing he's not to be trusted?"

Gillian shook her head again.

"What about Quinn? Callum Hayes is still here. Has Bethan been around?"

"No one's seen hide nor hair of her. She took half-day, I were told, but her car's still here. Quinn went about same time. I asked Rogers in Site Services what's happened, but he don't know fuck all."

Iain and Glyn. Callum and Bethan. God, what were they doing to each other? Rachel shuddered. Then Gillian's comment about the town sent a chill through her body.

"Shut down. All roads closed off?"

"Aye. All a blind. They'll be coming here next. That's why we've gotta move." Another glance at her watch. "I watched what was happenin' with telescope in OT room. All designed to make it look like focus is on t'town, but mark my words: it's this place they'll be shuttin' down."

Dad. Where are you?

"So where do we go? They'll be here any minute, surely?"

"To the lighthouse," Ant said quietly. "That's where we go."

Gillian frowned. "Nowt there, Ant. We gotta get to the lower levels, hide there until they've finished. I left the door to Sun Garden wedged open, so it looks like folk've left, but if they do a full search, we're buggered."

"Why the lower levels? What's down there?"

Gillian sighed as she shut the fridge door. She fingered the laminated keycard and twisted the lanyard around her fingers. "If I guess right, Glyn will try to free Callum. I want to make sure that bastard stays where he is. And then...then we hide out. There's a place down there t'authorities know bugger all about."

Rachel made no attempt to move. Callum Hayes...the prospect of coming face to face with the man of her nightmares was like a punch in the stomach.

"Don't worry, you won't have t'face him." Gillian patted her shoulder and picked up her iPhone. Shining the handset into the dining room, she moved past. Rachel was left staring at Ant.

The younger girl had regained composure. She no longer looked worried, but neither did she have that far-off, otherworldly look in her eyes that had been her hallmark, either.

And perhaps…Callum might be scared of me. The look on his face when that blast blew him out the building - that was total fear. No one's looked at me like that, no one. And Ant…Ant even scares me. Perhaps if we do come face to face he'll be too scared to do anything.

"Are you cold? Do you need to get some shoes?"

Ant shrugged. "I've walked on worse than cold floors. I'll manage."

Hand in hand, they left the kitchen and followed Gillian's erratic flashlight.

Down the main corridor, Rachel found herself tiptoeing, subconsciously afraid of alerting anyone left in Fairlight to their presence. Ant followed behind; her bare feet were soundless. It made no odds; Gillian's heavy trainers, squeaking and thumping, made enough noise for all of them. Rachel winced.

The young nurse lowered her iPhone and peered through the window. She was about to swipe her access card down the panel when she froze. "Shit." She pocketed the phone and turned to face the girls. "Back! Quickly!"

Rachel froze, unable to read Gillian's expression in the gloom. Then a pale shaft of light shone through the small window, cubed and dissected by the wire mesh between the glass panels.

The reception lights had come to life.

"They're here," Gillian said grimly. "Back the way we

came, quickly!"

Rachel waited until Gillian had passed and the flashlight app restarted, before grabbing Ant's hand and turning. She caught a brief glance of two soldiers entering the reception: one was armed with an automatic rifle, clad in a yellow Hazmat suit, his face obscured by a helmet; the other was in camouflage fatigues, with close-cropped grey hair and a hard, determined look about him. She didn't wait to see who followed them, but the flashing of blue lights told her these guys had come with a police escort.

"Where to?" Rachel hissed as they made their way back down the corridor.

"We'll have to chance going t'back way. If we hug walls, use cover of shrubs, we might be able to make it." There was little conviction in her voice, only desperation.

"I say we get out of here right now." Rachel's heart pounded. She didn't care what Gillian had planned, or why she was so determined to get them to the lower levels. All that mattered was getting her and Ant out of here – and to find a way to her father. "We take our chances with that bloody chopper, run across the headland."

To the lighthouse. Ant's eyes sparkled in the gloom.

At the hungry smile that followed, Rachel Collins felt a chill run through her already cold body.

Callum Hayes woke in darkness. He lay pressed against a warm, vinyl-coated padding that felt familiar. The smell of his blood and the feel of his ruined eyeballs beneath his shaking, grasping fingers confirmed he had returned to Fairlight.

Standing was an effort – he was more drained than he'd ever been before, and the blast of Light from the Collins bitch and…

…what was that? Her mother?

…felt like he had been subject to some mad scientist's laser beam. He felt he'd been disintegrated and not wholly reassembled.

Outstretched fingers felt for the small portal in the doorway. They found it, and he pressed his cheek against the door, trying to see through.

Nothing. But the lights in the corridor beyond were never switched off. So what –

The memory of the torn, squashed, grape-like things under his fingers had him mewling in despair.

"But I could see without them! You granted me your gift, your vision!"

The padded walls soaked up his words; his protest was silenced. He sank to his knees. He wanted to weep; shudders wracked his body, but only a dull ache from his eye sockets accompanied his sobs. And with it, the memory of tears.

He felt empty. Hollow. All power, all potential to become the leader of a new generation, was gone.

Defeated. Just like that? He fingered the holes in his palms. The skeins were there, but they felt fragile, like tissue paper. They hurt.

His fingers went to his eye sockets. He hesitated, fearful of feeling the emptiness; confirmation that his sight – his human sight - had gone for nothing. He remembered witnessing the horrified faces of the funeral congregation, the powerless face of his father, the thousands of supportive emails, Tweets and comments on his blog posts and TikTok videos.

The joy of beholding the Sightriders, the alien vision of the old man and Rachel's father in the village pub and witnessing what the power within him did to them. Would he be able to see in his dreams? Would his sight return when he was unconscious?

Who cares? What fucking good is that to me? I need to see

here and now! His eyelids were flaps of skin that stuck to his sweating fingertips, pulled outwards like curtains through an open window when the wind changes.

He lowered his hands. They slumped to his thighs, lifeless.

Now he screamed. He shouted to the ceiling, yelled his frustration and betrayal. He felt the ground tremble, but knew it was only his quaking body that gave that impression – his ability to move the earth was no more.

Only when his screams echoed down the corridor – no longer soaked up by the padded walls - and warmth spilled onto his face did he realise the door to his cell was open.

He heard a sharp intake of breath and a muttered curse. A male voice.

"Is that you, Quinn? Come to gloat?" He felt the tremble in his voice, the quavering tone of a small, frightened little boy, and he both hated and pitied himself for it. He was aware he was rocking back and forth on his ankles, his arms wrapped around his chest, and forced himself to keep still. Regain control.

"No, mate. It's Glyn. Glyn Dolan. Remember me?"

Callum almost fell backwards. "Glyn? You're kidding! They had tabs on all of us – how the fuck did you get a job here?"

"I thought I'd covered my tracks. Found out an hour ago that wasn't the case. The bastards played me." Firm hands took hold of Callum's. They were warm and slippery, coated in something slimy.

"Jesus, Callum. What have you done to yourself?"

Callum allowed Glyn to pull him to his feet. The lack of sight made his disorientation worse. He swayed, would have fallen had Glyn not put an arm around his shoulder and steadied him.

"What I thought had to be done," Callum said in a weak voice. He allowed Glyn to guide him towards the door. "It was worth it…at the time. But now…"

Glyn's trainers squeaked on the padded floor. There was a slight change in pitch, and a squishing sound, like grapes being squashed underfoot. "Oh, shit. *Jesus*…"

Callum swallowed, fighting back bile. He knew what Glyn had trod in. He took a deep breath before continuing. "What I had – what replaced my eyes – was something wonderful. God, the things I saw…"

Glyn's arm tightened. "Don't worry, mate. We'll get you fixed up. Remember what you said in your April blogpost?"

Callum shook his head. He hesitated when his feet made contact with a hard, tiled surface.

"Easy, mate. I've got you. Just take my lead, yeah?" Glyn guided Callum down the corridor. Callum's nostrils flared; he smelt disinfectant and floor polish, and the hint of blood and excrement. Something else as well: musky, sweaty. The scent of fear.

"You said removing the eyes was to be avoided, but stated that nearer the time the Presence will call on some of us to do just that. Why would that power ask us to do this if it left us blind? It needs us to be able to function in the real world, yeah?"

Callum considered this. *April*. God, so much had happened since then. "I can't remember…"

"You're our leader. If it ordered you to do this, it must be for a good reason. It won't leave you sightless." Glyn stopped. Callum heard fingernails on laminated plastic, then the click of a card-activated lock spring open. A door was pushed open, and with the air-conditioned chill came the full force of the stink. Blood, shit and fear: human terror and pain filled his nostrils. Sweet perfume. He was overcome with it, felt strength return.

"The Presence left me. It was that Collins bitch. She wasn't alone."

"Yeah, nutty Ant was with her, wasn't she?"

Callum nodded. "And someone else. Some*thing* else. Claimed to be the bitch's mum."

Glyn whistled. "Shit. That *is* new."

"She wasn't human, whatever she was. The look she gave me – her and her daughter – blew me back here. Stripped my ability."

Glyn guided him forwards, closer to the source of the smell. Callum heard shuffling and rattling; the sounds of someone secured to bed railings with canvas straps.

"No, mate. Just temporary." Glyn paused. "You probably don't know what's happening out there."

"Yeah. Broadband reception's crap in that cell."

"TV and internet wouldn't tell the full story, anyway. The town's under complete lockdown. An explosion in the pub on the quayside – they're blaming us."

Callum turned his face in the direction of Glyn. He heard his rescuer attempt to stifle his gasp. "An explosion? That's bullshit, we don't do bombs." *We don't need earthly weapons.*

"'Course it's bullshit. But they're pulling the same blind – sorry – the same story they did about your hometown. Army and Old Bill all over the place, roadblocks. You name it, they've got it."

Callum paused. He inhaled the smell from the prisoner before him, and slowly exhaled. "Fear. They're panicking."

"Got it in one. And guess who they said planted the bomb?"

Callum smiled. He caressed the raised sheets before him. The foot beneath jerked once, and the buckle on the rubber restraint jingled against the rail. "Surprise me."

"According to a statement from the Counter Terrorism Unit, you escaped three hours ago. You and your accomplice…Glyn Doran."

Callum laughed. "So that's how you got a job here. Yeah, they played you all right."

"I don't think Gilly saw the broadcast, but she's been outside hunting for the girls. Doesn't matter, though: we've got to move quickly. As soon as the town is finished, they'll come here. And if that's the case, we ain't getting out alive."

Callum stroked the bedsheets. The body thrashed as he moved his hands up the torso. "So where's everyone else?"

"Quinn and that Jim bloke overpowered Bethan. She was working on young Iain here. They're on their way upstairs."

"Iain, eh? Nice to meet you, mate." Callum placed a hand on the youth's bound hand, then followed the arm up to Iain's head. The forehead was cold and clammy, but the cheeks and chin were coated in warm, sticky blood. A tingling sensation filled Callum's hand, and he smiled at the churning, knitting sensation in the centre of his palm. The skeins *fed*. Iain's cheeks flapped back and forth, against empty gums. Callum nodded, realising how the kid had answered the call of the Presence.

"They gave her quite a hiding," Glyn continued. "Real gentlemen."

"She okay now?" Callum placed his other hand underneath Iain's drooling lips.

"She will be. I patched her up, gave her some painkillers and told her to rest. Tough old bitch, that one. She's looking forward to dishing out some on Quinn."

"I bet." Callum removed his hands and held them to his cheeks. They felt warm, comforting. Invigorating. "We'll help her."

"We'd better lie low for a bit. The Old Bill and the army will be here any minute. First thing they'll do is change the access codes for all the keycards. Mine'll be useless then."

"And they'll be able to check your last movements, know exactly where you are," Callum said. "They'll think they have you trapped."

"Yeah. Got any suggestions?"

The warmth transferred to his face was now heat. He felt

dark energy course through his skin, and his sense of self-defeat began to evaporate.

But it's not enough. He sighed. "I'll think of something. Tell me: did Bethan keep all of Iain's teeth?"

A multiple rattle of dental enamel on steel answered him. Glyn passed the kidney dish to Callum's free hand and closed his fingers around the lip.

"Good. Take me to her. She wanted to help the Evolution. Now's her chance.

CHAPTER THIRTY-THREE

There was a sharp grunt, and the pressure on Tony Collins's throat lessened. Frank beat Tony to unconsciousness. Tony fought the oncoming dark, and did his best to push the bulky policeman away from him. He had to push and roll to free himself.

He spun away from his assailant, gasping for breath. His head was still pounding, but his vision cleared. He saw the carbon dioxide extinguisher.

Then he heard a thud and a metallic clang, as the water extinguisher slipped from Karen's grip and rolled on the carpeted floor to rest against his own weapon. Blood and matted hair coated the bottom rim. He looked up, saw Karen stagger backwards in horror at what she had done. Her hands were still bound, but were now before her.

Slipped them under your bum and legs and freed yourself that way, he thought dizzily. *Clever girl.*

Then he saw the other copper, backing away from Karen, his right hand on the Taser retrieved from his utility belt. Napier unclipped it and raised the weapon, while his other hand flicked the transmit button on his two-way radio.

"Karen!" Tony's voice was hoarse, barely a whisper. He pulled the CO2 extinguisher towards him, ignoring the fresh pain signals of burned wrists. "Get down!"

Karen made the mistake of turning, following Tony's stare. She froze as Napier pulled the trigger.

The Taser's air cartridge broke open and compressed gas shot the twin wires through the air. The electrodes' barbs would have caught Karen in the face had Tony not got to his feet and thrown the extinguisher towards the policeman. The wires became entangled around the canister and pulled the stun weapon from Napier as it flew to the other end of the reception desk.

Tony broke into a run, taking advantage of Napier's momentary surprise. The policeman's left hand was still at the radio on his stabvest, but his fingers had slipped from the button.

Tony reached for the vase of orchids as he passed the reception desk. He threw it in Napier's face and then raced past him, crouching down for the extinguisher.

Napier swatted the vase away, but not before the flowers and water spilled onto his face and stabvest. He spat green water, coughed, and turned.

Tony lifted the extinguisher by its handle, taking care not to touch any part of the Taser wires entangled around the canister. He pulled the pin, turned, and depressed the lever.

Freezing mist enveloped the policeman's head and torso. Orchid petals and stamens flew in the air. The blast muffled Napier's scream.

Tony stood motionless, the canister trembling in his hand, but his grip on the depressed lever firm and unyielding. When Napier fell to the floor, Tony lowered the horn so that the directional flow of escaping carbon dioxide continued to hit the policeman in the face.

Ten seconds to empty the extinguisher. The plastic horn felt cold in his hand, and the base of the canister was coated in icy droplets. It felt like an age, but when the remaining cloud of carbon dioxide faded, Napier was on his knees, his palms pressed against his frostbitten eyes. He made sounds that were a cross between moaning and keening, as if he knew the permanent damage that had been done to his sight.

Tony carefully lowered the extinguisher and unthreaded the Taser's tangled wires. Then he raised the canister and brought it down hard on Napier's temple.

Tony glanced at Karen; she was sat on the edge of the reception sofa, her bound hands on her knees, fingers interlocked and twisting, kneading each other. Her eyes were rooted on the first cop to fall, the one she had incapacitated with the water extinguisher. He wasn't moving.

Tony inclined his head to see through the glass panel of the door Rawlings had exited. He fully expected the general's armed escort to come hurtling back into the reception area, automatic rifle raised…he picked up the Taser and ejected the spent electrode wires. The weapon had a set of two replacement pairs in the grip.

Better than nothing. He examined the Taser, surprised how easy it was to reload, and placed it in the thigh pocket of his work trousers, then went to the sofa. He crouched down and took Karen's hands in his.

"I k-killed him," she said in rapid, gasping breaths. "He's d-dead…"

Tony said nothing. He pressed his hands around hers and gently stopped her fingers. The arms still trembled. Tony looked over his shoulder. Karen's handbag had been thrown to one side by Frank. It now lay soaked in orchid water.

"Karen, if he's dead, it's no fault of yours. You saved my life. If he hadn't throttled me, he'd have taken us down to…wherever it is, and we wouldn't be getting out alive. And neither would Rachel. Rawlings would make sure of that." *If she is harmed, Mr Collins, it won't be by our hands. It'll be by hers. Or yours. 'Translocation'…it proves you and your daughter have something in common. Now we have to work out how that connection works.*

"Here." He released her hands and led her to the reception desk. "Just look straight ahead, not at the ground."

Her legs shook. He placed her hands on the visitors' book. "Grip the desk with your knees, okay? You won't fall. I'm getting your bag."

He picked the leather bag from the floor and dusted off the pollen and water. He put it on the desk and opened it.

"Trust me: I don't make a habit of going through ladies'

things." He forced a smile to accompany the weak joke, tried to ignore the half-litre bottle of vodka. She flashed an all-too brief smile back, tight and ephemeral. "You got a nail file in here?"

She nodded. "In that section. Next to the compact."

"Got it." He retrieved the file, feeling comforted by the presence of the printouts of Rachel's maps.

Karen seemed a bit calmer. Her knees ceased drumming the desk's modesty panel, and she looked over her shoulder, at the dark car park. Running lights from the Merlin helicopter made the shadows move.

"Why haven't they come in force? Two policemen, one soldier…it doesn't make sense."

"I wondered that." He removed the file's vinyl sleeve and began sawing at the fastening of her PlastiCuffs. "That chopper's on standby, waiting for orders. I'm guessing what Rawlings has planned hasn't been officially sanctioned; he's treading carefully. He went to Quinn's office first, for some reason." He shot an occasional glance at the corridor door while he worked. "Didn't want to use my lighter on you. Doesn't matter what happens to my hands – they've been through a hell of a lot worse – but yours…" The plastic strip fell apart. She clutched his hands. "Yours are…well…"

She caressed his knuckles, the scraped skin from his assault on the roller shutter door now fully healed. The burns from his lighter were still there, though, but even they weren't as severe as they should've been. *Healing*, he realised. *Another self-inflicted wound…*

There was tenderness and wonder in her eyes as she held his hands. "Fast healer."

"Runs in the family." He smiled, then shuddered.

Karen nodded. She released his hands and pulled the printouts from her handbag. "Okay. Let's go and find your daughter."

Jon Rogers stared at the opening door, frozen. The Beconase nozzle was still in his left nostril; he didn't have time to snort the antihistamine fluid back before the door opened and General Rawlings entered with his armed escort.

The site services manager found himself staring down the barrel of an MP5 submachine gun, but it was the silver-haired commanding officer that scared him more.

"Hello, Jon. Don't get up." The general pushed the clutter of lever arch files and paperwork from Rogers's desk towards the PC monitor and rested the backs of his thighs on the beech wood. He folded his arms. "You don't seem surprised to see me."

Rogers took his hand from his nostril. The Beconase bottle didn't tremble in his fingers.

"Not scared, either," Rawlings added.

"You're…prepared."

Rogers snorted and swallowed the hay fever-relief fluid. The fluid, so rank and bitter, now tasted like nectar; he knew it was the last thing he would taste.

"Aye. Soon as I heard the explosion in the town, I knew it was coming to an end." He swallowed, his eyes flicking back and forth between the steady barrel of the MP5 and the equally steady gaze of General Rawlings.

"Where's Quinn?" The general inspected his fingernails. To Rogers, there was no need; they were trimmed and clean. He suspected this was a habit of the general's, a mental preparation before a killing. "He's not in his office, despite explicit orders to stay at his desk."

"I dunno. Last I saw of him on the monitors, he was heading into the Acute Ward. That was an hour ago. He ain't come out since." Rogers pointed towards the bank of monitors at the far end of his office.

Rawlings didn't take his eyes off his fingernails. "I see. Did he say why he was going there?"

Rogers shook his head. He could smell gun oil and cordite through the odour of Beconase, and knew the machine gun had been used and cleaned earlier today.

"Bethan Appleton? Is she down there as well?"

"Aye. Figured that's why he ain't come out yet. You were right about her, General. She's been waiting for the Hayes boy, but as soon as ol' Jim was admitted she…she spent most o' the afternoon with him."

"Good God." Rawlings lowered his hands and stared hard at the site services manager. His eyes were steel. "I doubt there'll be anything left."

Rogers briefly wondered who Rawlings meant – Bethan, Quinn, or Jim Dawson. It didn't matter, though; soon there'd be nothing left of any of them. There was only one possible reason for Fairlight to be under lockdown and for the architect of the Orpheus Project to be here in person at the institute.

"And the others? Glyn Doran and Gillian Vassey are on duty today, yes?"

"Aye," Rogers said. "Glyn went down with one of the other kids – Iain, I think – but Gillian's easy enough to find."

Rawlings followed the pointed finger, aimed at screen five. In digital colour, Gillian was clearly visible crouched by the door leading to the Sun Garden. Two other girls were with her.

"Well, well. Would you mind explaining why that nurse is trying to help those two patients to escape?"

"See for yourself, boss." Rogers's fingers flew over the keyboard. Rawlings watched the reversing footage. Dusk became evening, and bronze sunlight filled the Sun Garden. The two girls' hair wavered in the gloaming, one mousy and one golden, as they pressed bleeding palms to each other. A brief flash of black stabbed from the sundial towards the ruined lighthouse.

"Okay. Roll it from there. Slow-mo, if you please." Rawlings eyed the time display in the top right-hand corner as the black beam flared from the Oratory to strike the two girls. His eyebrows rose.

"They were gone for over an hour," Rogers said. "Gillian went out all over the grounds looking for 'em, but it was obvious they hadn't done a runner."

"Indeed. Please forward to the moment they returned."

Rogers had to admire the professionalism of Rawlings's comrade. The soldier was a complete automaton, not showing any interest in the incredible events playing back before him. His stance didn't alter, the MP5 didn't move, and the black-visored helmet remained fixed in his direction.

Rogers had spent the last hour watching just what Rawlings ordered him to show now. He still couldn't believe it, and each repeated viewing merely reinforced the impossibility of what happened to Rachel Collins and Antoinette Penner.

The dark flash from the Pharos hid the disappearance of the girls, but there was no obstruction to the camera upon their return.

A patch of lawn, the brown grass barely moving in the wind, and a clear indication of where the two girls had lain: flattened grass formed an indentation in which shadows played.

Then they were back. No fading into view, no transparency or opacity, no shimmering or heat-haze or anything that Hollywood CGI would have used. They just appeared. No matter how slowly Rogers ran the feed, a finger tapping the 'frame advance' on the stilled film to move from one millisecond to the next, Rachel Collins and Antoinette Penner appeared, fully fleshed and lying in exactly the same position they had collapsed into an hour previously.

A few seconds later, Gillian's head appeared at the bottom of the camera's view.

"So she witnessed this," Rawlings said evenly. "No wonder she's trying to get them out."

Rogers watched Rawlings carefully. The general was trying to hide his astonishment – admiration? – for the length of time the two girls had disappeared, but there was no hiding the gleam in his eye, the thin lips parted like a freshly opened flesh wound. The unforeseen side-effect of the failed Orpheus Project would reap dividends for him and his paymasters. Rogers slumped in his swivel chair, suddenly exhausted, and sick to the stomach.

I've had enough. I want it all to end now.

"The Hayes boy? Is he still secured?"

"Aye," Rogers muttered. "Nothing happened down there. Lemme show you."

Camera three's display came up. A pristine, white-tiled corridor terminated in a low door with a small, circular viewing portal.

"He ain't moved since. Bethan visited him a coupla times, but -"

Rawlings almost leapt from the site service manager's desk. "What the hell is going on?"

The change in tone – calm, measured and authoritative – to one of anger, filled with incipient violence, made even the armed soldier look away from his target. All three men stared at the screen.

"Bloody hell," Rogers whispered.

The door was open. Callum Hayes was being helped down the corridor by the only present nurse within Fairlight.

Rawlings rounded on Rogers. His teeth were bared, his eyes ablaze. "All Fairlight staff keycard access: deny permissions. *Now.*"

Rogers opened another window on his computer, bringing up the complete lists of access cards and the names assigned to them. Six people: four staff members, and two 'guest' passes, that only Rawlings possessed.

The codes to those were unviable from Rogers's console; only Rawlings and his superiors could change the permissions on those.

Rogers highlighted all four staff members' names, then selected the 'deny access' option. The names flashed red on his monitor. Even his own.

Now everyone's trapped. He watched Rawlings retrieve a two-way radio from an inner pocket, and turned to the display from camera one.

It was a peaceful scene, usually. The front facade of Fairlight Hospital: modern, glittering chrome and steel surmounted by Victorian red-brick neo-gothic. Past and future, juxtaposed. Incongruous, yet oddly comforting; especially when the sun dipped behind the finials and spires of the older building and turned the red brick into gold and copper.

Now the building was shrouded in darkness, the solar lamps from the car park mere pinpricks of light that did nothing to dispel the pall of imminent destruction that awaited Fairlight and all within. The running lights of the circling helicopter were demon's eyes, casting unholy light on the building. The barrel of the 7.62mm general purpose machine gun in its belly gleamed.

Strange things to think about, Rogers thought, as Rawlings issued commands to his men. The helicopter rotated, and Rogers saw the other cargo door slide open, illuminated from within by the twin-torches on each soldier's helmet. Rappel lines spilled forth.

Rogers's hand moved the mouse to the *start* icon. There was no point logging off really, but…

He looked up. The helmeted soldier was hastening through the doorway, back to the corridor and the reception. *Now what?* Rogers turned back, saw the handgun in Rawlings's hand. The two-way radio was gone, and the general's left hand worked the slide on his sidearm. He placed the muzzle on Rogers's temple. Rogers's index finger tightened and depressed the mouse button.

The SIG-Sauer spat fire. Blood and grey matter spattered the monitor, obscuring the message *Logged Out.*

CHAPTER THIRTY-FOUR

Quinn stared in horror at the swipe pad on the sealed door. He retried his card.

A 'click' to signify the card had been registered, but no sound of door bolts loosening. He tried again.

Access Denied, he realised. His heart sank. He rested his head on the steel door.

"They's locked us down?"

Quinn didn't reply. He dropped the card from the panel. It dangled on the twisted lanyard around his neck, spinning in the direction of the uncurling cord. Mocking him.

"Well," Jim said in a casual tone, "they chose a great place to trap us."

Quinn sighed and turned to face Jim. In his threadbare hospital gown, emaciated and ancient, the old man looked disturbingly at home in the old Victorian storeroom. Of course, Quinn reminded himself, Jim had been an inmate here before the old asylum had been taken over and 'rebooted'. But the modern extensions were just that: extensions, a façade to hide the older building rather than wipe out its history and original purpose.

You spent your formative years here, Jim. And yet you don't fear Fairlight, seem unconcerned about your own future. Now the old inmate was backtracking, peering through the meshed panels of the door leading back to the original asylum access corridor they had traversed.

"No use, Jim." Quinn winced at the sound of his voice. The makeshift dressings did little to prevent fresh blood flow from his nose, but the cotton wool swabs had at least forced him to breathe through his mouth, not the remnants of his nose. That, with the painkillers, made his words sound alien, distorted – a voice from a dream, or a nightmare, rather than his own. *How much we take for granted*, he had mused as Jim applied the dressings. *Even our own voices…but what is my own voice, really? Who have I been speaking for all these years?*

"Aye. This'll be locked down as well – 'bout the only bloody refurbishment they done to this section."

Quinn suddenly felt exhausted. He sank to the floor, rested his throbbing head against the wall and stretched out his legs. Pieces of plaster and flaked paintwork pressed into his hair, irritating his bald spot like burrowing insects.

Why had Jim insisted they come here first? If they'd raced to the elevator as Quinn had planned, they'd be on the ground level by now. Then again, they'd be easier prey to the armed soldiers, waiting for the elevator doors to open…

He stared at the dusty shelving, empty save for a few cork-stoppered bottles and retort stands. Leaning against a wooden bookend with a centrepiece carved into a globe of the Earth were a few large, thick hardback books - nineteenth-century ledgers, Quinn figured. He noticed a few dust-free sections on the shelves. Books – and taken recently. Why the hell hadn't he paid more attention down here?

"I remember this room," Jim said with a wistful sigh. "Me an' some o the other kids used to play hide and seek when they let us out o' the ward."

"Good God. Is this really the time to be nostalgic?"

"It were a proper storeroom back then. They kept all their old books and medical stuff – 'part from the sharp things, obviously. I got me education here…"

Quinn felt the wall vibrate. His scalp tingled. He turned his head and pressed his ear to the wall.

One thing he had realised about the older part of the asylum was how solid the walls were in comparison to the more recent additions. Sound scarcely travelled in these sections, and it was unlikely he would hear the footsteps of approaching armed soldiers.

So what's that banging?

"Them warders fair near shit 'emselves when they caught me here the third time. I acted all innocent like, kept me nose buried in one o' the books…but didn't let on that I knew what this room joined onto. I'd discovered it the first time I came here…"

Jim crouched next to Quinn. The gown rode over his midriff, exposing stick-thin legs and a withered scrotum, and the thin scar leading up to the horizontal slit in his belly. He tapped on the wall. More paint flakes rained down on Quinn's head.

"There was a door here. Another room – well, more of a pantry. That's where they kept their exhibits." Jim knocked again. Echoes answered him. Quinn leapt to his feet and turned, backing away from the wall. "Plasterboard an' paint. No real security. Guess they must've moved 'em."

"Moved what?" Quinn's voice was shrill, and his nasal passages screamed in protest at the vibrations.

"Specimen jars. Full o' starfish-like things, but with only three legs." Jim turned. "Guess that's sommat else yer guv'nors didn't tell you about? How much o' the old section have you actually *seen*?"

Quinn's cheeks flushed with embarrassment, but he ignored the question. It was possible Rawlings and his company didn't know about it, either; they were more interested in the current project and Fairlight's newest inhabitants, not ancient history.

Jim watched Quinn intently and nodded. "Right. Let's see if there's anything left. Something that may help us greet them soldiers in style…"

Quinn went to the shelves on the opposite wall. He picked up the bookend and pushed the ledgers back. The globe, painted to represent the Victorian perception of the world – mostly one colour, representing the Empire – fit easily in his palm. The bookend itself was a heavy slab, and an ideal weapon. He walked back to the wall and slammed it into the centre.

The shower of plaster and paint came in an explosion. Quinn's hand disappeared into the hole, his wrist scraping on rough edges of plaster and splinters of plywood as it powered through the rotten partition.

Instead of withdrawing his arm, Quinn pressed onwards, widening the breach with his forearm and elbow. He raised a foot and kicked.

He kicked again, withdrew his foot and his weapon hand, and barged into the crumbling partition wall with his shoulder. Dust filled his eyes, and he closed his mouth, thankful the dressings prevented access to his nasal passages.

He stood in the dark annex for a moment, eyes closed, and exhaled slowly. He waited until it seemed safe to take a breath.

Behind him, Jim broke the remainder of the thin wall down, allowing faint illumination from the storeroom's lights to spill into the newly revealed room.

It was about five foot square, and empty. Whatever Jim had believed to be stored here was long gone. But perhaps there might be another way out, into another passage that would give them an advantage over the approaching troops. It was worth a try. If the wall they had broken through was nothing but a plasterboard partition, perhaps another would be as well.

He stepped forwards and tapped the adjacent wall with the bookend. A more solid thump greeted him. The same with the three other walls.

Good, solid, Victorian brick. No way out.

"Shit!" He threw the bookend at the first wall again. A hand fell on his shoulder. He whirled.

"Listen," Jim said softly. He stepped forwards, guiding Quinn to the wall. He lowered and pressed his ear to the wall. His eyes widened.

Quinn heard it too. Faint, almost completely swallowed by the brick barrier, but unmistakeable.

Screaming and laughter. Screams that sounded like they came from a young male – Quinn couldn't make out who – but the laughter was all too familiar. There was no denying its source.

"Callum Hayes," Quinn whispered.

The eyeballs were warm and slippery. Callum rolled each one between forefinger and thumb. They felt like marbles soaked in oil.

Could it work? Iain had willingly gouged them from his own sockets, but it was Glyn who had severed the optic nerves.

But he'd had to. The pain – and the ecstasy that followed - was too great for Iain to concentrate on completing the task.

"It's still a self-mutilation," Glyn said as he replaced the scalpel. "It's a willing sacrifice. An offering. It'll work."

Callum lowered his head. He held the severed eyeballs close to his sockets. He had lost the ability to open his eyelids; they were useless flaps of skin, sucked into the concavity of his empty sockets.

"Hang on, Callum. Let me."

Callum felt his eyelids pulled out from the sockets. They resisted; it felt like sunburnt skin being peeled away. Callum stiffened, ground his teeth, and realised he was crushing the gift of eyeballs. He forced himself to stop.

What's wrong? Surely the Sightriders should be twitching with anticipation?

"Okay. One at a time." Glyn released the left-hand eyelid. It sucked back into place. Callum's right hand was guided to the corresponding eye socket and his thumb and forefinger were loosened. What felt like a cannonball pushed into his head. Then Glyn pulled the eyelid down. It hurt; the skin was no longer accustomed to being stretched over an eyeball.

"Okay. Shall we do the other one now?"

Callum was hyperventilating. In many ways, this felt worse than removing his eyes. This was wrong. It didn't feel right. *It's not going to work.*

"Yeah. Let's do it." He took a deep breath and raised his left hand. He braced himself for the pain.

Minutes passed and Callum felt uneasy in the silent darkness. He heard Bethan's deep breathing, fast asleep from Glyn's painkillers, and the pleasured moaning of Iain, his body rocking back and forth in his bed with ecstasy. There was no need to tie him again.

Still nothing. Iain's eyeballs felt like ping-pong balls, and just as useful. Just as hollow…

Callum stiffened. His palms twitched. Knitting flesh, itching, healing…

…hungering…

His stigmata. Birthplace of the Sightriders. Finally, he knew what to do. What would work.

"Glyn. Pass me his teeth." He lifted his hands. Glyn wordlessly tipped the kidney dish's contents into Callum's upraised palms. "What do you see?"

"Jesus! It's…"

"Indescribable?" Callum smiled for the first time that day. The Presence was back – faint, tenuous, but here nevertheless. "Try."

"Whirlpools - no, it's like…oh my God!" There was clatter as the kidney dish fell from Glyn's hand and rolled on the floor. Scuffling trainers beat a hasty retreat.

Callum grinned. He felt the teeth burrowing, pulled into his holed palms by a current more powerful than any earthly whirlpool Glyn could imagine. His hands were on fire; he felt canines, molars and premolars – could feel each *shape* – swirl within his flesh. They rearranged themselves, twisting until the roots pressed through the backs of his hands; the crowns remained beneath the skin of his palms.

They formed ranks: serried rows each side of his skeins. Like rows of eyelashes. They pushed against the tautness of his remaining human flesh. His fingers twitched spasmodically.

He lowered his head and pushed his hands into his face, like a desert traveller whose thirst is now sated throws cupped water into his sunburnt brow.

He held them there, waiting for the teeth — freely given by Iain, and now the property of the Presence — to resume their biologically decreed task. To bite, chew, and enable the mouth they surrounded to digest flesh.

They took his eyelids first. That didn't surprise him — Iain had given both his teeth and his eyes, so Callum still had to offer *something* of himself - but he was shocked by the pain. Sunburnt skin again, ripped with the healing, still-tender flesh beneath. The eyeballs slid out, and his cry of pain became a sigh of pleasure.

Now there was a sign from the Sightriders. Now he felt twitching in the severed optic nerves, the writhing of eels coming to life.

"Yes! Yes! *Yes!*"

Liquid sprang from his eye sockets. He felt it spray through his fingers and the feeding of his palms became more ferocious, devouring. The absolute blackness lessened, became shifting greys. When he took his hands away, he gasped.

His vision was restored. But it was not his former, human eyesight; the face before him was his own. His hands dropped into his lap with the shock of seeing his ravaged, *wizened* face with black caverns, twisting with serpentine life, where his eyes were. Palms still upwards, his vision was of a plaster ceiling with flickering fluorescent strip-lighting. He turned his hands over and held them towards the far wall.

The vision, as before — but *better!* Not just shifting greys and sepia, but *colour.* The blood from Iain's grinning, toothless maw and the dribbling fluid from his eye sockets sparkled like rubies and diamonds.

Enhanced vision, just as in the other state. He laughed with delight and excitement. Iain shuffled on the bed towards him, his hands outstretched.

"Soon, Iain." Callum kept his left palm fixed on the adoring Iain and turned his right hand to scan the rest of the room. Two different views, each processed by his mind simultaneously. He saw Bethan stirring from her sleep, her eyes blinking in bewilderment as she rose from the bed. And he saw Glyn, his saviour, with hand repeatedly swiping his access card up and down on the access panel.

"Oh, ye of little faith." He turned both hands to Iain. "Open your mouth, mate. Let's see what gift the Presence has given you."

Iain's cheeks were no longer sunken. They bulged like a hamster's, the skin rippling and threatening to tear with the new harvest. Iain could only smile with his eyes as he obeyed his leader's command.

The gums were no barrier to the new teeth birthed. His most recent self-extractions provided a clear access for the three-pronged pieces of black chitin, but they still tore the remains of the jaw line in their eagerness to enter the world, enrobed in blood and scraps of gum. Writhing became scurrying as they slid down the trail of blood and saliva to Iain's bared chest.

To Callum's fresh eyes, these new creatures – each the size of a human tooth - were beyond beautiful. They were jewels of ebony-like darkness that sparkled more wonderfully than the finest cut diamond. As each baby Triskelion unfurled its miniature legs he cried in delight – and fatherly pride – at their twitching and trembling, as they sensed the new world they had been born into.

And then a second birth: each limb unfolded, the outer section glittering with the promise of razor-destruction. They stretched upwards, drinking in the last of Iain's blood and saliva, then retracted.

Feed, my children. He held his hands closer. He could swear the eyes in the centre of each palm watered. Tears of joy and wonder at this miraculous birthing.

He was oblivious to everything else in the room. He heard a muffled cry from Glyn and a banging from somewhere in the corridor beyond, but they didn't concern him. Glyn would share his joy in this birth eventually. As would Bethan.

Sandwiched between two layers of circular, hub-like shell, the spongy bodies pulsed as they ingested their host's life-fluid. The jelly-like flesh retained its leprous yellow and grey colouring, and the stink of putrefying organic matter filled Callum's nostrils. It was sweet, sweet, perfume.

The shells shuddered and tiny protrusions appeared, forming a circle around the rim. Raised indentations that split down the middle, parting like human eyelids. Callum's palms twitched again, and a thrill coursed through his body. He trembled.

Tiny, tiny, eyes, but eyes nevertheless. Pupils smaller than pinpricks floated in pools of sea-green irises. They moved as one, in the same direction, focussing on their midwife. The limbs rose once more. In salute.

Their first action is to salute me. An army, born to do one thing only: follow my command.

He was dizzy with the realisation that the Presence had regained its strength, its power to thrust organic representations of itself into this world.

And it's all down to me! My commitment, my belief wavered, but I made amends! Who else would think to make use of his own followers' flesh the way I did? His palms tingled again, and his vision briefly vanished when the eyelids, encrusted with human teeth, closed together. One blink, one crunch of dental enamel, then his vision returned, even clearer.

Still human – sort of.

The eyes of the Triskelions blinked in unison. It was a wonderful sight: all thirty-six creatures, all thirty-six eyes on each suit of armour, closing and opening in imitation of his.

The banging was louder now. It was a distraction. Callum's cheeks burned with anger, and the eyes of the Triskelions flared scarlet. He didn't look up.

"Glyn, find out what that is."

"I – I can't! The doors are locked – my pass has been disabled!"

Callum frowned. For a moment, his babies were forgotten. "So they're on their way…but they can unlock the doors. Who's -"

A shower of plaster and dust followed the splintering and cracking of the wall to his left. Callum turned, held his left hand to the barrier. What he had taken to be a solid wall like the others in this ward was revealed to be nothing more than a thin partition. Dust particles filled his palm-eye and he was too late to close the lids. The pulsing in his hand became a brief irritation and he backed away, his right palm held at waist height to avoid the cloud of plasterboard and paint fragments. A wooden block burst through, the hand grasping it painted white with streaks of blood.

Light spilled through and Callum saw a darkened annex and two men within. He took a sharp breath as he recognised his jailer.

The globe bookend fell from Quinn's bloody hand; his fingers loosened, and his hand dropped to the floor at the sight that greeted him.

"Doctor Quinn!" The irritation in Callum's left palm ceased. He raised both hands and fixed the new arrivals with both eyes and Quinn took a step backwards in horror and disbelief. Callum was pleased to see the bandages wrapped around the clinical psychiatrist's nose and cheeks seeping fresh blood. His grin broadened when he saw Quinn's companion, the old man whose admittance to Fairlight he had enabled with help from his new powers.

Bethan's playmate, he thought. He cast a palm over his infant army.

They too had registered the arrival of the two men. They found their earthly feet quickly; the padded tip of each Triskelion's third limb pressed against the cold body of Iain and raised the central section into a vertical position. Eyes on both sides of the hubs glittered.

"Quinn! Get back here!"

Callum hissed upon hearing Jim Dawson's command. Did the old bastard know what these creatures were?

Didn't matter. He stepped back to allow the Triskelions full access to the adjoining room. Quinn was retreating, Jim's hand on his shoulder pulling him further back into the room beyond the annex.

The Triskelions left little tears in Iain's skin as they launched to the floor. Blood from the wounds flew up, flecked the sheets and Callum's face.

Metallic clicking and whirring filled the room, echoing through both chambers, as the swarm flew on the tiles and through the broken partition wall. There was no order in their approach, no concerted, military-precision approach.

That will come, Callum thought. Individuals now, separate pieces of the Presence's earthly grip on the planet – but they would develop a hive mind when the Presence grew accustomed to its earthly representatives. *With me leading them, guiding them. Controlling them.*

For now, he enjoyed the spectacle of seeing some move faster than others, some with a more unerring sense of direction than their comrades, some of whom attacked the surviving sections of the wall rather than follow their brethren through the gap. These were the most joyous to behold: they showed their species' full lethal potential as they unfolded the razor-sections on their appendages and tore through the plasterboard.

Callum followed, eager to watch their first killing. He didn't hear the click of unlocking deadbolts, but the cry of shock from Glyn and metallic utterances – orders to freeze - made him turn.

New visitors. These ones had guns. He turned back, oblivious to the gunshots that filled the chamber he just departed.

CHAPTER THIRTY-FIVE

In the ICU, Tony Collins smelt Trésor, the perfume that Rachel had fallen in love with. It was faint, only a trace – more a memory of a smell – but it overrode the more powerful aromas of disinfectant and medicine.

It was also the only reminder of Rachel's stay here. The bed linen was gone, the mattress and pillow bare. The IV stands were as empty as the bedside cabinet, the hooks free of glucose and saline drip bags.

While he searched the bedside cabinet, Karen pulled the curtains back on the rails of the other cubicles. They were empty as well. No occupants, no bed linen.

"Nothing." He closed the cabinet door with a sigh and looked up at Karen.

"Were you expecting anything?"

"No." He stood and brushed his thighs. There was no dust or dirt on the floor – everything had been scrubbed clean prior to the evacuation, if that was the right word - but kneeling on the tiles that children had bled on made him feel soiled, unclean.

How many died here? How many lay in these beds, bleeding their last while they saw beyond this world?

He knew the answer. The map retrieved from Karen's handbag led the way to their *true* location. "But I had to see for myself before…before we went there."

Karen glanced at the site layout in her hand. The area they were heading for next wasn't highlighted, but it stood out like a beacon. The Acute Ward. The place where Rachel's predecessors went for death – or rebirth.

What did they see when they cut themselves? He glanced at his knuckles, then fingered the healed cut on his forehead. He forced the memory of his visions from his mind and picked up the map.

The only thing that calmed him was knowing Rachel hadn't gone the same way as the others. Rawlings had admitted that, and it was clear the powers behind Fairlight weren't going to let Rachel die. Not yet.

"Straight on, Karen. At the end of the corridor will be the last section of the new building."

She nodded and shouldered her bag, then set off in the lead. She'd recovered from the incident in the reception area well, Tony thought. The sense of emptiness and abandonment in the ICU unit had shaken her as well, but she seemed willing to move on to the next stage.

But what choice did they have? There was no going back now.

Her heels echoed through the corridor. His boots weren't much quieter. Tony fought the temptation to glance behind, convinced he saw the cubicle curtains move, but that must have been due to the passage of air as Karen opened the double-doors.

"Card's still working," she said, holding the door for him. "But how much longer for?"

"Until they find the bodies, we're safe. And that all depends on where Rawlings went." He stepped through the corridor and blinked when the sensors activated the overhead strip-lights. Behind him, just as the double-doors swung to, the overhead lights in the ICU flickered and went out. "He'll have to go to the Site Services office to block the keycards – with or without Quinn."

She studied the card thoughtfully. Unlike the others, there was no profile picture of the assigned user within the laminate; the pass bore the word "Contractor" but if this – and any others like it – had been issued to Rawlings's men, Tony assumed it would allow access to all parts of the complex, not just to the limited areas normally granted to outside contractors.

Let's hope, anyway. He pressed on, but Karen put her hand on his arm.

"Wait," she said. "Hear that?"

Tony paused, listening. He heard the hum of a distant generator, and the buzz of fluorescent tube-lights, and...something from below.

His jaw tightened. It was distant and muffled – no doubt emanating from one of the lower levels – but unmistakable. The second sound confirmed it.

Screams and laughter.

"Who *is* that?" Karen asked.

"The one screaming, or the one laughing?" *More to the point, what the hell are they doing to him?* His hand went to the Taser tucked into the waistband of his trousers. "Something tells me this isn't part of Rawlings's plan. Might be an ally…and we can deal with whoever the torturer is."

At the end of the corridor they were faced with a choice of elevator or service stairway. Karen pointed towards the latter. Tony grunted his approval. The service lift was an older model - built in the seventies, judging by the olive-green paintwork of the corrugated pull-to door. *Not taking any chances being stuck between two levels in this bloody place.*

She pulled the door toward her. It was stiff and unyielding, and when she managed to get it open, they both stared at the rough concrete steps of a switchback staircase. There were no lights in the stairwell, so Tony took out his phone and held it face-outwards to spill some light. Cold air scented with musty brick and masonry filled the stairwell. Karen hesitated.

"Not used much. I'll go first," Tony said, casting a longing gaze at the elevator.

They were halfway down the stairs when the screams came again, accompanied by the sound of hammering on walls, which cut the laughter that followed the scream. The phone trembled in Tony's hand and the shadows danced. He felt

Karen's hand on his, steadying the phone's light.

"You okay? We don't have to do this, Tony."

"I'm okay. We have to go on; this is the only access point to the lower level. Rawlings and co will come this way eventually." He took a deep breath and another step forwards.

More banging.

He pushed the door open. Another corridor awaited them, but this was a stark contrast to the one upstairs. Red-brick walls glistened with condensation; the smell of musty stone was more pronounced. The damp carried the chill of the sea and Tony shivered.

The floor was uneven, with pitted and cracked chessboard tiles. Fifty metres down, the corridor switched to the left. The three entrances leading off the corridor fit his idea of Victorian asylum cells. Heavy steel jambs, rusted but still sturdy, surrounded black-iron doors that swallowed light cast by bare light bulbs that dangled on exposed flex at regular intervals from the arched ceiling. On the nearest cell door, a steel flap hung open, revealing a wire-mesh grille. He held the phone to the grille and peered in.

Torn vinyl padding covered the walls, floor, and ceiling, but there was nothing to indicate the cell had been occupied recently. The noises hadn't come from here. He tried the door handle. It was locked, with good, old-fashioned lock and key. Keycards would be useless here.

He passed the phone back to Karen and glanced at the other doors. He frowned, realising one was slightly ajar.

His fingers touched the door. Cold iron, like the others, but no door lock. It made no sound when he pulled it open; the hinges had been well maintained, and the presence of the keycard panel told him this cell was in more regular use. He stepped back and pulled the Taser from his waistband.

"Jesus…" He lowered his arm. Karen looked over his shoulder.

"Oh, my *God!*" She turned away and began to retch. Tony stared in disbelief at the blood coating the padded walls and flooring. Read the words scrawled in blood.

Further down the corridor, banging started again. This time it culminated in a crash of splintering wood and tumbling masonry.

"Doctor Quinn!"

Tony froze, the slaughterhouse of the padded cell forgotten. He turned. The voice and the continued noise of breaking walls came from beyond the left-turning of the corridor. He didn't recognise the voice of the man who spoke, but the realisation that Quinn was down here had his mind racing. That meant Rawlings would know the clinical psychiatrist wasn't in his office, would know where to head…time was short.

"Quinn! Get back here, now!"

That voice he did recognise. *Jim Dawson – you're alive!*

Hope sprang. He was about to race down the corridor when Karen grabbed his shoulder. He turned, eyes widening when she dragged him into the padded cell. She pulled the door to, careful not to close it.

She raised a finger to his lips and inclined her head.

Tony's hand tightened on the Taser at the sound of booted feet echoing off concrete steps.

Rawlings's men were here.

The helicopter had moved. The noise of its engines was no longer directly above them; now it had shifted, and Rachel Collins looked through the open door.

The shadows in the Sun Garden lengthened, angled, then disappeared into blackness as the aircraft's running lights disappeared.

"Is it going?" Ant asked.

Rachel didn't answer. The only illumination came from the moonlight, painting the crests of the bay's waters cold silver. The Oratory's angled tower and buttresses were briefly highlighted with the same light against the black sky, before the moon slipped behind cloud cover and the lighthouse became a pillar of darkness once more.

Surely a source of light should be a source of hope? It looked so bleak and desolate, and even more distant than its twin in the shadow Fairlight.

"No," Gillian said, letting the door swing to behind them. "They're hovering over the front entrance. Main group's coming in that way." She turned back and held her card over the panel reader. "Just in time – they've disabled me swipe card. Another few seconds and we'd've been trapped in there."

Rachel was tempted to run across the Sun Garden and leap over the wall, take the most direct route across the headland to the Oratory, but bowed to Gillian's suggestion of sticking to the walls of the building until they reached the facilities store. Behind that the ground sloped to a tiny copse.

"Slower, but a bit safer. They're expecting us to take the way you wanted, Rachel." She glanced at the top of the complex. The helicopter's tail rotor was visible above the Victorian turrets, turning clockwise. The roar muffled the shouted orders of the men spilling down the rappel lines at the front, out of sight to the three women. "Come on. That bloody chopper'll float above the downland any moment, and we're buggered then."

"Ant," Rachel said, seeing the younger girl pause by the sundial. "Come on!"

Ant raised her head. "We're going to face the Manxome Foe. We need a Vorpal Blade."

"What?" Gillian snapped. "We ain't got time for that! Come on!"

Rachel clutched the nurse's arm. "Wait a minute. I think

she's right."

Gillian shook the arm away. "For Christ's sake! I dunno what Manxome Foe is, but there's no blades here, only blokes with guns!"

Rachel felt icy calm settle over her. She was light-headed and weak, knew her blood sugar levels were not sufficient to keep her going for an extended period of time – and if they didn't follow Gillian's lead, they wouldn't even get to the lighthouse – but Ant had put her finger on something with that Alice in Wonderland reference. *Manxome Foe...Vorpal Sword...*

Rachel turned back to the sundial, with its grim memories of their shared bloodletting, and stared at the gnomon.

The girls' blood had long since dried; the numerals on the dial were hidden by congealed spatters that looked like black ink blots. The gnomon, that slice of ancient steel from foreign lands, glinted in the moonlight.

Ant looked at Rachel with a sad smile. Her face was pale and drawn, and her eyes were dull, glazed, Rachel nodded, knowing just what they would have to do with the blade when – if – they reached the Oratory.

We won't survive a second self-cutting. We're too weak, and the last trip took too much out of us. But all that matters is getting to the shadow Fairlight, within the Pharos...let the Light shine once more...

Because the soldiers invading Fairlight would have no idea of Callum Hayes's true powers, or indeed his very nature.

"He'll come to us, with his own army. This is our only hope, Rachel."

Rachel nodded and turned to Gillian. "Gilly. We need your help to unscrew this thing."

Gillian rolled her eyes. "For fuck's sake."

The nurse only had a nail file and, on her keychain, a small pocketknife from a Christmas cracker. The screws resisted initially, but to Rachel's surprise the sundial's exposure to the elements hadn't resulted in rusted and seized screws. Site Services had kept the sundial in excellent condition.

"One of t'few things they bloody looked after," Gillian grunted as she threw the second gleaming screw to the grass. The gnomon, freed from the bolts on its left side, didn't wobble or give any signs of leaving the dial. The fastenings on its opposite side were more resistant.

The lights came on in the corridor and lounge. Silver painted the lawns and the brass plate of the dial gleamed.

"Fuck it." Gillian grasped the gnomon with both hands and rocked the dial back and forth. The pedestal lurched and swayed under her assault, the carved squirrels juddering, its base disgorging dried earth and clods of grass.

Rachel glanced at the lounge window. Yellow-suited figures swept the room, guns bristling. One turned its helmeted head to the window.

Shit. Rachel turned her attention to the sundial and bent to help free Ant's Vorpal Blade. The gnomon was almost free from the base. Gillian grunted with the effort. Sweat beaded her forehead and her knuckles were white in the light spilled from the lounge.

Rachel looked over her shoulder. Three figures appeared briefly at the window before vanishing. Any moment now they'd be in the corridor, then in the garden…

The pedestal fell to the ground. Rachel jumped back, just in time to prevent it crushing her feet. Flakes of dried blood fell to the disturbed earth; the Roman numerals on the dial glowed in the light. Time with no marker.

Gillian stared at the gnomon with a strange expression, as someone who finally sees a hidden purpose to an everyday object that up till that moment was just part of the scenery. Freed from the dial, it looked more of a weapon than a component of an ancient time-telling instrument.

Gillian held the piece out to Ant, almost reverently. The corridor lights came on, and there was a serene expression on the nurse's features when she turned to face the door and the intruders framed within the window.

Rachel's heart began to break. Tears filled her eyes as Gillian put an arm around the shoulders of each girl and bent her head forwards. She whispered soft words of encouragement, stroking their hair.

"I think I understand now. Rogers kept complaining that someone was moving sundial, playing silly buggers, but…now I know. This has been waiting for you…" she released them with a pat on the back of each. "Now get out of here. I'll buy you some time."

Ant stared questioningly at Rachel, the gnomon forgotten. Rachel shook her head, not trusting herself to speak. Instead, she took Ant's free hand and guided her to the wall.

Tears blurred Rachel's vision. The wall felt soft and spongy, unreal, and she took her hand away. She gazed ahead, to the facilities storeroom, and forced herself to concentrate on that. *Don't look back. Gilly wouldn't want you to.*

"Gilly?" Ant said in a small voice. Rachel didn't reply. She had to drag Ant– and herself – away from the Sun Garden; even her own feet were reluctant to move, to leave Gillian to die alone.

For once, the dark was their ally; shadows kept them hidden as they made their way. Only when they reached the next section of the institute, following the wall that bent left, did they pause.

The copse was about a hundred yards away from the generator housing. The transformers hummed, making discordant music with the helicopter's engines. Rachel peered around the wooden gate, her hand on Ant's arm.

"Wait here," she said.

Three figures in yellow Hazmat suits and helmets

surrounded Gillian. The nurse was pointing towards the low wall and putting on a show of anxiety and panic. One soldier left the group to investigate.

She told them we jumped, Rachel realised. One of the armed men pressed his hand to the side of his helmet, and a moment later the helicopter rose from behind the asylum, its searchlight sweeping the turrets and the Sun Garden. The investigating soldier held his arm up and thrust it downward three times, towards the low wall and the bay beyond. The searchlight followed his direction.

She turned back to Ant. The girl held the gnomon tightly to her chest, her arms crossed over it. Her eyes shone in the darkness, and Rachel knew she hadn't been the only one crying. "Okay, Ant. On the count of three, we run to the trees. Keep your eyes straight ahead, and don't look back. Okay?"

"Gilly…"

"Gilly's fine. She's misdirecting the soldiers." She didn't want to consider what would happen when they found out she was lying. "One."

Ant sniffed and took a deep breath.

"Two." Rachel's heart pounded. Ant lowered the sundial pointer and braced herself. She glanced at the copse. In the darkness and the rotor wash the trembling tree branches looked like writhing tentacles.

"*Three.*"

They ran. Each yard of the dash felt like a mile, each second an eternity during which Rachel expected the helicopter's searchlight to swing round and shine on their destination, for the three armed men to point their weapons and open fire.

She was twenty feet from the first line of trees when her resolve broke and she succumbed to the temptation to look back.

The sense of slowed time and extended distance continued. The tableau was a hundred miles away and less than a hundred yards; the movements lightning-fast and slow-motion.

The investigating soldier faced the illuminated bay. Gillian had pushed against the door to ensure his comrades faced her and had their backs to the running girls.

Now one moved. His helmeted head turned slowly, almost swivelling, scanning the Sun Garden and the buildings that surrounded it. He froze and Rachel knew he had spotted them.

Gillian realised too. Her eyes widened when she saw the soldier lift his machine gun and pull the slide back. Her hand moved in a blur which Rachel's brain processed into a series of slow-motion images.

Nail file, hidden in the sleeve of her right arm, dropped to the palm. Keychain with its multitude of sharpened steel detached from her belt and wielded in her left hand. Both arms raised and reaching for the retreating soldier.

Red blossomed on yellow. The soldier jerking, his head rearing back. Legs collapsing, body falling to its knees, machine gun's position changing from horizontal to vertical. Muzzle flashes joined the searchlight in lighting up the night sky.

Another muzzle flash, another MP5 firing. This time it was not accidental, not the reaction of an injured soldier. Gillian's body jerked like she rode a wave of electricity. Her stomach exploded in a shower of red and purple.

Rachel's mouth opened and the scream began to rise. Then a hand clapped around her mouth and she was dragged into the moment, into real time, as Ant pulled her towards the spinney.

The shadowy trees swallowed them, and not even the helicopter's searchlight could penetrate the darkness Rachel felt surround her.

CHAPTER THIRTY-SIX

Quinn closed his mind to the inhuman noises behind him as he tried to re-join Jim Dawson. The screeching of miniature buzzsaws cutting through wood and plaster, the insect-like scuttling of multi-limbed creatures making their way through the partition room, the discordant hissing of alien lung sacs taking in air and expelling God knew what.

All accompanied by the laughter of Callum Hayes. The boy's eyes were gaping black pits, stained with the remains of some viscous fluid that was drying in clotted rivulets on his cheeks and chest. But it was the sight of the liquid orb in the centre of the boy's raised left hand, staring at him, that almost made Quinn freeze. *Dear God, what has he done?*

Jim Dawson's own eyes were wide, but more with revulsion and grim recognition than outright shock and horror. His hand was on the door handle, to the corridor beyond; his desperation to escape the alien army had made him forget the locks were in place.

That's what Quinn thought. As soon as he joined Jim and saw the yellow-helmet with its black visor staring through at them, he knew different.

Jim Dawson was trying to stop the soldier entering. His arms strained as he fought to keep the door pulling outwards. Quinn joined him, took the strain off Jim - with the intention of letting the armed man in.

Jim tried to push him away. He took Quinn by surprise, and the psychiatrist's head was forced back to the broken room and the oncoming storm.

The shuriken-like creatures' advance slowed; they cartwheeled more leisurely now, their appendages less rigid and more fluid, balancing, due to their slowed momentum. Their topmost appendages bristled and the multitude of tiny orbs on their vertically raised carapaces glimmered.

Blinking, Quinn realised as the door fell away from him. In unison with the monstrous eye buried within the halo of teeth in Callum Hayes's left palm. *Good God, is this how he's controlling them?*

Bethan stirred on her bed, and Quinn narrowed his eyes with the realisation her bonds had been removed. Then he saw the door behind her and the male nurse open, and another armed soldier, identically attired in yellow Hazmat overalls and helmet to the one thrusting him and Jim away from the door, entered.

Callum Hayes stood rigid, arms outstretched in opposing directions, and Quinn realised the soldier on the opposing door faced an identical monstrous eye on the boy's right palm.

Both soldiers had their weapons raised, aimed at the centre of the room, but the stiffness in the men's movements suggested they couldn't believe what they saw. Quinn and Jim Dawson were momentarily forgotten. The alien creatures rocked on their appendages, chittering like locusts.

Then the eye facing Quinn's new visitor blinked. The glistening, glittering swarm shook with new life – new orders – and the rear wave retreated back into Callum's domain. They advanced in a single row, through the tears in the partition wall, and then split into two columns. The vanguard did the same.

The movement was chilling. Each creature moved with military precision, none getting in the way of each other. They waited in line, each impossibly balanced on one limb while their second and third twitched in the dusty air like antennae.

Sixteen in each room, composing two columns: eight in each. Quinn backed away slowly, his hand reaching for the door which threatened to close as the soldier advanced into the damaged stockroom.

The eye in Callum's palm blinked, and Quinn thought he saw the black pupil flare scarlet – as though it had seen him, and knew his plans. Quinn grabbed Jim by the arm of his gown and began to pull him towards the door.

Gunfire shook the room. Quinn's ears filled with thunder and the metallic clatter of spent casings falling to the floor. Then the creatures leapt into life. Cartwheeling towards the yellow-suited intruder. As they leapt, their limbs unfolded to reveal glittering, serrated edges.

The gunfire ceased and the machine gun fell from the soldier's hands when sixteen lethal-edged creatures tore through his coveralls and flesh as though they were paper. The whirring became a glutinous churning, and the soldier's back exploded; the creatures enjoyed a second birth.

Quinn didn't even bother to wipe the blood from his face as he dragged Jim Dawson through the door. He tried to pull it shut, but the door-closer would not be rushed, and Jim was exposed to the creatures.

"Go on, boy," the old patient hissed. He kicked the soldier's weapon towards Quinn. "Get out of yer. Them things can't be allowed outside."

Quinn stared at the gun. It was the first time he had ever held a firearm. It felt clumsy and awkward, as alien as the creatures that tore its owner to pieces.

"For fuck's sake, go! I's seen what them things'll grow into. You've no idea how *big* the ones in the specimen jars were..."

"Jim..." his words were muffled, his voice low. "I can't."

Jim didn't answer with words. With a strength that belied his withered frame and suffering, he pushed the clinical psychiatrist away and stepped backward into the slaughterhouse. His face was grim but resigned. His jaw dropped and the scream died in his throat, replaced by the churning arms of a creature that sprayed blood and pieces of cartilage into the diminishing gap between door and jamb.

The door closed, followed by a click of resetting electronic bolts that sounded like the crack of doom and sealed Jim

Dawson's fate. The thick triple-panelled door would resist fire and maybe even bullets – but it did nothing to lessen the screams of the old man.

"Dear God…" Quinn backed away, unable to tear his eyes from the door. It shuddered, hammering away in the jamb, and the sounds of angry locusts and miniature buzz saws reverberated through the material, echoing along the corridor he stood in.

There were no more gunshots. Only the noises of alien creatures, tearing through wood as easily as they had torn through human flesh, and the roar of triumphant laughter from the fifteen-year-old boy who commanded them.

Quinn turned and ran. Back through the corridor and the locked doors of padded cells, where once screams from occupants tormented by their own demons had been silenced and prevented from reaching the outside world.

After the muffled gunfire, Tony Collins heard the shrieking of wood churned beneath multiple blades and his stomach clenched. In the faint light from her iPhone, Karen's pale face told him she heard the noise as well, and she remembered what had caused it.

"They don't have flamethrowers," she whispered. Her voice sounded muffled, distant, by the bloodstained padding of Callum Hayes's cell. "Only guns."

The screeching continued. The gunfire didn't.

Tony peered through the crack in the doorway. His hand tightened on the Taser.

"Jesus," he said. "It's Quinn."

Karen stood. "Anyone with him?"

Tony shook his head and stared at the approaching clinical psychiatrist. Quinn staggered on legs of jelly down the corridor. He swayed, almost zigzagging as he tried to break into a run, clutching something heavy and black to his chest. Tony narrowed his eyes at the sight of the MP5 machine gun.

Tony stepped out and raised the Taser. His eyes widened at the state of Quinn – the soaked bandage that covered most of his face, the pale, sweating skin, the spattered blood soaking his shirt. Worst of all, the eyes that bulged like those of a madman escaped from one of the ancient, padded cells.

Quinn halted. He blinked. "Collins? What are you doing here?"

"What d'you think?" Tony snapped. Whatever ordeal Quinn had gone through, he had no time to waste on pity – or indeed, explanations. "I'm here for Rachel. Where is she?"

Quinn stared at the Taser in Tony's hand and looked down at his own weapon. He stared at it as if he didn't know what to do with it. Picked up from one of Rawlings's men, Tony thought. One less to deal with, but he doubted Quinn would be much cop against the rest.

"I don't...I don't know. I last saw her outside, in the Sun Garden...I left her with Gillian..." His words were drowned out by the sounds of destruction from the end of the corridor.

Tony swallowed. The Taser's grip was sweaty. "And where's she?"

"Still outside, I think. I was called down here and..." a shudder racked his body. The MP5 trembled in his slack grip, and his fingers were worryingly close to the trigger. Tony lowered the Taser and spoke to Karen.

"Take the gun off him. We're going back up."

Karen took a sharp intake of breath at the spitting of wood chips and the glint of black metallic teeth. Taking the weapon from Quinn's unresisting hands, she said, "Rachel's not here?"

"No." Tony took the MP5 and replaced the Taser. It didn't feel as intuitive as the electric stun gun; he didn't know how many rounds remained in the magazine, or indeed how to release it to check. He'd need the Taser after all. He pushed Quinn ahead of him. "You're coming with us, Quinn. You're going to tell Rawlings to pull back from whatever he's got planned."

"Won't do any good," Quinn mumbled as he stumbled to the stairwell. "Jim said those things can't be allowed out of here."

Tony resisted the urge to kick Quinn up the staircase. "So he's dead as well? What did you fuckers do to him?"

"Nothing!" Quinn's voice was a whine that echoed in the stairwell. "He saved me! Bethan was going to kill me...she'd already started on him..."

The door at the end of the corridor exploded in a flurry of wood chips and whirling ebony. A swarm of living, alien weaponry bounced over the remains of the door. Framed in the ruined, chewed doorway, a fifteen-year-old boy stared at them with sightless eyes. He held his hands aloft, palms outstretched, and Tony froze.

Karen screamed, and Quinn turned away, crouched on all fours and began scrabbling at the steps with his hands like a frightened rat.

Tony couldn't take his eyes from the things in the boy's palms. They couldn't be...then he saw the grin break on the owner's face as the glistening black pupils dilated, became pools of blackness that held Tony, transfixed in the hypnotic glare of eyes that had no right to exist, couldn't possibly see...

Then they closed, disappeared in twin-skins of knobbly skin that gleamed like shiny warts...

Jesus wept! They're fucking teeth!

...and opened again. The pupils flared scarlet and shifted downwards.

The waiting infantry, organic shuriken that had demonstrated their devastating ability to destroy in Karen's school, began cartwheeling towards them.

Karen pushed Tony into the stairwell and was about to close the door. She hesitated. A thin sliver of light from the corridor spilled onto the staircase. Quinn was half in darkness, half in the light.

"Karen! Shut the bloody door!"

"Wait a minute," she said. She craned her neck forwards. "They're slowing. Look."

Tony followed her gaze. She was right. They no longer flew across the floor like tiny shuriken; they ambled. The limb trio of each was still as sharp and skeletal as before, but the twin disc-hubs wobbled as they came forward. Their pinprick eyes were dull and glazed. The grey flesh within each disc was swollen, bloated, and pulsated; the clam shell opened and closed, like bellows. No longer glossy ebony, the clam shell of each was dull grey, mottled...

...crumbling...

"My God," Karen breathed. "They're dying..."

Callum Hayes's grin slipped. A frown crossed his features as his palms tracked the slowing progress of his army.

"No," Tony said, backing away. He slammed the door shut and waited for Karen to spark up her iPhone. When the light came it was a relief; it almost dispelled his mental image of the flesh within each hubcap – *new* flesh, *growing* flesh. "Moulting."

"What?"

"They're *growing*, Karen. The fuckers are growing." He prodded Quinn's rump with the barrel of his MP5. "Follow the light beam, Quinn."

Quinn didn't reply. He was breathing rapidly; panicked breaths reverberated through the brick stairwell. Blood droplets marked the psychiatrist's passage on the stone stairs.

Tony beckoned to Karen to follow Quinn. The psychiatrist had the door open and was in the process of getting to his feet. He wore a confused expression as he stood, blinking in the light of the modern corridor.

"Hope your card's still working, Quinn," Tony said as he slammed the door behind them. "We've…"

Now he knew why Quinn stood so bemused in the corridor. Tony raised his gun, but Rawlings was too fast; his SIG-Sauer was at Karen's temple before Tony's finger found the trigger.

Three armed soldiers advanced; one took Quinn by the shoulders and kicked him to the ground. His head knocked against the corrugated outer door of the elevator door, and he crumpled into a heap. He began to cry.

Rawlings grimaced in disgust. "Pathetic. Mr Collins, your gun, please. Give it to my man here."

Tony hesitated, but seeing Rawlings's own finger tighten on the trigger bar of his pistol made him comply. He threw the MP5 to the ground and spat on the floor.

The Hazmat-suited soldier whipped it away in one smooth movement, his own weapon barely wavering. Rawlings pulled Karen away from the stairwell and backed away, the barrel pressed so tightly on her forehead the surrounding flesh whitened. Her eyes closed, and her lips trembled, and Tony noticed her grip on her handbag tighten. Squeezing the leather, as though…

What's she got hidden in there?

"Let her go, Rawlings. She's got nothing to do with this."

Rawlings smiled thinly. "Everyone's involved, Collins. Your lady friend here witnessed the birth of those things in the school. Information that cannot be broadcast to the outside world." His smile vanished. "Besides, she's complicit in the deaths of two policemen – and I've lost two men down there."

"Yeah? And whose fucking fault is that?"

Rawlings held up his free hand. Another soldier was hurrying down the corridor. He gave a crisp salute, which Rawlings ignored.

"Sir. Ground floor secure." The voice was a metallic

reverberation.

"All personnel accounted for?" Rawlings said with a questioning eyebrow. "Everyone?"

The soldier hesitated. "The nurse was shot while trying to escape."

"You *bastards...*" Tony stepped forward, but Rawlings's guard pressed the barrel of his gun into Tony's belly. Tony winced and backed off.

"The two girls accompanying her," Rawlings said crisply. "What of them?"

A metallic throat-clearing. "They escaped, but we're on to them, sir."

Rawlings stared. Even though the soldier's face was invisible behind his tinted faceplate, Tony felt the soldier's fear, could imagine widened eyes and dry lips, sweat beading the brow...Rawlings had that effect.

"Let me guess, Corporal: they're heading for the lighthouse, yes?" He didn't wait for the corporal to reply. "Take them down, but I want the older girl alive. Shoot to maim only."

"Sir."

"And Corporal?"

"Sir?"

"If by any chance they reach the lighthouse before your men, it is imperative you prevent them from self-harming. Is that clear?"

Tony stared at Rawlings, the pain in his bruised belly forgotten. *What?*

Rawlings released Karen. The action was as sudden – and as surprising – as the general's words. Before Tony's disbelieving eyes, Rawlings smiled, turned, and holstered his sidearm.

"Your daughter will not be harmed, Collins. Remember what I said on the way here."

Tony frowned. "You said she wouldn't be harmed by *you.*"

"That's correct. The truth." With his left hand he reached into the thigh pocket of his combat trousers. "You see, there's only one person in Fairlight who wishes harm – harm of the non-self-inflicted kind – upon Rachel. And that person is Callum Hayes.

"We're going back down there, Collins. To the Acute Ward, and to prevent Callum and his little pets escaping."

Tony gave a harsh laugh. "You're kidding. Have you any idea what those things can do, Rawlings?"

"I know exactly what they can do. This isn't the first time I've come across them."

Rawlings retrieved something from his pocket. A Ziploc bag. He opened it deftly, withdrew the object within.

It was an old-fashioned cutthroat razor. Karen's eyes bulged, and she took a step backwards, horror, revulsion and recognition on her face.

Rawlings unfolded the razor carefully. "We were surprised to find this weapon at the scene of Master Fleischer's self-mutilation."

Karen paled at the reference to her first taste of the day's horror. Behind them, Quinn continued weeping, oblivious to the events.

Rawlings held the razor aloft. The handle was dark mahogany, even darker now it was stained with Stefan's blood, but the blade gleamed as keenly as the day it had first been sharpened.

"This little toy has a long and far from illustrious history. Your pupil's grandfather brought it with him from wartime Germany. A little souvenir of his Nazi past...and the forerunner of Project Orpheus."

Then General Rawlings did something that made Tony freeze in horror. He pressed a hidden button and unfolded another blade from within the handle. Both shining rectangles of steel glimmered.

And then, another. Three blades of steel unfolded from the body of the cutthroat razor. Three wickedly sharp strips of metal, designed to cut and slice, at equidistant angles to each other. In Rawlings's right hand the thing resembled a man-made approximation of the things that had birthed from the bodies of Stefan Fleischer and Callum Hayes's prisoner.

Triskelion.

CHAPTER THIRTY-SEVEN

Rachel could only just make out the lighthouse through her veil of tears. The trek up the slope from the spinney could only have taken moments, but it felt endless. Each step toward the dark tower made her realise just how isolated she and Ant really were. Gillian was dead, and her killers wouldn't stop until they'd taken her and the younger girl as well.

It was Ant who gave her the strength to continue. *They won't kill us, Rachel; what they'll do is far worse.* The younger girl's grip on the sundial's pointer became tighter with each word whispered in the sparse shelter of the tiny wood. *It's our ability to move between both Fairlights, don't you understand?*

Rachel believed she did. It explained why Gillian had been willing to give up her life for them. She'd seen their translocation with her own eyes, something that defied rational, scientific belief.

And touching the sundial had really brought it home to her, Rachel reflected. It wasn't much of a weapon – certainly no match for soldiers and their guns and helicopters – but it was what it might do in the other Fairlight that could well save them.

Guns and helicopters…she looked over her shoulder. In the dip in the meadow, the spinney seemed even smaller, more distant, but the old parts of the hospital loomed into the night sky, even seemed to be growing. Even the military helicopter looked small, despite its rapid approach. The running lights were tiny compared to the moon; merely brighter, more colourful stars.

More lights filled her view; this time on the ground, from the approaching soldiers and their flashlights.

Ant tapped her shoulder and beckoned to the outlying rubble of the Oratory. The gnomon flared and Rachel started, wondering if the Light had announced itself, until the flickers of light trailed away and painted the stones that littered the ground.

The town's on fire, she realised. She wondered where Dad was, if he was in the town burning far below, or in the medical complex, and the thought brought a fresh pang of pain.

Either way, he can't help me now. We're on our own.

They stepped over the rubble, the remnants of the ancient monastery that had once been part of the lighthouse. There was nothing holy about these stones. The granite also reflected the fire from the burning town below, while the main structure itself, the Oratory, the beacon that had guarded the bay and saved ships and countless lives from the darkness and the hunger of the sea, stood dark, hollow, and lifeless. Impotent.

She felt tired, drained and as lifeless as the barren Pharos. Enervated. Gillian would have told her that was down to insufficient fluids, salts and low blood sugar levels, but…

No, it's more than that. That last trip…it almost killed me. The Light had not renewed her this time. *One more journey to the shadow Fairlight…it'll kill me. I know it.*

Only Ant seemed unaffected by their recent ordeals. Her face was wan and her movements stiff, but her eyes shone bright in the reflected light.

Of course. You have your Vorpal Sword. But now Rachel was worried that the Light would not call for them. Would it be enough to open their veins here, without any kind of signal?

The helicopter's engines were louder; the rotor blades beat the humid night air and the wash swept over the two girls. The sweat chilled on Rachel's skin.

Ant looked up, and her face was silver, moon-like in the searchlight that flashed down on them. The darkness from the Oratory was banished, shadows retreating to the outlying stones. The perpendicular marks where the chapel had adjoined the lighthouse were clearly visible: black, rotting scars that marked forcible separation.

Cut away. Rachel shuddered. She shielded her eyes from the glare of the searchlight and looked back to the hospital and the spinney. The approaching soldiers were more visible, their yellow Hazmat suits brightened by the helicopter's lights and the fires from the village below the headland. The visors of the nearest pair reflected the leaping flames of the burning village below the headland – vistas of Hell, she thought.

She took Ant's shoulder, screamed above the roar of the engines: "*Not here, Ant. Inside the lighthouse.*"

The helicopter was right above them, hovering some ten metres above the pointed tip of the Oratory. Its searchlight spilled into the eight lozenge-shaped openings that in earlier times would have given light.

The curved archway loomed over their heads. Rachel led the way into the tower and blinked in the interior's sudden darkness. The granite swallowed up most of the light and Rachel hesitated, searching her memory for a recollection of what the interior looked like when she had visited it on family holidays a lifetime ago.

The smell of musty, damp stone aided her memory. She imagined the octagonal floor – uneven, slippery with moisture, and moss growing in the cracks – and the spiral staircase that grew out of the granite walls, with no safety barrier, leading to the top floor. Another archway, smaller than the main one, led into the landing.

Dad had wondered why the owners had never bothered to replace the doors, thinking the town's druggy crowd would see the Oratory as an ideal place to shoot up. She'd never thought about it until now. It seemed odd that such a building, ideal for nocturnal gatherings amongst disaffected teenagers, would be empty of used needles and foil wraps, empty vodka and cider bottles...

Their feet made sucking sounds on the floor. Ant lowered the gnomon and trailed it on the stone. It made a grinding noise and Rachel started at the sparks that flew into the air. They spilled into the archway before the helicopter's light swallowed them.

She looked behind her. Through the archway she saw the soldiers reach the outer rubble, slowing in their approach. Their guns were lowered, and one had his head cocked to one side, maybe listening to instructions from a radio-transmitter in his helmet. He raised a hand to his comrades: a signal to halt.

Rachel didn't pause to consider the ramifications of this. All she knew was that order had given her and Ant some time. She turned back. Her eyes were more accustomed to the gloom, and the shadows had form, substance.

Ant raced up the steps; small fragments of rock and puffs of dust fell to the ground and Rachel's heart fluttered, worried the younger girl would fall. Rachel took the steps more cautiously, facing the angled wall and keeping both hands pressed to the cold stone. She advanced crab-like, her right foot raised and finding purchase on the crumbling steps before pushing herself along and repeating the action with her left. The walls vibrated and the steps trembled beneath her. She assumed - hoped - that was due to the rotor wash from the helicopter.

The staircase ended. Ant stood in the arched doorway, a halo of light surrounding her. Her hair rippled in the disrupted air, and the gnomon was gold.

The walls of the top chamber were blackened, stained with the smoke of centuries of fire, and even now Rachel could smell the soot. It mingled with the musty stone and the scent of the sea, and calm descended on her as she glanced through the nearest opening, seeing the village of Fairlight burn. *As above, so below. One way or another, it ends here.*

Ant turned to her, her eyes shining with excitement. The gnomon trembled in her grip, but still retained its golden glow, and Rachel no longer believed it was reflected light from the helicopter's search beam.

"*It's time, Rachel!*" Ant shouted. "*Here, where the Lady of the Light told us to be! Are you ready?*"

Rachel walked across the floor and stared at the downland. A cordon of soldiers now surrounded the ancient lighthouse. Vehicle headlights shone from the approach road to Fairlight; Land Rovers and police cars were coming. A whole army for two girls? Rachel's hands tightened on the lintel. It felt loose, crumbling, and she took her hands away and stared at her fingers.

They were coated in soot, but the black dust barely obscured the thin scars on her wrists. They were white lines, healed flesh, the only purity.

She glanced at Ant, saw how she pressed the gnomon into her belly. The opposite end awaited Rachel. The message was clear.

But something wasn't right. She fingered the soot, remembering the dark vapour that had come like a blast of black fog from the Oratory when she and Ant had last cut themselves on the sundial's pointer.

And why don't I feel the call? Where is the Light? She turned and faced Ant. She gripped the central section of the gnomon. The thumb and first finger of her right hand made contact with Ant's. The brass casing was cool to her grip, belying the heat of the steel's fire.

Ant's eyes gleamed, but now had that far-off look Rachel had seen when she first met the girl. As though she didn't even need to self-harm to pierce the veil to the other side.

"*I see her, Rachel! Your mother, the Lady of the Light. Oh, she's so beautiful!*"

Ant pressed forwards. The pointer went deeper into her belly. Ant grimaced, but the joy never left her eyes.

The forward momentum pushed Rachel back against the

wall. Her grip was tight on the gnomon, but she couldn't bring herself to repeat Ant's action.

The rotors beat the thickened air into heavy slabs that weighed on her. The heat from the searchlight burned her neck. She heard - and *felt* - cautious, measured footsteps echoing through the walls as their owners climbed the steps.

She turned, looked down, and saw the first soldier approaching, his rifle held high.

She looked back, stared into Ant's eyes, and made her decision. She tightened her grip on the gnomon and pushed forward.

Tony Collins walked slowly down the corridor, back to the room he had tried to escape from. He was conscious of the two soldiers keeping a close distance behind him, guns trained on his and Karen's backs. He squeezed Karen's hand and tried to give her a reassuring smile. Behind their guards, Quinn shuffled along, Rawlings's grip on the psychiatrist's shoulder tight.

Tony longed to drop the triple-bladed razor. It was obscene, and the realisation of what it had done – before and after Stefan's acquisition – sickened him.

Rawlings had been dispassionate in his description of the pain and torture its victims had endured. The human cost of this terrible weapon's existence didn't bother him, only what practical usages it could be put to.

Military. Offensive...or defensive. The Children of the Evolution had made no mention of such a weapon – Stefan Fleischer probably hadn't even been aware of the two hidden blades.

And what sort of grandfather was it who created such a weapon? Even the Nazis couldn't come up with something like this.

I thought it was a ceremonial weapon, like the daggers the SS used, Rawlings had said. *Four blades, unfolding from the handle, to create a swastika … but there are only three sections carved into the wood, and the steel is far older than the handle itself. No, this is older than Hitler's Germany. The Tailor Man – that's what they called him in SOE, you know – fit a new handle, that's all. We have no idea where he obtained it. But it is no accident that it resembles the creatures that came from Fleischer.*

So why me? Why are you giving it to me?

Because you're going head-to head with Callum Hayes, that's why.

The door to Callum's cell was still open. Tony didn't even glance at it as they passed. The razor's handle was slippery with his sweat. His heart hammered as they rounded the corner. There was no sound of wood splintering, of flesh being chewed. No mocking laughter from a child older than his years and twisted with powers beyond human imagining.

Nothing.

Only the irregular scrapings on the concrete floor proved the existence of those shuriken-like monsters. The triple-bladed razor felt hot in his hand.

"Wait." Rawlings bent forwards, narrowing his eyes at the markings. He followed them back to the broken door. He raised his head and took a deep breath.

Tony watched closely, feeling a faint glimmer of hope at the general's baffled expression. That was extinguished when Rawlings turned and said, "They retreated. They went this far, then turned back. Wonder why that is, Collins?"

Tony cleared his throat. "Why ask me?"

Rawlings stepped back and nodded to the two men bringing up the rear. They advanced; one grasped Tony by his shoulder and thrust him forward. Tony resisted, raised the razor, but the MP5 barrel swung his way. The noise of a retracted slide and chambered bullet also forced him to stay his hand. He glanced at Rawlings, who had his pistol pointed at Karen's forehead.

"In you go, Collins."

Tony spat on the ground, glared at the faceless soldier, and turned to the broken door. He saw two bodies: one had yellow overalls identical to those worn by the soldiers behind him. Little of the protective material remained; only shreds of shiny yellow Tyvek, some scattered around the blood-soaked floor like snow. Little remained of the body it had failed to protect to identify it as fully human. The grooves on the stone floor matched the carvings on the chest and face, but were deeper, and had taken more of a toll.

The second body he only recognised by the shock of white hair. Everything else was a mass of pink and purple ribbons and shattered bone. Tony's jaw tightened and his fist clenched around the razor.

You poor old fucker. You didn't deserve this.

Fragments of partition wall and plaster framed the next doorway. Dust clouds obscured the room, weakened the light. Still there were no sounds. Ahead, at the far end of the adjoining room, he saw through fresh clouds of dust the remains of another broken door. This one was the twin of the one he had walked through, another chamber. He stepped over Jim's remains.

The air smelled mustier here, older; the room was more of a pantry, a small storeroom, but there was little indication of what it had stored. He looked ahead to the room beyond, the twin of the one Jim had met his end in, and the first thing he noticed was the grooves in the floor were deeper. They were also filled with blood.

The smell hit him then, and he staggered backwards, gagging. The slaughterhouse in the previous chamber was no preparation for what faced him here.

Blood had spattered the bare light bulbs and illuminated the chamber in a hellish red glow. The two bodies had undergone the same destruction as the soldier and Jim Dawson. Muscle and innards festooned the beds, the contents of shredded bowels coated the floor and in the right-hand corner the devastation had been so fierce, conducted with such furious energy, that ribbons hung from the ceiling; garlands of human remains that glistened with seasonal light.

And in that corner was the architect of their destruction, along with his unearthly tools. Callum Hayes leant against the brick wall with his arms by his sides, his head bowed and tucked into his chest. His breathing was shallow and even. Sleeping.

So this was the creature Rachel had warned him about. The leader of the Children of the Evolution, the one convinced he would lead the new generation to mutual slaughter and genocide, to pave the way for the next chapter of humanity's history.

He seemed so small and pathetic, even with the blood that coated his cheeks and plastered his hair to his scalp. Then his left arm twitched, his palm flicked outwards to reveal the closed eye in the centre, the creatures at the boy's feet stirred, and Tony remembered the full danger of this fifteen-year-old boy.

The eye half-opened, its toothed lids rolling back to reveal a pale blue gelatinous globe centred with a black pinprick. It floated in its jelly sea, directionless, unseeing, and the lids of molars and canines slid back together again. The palm folded inwards and the arm drooped again.

Tony frowned. The boy's breathing didn't alter, and his chest rose and fell in time with the pulsating of the putrid grey flesh sandwiched between new, harder clamshells on the floor.

Larger clamshells. Tony swallowed and took a step back. *I was right. They really were moulting. Now they've renewed their outgrown shells.*

But how could they do it so quickly? How could these things reach the size of a small dog, each of their three limbs match the length of a yardstick, in such a short space of time?

He glanced at the human remains, realised just how little remained of two grown men, and knew the answer.

They've fed, and now they're sleeping. Recharging and renewing, just like any other creature in the animal kingdom.

Callum's head rose and a smile played at the corners of his mouth. The scarlet light filled his empty eye sockets and they appeared full of blood. Below him, the creatures stirred. One raised an appendage and unfolded it, revealing newly generated rows of serrated, diamond-shaped hooks, then the limb closed and sank to the floor.

Was that a yawn*? Jesus wept!*

In answer to his horrified thought, Callum's jaw dropped, and issued a sleepy groan. He smacked his lips several times and gently shook his head, dispelling sleep. He bent forward and moved from the wall. Then he raised his arms. Held out his palms.

Once again, Tony Collins stared into what passed for eyes. The pinpricks grew; the pupils dilated. Shuffling and chittering from Callum's army filled the air.

"Rachel's daddy. Welcome to Fairlight, Mr Collins." His voice sounded weak, distant, and Tony realised just how weary the boy was. It was an effort for Callum to speak, to maintain his mocking, gleeful and condescending tone of voice.

In contrast to their master, the creatures at his feet stirred with new life and energy. Tony fought the temptation to step backwards. He had to show no weakness to this little bastard.

"You're not on your own, are you, Mr Collins?" The nearest palm shifted fractionally, looking past Tony's shoulder through to the annex and the chamber beyond. "But perhaps you are, in a way. Tell me: men with guns and flamethrowers, and they send you in first armed only with a knife. Why's that?"

"In wartime, army boys have no respect for civvies. Or perhaps they're scared shitless and don't want to admit I can do more damage to you with one poxy knife than a whole battalion armed to the teeth."

Callum chuckled. "Brave words, but utter bollocks. One warehouse worker instead of an army? You're a test subject, expendable. Just like your daughter."

Tony took a deep breath, refusing to rise to the bait, but his fingers tightened on the razor. Blood trickled down his clenched knuckles; his closed fist obscured two of the blades, and only the third – the original one, still coated in Stefan Fleischer's blood – was visible, but its companions made their presence known – to him alone.

"My only work is to get her out, safe, and away from you. And my job ain't over by a long shot." He raised his hand and opened his fingers, revealing the triple-bladed weapon in his palm. Callum's palm dipped forward, examined the weapon, and the alien pupil shrank.

Fear, recognition? Rawlings knew what he was doing after all. The pain was sweet, energising, and the chamber took on a different hue. A light shone from an indefinite source, replacing the ruby glow of the blood-coated light bulbs with the fresh, pure sapphire illumination he had glimpsed on two occasions before.

What do you see when you cut yourself?

And now he saw through the walls, beyond the cowering boy and his army of bristling monsters. He saw through the curtain of night and the shroud of earth and sea, saw glimpses of what waited beyond.

And he saw the lighthouse, the Oratory of medieval times.

He saw the Light shine briefly from its upper tier, blazing through the eight rectangular openings of the beacon chamber. Then the Light dimmed, dissipated like mist, and darkness shrouded the building once more. Only the two entwined figures at the top remained visible, an aura of pure, shimmering white partially obscuring their features and bringing out hidden beauty within. Two angels.

One he did not recognise, but the other, pushing herself closer to the other girl on an impaling spear of silver, was unmistakeable.

"Rachel!" Tony screamed. The physical barrier of brick came back; the sapphire Light and its angelic auras over the two girls were replaced by the blood-glow of Fairlight's light bulbs and Callum Hayes cowered beneath his thundering roar.

Hate filled Tony Collins then. Hate for what had happened to his daughter, the realisation that she was once again in a place of unimaginable peril, and that this bastard before him had dared to threaten her.

Monsters or no monsters, Callum Hayes would not be allowed to harm his daughter. *Never.*

The boy shrank to the floor, his hands held aloft and hiding his head in the primal gesture of defence, overriding the alien presence within him that demanded his palms be protected first and foremost.

You cover your eyes first. Too late, sunbeam. Tony's hand flashed forwards and the free blade sank into the gelatinous pool in the boy's right palm. Tony pressed the blade deeper, a grin of contentment on his face as the alien eye exploded in a welter of jelly and pus.

The pain in his own hand sharpened as the forward pressure dug the other two blades deeper into his palm and fingers. Other fingers, black, chitinous appendages, reached for him on all sides; they unfolded, and their front sections exposed diamond-shaped daggers that raced towards him.

His thumb was almost severed by the Tailor Man's torture instrument, but Tony drove his fist forwards regardless, *through* the hole in Callum Hayes's palm and striving for the human face behind it.

Hands merged, joined by ancient steel in a human housing whose sole purpose was to inflict pain and suffering, mutilation and bodily separation.

Callum Hayes and Tony Collins were joined instead of separated. Their blood mingled, and the Light blazed once more.

CHAPTER THIRTY-EIGHT

Karen Tyndall stared in disbelief at the empty corner Tony Collins and Callum Hayes had fought in. Even the soldiers, who had rushed in the moment the light exploded in the second slaughter room, had lost their military bearing and stood staring at each other.

Only Rawlings seemed in control. There was a faint smile on his face, and a nod of approval.

"Well, that went better than I expected," he said to Quinn.

Karen turned to Quinn, who sat on the end of one of the beds, oblivious to the streamers of flesh and pools of blood that decorated the railings and mattress. His eyes were wide, his jaw agape, and his head shook slowly from side to side. He glanced at the general, then back to the corner again.

"Blood, old and young," Rawlings continued. "And timing, of course."

Karen rounded on him. "Timing? Blood? What the hell are you talking about?"

Rawlings ignored her. He unclipped his R/T and thumbed the talk button. "Brennan, drop three bodybags. Carson will collect them and bring them to the unit." He glanced at the remains of Bethan and Glyn. "Actually, just make that two. They'll fit. Then prepare for immediate evac. Protocol 15 is nearing completion; you will detonate the explosives on my mark. I want all forces focussed on the lighthouse."

Karen felt ice water slush in her veins. *Detonate the explosives …* "You're going to blow up the hospital? In God's name, why?"

Rawlings released the talk button and stared at her. There was irritation in his tone. "It was only a temporary measure; it's served its purpose."

Karen saw Quinn look up sharply. Now there was hatred in the chief psychiatrist's face.

"Temporary measure? For God's sake, what's happening out there isn't a temporary problem! Fairlight was set up to research the problem, to find a solution!"

Rawlings sneered. "You had your chance, Quinn. That girl – and her father – hold the answer. And *we* hold them."

Quinn stood. All trace of bewilderment and despair had gone; righteous fury replaced them. He poked a finger into Rawlings's chest. "This happened before. Jim Dawson is proof of that. Destroying Fairlight won't prevent this happening again."

Rawlings stared at the finger pressed into his starched tunic with an amused expression. He waved away the soldiers' raised weapons. "Yes, it will. Because we won't do the half-arsed job our predecessors did. They underestimated the power of those things, and mental healthcare was still too primitive to understand self-harming." The amusement left his face. "You never saw the specimen jars, did you? Those little beasties that Callum Hayes unleashed – and the ones that said hello in your classroom, Ms Tyndall - are nothing compared to what came before. No one realised Fairlight was the staging post for an invasion. Not just the asylum – everything in the town: the Customs House, the fish market where Jim and his family worked, and most of all, that bloody lighthouse. That's where it all began, Quinn. And that's where it'll end."

Karen exhaled. The slush in her veins warmed at the sight of Quinn's defiance, and liquid anger course through her. "You seem so bloody certain, Rawlings. How can you be so sure of solutions when events like this -" she pointed to the corner - "happen before your eyes? Events that have no possible scientific explanation? Unless you know something we don't?"

Rawlings turned. "The actions of the Hayes lad and his group told us all we need to know. Jim Dawson's records tell us that what happened in the '50s was just a probe, an enemy's recce. Testing its own ability as well as ours. Oh, yes, they're stronger now – but they made a mistake. They used the same staging post.

"But we made mistakes as well. To ensure a fortress is never used by the enemy, you slight it." He smiled without humour. "But England had just come out of a war. The last thing the military had the stomach for was destroying a piece of its own country."

"How times have changed, eh, Rawlings?" Karen folded her arms. "This government has got used to waging war on its own people. You won't think twice about wiping out an entire town and its people just to complete a project?"

"Spare me the socialist claptrap, Ms Tyndall. The enemy uses our own children against us. They can't be saved, they can -"

"They can only be used," she finished. "Ends and means. The greater good. I call shenanigans."

"You call it what you like, Ms Tyndall. I call it war." He checked his watch. "Time's getting on. Follow the men ahead, please."

Karen snorted. "Where to?"

"Where else? The Oratory has been here long before the village of Fairlight. Everyone who walked the shadow Fairlight made reference to it. A beacon, a source of light. Whatever this enemy is, its battleground will be there – and that's why it drew its weapons to this very spot."

"Weapons. They're children, Rawlings."

"So is Tony Collins. A weapon in himself. A rusty one, decommissioned…but a weapon nonetheless."

Karen hesitated. She looked at the empty corner again, remembered the steel determination in Tony's face to find his daughter. Come what may, he'd go through Hell to find her.

He's already there, she thought. With the Hayes boy, those monsters…and Stefan Fleischer's mysterious razor blade.

There was something else, something she was certain she'd missed, but couldn't put her finger on – another, as yet unknown, factor in the grim drama unfolding around her.

Only one way to find out. Who's afraid of Virginia Woolf, anyway? "Okay, General. To the lighthouse."

The words were unfamiliar, but the voice singing them belonged to the Hayes boy; Tony Collins was certain of that. But the words were low, sung with no power, and easily carried away by the hot breeze that blew around him. He felt the warmth on his face and frowned.

He opened his eyes. The floor he sat on was as before: the same black and white chessboard tiling. But the majority of the tiles were cracked and when he shifted his weight he felt the warmth of them, noted the melting and restructuring of some of the ceramic squares – subjected to an incredible heat.

There was no ceiling. Rubble surrounded him. The remnants of the walls framed a vista of apocalyptic devastation that took his breath away. Seaside cottages blown to pieces, the slates of their shattered roofs and the bricks of the broken walls glowing scarlet like embers as the sea breeze blew the cinders and clinkers of what looked like human remains across the quayside.

And the source of the breeze…his eyes widened. It was the same blood-red ocean lapping at a shore made of bones he had seen before. The last time – and place – he had seen Rachel.

He felt the heat as he stood on legs that no longer trembled, walked forwards with a body that did not feel exhausted, battered and at the limits of human endurance. There was no pain. Not even from the wound in his hand.

The two razor blades in his palm had gone as far as they could. The two facing him had met bone – his thumb and little fingers were bent backwards, twisted hunks of flesh and gristle that hung by sinews. The third blade thrust forwards from his fingers. There was no blood. It shone, glowed golden.

He couldn't see the handle. He turned his hand over and took a sharp breath. It was scorched, blackened; no more than a charred piece of wood, fused into the meat of his palm.

Tony slowly turned to face Callum Hayes. The crouched figure of the boy was framed by the shattered wall behind him, a red glow from the seaside town imparting an unholy halo. There was nothing else impressive about him: the pits of his empty eye sockets were black and the hands he used to see, with God knows what optical organs, were cradled in his lap. Tony smiled at the black fluid dribbling from Callum's right hand, and lifted his own hand, palm upwards, in a mockery of greeting.

"How," Tony said, Native American style. Callum couldn't see him, but his face went white on hearing Tony's voice. The undamaged hand twitched, and Callum held it aloft, hesitant.

The eye didn't open. The circle of molars and incisors remained tightly shut. Tony smiled.

"What's up, son? Frightened of losing the other one?"

Callum swallowed. Behind him, black clouds drifted and obscured the hellish glow from the devastated Fairlight. His halo gone, his hand trembling like a sufferer of Parkinson's disease, he was just a frightened, confused teenager.

*Powerless, friendless…*Tony frowned. He turned, scoured the ruined chamber for signs of the creatures Callum Hayes had commanded.

"They're gone, sunshine. Your little pets, they've left you." He meant the words to sound harsh, another nail in the coffin of Callum Hayes's ego – Messiah Complex, whatever it was – but the realisation worried Tony.

Where had they gone?

Now Callum smiled. The lining of teeth in his palm parted

slightly, like a smile, and the black hole in its sea of yellow glittered. The reaction of his alien sight emboldened him.

"They'll come back soon," he said. "For now, they have other flesh to cut. Look."

Callum pointed to the ground. Amid the jumble of cracked and fused ceramic tiles Tony saw other, more recent damage: perfectly straight, parallel lines that neatly bisected them like the work of the world's biggest tile cutter.

Tracks, leading to a holed wall. Tony walked towards it, the crumbled floor protesting his passage with shrieks of porcelain and groaning of floorboards. The damage to this wall was, like the floor below it, more recent. In places, the red brick was scoured; powdered red dust blew in from outside on the hot breeze.

*The world's biggest tile cutters...the world's biggest angle grinders...*Tony fingered the powdered masonry with his left hand. It was warm.

"Your monsters have grown," he said without turning. The ground outside the ruined chamber was scorched earth: where once were neatly mown lawns and tended flower beds, there was ash and soot.

The tracks were more visible here. The ground was less firm than the asylum's floor, and the razor-limbs of the creatures had cut huge swathes through the dead ground, casting uninterrupted piles of dead earth and cinder that formed trenches.

A war is coming, Dad...

Tony frowned. So where had this strange army disappeared to? He turned back to Callum, and when the boy flinched, Tony had his answer.

"They abandoned you, didn't they? When we were in the asylum, they were all around us." He shuddered at the memory of the switchblade limbs and the black, diamond talons - or teeth - opening above him. They would have torn him to pieces here, so why…

He held his right hand up to Callum, and the boy didn't flinch this time; he backed away sharply, his hands scrabbling for purchase on the damaged wall. Tony lowered his hand, gazing at the triple-razor attachment in wonder.

"They're *scared*. They ran away. Scared of this – or me?" What was it Rawlings had said? *'Translocation' is the word. Oh, so brief, so very brief. But it proves you and your daughter have something in common. Now we have to work out how that connection works.*

"Translocation, sunshine. No, I didn't know I had it in me, either."

"You shouldn't be here," Callum hissed. "Only the Children of the Evolution were promised this power."

Tony laughed. The sound was strange in this bombed-out, ruined building, but it echoed satisfyingly enough and caused the self-styled leader to flinch even more. Even the eye in his palm seemed to tremble. "Haven't you figured it out, Callum? It's all in the blood. But who gave *you* that blood, eh?" He advanced. He stood over the teenager and grasped the lad's palm. The eye clammed shut: Tony's new appendages scraped against human teeth. Callum whined.

"Let me explain something, boy. This ain't the first time I've been here – wherever 'here' is - and you know why? Because I cut myself."

"You can't…"

"That's why I'm here now. This -" he trailed the exposed blade of the razor along the upper lid of teeth. "This did the same trick. It cut me, and my blood mixed with yours."

Callum remained crouched, trembling on his heels.

"That scares you, yeah? It should. It scared away your monsters. No, I wasn't here for long last time. Just long enough to see my daughter. And when I touched her, I was bleeding – so was she. I was sent back, so I guess she was as well.

So…what d'you reckon will happen if she's here, and I mix blood with her again?"

Now a smile broke on Callum's face. "She won't do that, Collins. She thinks she's here to fight a war. She won't go back with you. She'll stay here. And she will lose the fight and die."

Tony reached down with his free hand and grabbed Callum's neck. He pulled the boy to his feet. "So Rachel *is* here. Right, shitbag. Where is she? Which part of the asylum?"

Callum writhed within Tony's grasp, struggling for breath. Tony lessened his grip, but only slightly – just enough to discontinue strangulation.

"She's not in the asylum, Collins!"

"Town, then."

"Not there, either! Haven't you guessed, Collins? It was never about Fairlight! It's the Pharos – it always has been!"

"Pharos? You mean the lighthouse?"

"Yeah! The lighthouse – that's where the Presence will begin its great work. Midsummer's Eve – the time most precious to what you call the Light. I know this - its Annunciation came through me, made its plan known when my parents were burying my sister!"

Tony dropped Callum to the ground, disgust and contempt on his face.

"Annunciation. Stigmata. Let me guess: it's bringing a kingdom of heaven here, yeah? You're going to build a New Jerusalem? You thick bastard. You never figured how many evil fuckers have used religion as a cloak in the past?"

Callum stood, the trembling in his legs dying; fear had left him. His smile returned, but it was not the mocking, supercilious smirk of a teenager – it was beatific.

"Good and evil don't come into it, Collins. The human race is about to undergo a new stage in its evolution, and I've been chosen to oversee it!" A guttural laugh. "You're lucky, Collins. You'll be able to see it firsthand before it blasts you to ashes."

Tony snorted.

"Don't take my word for it." Callum extended his right arm, pointed with his ruined hand to the wall Tony had looked through. "Follow the tracks, see where my army has gone. They didn't run away from you, Collins – they went because they knew your daughter has appeared!"

Fresh ice filled Tony's veins. Rachel, in the Pharos…surrounded by those things. Callum's army, ready for war in two dimensions.

First strike, Dad. But the war's just beginning. And I can't do it on my own.

"Go on, Collins. To the lighthouse. I'll follow you."

Laughter echoed throughout the ruined chamber, rolled off the broken walls and filled Tony's ears as he raced through the hole in the wall. It followed him as he stumbled and tripped through the no man's land of trenches; it filled the sky, where black thunder clouds bristled and glimmered with the promise of an alien storm.

CHAPTER THIRTY-NINE

The dark shore looked different from the vantage point afforded by the lighthouse. The blood tide stretched far wider – and further into the horizon – than the bay of the physical Fairlight. On a clear day, Rachel remembered, you could see the Isle of Wight from the lighthouse – in the other Fairlight, of course. Here, she saw nothing but a tide of blood. The further out to sea she looked, the less signs of life – or animation – were to be found in the red waters. It was gelid, opaque; blood clotting in defiance of any tidal currents.

She shuddered. This obscene shore had always held horrors for her, but at least in her previous visits there was an unspoken goal, an obstacle to overcome. Clear the ossuary seawall, reach the headland. Beyond that she hadn't known what was expected of her.

But she'd done that. Wandered the shadow-Fairlight, found the secrets of the old asylum.

Found Mum. But now what? To her left, the cottages and seafront buildings of Fairlight were empty shells of incandescent ruby. The quayside smouldered and crumbled; great chunks of sticky concrete, coated in molten tar, fell into the blood tide and sank without trace. The Customs House was only visible by the current fires that raced along its tower. If she turned and looked through another window, she would see what this reality's version of the asylum was like.

I'm not ready for that yet.

Rachel felt Ant's hand in hers. The other gripped the gnomon of Fairlight's sundial. Rachel lifted it, surprised by the steel pointer's lightness, and disturbed by the golden glow.

I should be comforted by this. It means Ant was right to take the pointer with us. But...

Ant put her head in the crook of Rachel's shoulder. The hot breeze gusting from the ruined town to the south whipped her hair into hot strands that brushed and irritated Rachel's eyelids. She gently pushed the younger girl away.

Ant didn't seem offended. She gazed into the bloody sea, a serene smile on her face.

"The Lady of Light is here, Rachel. I can't see here, but I can feel her presence. Can you feel it as well?"

"I can't feel anything. Something's wrong."

Now Ant turned to her. The smile slipped. "We're where we're supposed to be, Rachel. We have the Vorpal Blade."

The gnomon flashed scarlet; the steel reflected dancing red light from the burning town.

"Now we wait for the Manxome Foe." Ant's eyes hardened, but the smile broadened.

Rachel thought back to the dream – or rather, premonition – she received on her first night in Fairlight. Callum Hayes, advancing along the ossuary seashore, with fire in his eyes and murder in his heart, and the monsters accompanying him: giant starfish with three limbs rather than four, conveying spinning discs of putrid, cancerous flesh to their prey.

Triskelions. Manxome Foe. Either name suited them; they were indeed monsters that would not have been out of place in a Lewis Carroll nightmare. She remembered the pictures of the book on her bedroom wall, the White Rabbit, and the one she'd taken down, unable to face the similarity of the battle between the small child brandishing a sword against the Jabberwock and the fight she'd known was her destiny.

*Long time the Manxome Foe she sought…*she stared at Ant. And this girl, the one she felt a connection with…she was the one who suggested the same thing that destroyed the Jabberwock.

A Vorpal Blade. Wielded by two warriors, not one.

I was never alone.

"What do we do, Ant?" she asked. "Do we go hunting for them, or wait?"

Ant shrugged. "This isn't a castle. And they can cut through stone as easily as hands and legs, so yes, I say we move. Won't be able to fight if we're buried under rock, will we?"

Rachel caressed the window frame. There was no soot this time, just pure, clean granite. The stone was smooth and recently dressed; even the mortar smelled fresh. She stepped back from the window and inhaled. Everything smelled new. There was no trace of that musty, damp, church-in-summer smell. Behind her, the stone steps jutting from the wall were as clean cut as the stones that formed the beacon room; no grooves and dips from centuries of passing feet marred them.

This was wrong. If the dark shore was part of a future Fairlight, shouldn't the lighthouse be even older than she remembered it? Why would it survive the holocaust that had turned the rest of Fairlight to ashes and rubble?

Why would it be…rejuvenated? And why was everything so bright? There was no sun to speak of, yet the interior of the beacon room and the stairwell were equally illuminated, by a light that had no source. Too soft and mellow for modern electric lighting; too bright and clear of shadows for candle flames. She inspected the gnomon. There was no light now that it was hidden from the fires of Fairlight.

The stone itself, she realised as she descended the steps. A sense of awe filled her, and she caressed the smooth granite. It was warm yet cool at the same time. She took her hand away and rubbed her fingers. They tingled.

"There's power here, Ant. I don't know what it is, but it's…something magical."

Ant patted her shoulder. "It's Midsummer's Eve. Always a magical time."

Rachel hesitated. The ground level vestibule seemed to sparkle, and no motes of dust travelled in the light beams. "That shouldn't mean anything. The sun at its closest to the northern hemisphere…why would that have any effect?"

Ant shrugged. Her lack of concern, her apathetic indifference to the strange phenomena was infuriating to Rachel. Her fingers tightened on the gnomon's protective sleeve and she felt the warning edge of sharpened steel. She took a deep breath.

A child's acceptance of magic, that's all.

Midsummer's Eve. Even Callum Hayes had said that was the time the Children of the Evolution would inherit the Earth. And this was the place.

So what's going to happen? How will we fight him? The gnomon felt thin and useless in her hand. How could this be enough to fight Callum and his monstrous army?

They reached the vestibule, her trainers and Ant's bare feet silent on the warm flags. She halted before they reached the arched doorway. This time there were doors, but that didn't concern her – the double-doors, of glistening oak and shining steel bands – were open to the headland, and nothing barred their exit.

It was the circular opening in the floor that made her halt. At two metres in diameter, it presented little in the way of obstacles – they could still get out by hugging the octagonal walls – but it was the sheer darkness of the opening, the pitch blackness that suggested a bottomless well, and its stink of rotting fish and marine vegetation that made Rachel halt.

It was a familiar stench. It reeked of the Triskelions, of their putrid carcasses, their rotting mass of tubes and gristle sandwiched between two razor-sharp hubcaps of alien shell.

"Ant?"

The younger girl stepped nimbly past Rachel, her toes on the edge of the precipice. She leant forwards and spat. There wasn't much in the way of saliva; Ant, like Rachel, was severely dehydrated.

Rachel watched the small gobbet disappear into the blackness and mentally counted.

One...two...three...

Ant leant back, standing upright, her depth test forgotten. Her eyes narrowed and her lips drew back from her teeth. She tapped Rachel's shoulder.

Four...five...six...

"What is it, Ant?" Irritation in her voice, trying not to lose count.

...eight...nine...no, wasn't it seven? It was useless.

"That," Ant said, excited. "They're coming."

Rachel followed Ant's rock-steady index finger. Her own hand shook, and the gnomon felt loose in her perspiring hand.

They were hard to see at first; the sky above the headland was so dark. But the sound of their whirling appendages tearing through the soil rumbled across the baked ground like thunder. Disturbed ash formed dust clouds in their wake, and a fresh burst of flame from a dip in the headland illuminated the Victorian turrets of the old asylum and painted the carapaces of the Triskelions metallic scarlet.

They were huge. As they crested the rise, Rachel gasped at the sheer size – and number – of them.

A row of whirling, scything, shuriken-like monsters. Each the size of a windmill. The gnomon slipped from Rachel's sweat-greased palm and clattered to the floor.

Ant turned back, her eyes widening at the sight of the sundial pointer falling to the ground. Rolling on the edge of the precipice.

The Manxome Foe army were less than twenty metres from the Oratory. Ant's precious Vorpal Blade tumbled over the edge and fell from view.

Quinn's head rose at the squawk of static from Rawlings's R/T unit. The general pressed the receive button. "Yes?"

"General, we have a problem. The two girls have disappeared."

Rawlings didn't even blink. There was no visible sign of dismay or thwarted plans.

"Both of them?"

"Yes, sir."

Quinn caressed the bandage on his nose. The pain was a dull throb, only just bearable. He felt tired, weak, but the report gave him renewed hope – and, in turn, energy.

The Penner girl and Collins's daughter, he thought. *Both translocated to the other side. Clever girls.*

"Very well. Keep your cordon intact, and be ready to retreat on my mark."

Quinn looked up. "They won't be back, Rawlings. You know this. Three translocations in less than two days? Their bodies won't be able to cope."

Karen looked stricken, and Quinn felt a momentary pang of regret for his harsh words, but it couldn't be helped.

"Even if they could, the Hayes lad and his creatures are undoubtedly in the same place. They'll die there, or they'll die on their return. Either way, you've lost."

Rawlings snorted and shot Quinn a baleful look. "Thank you for your *professional* opinion, Doctor, but this eventuality wasn't unexpected." He stood back as two more soldiers entered with yellow bodybags. They went to work on the corpses of Bethan and Glyn, while two others went into the back chamber to repeat the process with Jim Dawson. They left their fallen comrade alone.

Cold bastards. Rawlings trained them well.

"The MoD planned to dissect Dawson years ago," Rawlings said. "Did you know that? Of course you didn't. Perhaps that's just as well. We'll learn more from his remains than 1950s scientists ever could, along with the Iain boy."

Quinn laughed without humour. "Like you did with

Fairlight's previous guests? Don't make me laugh. You've got them all stored in a lab somewhere, with our government's scientists scratching their heads wondering what to do with them."

Karen stood. There was anger in her eyes. "My God, Quinn. Is that why there's only three left? What bullshit did you give their families when they had the bodies back?"

Quinn looked down, staring at the floor. He couldn't meet her eyes.

"They never got the bodies back, did they?" Her words were whispered, full of horror. "Jesus Christ. How did you pull that one off?"

"They never requested them, Ms Tyndall," the general said in a condescending tone. "They were in no position to."

Quinn closed his eyes at the memory of the news report from Haverton, the death of Callum Hayes's parents. It brought back the reminder of other deaths from the hometowns of his charges. Fatal accidents, disappearances…reports he had ignored.

For the greater good. How hollow his self-justification felt now.

The corpses and their Hazmat-suited pallbearers left quietly. Silence filled the chamber. Finally, Karen spoke. Her words were muted, low, but there was no hiding the fury and disgust in them.

"Murderers. You're fucking murderers. And the bodies of the parents? Are they in the same place as their children?"

"You're too hard on us, Ms Tyndall," Rawlings said. "We only eliminated a few, and only when their children died; the majority of the parents led…shall we say, rather dissolute lives. Some were victims of their own excess, some mutually destructive in their domestic abuse. A sad reflection of modern Britain, I'm afraid. But on the positive side, there are no more cases. There are only three children left in Fairlight whose origins can be traced back to the Ocean Wave Direct incident. I hate to admit, but yes: mistakes were made."

"Like Callum Hayes."

Rawlings's eyebrows rose. "The Hayes boy is a complete enigma. A threat, and one we…underestimated, sadly."

"Your human resources, then." She pointed an accusing finger at Quinn. He flinched.

"Doctor Quinn made mistakes with his staff." Rawlings's face darkened. "The Appleton nurse should have been flagged up. An unforgivable oversight."

Karen glanced at Quinn, then said to the general, "And what now? What happens when Antoinette and Tony's daughter don't come back?"

Rawlings chuckled. Quinn frowned.

"You don't have much faith in Rachel's father, do you?"

"What d'you mean?"

"Why do you think I trusted Collins with that razor? Why I left him alone with Callum Hayes? Call it a calculated gamble: the blood link between Collins and his daughter made me reassess the situation, and I'm certain their unique relationship will solve the crisis. Add the threat of his daughter's death into the balance, and I think you'll find Tony Collins will be more than a match for the Hayes boy and his monsters."

"Calculated gamble…no. I call it desperation."

"Call it what you like. Very soon, it'll all be over. For all of you."

He retrieved his sidearm and held it to her forehead.

We shall meet in the place where there is no darkness. Tony wondered why that quote came back to him. The first conversation he had with Karen Tyndall; the last words Becky had said to him…why now?

Becky's dead. She's not coming back. But how could he be sure? If he was in some hellish afterlife, was it possible she would be here?

Rachel's convinced she's here, in some form. But there's nothing except darkness here. Rachel…he focussed on the immediate task: *Find my daughter.*

The trenches were fresher and deeper the nearer he got to the rise in the blasted headland. The surrounding piles of ash and crumbled soil were lighter, and blew apart in the hot breeze. Tony paused, listening to new sounds above the sucking of the blood-tide and the whine of the nuclear wind. Metallic clicking and chittering; the same noises he had heard in the chamber with the Hayes boy and his obscene monsters.

This time they were louder. Their owners had grown. He gritted his teeth and resisted the temptation to clench his fists; the razor embedded in his hand was more painful.

He began to climb the rise, feet slipping in the churned ground. The conical tip of the lighthouse came into view, and Tony halted.

It stood clear and bright against the blackened sky. The stone was bright, belying its granite formation, but no light issued from the portals in the octagonal tower.

An inner luminescence, he realised, *one from the very building materials itself.* What the hell was this thing *really* made from? He pushed himself forward, and remembered the seawall made from human bone. Remembered how painful climbing it had been.

Keep upright. Don't try climbing this fucker on all fours. Not that the razor would have allowed it.

His lungs ached with the combination of physical exertion and breathing hot, oxygen-poor air. He felt light-headed, weakened, but the sight of the lighthouse gave him second wind.

The rest of the ancient Oratory slowly came into view. The

midsection was just as luminous as the conical roof.

Fresh. Clean. *Pure.*

The only purity to be found in this impossible landscape. Now he began to understand why Rachel was so captivated by the ancient lighthouse on their family visits to Fairlight. She had seen glimpses of this incarnation when no one else was able to.

It had been calling her, speaking to her through the centuries, in a language neither could fully understand. *It's wonderful, Daddy…but you wouldn't understand. I can't explain it.*

"Neither can I, Rachel," he whispered. It was a structure that inspired, gave hope, and …he halted, frowning. There was something wrong about it. Something incomplete. Weren't there marks on the south-facing walls to show where the monastery had been attached? Where were they now?

He tried to remember Karen's description of the Oratory's history. Hadn't the lighthouse been built before the monastery?

No, they'd been built at the same time. He remembered that now. Besides, this wasn't a building from the past. He wasn't sure what it was exactly, but the sense of the lighthouse's *incompletion* nagged at him.

It was waiting for something – or someone – to make it complete. He stiffened. *Rachel. It's been waiting for her.*

But how would it be complete with her? What could she do to – or for – an inanimate object?

What do buildings usually get from people? And what do the kids do to themselves in Fairlight? Blood and pain. That's what the buildings in Fairlight wanted.

But the lighthouse – the Pharos – is different. I know this, and Rachel knows it. It's a beacon, of light and hope…

His thoughts evaporated, like his sweat in the hot air. He had crested the rise, and the full extent of the lighthouse was revealed to him.

The creatures clustered around the base of the tower took his breath away. He knew from their tracks they would have grown, but the sight of the monsters, less than twenty metres away, was like a punch to the stomach. He stumbled, and sank to his knees.

Every element of their alien grotesquery was amplified, increased, by their new growth. The scything limbs were yardarms, unfurling great sails of grey ash and black, crusted soil in their wake; the clamshell discs of their carapaces were giant windlasses, powering their monstrous vessels to greater speed; the raised indentations along the crust were not just eyeballs, but older windows to ancient souls that gazed out from their ships' portholes, burning with a knowledge that was greater than the ages and an insatiable hunger for destruction.

All thirty-six creatures sailed at full speed towards the lighthouse; ships running under full steam to a beacon whose physical, earthly version's purpose was to warn vessels away.

But this navy wasn't racing toward its *own* destruction. Clearly outlined in the archway and its open doors, outlined in a halo of light that resembled that given off by the stones of the Pharos, were two figures, one clutching what looked like a brass ruler.

The one on the left he didn't recognise, and he paid no heed to her anguished expression when the length of brass slipped from her fingers and rolled towards the black pit behind them. But the other's blonde hair flamed like golden fire against the darkness. Her cornflower eyes shimmered like sapphires.

"*Rachel!*" Tony screamed. His cry was hoarse, torn from a parched throat via airless lungs, but it had power. It rumbled along the blasted plain and filled the air, momentarily drowning the anticipatory chittering of the creatures.

They spun in the direction of the human cry, disappearing in a fresh cloud of dust that rose to the empty windows in the lighthouse's upper chamber and momentarily hid the beacon – and his daughter – from Tony's view.

Tony ran down the slope, adrenaline fuelling his weary body; fear and disgust of these nightmarish creatures replaced by hatred, an overwhelming urge to strike down as many as he could before they tore him to pieces. It might just give Rachel and her friend a chance to escape…

It might not. But he was damned if he'd stand by and do nothing.

I failed your mother, Rachel. I won't fail you.

The razor felt light and powerful, an extension of his right hand rather than a foreign object brutally embedded in flesh. He felt no sensation in his fingers, knuckles, or thumb – just a righteous fire burned in their stead.

It hungered. Tony ran to feed it.

The slope was less steep this side, more a gentle incline, but still treacherous; fresh potholes were covered by the ash clouds thrown up by the passage of the starfish-things and Tony felt the earth quake beneath him, darted to the right just in time to avoid his ankle plunging into a fissure.

As he twisted, he saw a figure crest the rise behind him. Callum Hayes smiled; his face lit up at the sight of his army of darkness.

"See, Collins! Like dark moths to a flame!"

Fuck you! Tony regained his balance and ran forwards. The slope levelled, and the first creature was ten yards away. Tony drew back his arm.

Five yards. The eyes on the clamshell blazed with scarlet fury and the topmost limb opened up. Black diamonds gleamed.

Two yards. He halted, face to face with his enemy. The stench of putrefaction was overpowering, and the sandwich layer of grey, gelid flesh writhed with corruption. Tumours glistened and puffed out with each contraction of the two shells.

Tony smiled, aware he was too close to the animal for its limbs to be used offensively. But two more creatures had joined Tony's target, sliding behind him on retracted limbs. Only the scrape of talon on clinker and the hiss of disturbed dust told him he was surrounded.

First strike, Daddy, you told me. Well, darling, this is my first strike – and as it may be my first and only, my last strike against this evil, it's all for you.

His arm shot forward, the triple-bladed razor a silver blur. The two front blades struck the sandwich layer of the creature, where the topmost appendage joined, and the writhing flesh exploded in a welter of gristle and grey fluid. It scorched, it burned. He was baptised with alien blood and dark fire.

The appendage wasn't severed; he had to strike three more times before the jointed limb crashed to the ground behind the beast, thrashing like a scorpion tail. The creature faltered as it tried to retreat, its internal balance upset by reliance on two limbs. The Oratory was revealed again, along with its two inhabitants.

It was the appearance of the third occupant that made Tony halt. His jaw dropped, and he stood still with amazement and disbelief at the sight of the miraculous creature of light that stood behind its – *her* - daughter.

Light. A Light that will banish all darkness. Rachel was right after all. My God, Becky, what have you become?

"'We shall meet again in the place where there is no darkness,'" he murmured. "You *are* the Light."

Rachel's eyes were full of love and despair for her father, her mouth open in a scream of horror as the two appendages of the beasts behind Tony flashed forwards and drove their lethal talons into his back.

CHAPTER FORTY

The Land Rover rocked on its springs as Rawlings's lieutenant drove them to the lighthouse, and she concentrated on the headlights piercing the dark. She was thankful she couldn't see the sight of the asylum burning in the side mirrors.

"The mystery of death and resurrection – it's just a bloody opportunity for a new weapon, isn't it?"

The driver changed down a gear to negotiate the incline. Rawlings shook his head and gave Karen a supercilious smile.

"You seem to have forgotten just what we're up against, Ms Tyndall. A hostile force, an invasion, which fights us with our own children. What hope could we have of battling an enemy like that, unless we took the initiative?"

"And that's where Fairlight comes in, doesn't it, Quinn?" Her voice dripped venom, and the psychiatrist flinched. "Didn't take long for the military and the NHS to compare notes, figure out that what Jim Dawson experienced is exactly what the new batch of patients is going through. But to help them, cure them? No. To you and Rawlings they're still weapons; all you're doing is turning them against the invaders."

She had to shout her words to avoid being drowned out by the helicopter, but even if the Merlin HC3's engines hadn't filled the skies with thunder she would have being yelling anyway.

Rawlings smiled approvingly at her conclusions. He leant over, spoke in her ear. "That's all we could do."

The Rover crested the rise and its headlights flashed upon the ruined Oratory. The granite swallowed the halogen glare and the old lighthouse spat it out reluctantly through the arched doorway. Several Hazmat-suited soldiers shone bright yellow as the Rover reached the bottom of the incline and turned, side on, to the lighthouse.

One came to Rawlings's door and opened it. The general stepped out and indicated Karen and Quinn with a brief incline of his head. Two more soldiers opened their doors and dragged them out.

The night air was warm, the stretch of headland reluctant to relinquish the heat of the day. Even the Oratory, with its ancient stone, seemed to radiate heat. Or perhaps that was the rotor wash of the helicopter. Karen glanced across the bay to the tiny points of light in the village. Where streetlights and houselights should have shone there was only the bright glare of arc lights and military vehicles' headlights. Curfew, she thought grimly. Fairlight's last night, illuminated by its executioners. She wondered what dawn would look like.

She turned back to the Oratory, the ancient lighthouse that was once a beacon of light and hope in the treacherous bay. So this was where it would end. It was a chilling thought, to realise that Tony and Callum – and the last two inhabitants of Fairlight Hospital – were at this moment fighting in the very same spot, albeit in a different dimension.

So close, yet so far away. And they would all know shortly which way the battle had gone – Tony couldn't possibly survive for long against those monsters, and yet his daughter had a hidden advantage. Something Callum Hayes was terrified of, and which General Rawlings was convinced would lead to victory.

And what then? If Callum and his army are defeated, and Rachel and Antoinette manage to utilise a weapon they don't even know they have access to, what happens to us?

The bristling of firepower and military might – above and below – told her. That was why Quinn was so scared, why Rawlings was so unconcerned. Death for the psychiatrist, and a laboratory for anyone who came through from the other side.

This was a victory that would not be celebrated, would not even be public knowledge. And fringe benefits for the military:

working out just how Rachel's body could heal so quickly. Another bioweapon for Britain's armaments industry…one they'd sell to other countries.

That place they translocated to…it's death. But surviving it…that'll lead to a living death. She shivered, despite the heat, and part of her hoped Tony, Rachel, and Antoinette would not return.

Rachel sank to the ground and screamed to the heavens as the two Triskelions tore into her father. His agony was not just visible, it was palpable; she felt waves of his pain crash over and engulf her like a tsunami of suffering.

Ant was forgotten. The sundial's pointer, the weapon the younger girl was so convinced was required in the final fight against the Manxome Foe, had fallen into the pit and now there was nothing to stop Callum Hayes and his army of demons.

She had difficulty believing her eyes when Dad felled the first Triskelion, not trusting the ray of hope that flared in her heart. Even when the monster's appendage fell to the ruined ground, twisting and writhing like a severed scorpion's tail in the ash and clinker, and the creature keeled over and bled grey slime into the ashen earth, she dared not hope that Dad and the mysterious weapon that flashed pure silver could defeat the Manxome Foe.

I was right not to hope. He took one down and that's all. And now he's dying.

She closed her eyes, unable to watch the downed creature's comrades exact vengeance upon her father's body.

The mechanical noise of Callum Hayes's army increased, became an industrial frenzy. She expected, even welcomed, the whirling talons of the other monsters to tear into her and shred her body, scatter its pieces to the corners of this God-forsaken seashore. For her blood to be spattered against the glowing stones of the lighthouse, dimming its illumination and its false promise of deliverance.

It was all a lie. There's nothing to save us here. Nothing.

"Rachel! Look!"

Ant's voice was barely audible over the chittering and whirring of the Triskelions. But it wasn't a cry of despair or anguish. It was Ant's normal sing-song voice, uttering a song of hope and wonder. Rachel opened her eyes and blinked the tears away.

Her father lay belly-down on the ground, his head raised. He stared into her eyes and forced a smile while his life fluid poured into the ash.

Her jaw dropped. The two Triskelions didn't press home their advantage and whirl into the prone man; they retreated. Just a couple of metres, no great distance, but enough to prove they were unwilling to slaughter her father.

If it was possible for these alien creatures to look scared, Rachel was convinced they would have shown it. They spun on their lower appendages, facing each other, then turned and cartwheeled away, their chittering muted.

They didn't get far. The tips of the limbs smouldered and left black, gelatinous smears in their wake. The talons were unable to tear tracks through the ground. And they would never again cause physical harm to another living creature.

Blood, Rachel realised. It wasn't the weapon that caused them to back off. It was Daddy's blood that burned them.

Now Rachel saw the figure of Callum Hayes appear at the apex of the incline. His face was a mask of bewilderment, then anger. He screamed orders at the retreating Triskelions.

They ignored him. Rachel tore her eyes from Callum, and saw the other creatures slowly retreat from the lighthouse. Their eyeball-studded shells glittered scarlet.

Tony Collins was unaware of the retreat. His eyes were fixed on Rachel's, and despite the agony that pulsed through his body, he began to push his way along the wasteland with his feet. He held his right hand aloft, and the strange metal object in his hand gleamed with the blood spilt from his chest.

Blood that had burned the Triskelions who'd attacked him.

It would take an age for him to reach her. She took a step forwards, and then Ant's hand fell on her shoulder. Pulling her back into the lighthouse.

Ant's smile was unearthly. She'd either not seen what Rachel's father had undergone or didn't care. Either way, her attention was focussed on the things rising from the pit within the Oratory.

Rachel stared, and in that moment her father was forgotten.

"The Lady of the Light," Ant sang. "She's here!"

Rachel was overcome by the vision. The blackness of the circular pit, seemingly so impenetrable before, had vanished, replaced by a scintillating rainbow of lights that rose to cast its ethereal illumination upon the vestibule of the lighthouse. A kaleidoscope of glowing colours, of innumerable hues, swept over the two girls and painted the apocalyptic landscape with alien light.

Rachel had a vague impression of wings, of fins, engraved with a delicate tracery of light that *breathed*, that *lived*, coating a vast serpentine body — all shrouded by the Light that filled her soul with joy and ecstasy while it threatened to burn her eyes from their sockets.

Two glowing, moon-like spheres opened in the middle of this vision. Huge eyes that stared dead and fish-like yet were filled with the unmistakable — the unique — warmth and life of Becky Collins.

My mother.

Sinuous appendages, too thin and gossamer-like to be truly arms, unfolded with the delicate motions of sea anemones.

Extended towards Rachel.

And within the myriad, glowing fronds, caressing the metal like seaweed, was the bronze gnomon of Fairlight's sundial.

It was the bronze of a lake reflecting a dying winter sun. Metallic, impersonal. Cold and inhuman.

It was being offered to her.

"Take it, Rachel!" Ant whispered in awe and excitement. Her fingers pressed into Rachel's shoulder. "It's yours!"

Rachel reached out, and then hesitated. The apparition brightened and then dulled, and Rachel thought she detected a narrowing of those huge orbs. Displeasure.

She turned and stared at the headland that had been ordained to be the battleground between her and the Children of the Evolution. Callum Hayes had frozen, his eyes wide in terror at the Lady of the Light. His army rocked back and forth in their ranks, the eye-clusters blinking scarlet-black, scarlet-black.

Waiting for orders, Callum. Or perhaps they're waiting to see who the winning side will be.

Rachel turned back and placed her hand on the sundial pointer. It felt ice-cold. The fronds of the thing with her mother's eyes unfurled and rolled back into the dreamlike shrouds, and Rachel Collins held the gnomon in both hands.

Like Excalibur, from some unearthly Lady of the Lake. The eyes blinked once. A flash of brilliant sapphire bathed her.

Then the Triskelions began to move. She heard them advance, saw from the corner of her eye the monstrous black cartwheels with their flailing, dagger-tipped limbs surround the Oratory. She heard the cry of betrayal and disbelief from Callum Hayes and knew some of the army had surrounded him. Captured him.

They're just foot soldiers, she thought as the sounds of Callum's resisting feet, scuffing against the wasted ground, came closer. No hive mind, no alien intelligence guiding them.

Certainly not subservient to a human child. Not now.

"I know what needs to be done now, Ant." She saw the gleam of unhealthy anticipation in Ant's eyes, felt revulsion at the younger girl's obvious appetite for slaughter.

"Yes," Ant crooned. "Food for the fishies."

Yes. That's what it's all about. Food for the fishies. Rachel sighed and turned to face the two alien guards and their prisoner. The gnomon felt heavy in her hands now she knew what had to be done.

She gazed into his empty eye sockets, glanced at the surviving eye in his left hand, which blinked furiously. He whimpered - whether from the pain of the talons pushing him forward, or the prospect of what was to be done with him, she didn't know.

But I care. That's what they forget, these aliens fighting for possession of a world that isn't theirs, that never had a place for them.

"I care, Callum." She smiled sadly at his baffled expression, and then lifted the gnomon. Blue sapphire light glimmered along its edge.

For a moment Karen Tyndall felt that she could run down the headland and past the burning asylum and no one would race after her, order her to halt, or even fire one of their automatic pistols. A brief moment of invincibility, invisibility. The soldiers were busy, focussed on the lighthouse. She'd seen three go in with small packages of what could only be plastic explosive.

That's why I can't run. I have to stop them blowing this up. Rawlings came from the other side of the Oratory with her handbag.

Quinn was a defeated man. He sat cross-legged on the

ground, his back to the idling Rover, his head in his hands. She would have no help from him.

Or maybe…her eyes widened when the general opened her bag.

"Perhaps you'd like a drink," he said loudly above the distant roar of the helicopter engines. He withdrew the small half-litre vodka bottle and offered it to her. "It's been a good few hours since your last, I believe?"

She stared at it. Then she took the bottle and unscrewed the cap, breaking the seal. She raised the bottle in mock salute and pretended to take a swig.

"So you're going to blow the lighthouse up as well?" she said, inclining her head to the stone tower. The three soldiers who had entered had emerged. Now they were retrieving flame units from the Rover, helping each other secure them to their respective backs.

"When the time is right, yes." He smoothed the creases in his combat trousers and squatted before her. The soldiers approached. Their MP5s were gone; tubular nozzles of their flame units replaced the machine guns. Rawlings made a gesture with his fingers.

To the helicopter. Await my command.

"Taking no chances, though." She indicated the retreating flamethrowers. "Expecting something else to come through, to survive the blast? Maybe in the bodies of the girls, when they come back? Like Stefan Fleischer?"

Rawlings nodded. "It's possible." There was sympathy in his eyes. "I won't lie to you, Ms Tyndall. I don't know who will survive, as I don't fully understand what powers those girls have. But please believe me when I say it's all for the best. It's a war, and there will always be casualties."

Karen bit back her anger. She forced tears – easily enough with the strong alcohol burning her sinuses. Rawlings stretched out a comforting hand.

His guard was down; Karen acted. She thrust the neck of the bottle into Rawlings's groin. It connected with a meaty thud, and the general cried out in pain. He fell back, hands over his genitals. Karen got to her feet. She tightened her grip on the bottle, despite the slipperiness caused by the spilled vodka, raised it high above her head, and brought it down with full force on Rawlings's head.

The bottle fractured, and shards cut the heel of her palm. It also opened a large gash in the general's grey scalp which rapidly welled with his own blood before he slumped, unconscious, to the ground.

She threw the remains of the bottle away, wiped the blood from her hand, and reached for the general's sidearm. The holster's flap was sealed; she struggled to undo it, and the bleeding of her palm made the task more difficult.

Finally, she had the flap open and slipped Rawlings's SIG-Sauer pistol free. It was the first time she had ever held a gun, and the weight and deadly architecture horrified her. She glanced at the lighthouse.

The soldiers would gun her down without a moment's hesitation. She knew that. She didn't expect to leave Fairlight alive.

But knowing the plan was to destroy the lighthouse even before Tony and the girls had a chance – if any – to return, had sealed her decision.

She turned to the vehicle that had brought them to the lighthouse. She wondered if it had any form of armour-plating. The incline wasn't steep, but it would take a fair amount of time to build up enough speed to crash into the landed helicopter. By which time the soldiers would have opened fire and…

Where's Quinn?

She flinched at the hand that fell on her shoulder, turning and raising the gun. Quinn smiled thinly. He held out his hand,

and Karen stared at the small package.

"I could only take one – from the archway – but it should be enough. The detonation won't take place without the order from Rawlings, but they'll come down here soon to find out why he's not in radio contact. Least I can do. Karen, run and hide. You have to look after yourself, now. Forget Tony Collins…"

She shook her head. He gently pushed her away from the Rover, opened the driver's door.

"…and forget me. Forget I was part of this, one who made it possible." He prised her fingers apart and took the gun. He threw it in the passenger seat. "Just in case," he added with a faint smile.

She stood, speechless, as he put the Rover into reverse and popped the handbrake. With a clunk of engaging gears and a spin of tyres in the dried grass, the vehicle reversed up the incline. Slowly, then with more speed.

Quinn turned off the headlights and Karen was in darkness. When the first volley of gunfire rolled from the men at the helicopter, she realised why the psychiatrist was reversing up the incline.

The bullets wouldn't strike the engine this way. Four-wheel drive enabled the Rover to maintain its traction and increase its speed, and now more muzzle flashes lit the night sky. Bullets struck the boot and sparks flew, then the interior of the car exploded in a shower of glass and flying blood. A roar of the engine – Quinn's foot must have stiffened and pressed harder on the accelerator pedal at the moment of death – and the Rover flew in unerring direction towards the Merlin helicopter.

The light in Tony Collins's eyes faded and died with him. The last thing he had seen was his daughter and the creature behind her. Had he realised? Rachel closed her eyes and rocked on her feet. The gnomon felt heavier now, and she wanted – no, she burned with the desire – to strike a killing blow on Callum Hayes, the architect of all this misery and death.

"Go on," Ant whispered. "Take him."

Rachel turned. She saw the earnest eyes of the younger girl, still gleaming with hunger for blood. "Didn't you see what happened? My father is *dead*!"

"Then avenge him!" There was no sympathy, no shared sorrow for Rachel's loss. Just anger and impatience to get the killing done. "He's the cause of it! He brought the Manxome Foe here, and killed your father!"

Rachel stared at her. She couldn't feel angry at Ant, but for the creature behind her. She wanted to rage at it, strike it with the weapon it had urged its human puppets to bring here.

No. If I do that, we're all lost.

"Ant," she said slowly, her eyes never leaving the glowing orbs of the thing Ant called the Lady of the Light, "Callum's like us. He's been lied to. Those things aren't demons, or monsters; they're soldiers. That's all. Tools to be used by their master."

Ant turned, stared at the target of Rachel's statement. The clouds of light billowed and flickered. She turned back. "No. You're wrong."

"Did you think we were hunting the Jabberwock?" Rachel's laughter was full of bitterness. "To bring its head to the Queen of Hearts here?"

She dropped the gnomon. It sank into the ground with a puff of dust. She walked past Callum and his guards. They didn't react, but she heard Ant scrabbling in the dust for the sundial's pointer.

She walked to the prone form of her father. Tears trickled down her cheeks and splashed onto the ground where his blood had spilled. She stroked his hair and closed his eyelids.

"Thank you, Dad. Thank you for trying. I'm so sorry the last thing you saw was the thing that pretended to be Mum."

She lifted her father's right hand from the ground. It was limp, had yet to stiffen with death. The strange razor-blade slid easily from the terrible hole in his palm, and she felt a tremor rock her body as she took the burden.

It was a weapon of evil. Three razorblades joined within a nondescript wooden shaft at equidistant angles. Perhaps its creator hadn't understood the significance of the symbol he had created. Perhaps the shaft was originally planned to hold four blades, to form a swastika.

It was old, and it carried the burden of decades of pain and suffering. Wilful suffering, inflicted by one human being upon another.

Not now. Now it'll be used for something good. Its evil will be negated. She leant down and kissed her father's cold cheek, then stood and turned.

Ant held the gnomon awkwardly, trying to brandish it like a sword. *Like a little girl playing at knights and castles*, Rachel thought sadly. She lifted the triple-razor by its third limb. The one that had been buried in her father's palm. It was still warm.

Callum flinched as she approached. The eye in his palm blinked rapidly, the teeth lining its lids clattering, mirroring the panic – and fear – of its owner. The apparition in the pit glowed more brightly, and its own eyes gleamed with approval.

Rachel took Callum's right shoulder and gently, but firmly, turned him round to face her. He trembled, tried to retreat, but the talons of the two Triskelions prevented him.

"Callum," she said quietly, soothingly. "I'm not going to kill you. That's what they want, don't you see? This…this place, dimension, whatever you want to call it: it's a mirror to the future. A distorted one, yes, but one that shows pretty much what our planet will be like if we allow these things to break through. You're not to blame; you were lied to. Just like I was."

She ignored Ant's incredulous cries and addressed the creature in the pit. "You'll never understand human beings. Our capacity to forgive, to love…to sacrifice ourselves. And to walk through Hell for those we love. That's what my father did: he went into Hell for love." She gestured around her. "*This* is Hell. He knew what was waiting for him. He came here to rescue me, and the last thing he saw was a monster imitating his wife. I just hope that he didn't realise, that what he saw in your eyes is what remains of Mum. I wish I could take him back, but I can't. There's only one thing I can do to honour him, and that's make sure this Hell doesn't come to pass."

She raised the razor. The blood on the blades was her father's, the same blood that ran through her veins. Spilled in sacrifice for her.

Love. Self-sacrifice.

This time, more blood had to be spilled. And given.

What do you see when you cut yourself?

She smiled sadly. Self-harm within the shadow dimension…it had never been done before. And never for this purpose. She raised her left forearm and held the blade's tip against her wrist.

She cut.

Some of the soldiers clustered by the helicopter had the sense of mind to aim at the wheels of the hurtling Rover. Karen saw sparks flare from the tailgate and the hubcaps and then the vehicle listed, veering away from Quinn's target on pancake tyres. It tore ruts into the ground, shaking wildly and decreasing in speed.

Karen stood, willing the vehicle onwards with silent prayers. More bullets peppered the bodywork, but the Rover was slowing. Her heart sank.

She looked behind her, at the dead stone of the lighthouse. Now she had to act on Quinn's instructions. Run. Hide. Forget. But how could she?

Stirring and groaning filled the space behind her. She stiffened. There was a cough and a whispered curse. She turned.

Rawlings got to his feet, his face a mask of blood. Fragments of glass protruded from his forehead, glinting like dark rubies. His eyes were dulled steel, narrowed when they saw Karen. His hand went to his holster.

"Shit." His fingers twitched in the empty space. He blinked, removed his hand, and grasped at the R/T on his lapel. His eyes never left Karen's.

"Carson. D'you read me?"

There was no answer. Rawlings frowned at Karen's smile. He turned and saw the source of her pleasure.

The Rover had come to a halt, but there was stirring from within. In the glare of the helicopter's lights, Karen saw a bloodstained hand emerge, clutching a shining tube.

"Carson! Dust-off now!"

More gunfire, at close-range. Quinn's hand jerked as bullets tore into his body, firing the general's SIG-Sauer wildly. One soldier went down. The helicopter began to rise.

Rawlings moved forwards, Karen forgotten. "Detonate now!" he screamed.

"We can't, sir. You're in range of the -"

"Never mind me! You have your orders: explode the lighthouse *now!*" He turned back to Karen, his lips drawn back to reveal those white teeth that gleamed like a predator's fangs. It was a snarl and a smile. "Nice try, Ms Tyndall. But Quinn's little stunt will mean nothing!"

Karen didn't reply. She watched the helicopter's nose sink, its tail in the air. The full glare of its lights revealed the body dragging itself out of the Rover and onto the incline.

In the instant that the lights moved away from the vehicle and its thief, she saw a smile break on Quinn's features. She saw his other hand rise and reveal the package that now opened as the unseen Carson acted on Rawlings's order.

Now a new light filled the sky and thunder roared across the headland.

Rachel didn't see the wound that opened in her wrist, or the life fluid that welled from it. She felt nothing but a pure, cleansing fire that jetted into her eyes. And with that, the universe opened to her.

The veils of the universe were burned asunder, and all their treasures and mysteries were revealed to her. The unutterable coldness and darkness of interstellar space vanished in a fraction of a millisecond, and the stars paled into insignificance, became nothing but dull smears of light against this, the true Light that lay at the centre of all things that had passed, that were, and were yet to be.

She saw everything. She *was* everything. She was the moment of creation and the end of time. She was the mother of the universe and its midwife and its child. She was its death and its burier and its mourner.

And yet…and yet, the planet she was on, the planet she had spent her whole, short life upon, was the single most precious jewel in a universe of cosmic wonders. She understood why humanity was born, why it warred amongst itself, why it was capable of godlike wonders and demonic horrors. She understood why it was lusted after by alien intelligences and why those beings destroyed entire species and their own galaxies to possess it.

In an unending instant of time that encompassed aeons where even ice ages were but mere milliseconds, it was the fragments of humanity's past that shone the brightest.

She saw desert lands where turbaned wise men crafted strange metals into instruments that measured time by the passage of Earth's sun; heard secret incantations and understood how they imbibed the sundials with a power to direct cosmic power to singular locations on the planet, to open portals and allow the Light to shine through. She saw tribes war amongst themselves for possession of these keys to the portals, with spears and swords, then with bullets and missiles that contained the power of suns in their payloads. She saw the wise men rail against the misguided leaders and chieftains, felt their sacrifices as they battled to close the portals.

She experienced their pain and despair at their failure to close the one portal that remained. She suffered and inflicted suffering in the torture chambers of those who had appropriated the precious metals to fashion into weapons, inadvertently turning the power of forgotten incantations upon itself, so that the metal and its power became corrupted and fed upon human suffering and blood. How unconscious minds fashioned the weaponry into symbols that represented mankind's own destruction.

And, with joy in a heart that shrivelled and burned with the unearthly life-force that it could no longer pump through its chambers, she saw how the simplest of all human actions could turn that power back to a benign force.

That power flowed through her. It *was* her. She was the Light.

I am the Light of the World.

Not the Lady of the Light, who deceived and took from

those who crossed the borders of the night. Rachel could not even feel contempt or hatred for it; she was beyond those emotions.

But I am still human. I have one more task to complete. She registered the presence of two children her own age, felt their pain and confusion and fear. The blade moved to her abdomen.

Come to me, my brother, my sister.

She opened herself and bared her soul. Her organs and skin were mere vestments that had no use to one who was clothed with the sun. They were garments to be given to those who had need of them.

She experienced Callum Hayes's joy and gratitude as he saw the world through human eyes once more. She rejoiced in his happiness at being able to weep tears of joy and sadness. She held him as he wept his loss and regret away, the years of suffering and hatred melting away like candle wax.

She embraced Antoinette Penner with unearthly arms and sang a song to her sister in suffering. She imparted a message that could not be heard, could not be understood, merely *felt*. The girl would understand it when the time was right, for her role upon this planet and this part of humanity's story was not yet complete.

The only pain she felt was when she turned her back on her father to confront the thing in the lighthouse. She could not rejuvenate or revive him; the power behind the Light made that clear.

The true nature of the lighthouse – the Oratory, the Pharos – was revealed to her. She saw through the once-beautiful illumination, the transcendent glow of its bricks and mortar. Realised it was a false light, as treacherous and deceitful as that cast by wreckers on this shore from centuries ago, which would lure ships to their doom upon rocky cliffs.

I am the Light. I am the Pharos. It was time to close the

portal.

The Lady of the Light was no longer the angelic, ethereal figure of staggering beauty. The fins were demon's claws. The wings were serpent's teeth. The translucent robes of iridescent gems were the rotting shrouds of the corrupted dead.

Only the eyes were pure. The eyes of cobalt, the same colour Rachel Collins shared with her mother. Those eyes were all that remained as Rachel entered the Oratory and kindled a new fire. She extinguished the false light of the Lady and a new beacon shone through the shadow world.

Hot wind blew across Karen Tyndall's cheeks and grit prised her eyelids open. It carried the smell of burning flesh as well as ash. She coughed, gagging on the taste of fire and devastation, and blinked at the blinding ash in her eyes.

She stood on a shore that burned. The black sea roiled like oil, and her disoriented mind told her the sea was composed of blood. The ground she stood on was scorched, the few remaining blades of grass writhing their death-throes in shrouds of fire.

Fire...

Then the pain hit her. Her back was a sheet of agony, burning. She smelled burnt flesh and scorched hair.

It jolted her into awareness. She saw thin, angular shapes cartwheel towards her, elongated limbs tearing chunks from the ruined ground with their jagged talons...

Triskelions.

She got to her feet, swaying in the hot wind, and took a step back before the first creature could reach her.

Something stopped her. A solid, unmovable barrier of stone that burned her already scorched back. She screamed, but terror froze her into place and she could only watch as the cartwheeling thing came towards her.

Then it slowed, tilted. Fell. Remained still, lifeless.

She blinked the grit from her eyes. The hot wind carried scents of aviation fuel as well as death. Now she saw what the thing truly was.

To her left, another of the helicopter's twisted rotor blades fell flat, smouldering.

She fell to the ground, her skin coming free from her back with the sound of Sellotape. She lay, inhaling the smell of recently burned earth. When she twisted her head, she saw the third rotor and the body it had impaled to the devastated wall of the Oratory.

General Rawlings's face was black. The burning air had scorched the blood on his face, boiled it away before starting on the skin and flesh beneath. His lips were gone. His teeth no longer gleamed white.

She turned away and buried her face in the earth again. Her tears came easily, and the ground was softened, cooled. There was a faint scent of freshly churned earth, of a field ploughed to rejuvenate the soil and allow new life to grow.

It wasn't until the fires died and a new light rose into the sky, casting golden, life-giving rays from the eastern horizon, that she rose again.

Blue skies. Blue ocean. She turned.

The lighthouse was intact. The old granite blocks seemed new, recently dressed. The mortar had the aroma of freshly mixed cement. They seemed to glow with a strange, inner light, but that had to be the result of her gritty eyes and the rising sun.

There was no mistaking the movement of the figures within the vestibule, though. They approached her, naked as the day they were born, hand in hand. They too were untouched by the holocaust. Their skin was pure and unblemished, free of any scars they had once inflicted upon themselves.

Callum Hayes stared at Karen with cobalt eyes, not grey, and his smile was that of a saint. Antoinette Penner had also changed. She carried herself with a grace that belied her disability.

Her empty eye sockets seemed no hindrance to her; she navigated the floor and came through the archway as if she could see perfectly. Her sightless eyes scanned the bay, and the smile was as saintly as Callum's. She opened her mouth and spoke with Rachel Collins's voice, and Karen heard the message of the true Children of the New Evolution, spoken in the place where there would be no darkness.

THE END?

Not if you want to dive into more of Crystal Lake Publishing's Tales from the Darkest Depths!

Check out our amazing website and online store or download our latest catalog here: https://geni.us/CLPCatalog

We always have great new projects and content on the website to dive into, as well as a newsletter, behind the scenes options, social media platforms, our own dark fiction shared-world series and our very own webstore. Our webstore even has categories specifically for KU books, non-fiction, anthologies, and of course more novels and novellas.

AUTHOR BIOGRAPHY

Adrian Chamberlin lives in the small south Oxfordshire town of Wallingford that serves as a backdrop to the UK television series Midsomer Murders, not far from where Agatha Christie lies buried, dreaming in darkness. He is the author of the critically acclaimed supernatural thriller novel The Caretakers as well as numerous short stories in a variety of anthologies, mostly historical or futuristic supernatural horror. In his spare time he likes to walk dogs through decaying ruins and mend broken cuckoo clocks.

Say hello to Mr Golien at: www.archivesofpain.com.

Readers…

Thank you for reading *Fairlight*. We hope you enjoyed this novel.
If you have a moment, please review *Fairlight* at the store where you bought it.

Help other readers by telling them why you enjoyed this book. No need to write an in-depth discussion. Even a single sentence will be greatly appreciated. Reviews go a long way to helping a book sell, and is great for an author's career. It'll also help us to continue publishing quality books.

Thank you again for taking the time to journey with Crystal Lake Publishing.

You will find links to all our social media platforms on our Linktree page: https://linktr.ee/CrystalLakePublishing.

Follow us on Amazon:

MISSION STATEMENT

Since its founding in August 2012, Crystal Lake Publishing has quickly become one of the world's leading publishers of Dark Fiction and Horror books in print, eBook, and audio formats.

While we strive to present only the highest quality fiction and entertainment, we also endeavour to support authors along their writing journey. We offer our time and experience in non-fiction projects, as well as author mentoring and services, at competitive prices.

With several Bram Stoker Award wins and many other wins and nominations (including the HWA's Specialty Press Award), Crystal Lake Publishing puts integrity, honor, and respect at the forefront of our publishing operations.

We strive for each book and outreach program we spearhead to not only entertain and touch or comment on issues that affect our readers, but also to strengthen and support the Dark Fiction field and its authors.

Not only do we find and publish authors we believe are destined for greatness, but we strive to work with men and women who endeavour to be decent human beings who care more for others than themselves, while still being hard working, driven, and passionate artists and storytellers.

Crystal Lake Publishing is and will always be a beacon of what passion and dedication, combined with overwhelming teamwork and respect, can accomplish. We endeavour to know each and every one of our readers, while building personal relationships with our authors, reviewers, bloggers, podcasters, bookstores, and libraries.

We will be as trustworthy, forthright, and transparent as any business can be, while also keeping most of the headaches away from our authors, since it's our job to solve the problems so they can stay in a creative mind. Which of course also means paying our authors.

We do not just publish books, we present to you worlds within your world, doors within your mind, from talented authors who sacrifice so much for a moment of your time.

There are some amazing small presses out there, and through collaboration and open forums we will continue to support other presses in the goal of helping authors and showing the world what quality small presses are capable of accomplishing. No one wins when a small press goes down, so we will always be there to support hardworking, legitimate presses and their authors. We don't see Crystal Lake as the best press out there, but we will always strive to be the best, strive to be the most interactive and grateful, and even blessed press around. No matter what happens over time, we will also take our mission very seriously while appreciating where we are and enjoying the journey.

What do we offer our authors that they can't do for themselves through self-publishing?

We are big supporters of self-publishing (especially hybrid publishing), if done with care, patience, and planning. However, not every author has the time or inclination to do market research, advertise, and set up book launch strategies. Although a lot of authors are successful in doing it all, strong small presses will always be there for the authors who just want to do what they do best: write.

What we offer is experience, industry knowledge, contacts and trust built up over years. And due to our strong brand and trusting fanbase, every Crystal Lake Publishing book comes with weight of respect. In time our fans begin to trust our judgment and will try a new author purely based on our support of said author.

With each launch we strive to fine-tune our approach, learn from our mistakes, and increase our reach. We continue to assure our authors that we're here for them and that we'll carry the weight of the launch and dealing with third parties while they focus on their strengths—be it writing, interviews, blogs, signings, etc.

We also offer several mentoring packages to authors that include knowledge and skills they can use in both traditional and self-publishing endeavours.

We look forward to launching many new careers.

This is what we believe in. What we stand for. This will be our legacy.

Welcome to Crystal Lake Publishing—Tales from the Darkest Depths.

THANK YOU FOR PURCHASING THIS BOOK

www.ingramcontent.com/pod-product-compliance
Lightning Source LLC
Chambersburg PA
CBHW070231200726
48293CB00005B/1571